# THE
# JACKAL
# MAN

For more information regarding Kate Ellis
log on to Kate's website: www.kateellis.co.uk

# THE
# JACKAL
# MAN

## Kate Ellis

piatkus

PIATKUS

First published in Great Britain in 2011 by Piatkus

A CIP catalogue record for this book
is available from the British Library.

Hardback ISBN 978-0-7499-5352-2
C format ISBN 978-0-7499-5357-7

Typeset in Baskerville by M Rules
Printed and bound in Great Britain by
Clays Ltd, St Ives plc

Papers used by Piatkus are natural, renewable and
recyclable products sourced from well-managed forests and certified
in accordance with the rules of the Forest Stewardship Council.

**Mixed Sources**
Product group from well-managed
forests and other controlled sources
www.fsc.org Cert no. SGS-COC-004081
© 1996 Forest Stewardship Council

Piatkus
An imprint of
Little, Brown Book Group
100 Victoria Embankment
London EC4Y 0DY

An Hachette UK Company
www.hachette.co.uk

www.piatkus.co.uk

For Tom and Becky

# CHAPTER 1

*We are not of the servants' hall nor are we exalted with the angels above stairs. We are a sad and sorry sisterhood. Neither fish nor foul. Always underestimated and yet, as a body of women, our tastes are refined and we are frequently more educated than our so-called betters. We are the teachers of ungrateful young ladies and gentlemen. We are the forgotten daughters of impoverished gentility. We are the slaves of duty. We are the governesses.*

*I myself am possessed of many accomplishments. Painting. Singing. A broad knowledge of literature. A small talent for the pianoforte. An ability to converse in the French tongue. And a keen interest in history, particularly that of Ancient Egypt.*

*I have made a special study of hieroglyphics and the customs, practices and religion of those remarkable people. Indeed it was this interest that secured me my post here as Sir Frederick Varley is an aficionado of such matters.*

*When I was interviewed by Sir Frederick in Oxford, he asked me which Egyptian deity I favoured and I had no hesitation in saying that it was Anubis who claimed my particular attention.*

*Anubis. The Lord of the Mummy Wrappings. The Helper of the Dead.*

# CHAPTER 2

Half an hour to midnight and Clare should have been home fifteen minutes ago.

As she hurried down the lane, the high hedgerows looked naked and dead in the silvery darkness. The wind was gusting harder now and the cold seeped through her thin coat like icy fingers touching her flesh.

She broke into a run, grateful that at least she'd had the foresight to put on her flat boots. In high heels, this walk would have been impossible and maybe she'd always suspected that Jen was going to let her down. Jen's promise that she'd be there to provide a lift home from the Anglers' Arms had seemed half hearted but Clare had convinced herself – and her mother – that all would be fine. Besides, there'd always been the option of calling a minicab if the plan fell apart. Until she'd looked in her purse at five to eleven and realised that the last of her money had gone on a fourth Bacardi and Coke.

The other girls lived in the opposite direction and had already arranged their own transport so there'd been no room in their minicab. As they'd left, Vicky had given her a pitying look and told her that she'd be fine walking home: it was only half a mile away, across the main road into Tradmouth and then down a narrow country lane flanked by farmers' fields, so what was she worrying about? Vicky had always been a bitch. She'd always managed to make Clare feel dim and clumsy but she was clever enough never to cross that narrow and precarious boundary into bullying.

A tree ahead creaked in the wind and its bare arms waved to and fro as if warning of danger ahead. Clare walked on, avoiding the puddles that glistened like mercury pools in the light of the full moon. She could smell manure and damp vegetation as the moon suddenly disappeared behind a bank of clouds. Then, in the shock of the darkness, she stumbled over something lying in the lane. She put out a tentative hand to see what the obstacle was, hoping that her fingers wouldn't meet the soft dead corpse of some creature run down by a speeding car. But when she felt the rough, cold wood of a fallen branch she exhaled with relief.

As she levered herself up an owl swooped out of nowhere and the sudden movement of those silent, ghostly wings sent a shock through her body. But she forced herself to stand and ignore the stinging graze on her knee and the gaping hole in her new patterned tights. Just a couple of hundred yards to go now. Then she'd be in sight of home.

Suddenly a throaty noise shattered the darkness like the roar of a lion. She froze and pressed her body against the hedgerow, wincing as the twisted wood bit into her flesh. After a couple of seconds a pair of bright headlights lit up the lane. Temporarily dazzled, Clare shielded her eyes as the vehicle shot past. And as the sound of the engine receded, she stood quite still by the side of the road until her eyes readjusted to the moonlight.

She took a deep breath and began to walk on, trying to ignore the sounds of the night; the eerie scream of a distant fox, the predatory screech of an owl. She was nearly home.

But the animal she saw as she rounded a blind bend made no sound as it walked silently towards her. A strange creature the size of a man, stalking on cloven hoofs like the devil.

It didn't move particularly fast but she sensed its power. If she attempted to get away she knew it could follow and outrun her easily. But she had to make the effort to escape somehow, even though her limbs felt heavy and useless, as if some unseen force had fixed lead weights to her feet.

In the middle of the Devon countryside there was nobody to hear you scream and Clare knew that, even if fear hadn't paralysed her throat, any cry for help would be futile.

With a huge effort she turned away from the thing and attempted to run. There was a cottage back near the main road and if she could just reach it she would be safe. So with the vision of that glowing cottage fixed in her mind like some heavenly city, she began to move. There was no need to look back to see whether it was still following: even though it moved silently she knew it was behind her . . . and getting closer.

As it caught her waist she lost her footing and stumbled to the ground, unaware of the pain as the gravel bit into her knees. Then the thing's soft hands, like great paws, closed around her neck and something thin that felt like wire began to bite into her flesh. Her hands shot up instinctively to her throat and she tried with all her strength to wrest the thing off. But the thin ligature cut in deeper as she fought for each precious breath.

Clare's struggle for life seemed to last forever. But in reality it was only a few seconds before she was vaguely aware of the droning engine of another vehicle, approaching with frustrating slowness. All of a sudden she felt herself tumbling forward again onto the rough road surface as her body was released from the creature's murderous embrace, and she lay there stiff with terror, hardly daring to move. Whatever it was had let her go but it could still be there waiting in the shadows like a cat preparing to return to a bird half tortured to death for its pleasure.

Then headlights appeared around the bend, bathing Clare's body with light as she lay sprawled across the road. But by the time the van had screeched to a halt, she had lost her fight for consciousness. And the thing that had tried to take her life had disappeared off into the night.

February is the quietest month. The festivities of Christmas are a vague and rosy memory and spring, when tourists descend on South Devon like migrating birds, seems a long way off.

So when the phone by DCI Gerry Heffernan's bed began to ring at half past midnight on Monday morning, he was unprepared for the interruption to his deep, complacent sleep. He wrestled with the duvet that had wrapped itself around his plump body and at first the duvet won the fight. But as his brain began to function he managed to escape its clutches and flick on the bedside light.

He picked up the receiver and put it to his ear, rubbing his eyes and wondering if he had any clean shirts ironed. This was bound to be something that required him to get up and dressed and venture out into the cold night air. A phone call at that hour always heralds bad news. This was somebody's tragedy.

Once the officer on the other end of the line had conveyed all the details, Gerry asked the inevitable question, dreading the answer.

'Is the lass expected to live?'

There was a long silence. 'We don't know yet, sir. But if the motorist hadn't found her when he did . . .'

'What do they say at the hospital?'

'You know what doctors are like, sir.'

Gerry understood. He knew what doctors were like all right. Like lawyers they tended not to commit themselves to certainties.

'Inspector Peterson's already on his way to the scene, sir. Do you want me to organise a patrol car to pick you up?'

Gerry answered in the affirmative and fifteen minutes later, wearing yesterday's crumpled shirt, he stumbled out of the house and onto the quayside. A thin veil of mist had come down over the river but he could still make out the streetlights of Queenswear on the opposite bank. As he walked to the patrol car, hands in pockets and the scent of seaweed in his nostrils, he looked around, drinking in the night sounds magnified by the water and the night air; the gentle lapping of the river against the quayside and the distant metallic clink of halyards against the masts of yachts bobbing on the tide. There was no traffic on the river at this time of night – the fishing boats had departed hours ago and wouldn't return till dawn – and all the town lay in silent misty darkness. He sat in the passenger seat and looked out of the window as he was driven away from the town up the steep hill past the Naval College and out into the open countryside.

The car turned sharp left by the darkened bulk of the Anglers' Arms and Gerry noticed a patrol car pulled up onto the grass verge outside a cottage on the corner opposite the pub. But Gerry's car drove on past. The crime scene, the constable explained, was further down the lane.

As they rounded a bend Gerry saw another patrol car blocking the single-track road ahead. His car screeched to a halt behind it and he climbed out of the passenger seat slowly, yawning widely like some large, sleepy animal. Being half asleep when he left the house he had thrown on the first coat that came to hand, not his warmest, and now he shivered in the damp night air.

The road ahead was lit by dazzling arc lights and a trio of men in white crime-scene suits were conducting a painstaking search of the lane and the hedgerows either side. He looked about for a familiar face and he spotted a tall, dark-skinned man in his mid-thirties, leaning on the bonnet of the patrol car, arms folded, watching the proceedings with detached interest. DI Wesley Peterson was wearing a weatherproof coat, the kind worn by the hardier type of yachting enthusiast, and warm gloves. Unlike his boss, he had come prepared.

When Wesley saw Gerry his face lit up with what looked like a smile of relief.

'So what's the story here, Wes?'

'A motorist found a girl lying in the middle of the road. He almost ran over her but he managed to stop his van just in time. He called the ambulance then he got out and went to see if he could do anything.' He paused. 'He assumed she'd been the victim of a hit and run but . . .'

Gerry knew there was more to come. If it had been a simple hit and run he and Wesley wouldn't be there freezing their balls off at one fifteen on a chilly Monday morning. 'But what?'

'The bloke who found her works at Tradmouth Leisure Centre and he'd been on a first aid course so he tried to roll her over into the recovery position. Then he noticed her neck: she'd been strangled with something thin like a cord or twine which had bitten quite deeply into her flesh, but she was still alive. They've taken her to Tradmouth Hospital.'

'Where's the driver who found her?'

Wesley turned and pointed to a small white van pulled up on a section of wide verge a few yards behind them next to a farm gate. Gerry must have passed it on his way there but hadn't noticed with all the activity ahead of him on the road. There were two shadowy figures inside the van and the windows had begun to steam up.

'Let's go and have a word, shall we? What's his name?'

'Danny Coyle – he lives in a rented cottage in Whitely with his girlfriend and he was on his way back from having a drink with some mates in Tradmouth. He seems a bit shaken up. Paul's in the van with him taking his statement.'

'Bet your Pam wasn't pleased at having her beauty sleep disturbed,' Gerry said as they made their way slowly back down the lane to where the van was parked.

'You could say that,' Wesley replied quietly in a tone that told Gerry that further enquiries wouldn't be welcome.

When they came to the car Gerry rapped sharply on the steamed-up driver's window. The passenger door opened and as the interior light came on he saw a muscular, shaven-headed young man wearing a tracksuit in the driver's seat. Sitting hunched beside him with a clipboard on his knee was DC Paul Johnson. Paul was in the habit of running marathons and the driver had a decidedly sporty look so Gerry guessed the pair would have a lot in common.

The driver opened the door and sprang out eagerly, as though he was glad of a chance to get out into the air. Paul did likewise, uncurling his tall frame from the cramped confines of the seat and stretching out his long legs.

'Mr Coyle? I believe you found the young woman, sir,' Gerry began after introducing himself.

'Yeah. I've just given a statement. Can I go now?'

'Yes, no problem. But before you go, can you just go over what you saw?'

Danny Coyle nodded meekly. Too much exercise had deprived him of a discernable neck and the arms that bulged beneath the thin cloth of the tracksuit top looked powerful. Certainly powerful enough to strangle a woman.

'I've told him all I know,' he said, nodding towards Paul. 'I was just driving home when I saw a girl lying in the middle of the road. I presumed she'd been run over – hit and run – so I got on my mobile and phoned for an ambulance then I got out to see if I could do anything.'

'Did you see or hear any other vehicles? Please think carefully.'

Danny shook his head. Then he thought for a moment. 'Come to think of it, I might have heard a car engine in the distance just as I got out of the van. But it might have come from the main road. I don't know. I rolled her over into the recovery position and felt for a pulse. But when I touched her neck I realised it was all . . . well, all sort of cut. I'd kept my headlights on and when I looked more closely I could see that there was a sort of bloody line around her neck. I could feel a pulse so I knew it wasn't too late. I just wanted the ambulance to come before . . . Anyway, I thought I'd better

9

ring you lot as well. I mean that mark on her neck looked . . .
Have you heard how she is? Did she make it?'

Gerry and Wesley exchanged looks. That was the next
thing they had to find out.

There had been several occasions during Dr Neil Watson's
life when he had felt out of his depth and this was one of
them.

He wasn't really sure why he, of all people, had been contacted. But there were many, he supposed, who, on hearing
the word 'archaeologist', thought automatically of Howard
Carter and Tutankhamen's tomb or Schliemann's magnificent treasures of Troy. If only they knew that life in the
Devon County Archaeological Unit was mostly mud and
paperwork.

But Neil didn't feel inclined to enlighten anybody just yet.
For one thing he'd always wanted to see Varley Castle. The
concept of somebody building a forbidding granite fortress
on the edge of Dartmoor during the late nineteenth century
when there was little need to defend yourself against
marauding neighbours intrigued him. He had seen photographs of the castle perched on a gorge above a glistening
river, but photographs can never really capture the feel of a
place or give anything more than a hint of its breathtaking
magnificence.

Once he'd left the main A30 from Exeter, the castle hadn't
been particularly easy to find, tucked away down a single-
track lane as if its builder had designed it as his own secret
kingdom. He'd driven between a pair of massive granite
gateposts that wouldn't have looked out of place in a prehistoric stone circle, then up a meandering driveway flanked by
fields and mature woodland. Finally the castle came into view.

The moment of revelation had probably been planned carefully by the owner and architect to impress the approaching visitor and this theatrical sleight of hand – like a magician whipping off a velvet cloth to reveal some wonder beneath – had worked to perfection. Neil brought the car to a halt and sat there for a few moments, taking it all in.

To the casual observer it looked as though Varley Castle had been hewn from some great granite cliff. Only the tall windows betrayed the fact that it had been created by man rather than nature. It looked like something from another, more warlike age with its crenellations and its great square towers as it stood, dark grey against the soft green landscape. It was a statement of power but its creator had been no medieval warlord. This great building, Neil knew, was an expression of financial rather than military might.

As the watery winter sun emerged from behind the clouds, he put the car into gear and carried on. He had an appointment with Caroline Varley at ten o'clock and he didn't particularly want to be late – even though he feared that he was bound to be a great disappointment to her.

Leaving his old yellow Mini on the gravel circle in front of the castle's great oak door didn't seem appropriate somehow, like leaving a piece of chewing gum stuck to some great Rodin sculpture. But, lacking an obvious alternative, he drove carefully to the edge of the gravel, as far as possible from the door, and stopped the engine.

He'd brought the battered briefcase he used when he had meetings to attend. But when he took it off the back seat he realised how shabby and scuffed it was. This wasn't something that usually concerned him – he was a man who'd face wealthy developers wearing an ancient combat jacket and mud-caked jeans – but somehow this meeting felt different.

Caroline Varley wanted an archaeologist to advise her and he was sure that she'd be expecting some gentleman antiquary wearing tweed and a bow tie. Not a working field archaeologist like Neil Watson.

That wasn't to say that he hadn't made a stab at sartorial respectability. He was wearing his only pair of half-decent trousers and he'd managed to fish out a proper shirt from the back of his small wardrobe. He'd even found a tie lurking in the detritus at the rear of his sock drawer. On discovering the crumpled state of his rarely worn clothes, he'd been tempted to ring his friend Wesley who always seemed to dress smartly when he was out interrogating criminals and was sure to have something he could lend him. But a session with the steam iron had done the trick and now he felt uncomfortably smart. Even his best shoes had seen a bit of polish and his long hair had been washed the night before and attacked with a brush.

He straightened his tie as he climbed out of the car. The summons to Varley Castle had come via a letter handwritten on expensive deckle-edged notepaper. The missive had stood out from the rest of the Unit's routine correspondence – the bills and the reports – and Neil had stared at it for a while before opening it. It was rare nowadays to receive a handwritten letter, rarer still to receive such an upmarket one.

He locked the car door – he doubted whether such a security measure would be necessary in that particular location but it was hard to break the long-ingrained habit of suspicion – then he approached one of the most imposing front doors he had ever seen: studded oak and tall enough to admit a giant. But before he could raise the great lion-head knocker – not much smaller than the real thing – the door swung open silently.

Standing there in a pink cashmere sweater and jeans was a tall, slim woman, not much older than himself. She had a long face – horsy some would say – and wavy brown hair, newly washed and a little wild. Her nose was too large and her mouth too wide but, in spite of this, there was something attractive about her – but Neil didn't know quite what it was.

'Dr Watson, I presume.' Her voice was deep, her accent well bred but not cut glass.

Neil held out his hand. 'Ms Varley?'

'Caroline please.' She gave him a businesslike smile but he knew from her eyes that she was assessing him, weighing up his suitability.

'I'm a bit early.'

The corners of Caroline's mouth twitched upwards in a crooked smile as she stood aside to let him in. 'Eagerness. I like that in a man. Come through.'

He found himself in the entrance hall, granite-walled like the exterior. But here the stone was relieved by a set of large tapestries which, in spite of the faded colours, gave the illusion of warmth. He was struck by the abundance of artefacts from ancient Egypt displayed about the place: a large stone figure of a hawk-headed god; various smaller statues of gods and mortals; chairs, chests and a model boat, complete with rowing slaves. A cluster of stone jars with animal-headed lids stood near the doorway: Neil recognised them as Canopic jars, designed to hold the organs of a mummified body, and the realisation of their purpose made him give an involuntary shudder.

Either side of a massive stone fireplace stood a pair of life-sized Egyptian figures in black and gold, the sort left in tombs to keep the dead company. The figures watched his progress with painted eyes as Caroline led him into a book-lined room, the shelves packed with ancient volumes. The room was cosier than one would expect from the outside appearance of the castle with polished oak furniture and rich Turkish rugs on the dark wood floor. Caroline invited him to sit on a worn velvet sofa.

'Would you like coffee? I usually have one myself at this time of day.'

Neil nodded. He felt nervous, although he wasn't quite sure why, and coffee would give him something to do with his hands.

He had expected Caroline to tug the tasselled bell pull that hung by the great stone fireplace but, to his surprise, she excused herself and left the room. It seemed that she was going to make the coffee herself. He had assumed there'd be some kind of housekeeper at least.

He took advantage of her absence to look around. In the corner stood a grand piano supporting the traditional assortment of family photographs – he'd seen a similar arrangement in almost every stately home he'd ever visited. But instead of smiling grandchildren and the owner of the house shaking hands with a member of the Royal Family, these photographs were mostly black and white. And most of them featured one particular man.

This man was middle-aged, well built with the kind of weather-beaten good looks normally associated with heroic explorers of Queen Victoria's reign. He sported a fine moustache and in each photograph he posed triumphantly next to some notable Egyptian site: at the great pyramid of Cheops; in front of the mortuary temple of Rameses II; dwarfed by a colossal statue of a long-dead pharaoh. There were photographs of him with other men wearing light suits and pith helmets flanked by native Egyptians in their flowing robes, some smiling, some sullen. These were images of a more romantic age of flamboyant gentleman amateurs and great discoveries – a world away from the type of archaeology Neil knew.

He had heard of Sir Frederick Varley, of course. His name had cropped up occasionally at University but, as the topic of Egyptology hadn't featured heavily in the syllabus he'd chosen to follow, he knew only the bare facts about the great man's achievements. Varley had financed various expeditions to the Valley of the Kings and he had been a keen partici-pant in the excavations, although he always employed professional archaeologists to do the scholarly work and locals to do the physical digging.

However, for all his efforts, Varley had never experienced the glory of a really big find: he had been no Lord Car-narvon discovering Tutankhamen's virtually intact tomb. But he had a respectable record none the less, including the discovery of the tombs of a twentieth-dynasty queen, com-plete with intact sarcophagus, and the richly decorated tomb of a chief musician in the court of Amenhotep II when the culture of the New Kingdom was at its peak. For a gentleman amateur, Frederick Varley hadn't done too badly.

Neil walked slowly around the room. Most of the books around the walls were connected in some way with ancient Egypt and there were several small glass display cases con-taining jewels and amulets. All, no doubt, taken from tomb; objects intended to adorn the dead. Neil had always felt that the Egyptians had been obsessed by death and the preserva-tion of the body for the afterlife: perhaps that's why he'd preferred other branches of his chosen profession.

'I see you're admiring my great-grandfather's collection.'

Caroline's voice made Neil jump. He turned round with what he feared was an inane grin on his face and saw her standing in the doorway holding a large wooden tray. He hurried over to her, almost tripping over a well worn rug, and took the tray, hoping to impress her by good manners. He wasn't sure why he felt so eager to make a good impression: after all, it wasn't really something that would benefit the Unit. But there was something about this woman that made him feel he had to be on his best behaviour.

'In fact that's why I contacted your Unit. I thought it would be the best place to start,' she said as Neil placed the tray carefully onto a side table. 'My uncle died three months ago and I inherited the house and estate.'

'Wow.' Neil temporarily forgot to play the cool professional.

'It's more a burden than a blessing, I'm afraid. I'm negotiating for the National Trust to take the place over. There's no way I can afford the upkeep.'

'I'm sorry,' said Neil.

'Don't be. It's an old mausoleum of a place.'

'Did you move in as soon as your uncle died?'

'More or less. I didn't like to think of leaving the place empty.'

'Do you live here alone?'

She didn't answer for a few seconds. 'I have a flat in London – bought it as soon as my divorce came through – so I'm used to fending for myself.'

Her answer seemed a little evasive and Neil wondered if she was hiding something . . . or someone.

'What did you do in London?'

'I was PA to a company director.' She paused. 'And the director in question was a shit. When I inherited this place I told him where he could stick his job.' She smiled at the memory.

'Did you come here much as a child?'

She looked him in the eye as though she was about to share a confidence. 'My mother said that when I was very young I used to start screaming as soon as the car drove through the gates. The place really used to scare me.' She paused. 'Bad things happened here and I'll be glad to get rid of it.'

'What bad things?' Her words had aroused his curiosity.

She waved a hand dismissively and picked up her coffee cup, a chunky mug with a colourful design: Neil had expected bone china. 'It's not important.'

Caroline straightened her back, suddenly businesslike. Neil had caught a brief glimpse behind the confident mask but now the defences were up again. Something in that house made her uncomfortable and he suspected that her decision to give away her inheritance hadn't been influenced solely by financial considerations.

'The thing is,' she began, 'my great-grandfather amassed this huge collection of Egyptian artefacts. The castle's crammed with the things and they're not comfortable to live with, to put it mildly.'

'I can understand that,' said Neil with sympathy. It seemed that the hall and the library only contained a fraction of the collection. Elsewhere there would be more. And as the ancient Egyptians had put a lot of energy into creating and furnishing magnificent tombs, most of what was discovered by later generations was connected with death and funerary rites. The walls of this forbidding house were filled with the memento mori of an ancient civilisation. And this thought made him feel uncomfortable.

'The main collection's upstairs but it's probably best if we start down here and tackle that later. I'd like you to go through everything, Dr Watson. I need to know what's here . . . and if it has any value. There's always a chance the National Trust will want to keep the collection here intact of course, or it might go to a museum, but I'd like to know what I'm dealing with. Just an initial assessment. Nothing too detailed.'

He saw her looking at him expectantly. He was the first port of call. And he felt reluctant to admit his ignorance and tell her she was wasting her time. But he knew it was best to be straight with her. 'I admit I'm not an expert on this sort of thing but I'll have a quick look round and, if necessary, I'll get in touch with someone who can help.'

The truth was, he was anxious to see more of the place. He did his best to look knowledgeable, even though what he knew about Egyptology could be written on a couple of sheets of paper, and followed Caroline out of the room.

He was led down a corridor with towering granite walls. It was only the family portraits punctuating the expanse of stone that made the place look like a home rather than the interior of some ancient temple.

'What did you mean earlier when you said bad things had happened here?' he asked when Caroline stopped to open a tall oak door.

Caroline hesitated for a moment before turning to face him. She took a deep breath. 'Frederick Varley's son – my great uncle – was a murderer,' she stated with simple honesty. 'He killed four women.'

# CHAPTER 3

*I arrived at the castle in the middle of September 1901 – I forget the exact date, which is strange for it should have been imprinted forever on my memory. The trap was sent to meet me at the station and a taciturn man called Walter Hungate helped me with my trunk then drove me to my destination. I asked questions about the house and the family of course, but I received scant reply. Hungate sat up on the driver's seat, apparently without curiosity, addressing himself only to the horse he was driving. He was a large, ugly man whose face reminded me of a hideous gargoyle I saw once scowling down from a church roof and one of his eyes was half closed which gave him a sinister look. I decided to ignore his rudeness. I had been appointed as governess after all and had no need to ingratiate myself with the lower servants.*

*The journey took a full half hour and I felt ill at ease as I sat on the hard wooden seat, my bones jolted with every pothole on the narrow, winding lanes. I had come from the softer landscape of Oxfordshire and thought this part of Devon full of drama and beauty. The leaves were changing from green to russet and the sun was shining in an almost cloudless sky so, at first sight, Varley Castle looked almost inviting as we rounded the corner and saw the great building spread before us like some fortress hewn centuries ago from the granite of the moor.*

*When the trap pulled up before the house I felt that the place was towering over me, harbouring terrifying but delicious secrets. But I had no time to indulge my fertile imagination as the woman I was later to know as Mrs Ball, the housekeeper, was walking out to greet me, her stout shiny shoes crunching loudly on the thick gravel of the drive. She was a tall, well-built woman with a severe look and she said that the master wished to see me as soon as I arrived.*

*I followed her obediently through the tall stone passageways, wishing that I could have had time to rest a little and maybe change out of my travel-stained clothes. But I soon forgot my discomfort when I saw the painted coffins that lined the corridor leading to the drawing room. They stood like sentries with terrible painted faces, their staring, black-lined eyes watching my nervous progress. I knew that they contained the dead because Sir Frederick Varley had told me so during our interview when he had come to Oxford to visit the fellow of Christchurch, an aficionado of Egyptian history, who had recommended me for the post. I knew that inside these coffins were mummified corpses wrapped in linen, centuries old but still recognisable as human beings.*

*How I longed to see them.*

# CHAPTER 4

When Wesley arrived that Monday morning, bleary-eyed after the disturbances of the previous night, he made straight for Gerry's office. But before he could reach his goal he spotted DS Rachel Tracey bustling around the desks with an anxious expression on her face.

'Any news from the hospital about the girl?'

Rachel shook her head. 'I rang a few minutes ago. They just said she was comfortable. Trish is down there doing bedside vigil duty.'

'Have we identified her yet?'

Rachel pushed her blonde hair back off her face and nodded earnestly. 'Her name's Clare Mayers and she's in the sixth form at Neston Grammar. Her mother called to report her missing shortly after she was found. She'd been to the quiz night at the Anglers' Arms and she was due home by eleven thirty. She only lives half a mile away and she'd told her mum she was getting a lift.'

'What about the father?'

'No mention of a father. The mum gave us the names of the girls Clare was supposed to be with so we'll have a word with them. Paul and Nick have gone to the pub to talk to the staff.'

'And the mum?'

'A patrol car took her to the hospital.'

'Good,' said Wesley. It sounded as if everything was under control. But Rachel always made it sound that way.

He could see Gerry sitting in his office with the telephone receiver to his ear. He didn't look happy. As soon as he spotted Wesley through the glass-panelled door he began to make frantic beckoning signals.

Wesley suddenly felt even more tired as he made for Gerry's lair. The interrupted sleep was catching up with him. And his wife, Pam, hadn't been too pleased about being woken in the middle of the night either. For the past week she'd had inspectors crawling all over the school where she taught and, with the worry and stress, getting to sleep was hard enough. Wesley had made sympathetic noises and reminded her that the half-term break began soon. At least that thought had put a smile on her face.

He opened the door to Gerry's office and the DCI looked pleased to see him.

'I've just been onto Forensic,' Gerry began. 'Nothing apart from some tyre tracks in a passing place a bit further up but they could come from any vehicle that had been down there in the past day. I know it's hardly an A road but it's a short cut to Hugford so there's a fair bit of local traffic.'

'It was quiet last night: our man probably wouldn't have needed to use a passing place to give way to an oncoming vehicle.'

Gerry sighed. 'You're right. And by the time Danny Coyle arrived on the scene the attacker had buggered off. And the couple in the cottage on the corner didn't see or hear anything.'

'I think the sound of Coyle's car coming up the lane disturbed the attacker. Probably saved her life.'

Gerry looked up suddenly. 'Unless it was Danny Coyle who did the dirty deed and lost his nerve.'

Wesley shook his head. He couldn't see it himself. 'I think the attacker drove down the lane from the main road, saw Clare walking and stopped his car a bit further on just round the bend out of sight. Then he walked back to meet her.'

'She was attacked from behind. She might have seen him coming and started to run back towards the pub.'

'Which means something about him frightened her.'

'Or her mum warned her never to talk to strange men on dark deserted lanes.'

Wesley didn't let Gerry's comment interrupt his train of thought. 'Our man probably saw the headlights of Danny's van approaching and legged it, leaving the job half done. He could have run back round the bend and driven off before Danny had a chance to see him. It wasn't that long after closing time so someone might have seen a vehicle driving away fast.'

'Uniform did a house-to-house in Hugford first thing this morning but nobody saw a thing.' He rolled his eyes to heaven. 'All sleeping virtuously in their own beds for once. Just our luck.'

Wesley sat down and leaned across the desk. 'Gerry, I've been going over a few things in my head. Could this attack be linked with that one in Neston last month? I know the victim was unharmed but these things sometimes escalate.

23

Today's flasher can become tomorrow's rapist. What do you think?'

Gerry pulled a face, the one he pulled when he was deep in thought. The first attack had happened just after New Year in Neston, eight miles upstream from Tradmouth. The victim was a young woman who'd been walking home from a pub – just as Clare Mayers had been – and the attacker had been a man in a black hooded top and a mask.

According to the Neston victim's description of her attacker, he was average height. Average build. Average everything. He'd grabbed her from behind, thrown her onto the ground and tried to thrust his hand inside her clothing, fleeing when she started to scream. The victim had described the mask he was wearing as some kind of cartoon animal but she couldn't be specific.

The attack had left the victim more shocked than traumatised. But Wesley couldn't dispel the thought that sex attackers tend to grow bolder and more vicious with time.

'There's no indication that Clare Mayers suffered any kind of sexual assault,' he said. 'She was certainly fully dressed when she was found.'

Gerry snorted. 'If you can call what these young girls wear these days fully dressed. Skirts up to their knickers.'

Wesley grinned. 'You're showing your age, Gerry.'

'Maybe. But I never let our Rosie go out like that when she was at school.'

Wesley said nothing, certain that Gerry's daughter, Rosie, had had her wild moments when her widowed dad's back was turned.

Gerry changed the subject. 'Clare was strangled with some sort of thin cord or twine so he'd come prepared. If it was a spur of the moment thing, he'd have used his hands.'

24

After a perfunctory knock the door swung open to reveal Rachel standing on the threshold. 'Sorry to interrupt. There's a call for you, Wesley. An Inspector Petrie from the Met. He says you know him.'

Wesley's mind was so preoccupied with the recent attacks that it took him a couple of seconds to place the name. But as soon as he did he stood up, almost knocking his chair over. 'Ian Petrie's my old boss from the Arts and Antiques Squad at the Met. I'd better see what he wants.'

'We can't spare you to go poncing about after some art smugglers, Wes,' Gerry said, half joking, half concerned.

'Don't worry.' The boss looked as though he was in need of a bit of reassurance. But Wesley had experienced a feeling of curiosity and even excitement at the mention of Ian Petrie's name.

When he reached his desk he picked up the phone. It was a long time since he'd had any contact with Ian Petrie other than the obligatory card at Christmas. When he'd worked in the Met he'd liked the man. A gentleman copper, always dapper in suit, tie and a rose in his buttonhole, he had been the object of many snide remarks from officers in other, supposedly tougher, units like vice and serious crime. But the dandyish veneer had hidden a sharp intelligence. In spite of his appreciation of the finer things in life, Petrie had faced his fair share of violence and put away more than his fair share of villains over the years.

'Ian? It's Wesley.'

'Wesley, my dear chap. How are you?'

Wesley detected an air of forced jollity in his voice, as though he had something on his mind other than catching up with an old colleague.

'Well, thank you. And you?'

'Look, I need some help. As you're sunning yourself in the West Country, you're the first person I thought of.'

Wesley didn't know whether to feel flattered or horrified. It sounded as though Ian Petrie was assuming, like many London officers, that policing in Devon and Cornwall was an easy option; chasing stolen tractors and locking up drunken tourists.

'Hardly sunning myself at the moment,' said Wesley, keeping the conversation light but wondering how he could let his old boss down gently. He really didn't have time for distractions at that moment.

'Quite right. The weather's worse than it is in London.'

'But we do tend to get milder winters.' As Wesley said the words he wondered to himself how he had come to be discussing the weather. He gathered his thoughts. 'How exactly can I help you, Ian?'

'Look, can we meet up for lunch? Promise I won't keep you long.'

'You're actually down here?'

'Yes, I've just arrived. Didn't I say? How about that lunch?'

'Sorry, Ian. A girl was attacked last night . . . half strangled in a country lane. There was an assault in Neston last month and we're wondering whether there's a connection. I'll be lucky if I can grab a sandwich at my desk.'

'Please, Wesley. It's important.'

Wesley hesitated. 'Where are you staying?'

'I'm booked into a place called the Tradmouth Castle Hotel. How does twelve thirty suit you?'

'OK. I'll meet you in the Ship Bar on the ground floor.'

'Great. Look forward to seeing you. I need to pick your brains.'

As Wesley put the phone down he had an uneasy feeling

that he'd just committed himself to something he'd probably regret.

DC Trish Walton hated hospitals. She'd hated them ever since she'd watched her father die in a hospital bed with tubes and airways sprouting from his wasted body. She'd sat next to her mother, comforting her, while her sister had made herself scarce and gone off to her boyfriend's house because she couldn't stand their father's pain. Trish, the more dutiful daughter, had stuck it out, knowing that her mother needed the support.

As she sat outside the single room where Clare Mayers lay, it brought the memories back. The smell, the shiny linoleum floor, the pale pattern on the curtains around the beds, the sound of the machines. She'd peeped through the window in the door from time to time, just to reassure herself that nothing disastrous had happened and the machines were still bleeping as they should. Each time she'd seen Clare's pretty bruised face on the pillow she thought how young she looked . . . and how vulnerable. She hoped she'd pull through.

A nurse – middle-aged and reassuringly motherly – bustled past her to perform some routine checks and as she opened the door Trish slipped in behind her.

'Is everything OK?' she asked nervously as the woman checked the drip that was emptying itself drop by slow drop into Clare's arm.

The nurse looked round, her face serious. 'She's holding her own.'

'Any idea when she'll come round?'

'No idea, love,' the nurse said with a sympathetic smile. 'Could be tomorrow, could be in the next five minutes.'

Trish looked down at Clare's neck. The thin wound, like a necklace of blood, had been cleaned up and a couple of the deeper incisions had been sealed with stitches. Now it was hidden by a layer of gauze.

The nurse carried on with her tasks, talking to the unconscious girl every so often, telling her what she was doing as though she could hear and understand every word. Trish liked her for it.

'Would it help if I sat by the bed and talked to her?'

The nurse was washing her hands in the basin at the side of the room. She turned and smiled. 'I always like to think they can understand. It's just that they can't let you know. It certainly can't do any harm, can it?'

When the nurse left the room Trish took a seat by the bed, pulling the chair closer to the unconscious girl with a loud scrape of metal on linoleum. She took in a deep breath of disinfected air and began to talk. She started with the weather but after she'd exhausted the subject of the hospital she thought she'd better try and talk about what happened. In the gentlest possible way, of course.

'I don't know if you remember anything about last night,' she began. 'You'd been to the quiz night at the Anglers' Arms with your mates. How did you do? I'm useless at quizzes – I can never get the sports questions but that's what we keep boyfriends for, isn't it?' She paused, her eyes fixed on the girl's face, hoping for a reaction. She was beginning to feel a little foolish, chatting away to someone who probably couldn't hear her. But she decided to carry on. At least it relieved the boredom.

'Your mum'll be back soon. She had things to sort out at work and she knows you're in safe hands here.'

It was hard work trying to sound positive. She searched

28

round for something new to say but failed. Then as she stared at Clare's face she thought she saw a slight movement of the eyelids. She leaned forward. 'Clare. It's OK, you're safe in hospital.'

For a few moments she was convinced that she had imagined the flicker of the eyes. But it was there again. Stronger this time. Trish froze, watching intently. And when the eyes flicked open then shut again, she searched for the button to summon the nurse.

When she looked back at the bed she saw that Clare's eyes were fully open. She bent to take hold of the girl's hand, careful not to disturb the drips and the sensor clipped to her finger and Clare's grey eyes slowly focused on her face.

Her lips began to move. At first no sound emerged but a low rasping mumble, incomprehensible at first. Then her dry lips began to form words.

The effort almost seemed too much for her but it was clear that she had something important to say.

'What are you trying to tell me, Clare? Do you know who did this to you?'

Clare gasped for breath as she fixed Trish's eyes with hers. 'Dog,' she mouthed, the sound coming out in a hoarse, painful whisper. 'Dog's head.'

Then the eyes shut and she collapsed back on the blue hospital pillow, exhausted by the effort.

# CHAPTER 5

*Sir Frederick Varley greeted me with great politeness and we conversed for a while before he made any mention of his children.*

*I had been informed at our interview in Oxford a month before that he had three children. There was a twenty-one-year-old son called John who, naturally, was not my concern. His mother, I was to discover later, had ended her days in an asylum and upon her death, Sir Frederick had married again. By his second wife, Sir Frederick had fathered two further children: Victoria, now aged eight, and Edward, aged seven. After Edward's birth the second Lady Varley had been called to meet her Maker and it would be my task to educate and care for these two motherless children. I had expected to feel some degree of apprehension about making their acquaintance but now I was at the castle, I found I possessed a new confidence. Surely these infants could be no more terrifying than the reminders of death that surrounded them.*

*It was Sir Frederick himself who took me to meet the children in the nursery. I had expected the sound of play or squabbling to reach my ears as we approached the room and I was surprised by the silence.*

*Sir Frederick pushed the door open and I took in the scene. The schoolroom and nursery were neat and well equipped with a large blackboard and many toys and puzzles set upon shelves in an orderly manner. The pictures adorning the walls all appeared to be connected with Sir Frederick's travels and interests: paintings of the pyramids and framed copies of wall paintings and hieroglyphics. There was a large chart on the far wall illustrating the various gods of Ancient Egypt: Horus with his falcon's head was there, as was my favourite, Anubis.*

*The children were sitting at desks, backs straight and arms folded. But their eyes bore into me as though they could see into my very soul.*

# CHAPTER 6

The call had come in from Trish Walton: Clare Mayers had regained consciousness. But when she told Gerry Heffernan about Clare's indistinct words, he made the assumption that the sedation the girl must have been given was making her hallucinate. A man with the head of a dog.

But Wesley couldn't forget that the Neston attacker had worn an animal mask of sorts, albeit a cartoon version. Maybe after the first attack he'd found that frightening a woman and robbing her of her dignity wasn't enough. Maybe he'd branched out into attempted murder.

Some of the team had gone over to Neston Police Station to talk to the officers who'd dealt with the assault investigation. Although the MO had changed there were enough similarities to ring alarm bells – the possibility of an animal mask; the time of day, and the fact that the victims were both walking home from a pub.

Gerry had given orders that all known sex offenders in the

area were to be traced, interviewed and, where appropriate, eliminated from the enquiry. Wesley looked at his watch: he didn't have long to grab some lunch. Just long enough to meet Ian Petrie for half an hour at the Tradmouth Castle Hotel. After squaring it with Gerry he grabbed his coat from the hooks by the incident room door and hurried out, hoping that nobody would comment on his departure.

He dashed out of the building, hugging his coat around his body against the biting wind blowing in from the grey river. It had started to rain and the drops felt like bullets of ice as they landed on his warm skin. In summer the seats in the Memorial Gardens were always occupied by tourists and those with too much time on their hands but today they were empty and glistened with damp. As Wesley rushed past them some of the little plaques fixed to their backs caught his eye: people who'd loved the place and people who'd enjoyed happy hours there; touching little messages from the dead.

The tide was in and the small boats in the enclosed harbour bobbed energetically like excited children. Wesley could see the hotel to his right and the entrance looked welcoming. And warm.

He made his way to the Ship Bar, a perfect example of the cosy English inn with deeply upholstered seating and maritime knick-knacks hanging from low beams. He stood for a moment in the doorway and the enticing aroma of hot pub lunches made him realise he was hungry. He spotted Ian Petrie sitting in an armchair in the corner, a half-full pint glass in front of him, staring into the dancing flames of a log fire. As Wesley approached he looked up and his pensive expression became a fixed smile of greeting.

'Wesley. Good to see you.' He held out his hand and

Wesley noticed that it was shaking a little. 'Congratulations on the promotion, by the way.'

Wesley thanked him and as he sat down a young waitress came over to take their order – sandwiches for Wesley and fish and chips for Ian. Wesley stuck to shandy, explaining that he needed to keep a clear head. Ian ordered another pint of a Devon brewery's strongest offering.

They spent five minutes catching up on news – old times and past crimes – and of course old colleagues: who was still in the squad; who had left and what they were doing now. When Wesley asked after Ian's wife, Sheila, Ian gave an enigmatic smile and said she was fine. Wesley wondered if something was wrong with the marriage. 'Fine' covered a multitude of possibilities.

For all Ian's attempts to appear relaxed and casual, Wesley sensed a tension, a forced quality to the smiles and jokes. Ian looked tired. He had also lost quite a bit of weight and the lines around his bloodshot eyes had deepened into furrows – but then it was over six years since they'd last met.

Ian suddenly abandoned the subject of the Met and looked Wesley in the eye. 'Tradmouth's a nice place. Can't blame you for settling here.'

'It was originally Pam's idea. She's from round here and she was worried about her mother being on her own after her father died. Not that her mother needs any looking after,' he added with a rueful smile. He had always found the subject of his mother-in-law, Della, an awkward one. 'My sister's down here too now: she married a vicar and she's working as a GP in Neston, eight miles away.'

When Ian didn't reply Wesley feared that his family ramblings were boring him. He glanced at his watch, recalling the scene of industry in the incident room and Clare Mayers lying in the hospital nearby. It was time to get down to business and discover exactly what Ian Petrie wanted.

'I really haven't got long, I'm afraid. As I told you, a girl was attacked last night and we're pulling out all the stops.' He smiled apologetically. 'You said you wanted to pick my brains.'

Ian took a long drink then replaced his glass carefully on the table. 'I'm investigating a case of smuggled antiquities and the trail's led here, to South Devon.'

Wesley straightened his back, suddenly interested. He knew his time would be fully occupied with the Clare Mayers case but it would do no harm to listen to what Petrie had to say. 'Go on.'

Ian took another drink and began. 'Various valuable Egyptian antiquities have been turning up in auction rooms around London. It started a year ago when an expert from the British Museum identified one of them as coming from a certain dig in the Valley of the Kings in the nineteen seventies and when we started looking closer we found that the provenance of the treasure in question was a bit dodgy to say the least. We found more antiquities in a warehouse we raided. The artefacts were hidden inside crude statues and tacky trinkets made for the tourist market and once they were back in this country the outer clay was broken off to get at them. They shipped crateloads of the stuff over from Egypt under the noses of the authorities that way and then sold them over here and in the States with fake provenances. I have to hand it to them, they were clever.'

'Why Devon?'

'One of the men we arrested – just a foot soldier as far as we can tell – said that an artist from this area created the fake statues and trinkets. Whoever's behind it – and we think we know who it is – sourced the dodgy artefacts in Egypt and paid for this artist to go over and do his bit before exporting the stuff back to London as cheap tourist crap. Any ideas who this artist might be?'

'South Devon's full of artists, Ian. You can't move for them.' The food arrived and he waited until the waitress had gone before he continued. 'And I can't think of any who'd do that sort of work.'

'A sculptor perhaps. Someone who's come into money recently. The name Neston was mentioned.'

'A lot of artists operate in Neston. It's an arty sort of place.'

Ian leaned forward. 'We need to find this man. The people we've got so far don't know who's organising all this but I reckon the artist is pretty high up in the organisation. We think he's called Ra, if that's any help. Very appropriate – the Egyptian sun god.'

'It doesn't ring any bells.'

Ian Petrie looked a little disappointed. 'You were one of my best officers, Wesley. Pity you transferred to this backwater. Wives often have a lot to answer for.' He touched Wesley's arm. 'Look, if you ever fancy a return to the Met . . .'

'Sorry, Ian. As backwaters go, this isn't a bad one.' He finished off his sandwich and pushed his plate away. 'I'm sorry I haven't been much help. But when I have a minute I will ask around and I'll let you know if I find anything.' He looked at his watch and stood up. 'I've got to go, I'm afraid. It's really good to see you.' He held out his hand and Petrie shook it firmly. 'I'll be in touch.'

As Wesley left the bar to walk back to the police station he fastened his coat against the blast of cold that met him outside the front door.

At one time he'd known Ian well. But now he felt that his

36

old boss almost seemed like a stranger, although he wasn't quite sure what had changed. A new weariness perhaps; or a strain that hadn't been there before: the smile too forced, or a false note when he'd discussed the case. Or maybe he was imagining things.

He hurried back to the police station. He'd hardly liked to spell it out to Ian but the smuggling of Egyptian antiquities was pretty low on his list of priorities at that moment.

Clare Mayers was asleep when Wesley arrived at Tradmouth Hospital with Gerry Heffernan by his side. Although they'd agreed that Trish Walton should do most of the questioning, Gerry wanted to hear for himself what the girl had to say. Wesley knew this would have the added advantage of re-assuring her anxious mother that the man in charge was taking a hands-on interest.

Wesley was surprised to find that the mother wasn't hovering at her daughter's bedside. According to Trish, Karen Mayers had gone to work but she'd be there as soon as she could. She was a single mother and there was no regular partner about so she couldn't afford to take much time off. When Trish had asked Karen some probing questions about Clare's biological father, she had said that there was no way she wanted him traced and told about his daughter's misfortune. Wesley asked Trish to keep on probing gently; the man was the victim's father after all, and he was bound to want to know. Trish gave him a conspiratorial smile and said she'd do her best.

Gerry had told Trish to go and get herself a cup of tea before slumping down on the chair she had just vacated.

'Has someone been in touch with her school? We need to talk to the friends she was with. The attacker might have been in the pub watching her – he might have seen her go off down that lane on her own and followed in his car. The friends might have seen him.'

'Rach is going to the school this afternoon to take their statements.'

As Gerry opened his mouth to answer a young man appeared, walking towards them down the corridor. He had dark curly hair and the stethoscope hanging around his neck like a chain of office indicated that he was a doctor, albeit a youthful and junior one. He was making straight for the room where Clare Mayers lay asleep and, as this was the first medically qualified person Wesley had seen since his arrival, he wasn't going to let the opportunity pass him by.

He approached the doctor and flashed his warrant card but the medical man looked unimpressed. 'Can you tell us when we can interview her?'

The doctor didn't answer. Instead he pushed open the door to Clare's room and disappeared inside. A minute or so later he appeared again with a file in his hand. He studied it for a few moments then looked up at Wesley.

'She's been lucky. If she'd been found a couple of minutes later . . . Curtains.'

He made a slashing motion across his throat and Wesley found himself hoping that he used a gentler approach when relatives were present. Wesley, like all policemen, understood the appeal of gallows humour but there was a time and a place for everything.

'Will she be able to talk to us soon?'

'Someone's just tried to garrotte her so she won't be giving any long speeches or singing the lead in *Tosca* any time soon but she might be able to manage an inelegant croak.'

'So she'll pull through?' Gerry asked.

Wesley could tell from the way his boss asked the question that the doctor was starting to irritate him.

'The vocal cords are bruised but there's no lasting damage as far as we can tell. She should be fine. Fortunately chummy didn't have time to do his worst.'

'Chummy?'

Wesley couldn't tell whether Gerry was mildly amused or about to tell the young medic a few unpleasant facts of life.

'I thought that's what you called them. Criminals, I mean.'

'Not since Dixon of Dock Green was a lad,' Gerry muttered, rolling his eyes.

The doctor grinned and reopened the door to Clare's room. 'I'll put this file back and then my shift's finished. If she's awake when I go in you can try and have a word with her.'

'All right for some,' Gerry muttered under his breath as he watched the young man enter the room.

But when he re-emerged their luck was out. Clare was still fast asleep, sedated, no doubt, to aid her recovery. As they prepared to leave they heard a noise. Trish was coming down the corridor towards them and the woman by her side was walking in step, plucking at her sleeve anxiously, asking questions. Wesley recognised an anxious mother when he saw one. And this one looked worried. He looked round for the young doctor, hoping he would talk to her and put her mind at ease, but he'd disappeared off in the other direction. So much for communication.

Trish made the introductions and Karen Mayers shook their hands limply.

'We've just been talking to the doctor,' Wesley said, thinking that the woman deserved some sort of reassurance. 'He doesn't think there's any lasting damage.'

Somehow this news didn't improve Karen's mood. She still wore the strained expression of someone who's expecting the worst.

She ignored Wesley and looked Gerry in the eye. 'Has he touched her? Has he . . . has he interfered with her?' She jerked her head towards Trish. 'I've asked her but she won't tell me.'

'No, love,' Gerry said gently. 'He's not touched her. We're sure about that.'

Karen didn't seem very reassured by Gerry's words. 'I'll kill him.' She almost spat the words. 'When I find him I'm going to kill him.'

'Don't worry, love. We'll get him.' Gerry's voice was soothing. 'We've got the whole team after him.'

'But he's buggered off. I don't know where he is.'

Wesley suddenly realised that she was talking about one man in particular rather than some nebulous attacker in the shadows. 'Who do you mean, Karen? What's his name?'

'Alan Jakes, of course. My ex. He said she needed teaching a lesson but I never thought he'd do something like this.'

Neil Watson sat in Varley Castle's palatial kitchen amongst the tall oak cupboards and its racks of crockery eating the vegetable soup that Caroline had heated up for their lunch and, try as he might, he couldn't get her words out of his mind. Her great-uncle had killed four women.

Instead of elaborating, as soon as the words had left her mouth she'd changed the subject and began to tell him all about Sir Frederick's many expeditions to Egypt. To Neil it sounded as though the great amateur Egyptologist had been a rather hyperactive man, juggling his business empire with his passion for all things Egyptian. Neil himself had never been bitten by the Egypt bug, although he had known quite a few people in the course of his archaeological career who had succumbed.

As Neil pushed his plate away and made appreciative noises, he saw Caroline watching him closely, a slight smile playing on her lips, like a nurse watching her patient take his first nourishment after a long illness. Perhaps, he thought, he looked as though he was in need of a good meal. Living on his own, he tended to neglect domestic matters.

'Was that all right? I made it myself.'

'Lovely, thanks. Delicious. Look, I need to call someone in London . . . at the British Museum. They should really assess all this stuff and . . .'

Caroline stood up. 'As a matter of fact someone from the British Museum did contact me just after I wrote to you. He rang out of the blue saying he'd seen a piece about the castle in the paper and it mentioned Sir Frederick's collection. He asked if he could have a look at it.'

Neil's first reaction was suspicion. 'So who is he?'

'Hang on.' She crossed the room to the dresser and took some scraps of paper from underneath an old bakelite telephone – messages filed under D for Deal with One Day. 'Here it is. Dr Andrew Beredace. He works in their Egyptology Department. He sounded very keen. I said I'd get back to him.'

'OK. If he's genuine it might be just what we need.'

Caroline looked alarmed. 'You don't think he could be a fraud?'

Neil took pity on her. 'Tell you what, I'll call the British Museum later and speak to him myself.'

'Thanks.'

41

'I'd better take a look at the rest of the collection now if that's all right with you,' he said as he stood up.

'Of course. That's why I asked you here.' She picked up his dish and carried it over to the row of wooden sinks that dominated one side of the room, a relic from the time when an army of cooks and kitchen maids toiled in this space. The octagonal kitchen with its vaulted ceiling hadn't changed much in the intervening years and there was certainly no sign of a dishwasher, although a large fridge of indeterminate vintage wheezed in a distant corner.

She left the dishes unwashed in the sink and turned to face him. 'Like I said, the bulk of the stuff's upstairs. I'll show you the way.'

'Thanks. That'd be great.' He hesitated for a moment. There was something he wanted to ask and he hoped she wouldn't find his next question too intrusive. 'Were you close to your uncle?'

She considered the question for a few seconds. 'I didn't see him that often but I liked him. He was a lonely man, socially awkward if you know what I mean. But he was kind: when I was scared of the mummies he used to give them silly names and he let me try on jewels. He told me they belonged to an Egyptian princess.' She smiled. 'And he said the dead couldn't harm me. That's true, isn't it? Once you're dead, you're dead.'

Neil nodded. 'I'm surprised he didn't think of donating the collection to a museum.'

'My uncle George wasn't a decisive man. He tended to leave things as they were . . . hence the state of this kitchen. He thought of the collection as part of the fixtures and fittings so he never considered getting rid of it. My mother always said that he was even too lazy to find himself a wife.

He ran the estate and took an interest in wildlife and that's about it.' She looked Neil in the eye. 'But I feel an obligation to make sure this place is looked after. That's why I hope the National Trust will keep the collection here. Can you understand that?'

'Yes. Look, I'd better make a start. Thanks for lunch.'

'You're welcome. I'll show you upstairs.'

He let her walk ahead, out of the kitchen wing and back into the main house. Both parts of the house boasted plain granite walls which gave the place an austere look. It was only the rich carpets on the floors of the family wing that differentiated it from below stairs.

'Sir Frederick's father, Albert Varley, built the castle – he later became Sir Albert because of the baronetcy,' Caroline said as they walked through the wide corridors, lit on one side by tall Gothic windows. 'He hired the architect Sir Edward Harding to draw up the plans and he rejected the first lot for not being grand enough.'

She sounded like a tour guide, Neil thought. Maybe she'd end up as one if she decided to remain on the premises when the National Trust took over the running of the castle. He could see her in that role.

'Sir Frederick,' she continued, 'inherited in 1897. He'd been running the family business long before then, of course, ever since his father handed over the reins.'

'Remind me what the family business was,' Neil asked. Whatever the Varleys had made it must have been lucrative but Neil couldn't remember what it was that had brought them their fortune.

'Pickle. Varley's Vegetable Pickle.' She stopped and smiled, as if she could tell what was going through Neil's mind. 'How could a humble pickle manufacturer from Bristol fancy himself as a mighty medieval baron and build himself a huge castle on Dartmoor, eh? I suppose that was just the Victorian way. They were hardly lacking in confidence, were they?'

Neil didn't answer.

'Anyway, like many wealthy industrialists in those days Sir Albert tried to emulate the life of an aristocrat and he sent his eldest son on some sort of grand tour. Frederick eventually found himself in Egypt and that's when his obsession began. By the time Frederick took over the company it was well established and he was able to leave business matters in the hands of reliable managers while he indulged his passions and built up his collection. This place is packed with all the stuff great-grandfather Freddy brought home from Egypt in the latter years of the nineteenth century.' She hesitated, shooting him an uncertain glance. 'Did I tell you about Robert Delaware?'

'No. Who's Robert Delaware?'

'He's writing Freddy's biography and he's been coming here on and off for a couple of months now to look through the family papers. He lives in Tradmouth but I told him he can stay over when he needs to. It's not as if I haven't got the room and it saves him driving all the way back to Tradmouth. No doubt you'll meet him at some point.'

'No doubt.' Neil took a deep breath. All through lunch he'd been longing to ask a question but Caroline had filled the time with chatter so the opportunity hadn't really arisen. 'You mentioned something about your great-uncle murdering four women.'

Caroline stopped in her tracks. 'Yes, I did, didn't I?'

'What happened?'

'All I know is that four local women were murdered, then

my great-uncle – John, I think his name was – hanged himself in the woods on the estate and the killings stopped.'

'Was he Sir Frederick's son?'

'Yes. I think that's why I don't know much. It was all hushed up and it never came to trial. And of course the family never talked about it.'

She began to walk again, faster this time. Soon they were climbing a grand staircase, seemingly carved out of solid stone. The winter sun must have come out from behind the clouds because the space was suddenly flooded with light from the tall windows. As Neil followed he could see clouds of dust particles dancing in the beams. The place probably needed a good clean but he was sure that the National Trust would see to that when the time came.

He couldn't get the deaths of those four women out of his mind and the fact that Caroline either couldn't or wouldn't go into detail about them made him even more curious. Her words had started to insinuate their way into his mind like a burrowing worm and when he got home to his flat he'd see what he could find out on the Internet. But in the meantime he had to show the flag for the County Archaeological Unit.

They had reached the landing now. It was lined with painted mummy cases standing upright like sentries. He half expected them to creak open to reveal bandaged mummies who would step out, arms outstretched like in the horror films of his teenage memory. But they stood still and inscrutable, their painted eyes watching him as Caroline led him to the end of the dimly lit passage. She stood there for a few seconds before pushing a pair of tall double doors open with a dramatic flourish. The room beyond the doors was as dark as an impenetrable underground cavern until Caroline

45

reached inside and flicked on a dim overhead bulb. She stepped to one side and Neil realised that he was meant to enter. But he suddenly felt reluctant when he saw what was inside.

He had never seen so many dead bodies in one room.

They had an address for Karen Mayer's ex-boyfriend, Alan Jakes – a maisonette at the edge of the Tradmouth council estate. But when a patrol car called round there was nobody at home and the neighbours hadn't seen him for a couple of days.

According to Karen, Jakes worked at a small garage on the outskirts of Tradmouth. It was the sort of establishment often found underneath railway arches in big cities: but, as Tradmouth was rather short of railway arches, it was situated on a small industrial estate on the edge of the town.

The officers who went there were told that Jakes was taking a few days off to, as he'd put it, 'get his head together', which had annoyed his boss because he'd already taken a fortnight off in January to go to Florida with his sister.

One of the mechanics had heard that Jakes had been moonlighting, working on boat engines for a mate. The boss wouldn't be pleased with this arrangement, the colleague said ominously, and if he found out, Jakes would be lucky to keep his job. From time to time Jakes had talked about his tempestuous relationship with Karen Mayers and he'd called Karen's daughter, Clare, an interfering little bitch who needed 'sorting out'. His colleagues had found this embarrassing as, like most men, they preferred to confine the workplace conversation to sport and cars.

At that moment Jakes seemed to be the best suspect they had. But had he attacked Clare? And could he also have

46

attacked the woman in Neston back in January? A copy of the victim's statement had been sent over from Neston CID and Wesley sat at his desk reading it, searching for any similarities to the attack on Clare Mayers. However, for every similarity there was a thumping great difference. But criminals don't always work to a set script. Like everyone else, they get sick of the old routines and try out new ideas.

'Wesley.'

He looked up. Rachel Tracey was standing there, well wrapped up in a long brown wool coat, complete with gloves and scarf.

'I'm going to speak to Clare's friends at Neston Grammar. I've been in touch and asked them whether they preferred to be interviewed this evening at home or after school. They opted for school. They probably want to keep their parents out of it.'

Wesley nodded. The parents would be liable to panic at the reminder that the world was a perilous place for a young woman on her own. And the last thing an eighteen-year-old girl needs is parents fussing about and clipping her social wings.

'Want me to come with you?'

'Might be helpful.' She tilted her head to one side and gave him what looked like a wink. 'It's a girls' school so they'll be falling over themselves to make a good impression.' When he'd first known Rachel she had been inclined to flirt a little but she hadn't done so for a while. It made him feel a little uncomfortable and he looked away.

'I'd better tell the boss.'

'For heaven's sake don't suggest he comes with us. He'll do his jolly Uncle Gerry act and that'll shut them up altogether.'

Wesley knew Rachel was right. He looked into Gerry's

office and told him where he was going, then darted out to rejoin Rachel before Gerry could offer to tag along.

They drove the eight miles or so to Neston Grammar School for Girls, a fine example of nineteen thirties neo-classical municipal architecture. It was a quarter to four now: in fifteen minutes the girls would be released, giggling and swaggering their way down the school drive, hitching up their navy-blue uniform skirts once they were off school property as generations had done before them.

Rachel checked her appearance in the rear-view mirror before climbing out of the driver's seat and as they walked towards the school building, Wesley let her go first.

They were shown straight to the headmistress's office and found the woman in charge sitting behind a massive desk. She wore a smart trouser suit and reminded Wesley of some city director, businesslike and efficient.

She shook hands firmly, an expression of concern on her thin face. The girls in question, she said, were under instruction to report to her office at home time. As they were all over eighteen, there was no need for a parent or member of staff to act as an appropriate adult, she said, sounding rather disappointed. She went on to enquire about Clare's progress, each word carefully chosen so that she breached no guidelines or policies concerning confidentiality. Wesley answered in official terms. She had regained consciousness and was out of danger.

The electric school bell rang at four o'clock on the dot, shattering the silence. Then came a rumble like an approaching avalanche as home-bound footsteps echoed down corridors along with the sound of a thousand chattering female voices, like birds disturbed in an aviary.

'Before the girls arrive, Mrs Benson, could you tell me

everything you know about Clare Mayers? Her family circumstances and her relationships with staff and students.' Wesley tilted his head to one side expectantly.

'Clare is an able student, if a little on the lazy side. She is an only child and her mother is divorced. As far as I know she had lost touch with her biological father.'

'Would it surprise you to know that her mother was in a relationship with a man called Alan Jakes who is alleged to have threatened Clare?'

Mrs Benson opened her mouth and closed it again. 'The school wasn't made aware of this. If we had been there are procedures in place to . . . I can only follow the guidelines.'

'Of course. How would you know if nobody brought it to your attention at a meeting?' said Wesley pointedly. If the head had kept her eyes and ears open and got to know her pupils instead of playing at being Chief Executive, she might have picked up on what was going on. But he knew only too well from Pam how the world of modern education worked.

'Clare's form teacher says she's very quiet,' the head continued.

'So she goes unnoticed?' It was the first time Rachel had spoken. Mrs Benson gave her a wary look.

'That's always a danger with the quieter student.'

'Was she bullied?' Rachel asked.

This hit the spot. Mrs Benson rose from her seat, like an animal on the defensive. 'We have a very strict anti-bullying policy at this school.'

'But girls can be subtle about it. The staff might not know.'

Wesley looked at Rachel and saw that her cheeks had turned red. Once when they'd been working closely together and had been filling the time during a long and boring evening of surveillance by swapping childhood memories, she'd confessed to him that she'd been part of a group that had bullied a younger girl at school. He knew she found the memory painful and embarrassing. She hated what she'd done back then and she'd said that if she could have made it up to her victim she would. But the girl had left the school and Rachel didn't know what had become of her.

There was a knock on the door, nervous and tentative.

'That'll be the students. I have things to do. If there's anything you need . . .'

After Wesley assured her that they'd be fine, Mrs Benson opened the door to admit three girls and slipped out of the room.

The term 'girls', in Wesley's opinion, was misleading. These were young women. And, in spite of the neat school uniforms they wore, they had the worldly-wise look of women ten years their senior. In September they'd be at university, he thought, wondering if Pam had ever seemed that sophisticated during their student days. He thought not.

The girls sat down as invited. Wesley and Rachel had already decided not to place themselves behind the head's desk, in the position of authority. Instead they drew their seats into a cosy circle, like a group of friends meeting for a chat.

The girls introduced themselves one by one as Vicky Page, Sarah Salter and Peony White. They seemed confident, unfazed by the fact that they were being interviewed by the police. Wesley couldn't help wishing that they looked a bit more nervous. But then over-confidence has tripped up many a liar. He sat back and listened while Rachel began the questioning.

Vicky Page did most of the talking. She was tall, blonde

and beautiful but her lips were rather too thin and there was something hard about her blue eyes. She was the sort of girl who should have been irresistible in theory but there was something distinctly unattractive about her demeanour . . . and Wesley couldn't quite put his finger on what it was.

'So whose idea was it to go to the Anglers' Arms?' Wesley asked.

'Peony's,' Vicky said quickly, as though she was trying to shift the blame. Peony herself sat quite still and said nothing. 'Her brother worked there once and he said the quiz night was a good laugh.'

'How did Clare seem during the evening?'

'Quiet.' This was a simple statement of fact but Wesley thought he could detect something else behind the words, some criticism perhaps or some indication that Clare was regarded as the outsider of the group, the lowest in their teenage pecking order.

Rachel looked at Vicky and smiled sweetly. 'How come Clare was walking home alone? Her mum thought she was getting a lift.'

Vicky cleared her throat. 'Yeah. Jen offered her a lift back but she cried off at the last minute.'

'So how did you get back?'

Wesley looked round the group and saw that they were avoiding Rachel's eyes.

Vicky hesitated. 'Er . . . we shared a taxi.'

'Why didn't you give Clare a lift?'

'We were going in the opposite direction. She said she'd be OK 'cause it wasn't far.'

Wesley noticed a meaningful look pass between Sarah and Peony and he knew that Vicky was lying.

He'd had enough. It was time they talked to each girl

alone and found out what Sarah and Peony had to say away from Vicky's influence. He nodded to Rachel and they left the room to discuss tactics. They decided to start with Peony. Vicky they would save till last. The wait would do her good.

Peony was a plain girl, the sort bullies often used as a right-hand man – or woman. She was heavily built with dark hair and eyebrows that were in danger of meeting in the middle like a pair of over-friendly caterpillars.

Wesley began by asking Peony's opinion of Clare. The answer was as he expected. Clare was great. But the unconvincing way she said the words told him that she was lying.

'Did Clare ever mention her mother's boyfriend?'

Peony nodded warily. 'I don't think she liked him.'

'Did he ever hit her?'

Peony shook her head. 'She never said anything like that.'

'Or try to do anything she was uncomfortable with. I'm talking about kissing her or . . .'

Peony looked up sharply. 'I don't know. She never talked about it.' There was a long silence before Peony spoke again. 'I wanted to let her in the taxi but Vicky said it would be too much trouble to go out of our way like that to take her home.'

'Why would it be too much trouble if it wasn't far?' Rachel asked.

Peony stared at the floor, unable or unwilling to answer.

'Why did you want to let her in the taxi, Peony? Why were you worried about her walking home alone?'

Peony looked him in the eye. 'Her mum's ex was there in the pub, wasn't he? Clare saw him. She was scared.'

Wesley and Rachel drove back to Tradmouth in silence. Sarah and Vicky had admitted that they knew Clare had spotted Alan Jakes in the pub but Vicky had dismissed her fears, saying that he was hardly likely to do anything with all those people around. Sarah, like Peony, had gone along with it.

When asked about the taxi, Vicky had blustered. It wasn't her fault if Clare happened to meet some kind of psychopath on the way home, was it? Wesley had a feeling that nothing was ever going to be Vicky's fault. She would go through life shifting the blame onto others. And she would probably get away with it.

It was coming up to six when they returned to the incident room and found Gerry Heffernan staring at the notice board which covered one wall of the large open-plan office. Clare's picture was there in pride of place, together with scribbled details of the Neston attack. It seemed that Gerry had made up his mind that Clare's mumbled words about the attacker having a dog's head were significant. The Neston attacker had worn some kind of cartoon animal mask so the two attacks were probably connected. The possibility of getting a psychological profiler in had been mentioned, budget permitting: CS Nutter had promised to think about it.

As they walked in, Gerry emerged from his office to greet them. 'How did it go?'

Wesley told him.

'So this Vicky bullied Clare and the other lasses went along with it?'

'Oh she didn't beat her up on the way home from school or hide her PE things. The bullying was more subtle than that. Snide remarks and veiled threats to exclude her from the group, that sort of thing. I think Vicky enjoyed the power and when Clare saw a man she was afraid of in the pub, Vicky still wouldn't let her share their taxi.'

'Cruel.'

'Yes. I think the other two would have given in but Vicky's the dominant personality. What she says goes.'

'You think the other girls know something?'

'I've left my card with them and told them to contact me if they remember any more. But I'm not getting my hopes up.'

'Well, at least we know Alan Jakes was on the scene. We'll send someone round to the pub to see if anyone knows what he did when he left.' He grinned. 'But not tonight. I want everyone in bright and early tomorrow. No hangovers.' He sighed. 'Why don't you get home, Wes? Early start tomorrow.' He called across to Rachel who was checking messages on her desk. 'You too, Rach. Seven o'clock start tomorrow. But give Trish a ring at the hospital before you go, eh? See if Clare's up to questioning yet.'

As Wesley put on his coat he watched Rachel make the call. From her expression, he sensed that the news was neither good nor bad. Clare was on the mend . . . but slowly. They'd have to be patient.

He walked home up the steep narrow streets to the top of the town. It was dark and the street lamps reflected off the damp pavements as he walked on, longing for spring when the rows of cottages he passed would be festooned with bright flowers. When he arrived at his house the lights were on, warm and welcoming, and as he opened the front door he called Pam's name.

She appeared from the kitchen, a tentative smile on her face, and somehow he knew she was about to impart unwelcome news. But before she could speak two children erupted from the front room, charging at him with shrieks of 'Daddy'. Amelia took his hand and dragged him into the room while eight-year-old Michael followed behind, his face serious.

As soon as Wesley had taken his coat off Amelia sat beside him on the sofa, snuggling into his side and offering up her new reading book to be admired. She began to read unprompted and he was aware of Michael sitting silently on his other side, awaiting his turn to speak. Michael was quieter than his younger sister, something that worried Wesley from time to time. But, according to his mother, he himself had been an introverted child while his sister had claimed all the attention. Perhaps it was just a case of history repeating itself.

As Amelia prattled on, reading the text fluently, he turned to Michael and smiled. 'OK, mate?' he whispered.

Michael nodded, slid off the sofa and gathered up a heap of books lying on the floor; library books by the look of their glossy plastic covers. The top book bore a large image of Tutankhamen's blue-and-gold death mask and Michael began to flick through the pages.

'That's brilliant reading,' Wesley said gently as Amelia reached the end of her paragraph. 'Shall we see what Michael's got there?'

Michael passed the book to his father. 'I'm doing a project on the ancient Egyptians. I'm going to ask Uncle Neil to help me.'

'I don't think it's really Uncle Neil's branch of archaeology but I'm sure he won't mind.' The mention of Neil's name reminded him that he hadn't seen him for a while. Neil tended to burst into their lives from time to time and then disappear to immerse himself in his work. Wesley could have pursued the same career path after university and he sometimes wondered whether he'd have been happier as an archaeologist. He certainly wouldn't have had to face women traumatised by violence like Clare Mayers.

He whispered a few encouraging words to Amelia before joining his son on the floor.

'So what do you know about Ancient Egypt?' he said, ruffling Michael's dark curls.

But it was Amelia who spoke. 'Della's getting us a kitten.'

There had never been any question of Pam's mother, Della, being Nanna or Granny to her grandchildren. Della didn't like anything that might make her sound her age.

'When's this kitten arriving?'

'Della's friend's choosing one for us. She runs an animal sanctuary,' said Michael, matter of factly.

'I'd better go and get my supper.' Wesley was hungry. And he wanted to find out what his mother-in-law was up to now. Getting a kitten was news to Wesley. Knowing Della, one kitten probably meant a houseful of cats, none of them house-trained and each bent on destruction.

He found Pam at the kitchen table with a pile of exercise books by her side. 'I've got to get this marking done tonight,' she said as she looked up. 'Can you help Michael with his Egypt project? I tried to phone Neil earlier but there was no answer.'

'I'll do what I can. What's this about a kitten?'

Pam sat up straight and pushed her hair back from her face. 'Why? Don't you want one?'

'Well, I like cats but . . .'

'But?'

'Why do I get the feeling that this is something your mother's foisting on us?'

Pam sighed and sat back in her chair. She looked a little tired after a long day's teaching but Wesley thought she looked good and the blue top she was wearing brought out the colour of her eyes.

'I admit it was Della's idea. Her latest thing is playing lady bountiful to a load of stray animals. I can't see it lasting myself.'

'Michael said something about a friend with an animal sanctuary.'

'She went to a university conference and met this psychology lecturer. They got talking and he mentioned that his mother ran an animal sanctuary in Hugford. Between you and me she probably fancied the lecturer and thought it was a good way to ingratiate herself. You know what she's like about younger men. Anyway, one of the sanctuary cats had kittens a couple of months ago and Della thought it would be nice for the kids to have a pet.'

Wesley said nothing. If it had been anybody but Della, he would have been all for it but, in his experience, everything Della ever did for them came at a price.

The doorbell rang and Pam leapt up, meeting the children in the hall. Wesley watched the three of them dash to the front door.

Sure enough their visitor was Della and she was carrying a wicker cat basket. As Wesley stepped forward his eyes were drawn to the little creature inside and it would have taken a heart a lot harder than his not to warm to the small, inquisitive face with its large eyes and whiskers.

Pam did her best to calm the children's excitement as Della took the basket into the front room and placed it on the floor, turning to look at Wesley, a challenge in her eyes.

'Hope you aren't going to arrest me for being in possession of a vicious animal.'

Wesley had heard it all before, the jibes against his chosen profession. And over the years he had learned to ignore it. Della still lived back in a time when all police were 'pigs' and agents of an oppressive state. He'd given up trying to convince her of his good intentions long ago.

She sat down on the sofa, spreading out her ankle-length black skirt. She still wore her greying hair long, a couple of starry hair slides holding it back from a high-cheekboned face lined from years of smoking and too much wine.

It had taken Wesley a while to get used to Della; his own parents, who had travelled to London from Trinidad to study medicine, were upright, churchgoing people, concerned with the importance of education and establishing themselves amongst the professional middle class of their adopted country. In contrast, the feckless Della brought chaos in her wake and possessed an unpredictable quality that still made him slightly uncomfortable. Fortunately Pam had inherited the temperament of her conventional and long-suffering late father: she certainly wasn't her mother's daughter.

Della bent down and released the kitten from its basket. It was jet-black and elegant for its age and before it could begin an inspection of its new surroundings, Amelia picked it up and held it to her cheek while her brother tried to pat any visible patch of fur. The kitten didn't seem to mind the attention in the least. In fact it began to purr, a loud noise for such a tiny scrap of life.

'What shall we call it?' Pam asked, trying to bring some order to the proceedings.

'Kitty,' Amelia shouted, frightening the little creature which leapt from her arms and disappeared under the sideboard.

'The Egyptian cat goddess is called Bastet,' said Michael earnestly.

'Sounds a bit rude,' Pam muttered under her breath.

'We've got plenty of time to decide,' said Wesley, retrieving the kitten from its refuge. As he stroked its head, the volume of the purring increased until it sounded like a small motorbike engine idling outside in the street.

Hospitals have many places to hide at night. Unused consulting rooms; store cupboards; curtains pulled around an empty bed.

But Clare Mayers's attacker opted for a bolder approach. After discarding a heavy coat in an empty side ward, the attacker grabbed a stethoscope left on a trolley by some careless medic and walked confidently along the corridor without attracting a second glance from passers-by.

However, after peeping through the window into the room where Clare Mayers slept and seeing a young black nurse standing by the bed, writing furiously on a clipboard, the attacker continued down the corridor before marching purposefully back. But the nurse was still there, sitting in the chair by the bed as though she was settled there for the night. The attacker wondered whether to wait. The nurse was bound to have to see to another patient or answer a call of nature sooner or later.

Then a uniformed policeman strolled slowly down the corridor, paying the attacker no attention. The policeman knocked at Clare's door, said a few whispered words to the nurse and stepped inside.

The silencing of Clare Mayers would keep for another time.

# CHAPTER 7

*Edward was a lively boy and, as a new teacher with little knowledge of the young, I found his exuberance difficult at times. He loved his father's collection and would delight in reciting the more gruesome customs of that ancient civilisation. Edward was very keen to tell me that the brains of the dead were removed by a hook inserted up a nostril and that the internal organs were removed and stored in Canopic jars. I felt that perhaps this wasn't altogether a suitable subject for so young a boy but it seemed that his father had furnished him with the information so I was in no position to chastise him for his precocity.*

*Victoria, in contrast, was a quiet child who would lay her dolls in little coffins her father had ordered the estate carpenter to make for her. She would then conduct funeral rites of her own devising, often based on those of the Egyptians. I felt that those children, exposed as they were to their father's collection of mummies and grave goods, were perhaps developing an unhealthy obsession with death. However, as Sir Frederick's paid employee, I felt I could raise no objections. Besides, I myself found* those things fascinating so how could I deny that rich area of knowledge to young minds?

I had little to do with the servants although when I encountered Walter Hungate in the grounds on one occasion, he chided me for allowing the children to follow unchristian ways and for omitting to take them to church on Sundays. I merely smiled and stated that Hungate could think what he wished. I answered only to Sir Frederick.

On another occasion I found Hungate drunk one evening by the kitchen garden. He seized my arm but as I shook off his hand he put his face close to mine. I could smell ale on his stale breath but it was his words that most disturbed me.

He said he'd seen him walking. A creature with the head of a dog and the body of a man. A Jackal Man.

# CHAPTER 8

Neil Watson had promised to visit Varley Castle again that morning. But before he set out from his Exeter flat he searched the pocket of his jacket for the number of the expert from the British Museum who'd contacted Caroline Varley. When he found the crumpled scrap of paper he flattened it out and dialled the number on his mobile phone.

Dr Andrew Beredace answered after two rings and when Neil explained the reason for his call, Beredace sounded excited, like a child promised a thrilling birthday treat. Barely able to contain his enthusiasm, he'd said he'd drive down to Devon as soon as he could get away from the meeting he had to attend that morning. He'd ring the castle when he knew what time he'd be able to make it. Neil wanted to be fully prepared for his arrival so he called into his office and told his colleagues to hold the fort at the Unit until he got back. Suddenly the more glamorous and mysterious world of Egyptology seemed more alluring than a desk-based archaeological assessment of some muddy Devon field earmarked for new housing.

It began to rain as he drove over Dartmoor, a fine misty drizzle that blurred the greens and greys of the landscape. When he reached the castle Caroline looked pleased to see him and offered him coffee. He imagined that it was lonely for her in that great, grim house and he told himself that she probably enjoyed the company. He was reluctant to acknowledge the frisson of attraction he felt: over the years he'd been in too many disastrous relationships to hurtle headlong into anything sexual.

After telling her about Dr Beredace's imminent arrival, he followed her into the kitchen and sat on a bench by the long wooden table in the centre of the room while she stood by the boiling kettle, heaping instant coffee into mugs. Water dripped from somewhere into a brace of plastic buckets on the floor. Caroline saw him looking at them.

'Sorry about the water features. You'll find them scattered all over the house, especially upstairs. The kitchen's lost a few roof tiles over the years and if you will build a place like this in the bleakest part of Dartmoor . . .' She shrugged her shoulders and began to make the coffee.

Suddenly Neil's mind registered the fact that there were three mugs on the worktop. 'Who's the extra mug for?' he asked, trying his best to sound casual.

'Robert – the biographer I told you about yesterday.'

Neil nodded. He had almost forgotten about the unseen Robert Delaware.

'He's up in the library. I'll introduce you.'

He took the tray from her hands, playing the gentleman, avoiding the buckets on the floor.

There seemed to be a lot of stairs between the kitchen and

the library and Neil couldn't help sympathising with all those servants of the past who had had to trudge up and down them every day, obeying the whims of the Varley family who paid their wages and ordered their lives. Pickle, it seemed, could buy a man a lot of power.

They arrived in the library where an array of table lamps shed pools of golden light on the polished wood furniture and floor. A fire blazed in the grate and, in spite of its grand dimensions and the grey granite walls, the room looked positively cosy.

The man sitting on the sofa near the fireplace stood up as they entered. He was in his thirties, well-built without being fat, with dark hair and a well-scrubbed face. He wore a pale blue V-necked pullover with a pair of beige casual trousers and he looked the clubbable type, sporty without overdoing the exercise. Neil could have mistaken him for an escapee from a local golf club. The last thing he looked like was a writer.

He fixed a smile to his face and held out his hand. 'Robert Delaware. I'm working on a biography of Sir Frederick Varley. So Caro's called you in to have a look at the great man's collection?'

'I'm just having a preliminary look. I've contacted an expert from the British Museum and he's due to arrive later.' Neil noted the shortened form of Caroline's name and wondered how close the pair had become. 'How long have you been working on the biography?' he asked politely, hoping the answer might give him a clue.

'Only about a month. Caro's late uncle wasn't very happy with the idea. But as soon as Caro took over at the helm as it were . . .' He didn't finish the sentence but the smug expression on his face suggested to Neil that Caroline was being more than co-operative.

He glanced at Caroline who was warming her feet by the fire, holding her mug in both hands and staring into it as though she expected the brown liquid to provide an answer to some long-pondered question.

'Found anything interesting?' he asked, nodding towards the heap of old papers on the occasional table beside the sofa where Delaware was sitting.

'Oh yes. There's fascinating stuff amongst the family papers. I found all the notes Sir Fred made during his trips to Egypt stuffed in cupboards and there were boxes of letters in the muniment room downstairs. By the look of it nobody had touched them since his death.' He reached out and touched Caroline's hand. She pulled hers away gently but firmly. 'It's going to take months to go through it all and I can't finalise my first draft until I've finished. Imagine me stating something as fact then finding a letter that contradicts it. Wouldn't do at all.'

'I suppose not.'

'There are some who wouldn't be so scrupulous of course.'

Neil said nothing. If Delaware was being cautious about his primary sources, he guessed that it was because he didn't want to make a fool of himself by using duff information in his book. Or perhaps he just wanted an excuse to stay at the castle.

'I heard about the tragedy . . . Sir Frederick's son, John.'

Delaware's expression suddenly became a little guarded, as though he didn't like the way the conversation was going. 'My book will focus on Sir Fred's achievements as an Egyptologist. From the pickle factory to the Valley of the Kings and all that.'

'So John won't get a mention?'

'Probably in passing,' he answered quickly. 'Sir Frederick endured personal tragedy when his son committed suicide and all that.'

'What about the murders?' Neil wasn't sure why but he didn't feel like letting the subject drop. 'Caroline told me that four women were murdered. Surely that warrants a mention.'

Delaware opened and closed his mouth but before he could answer, the phone on the table by the window began to ring. Caroline rushed to answer it, as though she was relieved to escape. She returned a few moments later, holding the telephone out like an offering.

'It's for you, Neil. Dr Beredace from the British Museum.'

As Neil took the instrument, Robert Delaware stood up, drained his coffee mug and left the room, giving Caroline a charming and apologetic smile.

According to police records, Alan Jakes had been charged with sexually assaulting a woman he'd picked up in a night-club ten years ago. However, there'd been no conviction. It had been her word against his and for some reason the jury had believed his version of events.

The phone on Wesley's desk began to ring and he rushed over to answer it. It was Trish Walton on the other end of the line and she sounded worried.

'Clare Mayers is wide awake and she wants to discharge herself.'

'Is she well enough?'

'I wouldn't have thought so.'

'I'll come straight over.' Wesley put the phone down, wondering why he'd been so hasty. If the girl had made up her mind to leave hospital there was nothing he could do. But he couldn't help feeling that she was safer there in the hospital than back at home. Especially if it had been her mother's ex, Alan Jakes, who had attempted to strangle the life out of her.

As he made his way out of the CID office Gerry Heffernan was on his way in. He looked harassed – late as usual – and when Wesley told him where he was going the DCI just muttered 'silly girl' before explaining that he was in a hurry: the DS from Neston who was dealing with the January assault enquiry was coming to see him in ten minutes to compare notes.

Wesley left the heated police station and walked in the cold drizzle to the hospital nearby where Trish was waiting for him, pacing up and down the corridor outside Clare's room.

'The doctor's in there with her now. Let's hope she can talk some sense into her.' Trish looked anxious, as though she was getting too involved.

'There's nothing we can do if she's made up her mind, Trish. We can only advise her to stay put.'

The door opened and a young woman doctor came out. As she swept off down the corridor, Wesley could tell by the look on her face that she'd been trying to talk some sense into Clare and failed. Wesley gave a token knock and entered the room, Trish hovering behind him.

'Hello, Clare. I hear you want to go home?'

'Can't stand hospitals,' she said in a coarse, barely audible whisper. Her hand went up to her bandaged throat.

'Neither can I but it's really the best place to be at the moment.'

'I'm fine,' she croaked weakly.

'Is your mother picking you up?'

She shook her head slowly as though the effort was agony.

67

'I'm getting a taxi.' She winced as she sat up and tried to loosen the bandage around her neck.

'Painful?'

She didn't answer.

'You're safer here, you know. But I expect the doctor's told you that already.' When he got no reaction he carried on. Now he was there and she was alert, he thought he might as well ask a few pertinent questions. He sat down on the visitor's chair and glanced at Trish who was standing at the end of the bed with a benign expression on her face like an actress trying to play the part of Florence Nightingale.

'Alan Jakes was at the Anglers' Arms the night you were attacked. I take it you saw him?'

She gave a feeble nod.

'Did you speak to him?'

With a great effort she cleared her throat. 'He just said hi. That's all.'

'Did he have a car?'

'He has different cars all the time. He works in a garage.'

'Do you think he could have seen you leave and followed you down the lane in his car?'

There were tears in Clare's eyes now. The question had upset her for some reason. 'No . . . I don't know. But whoever it was had a dog's head. He was wearing a dog's head. I want to get dressed. I want to go now.'

'Do you mean a mask . . . like a cartoon dog? The Disney dog maybe? What's his name? Goofy is it?'

She shook her head and gasped with the pain.

'No, it wasn't like that. It was a head . . . with pointed ears. I want to go home.'

She flopped back on her pillows, exhausted. Trish caught Wesley's eye and gave a small shake of her head. It was useless. The girl was going home whether they liked it or not. And she was sticking to her story.

Suddenly Wesley wanted to speak to Alan Jakes more than anything else in the world.

It seemed that Alan Jakes had vanished into thin air. None of his workmates or known associates had seen him since the weekend. Which, for Gerry Heffernan, rather seemed to suggest guilt. Clare's story about the dog-headed man might well have been concocted to throw them off the scent. Jakes wouldn't have been the first man to become entangled with his lover's teenage daughter and he probably wouldn't be the last.

When Wesley returned to the incident room he found Gerry in his office, swivelling to and fro on his black leather executive chair, reading a lab report. When he heard Wesley enter he looked up.

'There's something odd about this case, Wes. I don't think it's a straightforward sex attack. After all, the girl wasn't interfered with, was she? He just tried to strangle her – nothing else.'

'He didn't have time to do anything else, Gerry. Danny Coyle came along in his van and disturbed him.'

'The popular theory of the moment seems to be that this Neston attacker's changed his MO. Maybe he intended to assault her when she was unconscious, then kill her.'

Wesley shrugged his shoulders. 'Maybe. They say that sex attackers have to up the stakes all the time to get the same thrill. But in this case don't you think the change is rather . . .' He searched for the right word. 'Drastic. He went from a quick fumble to calculated attempted murder. If it was the same man, surely there would have been something in between.'

Gerry looked up. 'Who needs criminal psychologists when they've got you? Anyway I've had people out asking all the known sex offenders in the area where they were on the night in question. They've all got alibis and there are only two dodgy ones – a kiddy fiddler who lives alone, hence no witnesses, but I don't think this is his style at all. Then there's a character with two rape convictions who lives with a mother who'll swear black was white for her nasty little darling.'

Wesley raised his eyebrows. 'Is he a possibility?'

'He would be if he hadn't broken his leg last week falling off a ladder. Who says there's no justice in this world? Then there's Alan Jakes – I reckon he's our number one at the moment. I take it someone keeps trying his address?'

'Oh yes, but there's still nobody home. Karen Mayers gave us his sister's address in Dukesbridge but no luck there either.'

Wesley's mobile began to ring. He muttered an apology to Gerry and pressed the key that would stop the tinny rendition of *Eine Kleine Nachtmusik*.

After a brief conversation he ended the call. 'That was Ian Petrie, my old colleague from the Met. He says he's got some information. If I go now, I'll only be half an hour.'

Gerry frowned and looked at his watch. 'Go on, then. Assure him of our co-operation . . . providing it only takes ten minutes. Tell you what, while you're out will you get me a pasty? I just fancy one.' He patted his large stomach. Since his lady friend, Joyce, had gone off to stay with her recently widowed sister, his noble attempt at healthy eating had been abandoned, confirming Wesley's suspicion that it had been rather half hearted in the first place.

'Large or small?'

Gerry gave a wicked grin. 'Large. I'm a growing lad.'

Wesley took his coat from the stand and hurried out of the office before any of the DCs could waylay him.

It was just coming up to midday when he found Ian Petrie in the Ship Bar. He was sitting at the same table, almost as though he hadn't moved since their last meeting. In front of him sat a half-drunk cup of coffee. Wesley ordered one for himself before sitting down.

Ian looked up and gave him a nervous smile. There were dark circles beneath his eyes, as though he hadn't slept. 'How's your investigation going? I take it you haven't found out who attacked that girl the other night?' The question sounded more than casual somehow.

'I'm afraid not.'

'Any progress?'

Wesley leaned forward. He didn't want to be overheard. 'We're looking for the girl's mother's ex-boyfriend. He was in the pub the night she was attacked and he's done a runner.'

'Sounds promising. I read in the local rag that a young woman was attacked in Neston a few weeks ago. Could it be the same man?'

Wesley's coffee had arrived. He took a sip. It tasted good. 'There are as many differences as there are similarities.'

'That's not what the paper said.' Ian leaned over and picked up a discarded copy of the *Tradmouth Echo*. He passed it to Wesley who read the headline: 'Dog Head Mystery of Tragic Girl. Is there link with Neston attack?'

Wesley didn't normally swear but this was an exception. This had been something they wanted to keep to themselves but somebody had talked to the local press. Gerry wouldn't be pleased.

'Dog's head indeed. I take it the girl was on something. I've heard drugs are a big problem in these rural places.'

'They are. But there's no evidence that the victim had anything stronger than a few Bacardi Breezers on the night she was attacked.' He glanced at his watch. He had promised Gerry he'd only be half an hour. 'Anyway, Ian, why did you want to see me? Has there been a development?'

Ian Petrie drained his coffee cup and sat for a few moments, deep in thought. Then he spoke. 'You know I mentioned Ra?'

'Yes. Have you found out who he is yet?'

'I've been making enquiries at various art galleries but I've drawn a blank. We got the name Ra from an e-mail found on the computer of one of the people we arrested. "Ra will provide the usual service." Then there was a note we found in a crate full of dodgy artefacts. It was a list of numbers – prices we think – and the name Ra was at the top. Either they have great faith in an Egyptian deity or this Ra is a codename for somebody involved in the organisation. Who knows? It would be really helpful if you could look through your files and ask around – see if the name Ra rings any bells.'

'I'll do that, Ian. I'll be in touch if I find anything.' Wesley suddenly realised that Ian was expecting him to slip back into his old role as right-hand man. And he really didn't have the time.

He looked at his watch. He had to get to the pasty shop on the High Street to feed Gerry's craving: he'd pick a pasty up for himself while he was at it. At least it wasn't the tourist season so there wouldn't be any long queues.

'Sorry, Ian, I've got to go. I'll be in touch.'

He finished his coffee and as he stood up a young woman appeared at the door. She spotted Ian and homed in on him like a guided missile.

'Excuse me, Mr Petrie. Sorry to interrupt but when you arrived on Saturday you didn't tell us how long you were staying . . .'

'I'll leave you to it,' Wesley mouthed.

Ian raised a hand in farewell and as he left the young woman took his vacant seat.

But it wasn't until he was inside the warm, steamy pasty shop, trying to peer through the condensation running down the windows to see if had started to rain, that a thought suddenly struck him. Ian Petrie hadn't been specific but Wesley had assumed that he'd arrived on Monday morning. But now it seemed that he'd been there since Saturday.

Dr Andrew Beredace didn't wear tweeds or a bow tie. Instead he wore jeans, sweatshirt and a weatherproof coat suitable for a late February day on the edge of Dartmoor. He was about Neil's age, or maybe a couple of years younger, and he had a shaven head – sensibly covered by a woollen hat – and a gold stud in his ear. Neil Watson, unsure what to expect of an expert in Egyptology from the British Museum, was pleasantly surprised. This was a man he could do business with – maybe even share a pint or two down at the local with.

Andrew arrived at three o'clock and, after the initial introductions had been made, he and Neil made their way to the room where Sir Frederick's main collection was kept. So far Neil had only had a swift peep inside and had retreated, thinking he'd wait for Andrew who knew so much more about that sort of thing than he did. In the dim light he had seen the statues and upright mummy cases, standing there as if they were waiting to be discovered by some latter-day Howard Carter. The contents of Tutankhamen's tomb had been described as wonderful. But as Neil gazed on the shadowy figures of death he thought the word terrible was more appropriate.

Some of the statues were recognisably human with blank, staring eyes outlined in black; others were fantastic creatures with the bodies of men and the heads of beasts.

But it was the mummies themselves, desiccated human forms swathed in grey bandages lying in coffin-like glass cases, that had discomforted him the most. He'd felt that they were about to rise up and turn their terrible, featureless heads to watch him, resentful of his intrusion on their centuries of sleep. He wasn't superstitious by nature but he could imagine why some people thought they had the power to bestow terrible curses upon the living.

Andrew, however, had no such qualms. When Neil led him up to the room and pushed open the doors, the expert's eyes lit up like a child's on Christmas morning. He strode across to open the shutters and then he obtained a stronger bulb from Caroline which he fitted himself with the aid of a stepladder from a storeroom near the kitchen. Neil followed him round as he examined the collection and watched him open the glass cases carefully to get a closer look at the dusty, bandaged remains inside. Neil turned his attention to a display of miniature boats and small figurines depicting everyday activities. Although he knew these had come from tombs, they didn't bear the obvious taint of death.

After half an hour Neil had decided to leave Andrew to it. He'd had enough of Egyptian artefacts for one day and Caroline had mentioned that somewhere in the grounds lay the ruins of an earlier house; a medieval stone manor house, abandoned since the eighteenth century. This appealed to Neil more than all the tombs in the Valley of the Kings, although he wouldn't have admitted it to Andrew Beredace.

Andrew was too preoccupied to comment on his discreet departure and, relieved to be out of that airless shrine to death, Neil made his way out of the front door and rounded the castle, keeping the towering granite walls to his right. From every angle the views were spectacular; rolling hills of green and brown with skeletal trees reaching for the wide grey sky. In summer the landscape would contain a hundred varied shades of green. But now it was bleak, cold and damp.

The back of the castle overlooked the river and a series of steep formal gardens led down to the river gorge. To the left of the gardens was a large area of woodland where, according to Caroline, the remains of the old house could be found. Neil walked down the gravel path and headed for the trees, trying to ignore the biting wind.

When he reached the wood he stopped and looked up at the bare branches overhead where crows cackled at him from their straggly nests. Maybe this place would be lush and beautiful in summer but in winter it felt hostile and forbidding. Caroline had instructed him to keep on the path and then turn off left at a large clearing so he walked on, alert to every sound: every rustle of dead leaves and every twig that cracked like an echoing gunshot under his feet.

Suddenly he had an uncomfortable feeling that he wasn't alone so he stopped and stood perfectly still. Sure enough he heard a faint snapping of twigs a short distance away. Someone else was in that wood. And that someone was getting nearer.

He scanned the surrounding woods for any telltale sign of movement and after a few seconds he saw a figure walking casually through the trees. Robert Delaware's hands were thrust in the pockets of a new-looking waxed jacket and he seemed unaware of Neil's presence until he stepped into his path and waited for the moment of recognition.

When Delaware saw him he stopped, a slightly guilty look on his face as though Neil had caught him doing something he shouldn't.

'I'm going to have a look at the medieval ruins,' Neil began. 'To tell you the truth, that's far more my thing than all this ancient Egyptian stuff. I take it I'm on the right path for the old house?'

Robert Delaware gave Neil a smile that was probably meant to be friendly but came out as an insincere grimace. 'It's not far. You pass a large clearing – take the path to your left then you'll see the walls. They're over six feet tall, some of them, and the footprint of the house is quite clear. This must always have been regarded as a desirable place to build.'

'I'm surprised Sir Albert Varley didn't restore the old house instead of building that monstrous place.'

'It wouldn't have been nearly grand enough for him. He was a self-made man and self-made men like the world to see the end product, as it were. His son, Sir Frederick, might have seen things differently, of course.'

'At least the castle was big enough to house his Egyptian collection.'

'Yes. That was very important to Frederick. Almost an obsession, I'd say.'

'I've heard that people working in that particular field can get a little bit obsessive,' said Neil lightly.

'I think it's true of most historians and archaeologists,' Delaware replied with a frown. 'Sometimes the past becomes more real than the present, doesn't it?'

Suddenly Neil remembered something. 'Didn't Frederick's son John hang himself somewhere in this wood?'

Delaware's face grew pale, as though the blood had drained from his cheeks. Perhaps he had become so caught up in researching Sir Frederick Varley's life that the source of his subject's grief actually caused him pain.

'Yes,' he said after a few moments. 'I'll show you where it happened. It's just down here.' He began to stride ahead and Neil felt he had no choice but to follow.

The track was muddy in places and Neil could see that the bottoms of Delaware's trousers had become wet and stained. He followed him through the trees until they reached a large clearing where a flock of crows in the surrounding trees cried out raucous warnings of their arrival. Delaware stopped in the centre of the clearing and pointed to an ancient oak tree with gnarled and crooked branches that reached into the open space like predatory arms, beckoning.

'He took a rope he found in one of the outhouses and slung it over there.' He pointed to a thick, twisted branch about eight feet off the ground; high enough to hang a man. 'He tied a noose then climbed onto one of the lower branches. Then once he'd put the noose around his neck he launched himself off. It must have taken him a while to die.' He stared at the tree as though lost in another time, another world. 'On a day like this you can just imagine it, can't you? The sudden crash and the crows rising up in a cackling black cloud. Then the rhythmic creaking of the branch as the body swung to and fro.'

'Oh for God's sake,' Neil said, suddenly anxious to bring the man back to reality. 'Which way is it back to the path?' With all the talk of hanging, he'd lost his bearings amongst the trees.

Delaware pointed to the right of the oak. 'If you carry on down there you'll find the old house. It's not far, only a couple of hundred yards.'

As Neil watched Delaware disappear through the trees he realised that he should have taken the opportunity to ask again about the murders John was supposed to have committed. However, the encounter with Delaware had disturbed him and he hadn't been anxious to prolong it. But there'd be other times – other opportunities. There was unfinished business that he still had to face.

# CHAPTER 9

*It was all in Hungate's mind, of course. I realised that he had seen the life-sized statues of Anubis in Sir Frederick's collection and therefore it was hardly surprising that, when in his cups, he imagined that the jackal-headed god stalked the corridors and grounds of the castle look-ing for souls to claim. I myself rather liked the god with his jackal head and his lithe human form. He cared for the dead, preparing their earthly bodies for the afterlife. In my mind Anubis did no harm.*

*After a while I forgot all about Hungate's foolishness, for the care and education of the children occupied most of my time. That winter of 1901 was a peaceful time, although the weather on this fertile fringe of Dartmoor was harsh as it always is in winter. The year up to then had been eventful: the old Queen had died in January, although our new King Edward would remain uncrowned till August the following year. But these were events of national note and history would never record how I myself had moved into a new world, a world I was finding most con-genial, despite my lowly social standing.*

*However in the spring my new and satisfying life was to change. In*

*March Sir Frederick's elder son, John, came home from Bristol. He was a slender, tall young man with very black hair and brown eyes. I picked up from kitchen gossip that he longed to join the army but injuries incurred in childhood had left him with a severe limp and his country had no place for an officer with such a disability. Yet although he walked with a stick he still possessed the strength of any healthy young man. Strange, I thought, that the British Army should reject a man strong enough, and willing enough, to kill.*

# CHAPTER 10

The attack on Clare Mayers was something DS Rachel Tracey felt strongly about, just as she felt strongly about all attacks on defenceless women. During her time as a police officer she had sometimes worked with men who didn't seem to care. Wesley's predecessor had been one of them and DC Steve Carstairs had been another – although Steve had redeemed himself by dying a hero's death, thus putting himself beyond criticism. A sly move, in Rachel's opinion.

Rachel didn't intend to let the search for Clare's attacker run out of steam like some investigations tended to do. The same went for the Neston case. The victim might not have been hurt but she'd been badly frightened. All women should have the right to walk the streets unmolested. And who was to say that the attacker wouldn't grow bolder over time and do serious damage . . . like that done to Clare?

She wanted to talk to the Neston victim just to see if

anything had been missed. With men in charge, she suspected that the woman's ordeal wouldn't have been taken seriously enough and she needed to know every tiny detail, even the things dismissed as unimportant. After making a phone call to ensure that her journey wouldn't be wasted, she hurried to Gerry Heffernan's office to tell him where she was going. It was a formality of course; the DCI merely looked up from his paperwork and grinned his approval, showing the space between his front teeth. She noticed a small gravy stain on the front of his shirt: he and Wesley had been feasting on pasties earlier. She'd watched them chatting in the DCI's office and felt a pang of envy at their relaxed camaraderie.

Gerry suggested that she should take Trish with her and she saw the sense of this. Trish was the kind of person people confided in.

By the time they left the station the sky was dark grey and it had begun to drizzle. Rachel nosed out of the car park and waited for the parade of headlights to pass before revving the engine and taking her place in the traffic heading for Neston.

'I got the address of the assault victim from Neston CID.'

Trish looked at her, her eyes wide with shock. 'Shouldn't we speak to the officer who's dealing with the case? Maybe we shouldn't go barging in like this.'

'Are you saying I'm insensitive?'

'I'm just saying that we should think about the victim having to relive what happened, that's all. We've got her statement – surely that's enough.'

Rachel put her foot down hard on the accelerator pedal. She shared a house with Trish and most of the time they got on fine. But sometimes Trish's caution irritated her. 'We need to find this man before things escalate – if they haven't already. She'll understand that.'

Trish didn't reply. They drove on in silence until Rachel crossed the bridge over the River Trad and brought the car to a halt outside a block of flats that had begun its life as a waterside warehouse in the days when the town of Neston had exported cargos of wool and grain.

Rachel climbed out of the car and marched up to the door, aware that Trish was following behind reluctantly. The rain was falling heavier now and both women huddled in the shelter of the doorway while Rachel rang the bell marked Flat 2. After a few seconds a disembodied voice uttered a timid hello and when Rachel announced who they were, they heard a buzzing sound, like a bee who'd lost the will to live, and Rachel pushed open the heavy glass door.

'Just go easy on her,' Trish whispered as they waited for the flat door to open.

'What do you think I am?'

'Bossy,' came the quick answer. Rachel turned to face her friend. There was no smile on her face. Trish meant what she said and Rachel felt rather shocked. But before she could say a word in her defence, the door opened a crack, then a little wider.

Rachel held up her warrant card and made the introductions. 'Andrea? We're really sorry to bother you but can we come in for a quick chat? We wouldn't ask if it wasn't important.' Mindful of Trish's misgivings, she didn't move until the woman opened the door wide and gestured them to come in.

Andrea Washington was a skinny young woman with short dark hair. Her eyes appeared large but it was probably the thinness of her face that made them seem so. She

83

hugged a baggy cardigan around her body defensively as she walked through to the lounge, turning her head every now and then to see if they were following.

No tea was offered as they took their seats on a black leather sofa designed more for fashion than comfort. Andrea perched on a red chair opposite, sitting on the edge as if she was preparing for a quick getaway. All the furniture in the room was modern, monochrome and harsh and the lack of pictures on the wall gave the place an empty, clinical look. Rachel preferred something more homely.

'Have you heard about the girl who was attacked near Hugford on Sunday night?' Trish asked gently.

'It was on the news.' Andrea spoke almost in a whisper.

'We think it might be the same man who attacked you. That's why we need your help.'

Andrea shook her head. 'I've been over it again and again. I just want to forget about it. Please go.' She stood up and turned her back on the two women.

Rachel gave Trish an exasperated look. 'We only came to ask you if you'd remembered any more about your attacker. Please, Andrea. We really need to catch this man before he hurts someone else. The girl in Hugford was nearly strangled. A passing motorist scared him off but the next victim might not be so lucky. Please, if there's anything you can remember, however small, that might help . . .'

Andrea slumped down in her seat again and sat there, staring ahead. Rachel watched her, hardly daring to breathe in case it broke the spell and made what little courage Andrea was mustering disappear.

'I suppose I was lucky,' Andrea said after a long silence. 'He just grabbed me then he pushed me to the ground and tried to touch me . . . you know. But even so it's on my mind day and night playing over and over in my head.' She suddenly looked Rachel in the eye. 'Even though I wasn't raped, I keep thinking of what might have happened. Wherever I go and whatever I do he'll be there . . . like a stain you can't get rid of however hard you try.'

'You don't have to let him win, Andrea,' said Rachel, trying to hide her rising anger. 'You were on your way home from a pub, weren't you?'

Andrea nodded.

'In the statement you gave after the attack you said you'd met a man there.'

'That's right. It looked promising at first but we didn't really hit it off. If we had, I wouldn't have been walking home alone, would I?'

Rachel caught Trish's eye. 'What was this man's name?'

'Rory. He was full of himself. Said he was a successful businessman – I reckoned he was a prat. Fancied himself something rotten.'

'Did he tell you his surname?'

Andrea shook her head.

'Could he have followed you from the pub?'

Andrea thought for a moment. 'I don't think so.'

'You don't sound very sure.'

Andrea didn't reply.

'Can you remember what this Rory told you about himself? We'd like to speak to him.'

'He said he owned a yacht in Tradmouth. And he had a flashy car – a Ferrari, I think – but it was in a garage. He lived just outside Tradmouth near the golf course and he owned a hotel or something. I wasn't taking much notice 'cause I thought it was a load of bullshit.'

'Can you describe him?'

85

'Around five feet ten. Short dark hair. Good looking. Blue eyes. Nice leather jacket. Not bad really but I felt there was something not quite right about him. He talked quite posh but occasionally he slipped back into a local accent. I think he was putting on an act to impress me.'

'The man who attacked you – could it have been this Rory?'

Andrea frowned. 'I didn't think so at the time. The man who . . . well, he was wearing a dark anorak with a hood but I suppose he could have slipped it on over that jacket. He was around the same height, I suppose but . . .'

'He was wearing a mask.'

'Yes . . . a silly cartoon thing.'

'Was it a dog?'

Andrea shrugged her shoulders. 'It might have been. I didn't have a chance to look that closely.'

'You say you keep thinking about the attacker – you must have remembered more since you last spoke to the police. Something small maybe. Something about his clothes. Something he did or said.'

Andrea looked round, as if she feared someone was hidden in a dark corner, listening. 'There is something.'

'Go on.' Rachel glanced at Trish who was sitting by her side, enthralled.

'It was a smell when he put his hand over my mouth. I tried to describe it to the police but I didn't know what it was. Then I went to the Arts Festival at the museum last week and I smelled it again . . . or something like it.'

'What was it?' Trish couldn't help asking the question.

'There was an artist painting the church. He was going to auction the picture for charity.' She hesitated. 'It smelled very similar.'

86

'What did?'

'The paint he was using. Oil paint. He smelled of oil.'

It was almost six o'clock and Wesley sat at his desk, deep in thought, turning his pen over and over in his fingers. The sound of the phone shattered the silence and made him jump. He picked up the receiver and after a brief conversation he made his way slowly to Gerry's office.

'Rachel's just called,' he said. 'Her and Trish visited Andrea Washington, the Neston victim. Andrea said she thought the man who attacked her smelled of oil – maybe oil paint.'

'She didn't mention it in her original statement.'

'She's only just remembered. She smelled some oil paint at an art exhibition and it brought it all back.'

Gerry took a deep breath. 'Oil. Oil paint . . . or maybe engine oil? What do you think?'

'Alan Jakes works in a garage.'

'We've got to find him, Wes. The fact that he was in the Anglers' Arms on the night of the attack on Clare is ringing ruddy great alarm bells in my head. All patrols are on the lookout for him but now I think we should put the message out that it's urgent.'

'Andrea Washington said she met a man in the pub before she was attacked. His name was Rory and he said he was some sort of businessman. She doesn't think he's got anything to do with the attack but you never know.'

Gerry put his head in his hands. He looked tired. And he hadn't had anything to eat since his lunchtime pasty. He raised his head and surveyed his paperwork. 'Does she know this Rory's surname? He might have seen something.'

Wesley shook his head. 'He just chatted her up. I don't think they got as far as surnames or addresses.'

'Let's make a real effort to find Jakes. He's our most likely candidate for the attack on Clare Mayers.'

'Wouldn't she have recognised him?'

'Not if he was pissing about in some kind of mask. That must be what she meant by a dog's head, don't you think?'

Wesley suddenly remembered something he'd seen when he'd been reading through the heap of statements and interview reports that had accumulated on his desk during the last couple of days. 'Didn't Jakes's boss say he'd been to Florida with his sister recently? Disney World's in Florida. I bet you can buy cartoon character masks in Disney World.'

Gerry smiled approvingly. 'Good thinking, Wes. Hadn't you better go? I'll give you a call at home if uniform have any luck.'

The walk home seemed shorter than usual, maybe because he was hurrying, anxious to be out of the cold. The streets leading up to his house were so steep that they left summer visitors breathless. But Wesley had become used to them over the years; he reckoned that few residents of Tradmouth really needed to visit a gym.

As he walked he had the idea of inviting Ian Petrie over one night for a meal, if his stay in Tradmouth was going to be prolonged. A hotel in a strange town could be a lonely place. Pam would need some notice to feed an extra mouth, of course; particularly one she didn't know well. When Neil arrived on their doorstep he was always happy to accept any leftovers that were going but Wesley's old boss was a different matter.

As he turned into their cul de sac the first thing he noticed was Della's car parked in their drive. This was all he needed after a hard day. He steeled himself and unlocked the front door with his key. He could hear Della braying in the kitchen. And an unfamiliar male voice saying something in reply. As he stepped into the hall, Pam emerged from the living room, an exasperated frown on her face.

'What's going on?'

'My mother's brought someone round – the son of the woman who runs the animal sanctuary. She claims it's to show him how the kitten's settling in. But, knowing Della, she'll have another agenda . . . not that he'll be suspecting a thing.' She rolled her eyes to heaven. 'I was hoping to get the kids off to bed so I could prepare my lessons for tomorrow.'

'Shall I have a word?' Wesley had no idea what he'd say but he thought he'd better make the offer. He'd been about to mention a possible dinner invitation to Ian Petrie but he knew that the time wasn't right. Pam had enough on her plate and her mother's visit wasn't helping.

Wesley took off his coat and pushed the kitchen door open. Della was sitting at the table, a glass of white wine in her hand. A man stood by the sink, holding the kitten which looked tiny in his large hands. He was at least twenty-five years Della's junior with the lean look of a regular gym attendee and tousled dark hair. He didn't look Della's usual type somehow. She usually went for rogues, wastrels and men more interested in the fact that she had a steady job and her own house than her looks and personality. If she had her eye on this one, he was certainly an improvement. And there was something familiar about him, although Wesley couldn't think what it was.

'Guy, this is Wesley, my son-in-law. I told you he was a policeman, didn't I? But don't hold it against him.'

Guy put the kitten down gently on the floor and offered Wesley his hand. His handshake was firm and rather hearty.

89

'I've done some work for the police myself. I teach psychology at Morbay University.'

'I thought you worked at an animal sanctuary.'

'Oh no. That's my mother's brainchild.' He smiled. 'I've done profiling work for the Devon and Cornwall force – the two murders in Plymouth last year and the attacks on elderly women in Truro.'

'Of course. That's where I've seen you before. You came to Tradmouth to observe an interview with one of the Plymouth suspects.'

'That's right.'

'You had some success I seem to remember.'

Guy smiled modestly. 'He got life with a recommendation that he serve at least twenty years. Della tells me you're trying to find out who attacked that girl on the road to Hugford. My mother's sanctuary's in Hugford and the police came round to ask if she'd seen anything. Have you made any progress?'

Wesley really didn't want to talk about work so he muttered the usual platitudes about the investigation being on-going and following a number of leads. Guy looked a little disappointed: he probably wanted chapter and verse so that he could report back to his nervous mother. Or maybe he was after another paid assignment with the police.

But Guy wasn't to be discouraged. 'From what I've read in the press, it sounds as though it might be connected to that attack in Neston last month.'

Wesley forced his mind back to the case, even though his stomach had started to rumble and he could see a plate of curry and rice sitting beside the microwave – his dinner. 'We're considering the possibility,' he said. 'Masks were involved in both attacks.'

'The perpetrator wanted to hide his identity . . . and frighten the victim. He wanted to be in control.'

'So, in your professional opinion, you'd say the attacks were definitely linked?'

'Well, of course I don't have access to the finer details but I'd say yes. They're too close geographically for there to be no connection.'

'But the first victim was unharmed and he ran away after a quick grope and in the second attack there didn't seem to be a sexual element – he just tried to strangle her.'

'Maybe he found a quick grope wasn't enough for him. The first attack would have been experimental.' He hesitated. 'Look, I'm not touting for business or anything like that but I really think I could be of use if . . .'

'Thanks. I'll mention it to DCI Heffernan – he's the Senior Investigating Officer.'

Guy nodded. 'I'd be happy to help.'

'Thank you for the kitten, by the way,' Wesley said. 'The children love her. Did Pam tell you they can't agree on a name? Michael suggested we call her after the Egyptian cat goddess but Amelia hates that and wants to call her Kitty. At the moment she's just The Kitten but we'll have to come up with a compromise soon.'

'I'm sure you'll think up something suitable,' Guy said, squatting down to stroke the little creature who had started to paw a toy mouse, batting it to and fro.

Wesley could smell the curry and his stomach churned again. It seemed rather rude to help himself while there were guests in the kitchen but as he was considering the problem Della announced they were leaving. She was going out for a drink with friends and Guy had to get back to Morbay, she said, almost with a schoolgirl giggle. Wesley made polite noises and shook Guy's hand again. As soon as they'd shut the front door behind them, Pam rushed in.

'Before I forget, Neil phoned earlier. He said to ask you if you knew anything about four women being murdered.'

Wesley raised his eyebrows. 'When and where?' he asked as he put the curry in the microwave.

'Don't ask me.'

Wesley pulled out his mobile phone and dialled Neil's number. But all he heard was a voicemail message.


Karen Mayers had promised her daughter that she'd be in by seven. But it was ten past now.

Clare felt uneasy in the empty house and kept asking herself why she had discharged herself from hospital so hastily. The food left a lot to be desired there but at least she hadn't had to make it herself.

The bread she found in the cupboard was cheap, white and a little stale and the packet of ham in the fridge was a day past its sell-by date, but Clare was hungry so she made herself a sandwich. She had assumed that the excruciating pain she felt when she swallowed would disappear now that she was out of a hospital bed but her first bite of the sandwich tasted like a mouthful of barbed wire and she spat it out into the sink.

Luckily, she found a half-empty tub of vanilla ice cream in the freezer, tore it open and spooned it into her mouth. It tasted good and it slipped down just fine, its coolness soothing her tender throat.

As she was scraping the final precious spoonful from the tub the doorbell rang and she froze, holding the spoon in midair.

Creeping into the unlit hall, she could make out a

shadowy figure behind the glass in the front door. When the doorbell rang again she tiptoed into the living room and crept over to the small bay window, craning her neck, holding her breath, praying that whoever it was wouldn't look in her direction.

But when she saw that it was Vicky Page standing there, arms folded, beneath the outside light, she felt a wave of relief. Vicky reached out her hand and rang the bell again and the angry determination of the gesture told Clare that she was annoyed.

Clare hurried into the hall, flicking the light on as she passed the switch. She had kept Vicky waiting long enough and she wouldn't be in a good mood. As soon as the door opened Vicky stepped indoors, scowling impatiently, almost pushing her out of the way.

'I want a word,' she said as she stalked through to the kitchen. When she reached the table she sat down on the chair Clare had been using and looked her in the eye. 'I need you to promise you'll keep quiet about what I told you on Sunday night. The others have all agreed. I don't need you ruining things. If my mum and dad got to hear about it . . .'

Clare nodded meekly. Vicky wasn't the sort of person you crossed.


For Analise Sonquist Tuesday nights were special. On Tuesdays she moved in another, more exciting world.

Since moving to England she'd discovered that the life of an au pair has its downside. Mrs Crest insisted on everything being done her way but Analise could deal with that. She spooned the organic vegetarian baby food into young Alexander's mouth obediently first thing in the morning while Mrs Crest was tearing round the huge kitchen, preparing for work. But once Mrs Crest wasn't there to see, all that changed and Analise was glad that Alexander – she was never allowed to call him Alex – was too young to tell his mother about the turkey nuggets, the packets of crisps and the biscuits she gave him to ensure his good behaviour.

Analise knew that Mr Crest – do call me Clive – would have tried to get her into bed, given half the chance. He was a small, smooth, balding man – a partner in a firm of Morbay solicitors – and the thought of him running his little hairless hands over her naked body made Analise feel slightly sick, although there were times she suspected that there might be another woman somewhere in the background; a secret he was careful to keep to himself. She had always had a nose for such things.

However, Clive wasn't the person to fear in the Crest household. Mrs Crest – Suzie – was firmly in charge – or, to quote a peculiar English phrase Analise had heard, she 'wore the trousers'. Suzie was something quite high up in Morbay's local government offices: Analise wasn't quite sure what she actually did but whatever it was, it took up a lot of her time and ensured that most nights Alexander received little more than a goodnight kiss from his loving mother.

And when Suzie wasn't at work she always had something to occupy her time: yoga class on Monday; French evening class on Wednesday; badminton on Thursday; amateur dramatics on Friday; and an assortment of social activities at weekends. Tuesday was the one night Suzie set aside to dedicate to her baby – although he was usually in bed – therefore Tuesday was Analise's night off. Her only night of freedom.

Before leaving the house, Analise studied her reflection in the hall mirror. She looked good and she knew he wouldn't be able to resist her tonight. She zipped up her white quilted jacket and pulled on her woollen beret. It was cold out there with the wind blowing in from the river.

Tonight the meeting place was Tradmouth Castle but she had to meet Kristina first. Kristina, also from Norway, was her fellow au pair, stationed with a family in nearby Stoke Beeching. They usually met up for a drink in Tradmouth on Tuesdays with two other girls from the Hands Across the Sea Agency – one French, one Spanish – to compare notes and air grievances to sympathetic ears. But Analise wouldn't be staying long. She had a more exciting meeting arranged.

She slipped out into the darkness and began to walk the quarter of a mile into Tradmouth. In the summer there would have been a lot of people around; tourists strolling in the evening sun. But on a damp night in late February the road was deserted.

She spent fifty minutes with the girls in the Tradmouth Arms down by the quayside, making a single bottle of lager last the whole time. But her mind wasn't on the shared gossip and the laughter of an evening's precious freedom: she knew he would be waiting for her up by the castle and she longed to see him and feel his arms around her. The girls knew about him, of course – it wasn't something she'd been able to keep to herself – and they wished her a slightly envious goodnight as she left the pub, tingling with delicious anticipation.

She retraced her steps along the road leading to the castle, thrusting her hands into her pockets as she passed the houses on the fringe of the town; houses with nautical names, built for retired naval officers, unwilling to move beyond the sight and smell of the sea. The road became steep here and she could just make out the lights of Queenswear shining like stars through the veil of sea mist that reached down to the black shifting waters of the River Trad. The trees ahead formed a tunnel over the narrow road and the descending mist swirled like spectres around their bare branches. She could hear her footsteps echoing in the darkness. Or perhaps it wasn't an echo; perhaps it was someone following behind. But when she turned her head the road seemed empty and she told herself it was just her imagination.

Last time she had been down this road it had been a crisp sunny day but now it resembled the set of a horror movie, scented with the clinging smell of rotting vegetation, the scent of decay. But he was meeting her at the end of the road so everything would be OK. It was always OK when he was around.

She carried on, her sheepskin boots slipping from time to time on the rotting leaves, remnants of a distant autumn. She couldn't see the castle yet because it was hidden behind a sharp bend in the road but she knew it wasn't far. And he would be there, waiting.

Somewhere behind her she heard a shuffling and a sharp crack of twigs, like a pistol shot in the mist. She resisted the temptation to look round and quickened her pace, trying to convince herself that it was some animal in the woodland. But when she heard the sound again she recognised it as stealthy, predatory footsteps creeping through the rotten leaves beneath the trees.

Analise tried to break into a run but, like in some night-mare, her feet wouldn't obey her brain. Whatever it was was getting closer and she could almost hear it breathing. Closer. Then her mobile phone rang and as she slowed down to fumble for it in her bag, she felt something being slipped around her neck from behind.

She reached up in a desperate attempt to scratch her assailant's face. But her bare hands met not with live flesh but with something cold and hard.

And that was the last thing she touched on this earth before the thin cord tightened around her neck and the spirit left her limp, lifeless body.

# CHAPTER 11

*John Varley had no time for his father's interest in Egyptology. I once overheard him saying that if Sir Frederick were to die, he would make a bonfire of his whole collection and rejoice at the sight of those desiccated mummies going up in flames. The very thought struck me with horror. How could a son be so insensitive to his own father's passions?*

*I had been told that when John had completed his education at Rugby School Sir Frederick had sent him up to Varley's Pickle Factory near Bristol where he was to learn the business his grandfather had founded with a view to taking over on Sir Frederick's retirement. As an orphan who had had to make her own way in the world I considered John to be a young man in possession of many of life's privileges, even though he himself seemed quite unaware of his good fortune. I had met several such spoiled young men from wealthy families before in Oxford: having nothing to fight for in this life can make us weak and soft.*

*The accident John had suffered as a child had been a fall from a tree in the woods beside the castle. He had broken his right leg very badly and, as a consequence, it had been left deformed and twisted. Because of this misfortune he limped badly and he was very sensitive about his disability. He had a strong hatred of being looked at and one day when I was outside with the children, he must have fancied that I was watching him. When he turned to address me his demeanour was most unpleasant, and his words quite unsuitable for use in the presence of young children. Naturally I remonstrated with him but he told me that a pauper like myself living on the charity of his family had no right to an opinion. I was shocked by the viciousness of his speech but I had no desire to show my feelings in front of my charges. I hurried them away and led them to the room where Sir Frederick kept his collection. Edward, of course, was delighted at this diversion from his lessons, as was Victoria. But for myself, the visit to the little museum of antiquities allowed me to recover from the shock of John's verbal assault.*

*It was when we left the museum to return to the schoolroom that I encountered Sir Frederick. When the children were out of earshot he enquired whether anything was amiss and I had to tell him the truth. We should always tell the truth, whatever the consequences.*

# CHAPTER 12

Wesley knew the road well. It led to the castle which stood high on the promontory where the River Trad met the sea. The castle had battlements affording a spectacular view and inside were cannons, dungeons and other delights for imaginative young minds. It was a place he and Pam often brought the children on a summer Sunday when he was off duty; a place of ice creams and fun with sheltered coves below its walls, perfect for skimming stones. But now he had an uneasy feeling that those pleasant associations would vanish forever.

The body lay to the right of the road in a leaf-filled hollow beneath a tall oak tree. Her hands had been crossed on her chest and she had been loosely wrapped in a linen sheet which stood out stark white against the brown ground. No attempt had been made to conceal her and she was quite visible from the road. Her killer had meant her to be found: to Wesley it almost seemed as if he was showing off – boasting of his power over life and death.

She had been discovered at seven thirty a.m. by a jogger who had dialled 999 on his mobile. He had watched enough TV police dramas to know that he shouldn't touch anything and he had waited patiently like a good citizen for the police to arrive.

The constable who was first on the scene told the jogger that he'd been wise not to look too closely. This was a nasty one. Touch of Jack the Ripper. Once the jogger had given his statement he had been allowed home for a restorative cup of tea, or maybe something stronger.

The panoply of Crime Scene Investigation had been mustered in what seemed like no time and the entire area had been sealed off for forensic examination. The dead girl had been in her late teens or early twenties, slim and fair-haired. In life she'd been pretty but now her face was twisted and discoloured above the deep, thin line left on her neck by whatever had been used to strangle her.

Wesley stood in the road by Gerry's side, watching the crime scene investigators in their white overalls crawling like fat maggots over the area, thinking of the young life so brutally ended and trying to stay professional. Sometimes it wasn't easy.

'Did you look at her, Wes?' Gerry's words, after a long period of contemplative silence, almost made Wesley jump.

He nodded. He'd arrived before Gerry and, foolishly, he'd accepted pathologist Colin Bowman's invitation to enter the tent that had been erected over the scene to view the body. One swift glance had been enough to make him flee and throw up his breakfast in the bushes at the other side of the road. He'd felt embarrassed and even when Colin had said that he wasn't the first officer on that particular crime scene to react like that, he still felt irritated with himself. He knew his limitations: in spite of coming from a medical family, keeping a strong stomach in the presence of a disembowelled corpse was something he had never been able to do.

'You look a bit green around the gills, Wes.' Gerry sounded concerned.

'I'm fine.'

'Strangulation with some kind of thin cord. Looks a lot like the wound on Clare Mayers's neck. If it's the same man, he's certainly spreading his wings.'

'You think it's the same man?'

'Colin reckons that she was strangled before . . . before he did the other things. I don't think it's very likely that there are two lunatics going round strangling women in this area. Clare might have had a lucky escape.'

If Gerry was right, Clare Mayers's importance as a witness had just rocketed. 'Maybe we should give Clare some police protection.'

'Just what I was thinking, Wes. We'll arrange it.'

Wesley looked round and saw Colin Bowman walking towards them. Today there was no congenial smile. Instead the pathologist looked rather stunned and his flesh had taken on a grey tinge, as though the blood had drained from his face. Wesley had never seen his mask of professional detachment slip like that before.

Colin stood beside Wesley in silence for a few seconds. Then he spoke quietly, almost in a whisper. 'Nasty business.'

'You can say that again,' Gerry replied.

Colin took off his plastic gloves and touched Wesley's shoulder, a gesture of concern. 'Feeling better?'

Wesley nodded. 'Sorry about that. It just came as a bit of a shock. What can you tell us?'

'She was strangled and then the killer made an incision in the abdomen post mortem. The internal organs were left in neat piles at the side of the body. Then he wrapped her in a linen sheet, arms crossed on her chest. She'd been laid out properly – I'd say there's a ritual element to this.'

'Jack the Ripper did something similar, didn't he?' said Gerry.

Colin considered the question for a moment. 'Similar, I suppose. But from what I recall of the Ripper case, this is far more controlled.'

'Would you say the killer had medical knowledge?'

Colin shrugged his shoulders. 'He was aware of basic anatomy but I don't think this is the work of a surgeon.' He managed a smile – the first of the day. 'Or even a pathologist.'

'Any ideas?' Gerry asked. 'A medical student? A butcher?'

'You can find it all out from the Internet these days. It's definitely not an expert job, Gerry.' He paused, shifting from foot to foot in an effort to keep warm. 'But I did find one very odd thing – apart from the mutilations, that is. There's damage to the nostrils, as though someone's tried to insert some kind of instrument.'

Wesley frowned. This was getting stranger by the minute. There was something familiar about the mutilations but he decided to say nothing for the moment until he was sure of his facts. 'Have we any idea who she was?'

Colin shook his head. 'She was naked and there's no sign of her clothes nearby. But something was found caught up in the sheet. Hang on.' Colin returned to the tent and whispered a few words to the officer in charge of exhibits who was waiting outside, trying not to look at the body. He handed Colin a small plastic bag which he carried back to the waiting detectives.

Wesley took it and examined it carefully before handing it to Gerry. It was a carved figure of some kind, dark in colour and about six inches long.

'I know what it is,' Wesley said softly. 'It's Egyptian. I think it's Anubis . . . the god associated with death and embalming.'

Gerry turned the thing over in his fingers. 'It's got a dog's head.'

'A jackal if I remember rightly. I think we should show it to Clare Mayers . . . see if it means anything to her. And it rather confirms a theory I have about the mutilations.'

Gerry raised his eyebrows but said nothing.

Rachel Tracey covered the receiver with her hand and called across the incident room. 'A Mrs Crest has just called. Her au pair didn't come home last night.'

Wesley walked over to her desk. He was about to ask whether the au pair in question was in the habit of staying out all night but then he realised this would be a stupid question. The young woman's murder wouldn't have made the news yet and if the au pair regularly went AWOL, her absence was unlikely to be reported to the police at this early stage.

'What's her name?'

'Analise Sonquist. She's Norwegian. The Crests describe her as a quiet girl. Tuesday is her night off and she usually goes out.'

'Do they know where?'

'She told the Crests she was going out for a drink with another au pair who works for a family in Stoke Beeching.'

'Do they know this friend's name?'

'It's Kristina. She's Norwegian too. When Analise didn't come home the Crests contacted the family Kristina works for. Kristina says she met Analise and a couple of other girls in the Tradmouth Arms last night but Analise left early. Mrs Crest gave me Kristina's phone number so at least we've got a starting point.'

Wesley looked out of the window. The sun had come out, weak and watery, but it still looked cold out there. 'We'd better pay the Crests a visit first – get a definite ID on the victim,' he said before heading for Gerry Heffernan's office.

He could see the boss was on the phone. As soon as Gerry saw him he beckoned him in with a large gesture, pointed to the mouthpiece and pulled a face. Wesley guessed he was talking to Chief Superintendent Nutter – and that his superior was telling him something unpalatable.

When Gerry put the phone down he looked up. 'That was the Nutter. I called to give him a full update but he's more concerned about how much the investigation's going to cost and filling in the right forms than he is about catching the lunatic who butchered that poor lass. Anything new?'

As soon as Wesley had finished telling him about the Crests, the DCI stood up and tugged his coat off the coat stand in the corner of his office, almost pulling the thing over in his enthusiasm.

'Of course it might not be this Analise, Gerry. It could just be a coincidence.'

'No, Wes, it's her. I can feel it in my water. I'll get Mrs Crest to identify her. It's not a pleasant thing to do but at least she's not family – not emotionally involved.'

'OK. I'll send Rachel to interview this Kristina. She'll probably know more about what Analise got up to in her spare time than Mrs Crest does: she'll only have been told the edited version.'

Five minutes later they were walking through Tradmouth

towards the Crests' house. The weak February sun had lured shoppers from their houses and the streets were fuller than they'd been since Christmas. To their left the light sparkled on the river's choppy surface. A chilly wind was getting up and Wesley zipped his coat up to the neck as they walked. Gerry, however, didn't bother doing up his well-worn anorak: in his days in the merchant navy he'd endured far worse weather than this.

Wesley knew Gerry was right. They needed to uncover all of Analise Sonquist's secrets. There was no privacy in death.

Neil Watson sat in his Mini parked in front of Varley Castle, staring at his tiny mobile phone and wondering whether to try Wesley's number again as he hadn't managed to talk to him the previous night. But when he saw Robert Delaware emerging from the castle's front entrance, he put the phone back in his pocket.

Delaware spotted him and raised his hand, then turned back to the front door as Neil got out of the car. Neil had the impression that he was trying to avoid him. But he wasn't going to get away that easily.

He shouted over to him. 'Robert. I've been wanting a word. I tried to call a mate of mine in the police last night to see if he knew anything about those murders . . . the ones John Varley was supposed to have committed.'

Delaware stood there, his hand hovering on the door handle. 'He's hardly likely to be interested. It's ancient history. Case closed.'

'Who exactly did John Varley kill?'

Delaware turned to face him. 'Just local women.' He looked cornered, as though he didn't want to be having that particular conversation.

'How did he kill them? What happened?'

'They were strangled, I believe. Why are you so interested?'

Neil couldn't think up an answer. Delaware had whetted his appetite. And the guarded way he'd spoken about the murders suggested that he might have some personal interest. Or maybe Neil was imagining it.

'Look, I really must get on. Caro's just found some more letters in the muniment room that I really need to have a look at. I meant to do it last night but I had to go back to Tradmouth to meet someone. I stayed there last night and I've only just got back.'

'Bet you missed the palatial splendour of this place.'

He saw Delaware's cheeks redden a little. 'Hardly palatial splendour. Caro's given me one of the old servant's rooms at the top of the house but it saves the journey to and from Tradmouth every day. Now if that's all I really must . . .'

'Maybe we can talk about the murders another time then?'

But Neil was talking to Delaware's disappearing back. He took his phone out again and tried Wesley's number. This time it was engaged.

Once they'd passed the shops Wesley and Gerry reached a narrow gap in the buildings to their right where a steep flight of stone steps led to the street above. Wesley began to climb upwards but when he realised he was outpacing Gerry, leaving him behind, he stopped and waited.

'Hang on, Wes. It's OK for you. You live up the top of the town so you're used to this sort of thing.' Gerry halted and clung to the handrail, trying to get his breath back.

'You should get more exercise, Gerry.' Wesley paused for

a moment until the DCI drew level with him. 'I had a visit from a friend of Della's last night. His name's Guy Kitchener and he's a psychological profiler. He's worked for the police before. It's just with seeing the state of that girl's body . . . I wondered if we should have a word with him.'

Gerry didn't answer for a few seconds. 'I'd certainly have no objection. But you know what the Nutter's like about his budgets.' He grinned. 'In the meantime, if you can get this Kitchener to give us any free hints and tips . . .'

'I'll have a go,' Wesley replied.

They reached the top of the steps and crossed the road, only to be confronted by another flight on the opposite side of the street.

'I told you the Crests lived Above Town.'

'We should have driven.'

'These streets weren't built for cars.'

'Then they should issue us with police donkeys,' Gerry said quickly.

Wesley smiled, enjoying the mental picture, and when they rounded a corner the Crofts' house came into view, its pristine creamy stucco glowing in the weak February sun.

'Nice house,' Gerry said as they walked up another flight of steps to the glossy green front door.

It was indeed a nice house. Probably built in the early years of the twentieth century, it had a balcony over the front porch which undoubtedly provided a spectacular view over the river.

The door was opened by a tall, thin woman with neat dark hair. She wasn't the sort who looked comfortable in jeans. And she didn't look particularly at home with the baby she carried on her hip either; a handsome boy around ten months old with a full head of hair and denim dungarees. The woman introduced herself as Suzie Crest and led them through the hall into an immaculate drawing room with cream walls, cream sofa and an impressive marble fireplace. Wesley sneaked a look around. It was the sort of house Pam would love – if ever they could afford it or find the time for house-hunting.

Suzie placed the baby on the beige rug with casual indifference and presented him with a wooden sorting box of the educational kind. Then she took a seat on the sofa and gave the two policemen a businesslike smile.

'I wasn't sure whether to report Analise missing or not. But she's never done anything like this before.' She hesitated. 'Even though she wasn't the most reliable . . .'

Gerry pounced on her words. 'How do you mean, love?'

She gave the DCI a look of distaste. 'She didn't have meals ready on time and often we would start looking for clean clothes in the mornings and then find the washing and ironing hadn't been done. And sometimes she'd be late back when she knew I had to go out. I had a word with her, of course, but it didn't seem to have any effect.' She pressed her lips together disapprovingly.

Wesley said nothing for a few moments. The concept of au pairs performing light duties in return for learning English had obviously passed this woman by. He suspected that Analise had been regarded as little more than a cheap servant, there to run the house while her mistress pursued her own agenda.

She glanced at the expensive watch on her wrist. 'I've had to postpone an important meeting this afternoon.' The baby started grizzling and she gave it a look of distaste.

Wesley caught Gerry's eye. This woman clearly had no

emotional attachment to Analise Sonquist so he thought he might as well opt for the direct approach. 'The body of a young woman answering Analise's description was found near the castle road first thing this morning. The pathologist thinks she died last night between eight o'clock and eleven.'

Suzie Crest's eyes widened for a second then her hand went to her mouth. There was something rather theatrical about the gesture and Wesley's instincts told him that she was merely going through the motions of shock.

'Have you a photo of Analise by any chance?' Wesley asked.

Suzie Crest stood up and hurried from the room. She looked cool, as if they had asked to see her driving licence after a speeding offence. Wesley thought the lack of any emotional response rather odd. In her absence Gerry knelt down to play with the baby, helping him put the shapes into the appropriate holes. Wesley watched with a smile on his face. There were many young DCs in Tradmouth CID who'd be very surprised to learn that Gerry Heffernan had a soft side. The child clearly enjoyed the attention for he held his chubby little arms up to the DCI but as he did so his mother returned carrying a blue-and-white photograph folder, and sat down, ignoring her child who was now watching her with a slightly puzzled look on his little face.

Suzie took the photographs out and sorted through them before selecting a couple and handing them to Wesley. 'These were taken just before Christmas. This is Analise with Alexander.'

Wesley studied the pictures. The last time he had seen this lovely face it had been twisted and cyanosed in the agony of

110

death, but he could still recognise her. In the pictures she was smiling and holding the baby on her knee and the contrast with that naked, mutilated corpse made Wesley feel slightly sick. He handed the photos to Gerry who regarded them solemnly and nodded.

'I'm afraid this is our dead girl, Mrs Crest. No doubt about it. I'm sorry.'

Suzie inclined her head, acknowledging the sympathy she probably knew she didn't merit.

'We'll need to contact her family,' Wesley said quietly. 'I presume you have an address for them?'

'The agency will have it. Hands Across the Sea – they're in Morbay. I've got their card somewhere.' She stood up again and rushed from the room. This time Gerry made no attempt to play with the baby: he had other things on his mind – like how do you tell parents that their daughter's just been killed and butchered in a foreign land?

When Suzie returned Wesley took charge of the agency's card, putting it carefully in the inside pocket of his jacket. Then he glanced at Gerry who gave him a small nod. It was up to him to start the questioning.

'What can you tell us about Analise, Mrs Crest?'

Suzie Crest shrugged her shoulders. 'She was like most of these girls, I suppose. No initiative. Had to be told what to do – what to feed Alexander and when. And I had to make her a timetable of when I expected the housework to be done or she'd have sat reading magazines and talking to her friends on the phone all day. I've had these foreign girls before. They're more interested in boys and sneaking out to meet their friends than hard work.'

'Did she have a boyfriend?'

Suzie shrugged. 'If she had, he certainly never called

here . . . not that we encourage that sort of thing, of course.'

'What did she do on her evenings off?'

Suzie thought for a few moments. 'Analise never said where she was going unless I asked her.'

'And you asked her last night?'

'She told me she was meeting Kristina but I suppose she might have been meeting a man instead. Some people tell you what they think you want to hear, don't they?'

'Do you know Kristina?'

'I know of her but I've never met her. She's with a family in Stoke Beeching.'

'So you contacted her when Analise didn't come home?'

Suzie nodded. 'I called her first thing this morning when I saw Analise's bed hadn't been slept in. I didn't have her number but I remember Analise saying she worked for a family called Barlow. I got their number from the book.'

'What did Kristina say?'

'Just that she'd seen Analise last night, but she'd left the pub early to meet someone – a man, Kristina said. But she didn't know his name or where he lived.'

Gerry stood up. 'We'll need to speak to your husband.'

'He won't be able to tell you anything,' Suzie said quickly.

'You say you're out a lot. If your husband and Analise were in the house together she might have talked to him . . . told him more than she told you.'

'I don't know what you're implying, Inspector.' She was prickling now, as if he'd hit a raw nerve.

'Nothing whatsoever, Mrs Crest. We'd like to talk to your husband, that's all. Just routine.'

'Of course,' said Suzie as though she'd just realised she had overreacted.

They took their leave and began to make their way back to the police station. At least it was downhill this time.

'What did you think?' Wesley asked as soon as they had shut the Crests' front gate.

'I wouldn't like to work for that cow, Wes. I wonder why Analise stuck it for so long. Maybe when we meet Mr Crest, we'll find out.'

Wesley grinned. 'Bit of a cliché, isn't it, Gerry? Husband knocking off the au pair?'

'They say clichés only become clichés 'cause they have a grain of truth in them.'

Wesley couldn't really argue with that. As they walked on in amicable silence, he tried to forget that he had to face Analise's post mortem later that afternoon. And then the even worse task of informing her family.

It seemed to Rachel Tracey that Kristina Haken was quite happy with her lot.

The au pair greeted her with a smile and a baby on each arm and led her into an untidy playroom where a woman in jeans and baggy T-shirt was cleaning paint off a toddler's hands. The woman looked up and smiled as Rachel entered and introduced herself as Jane Barlow, the children's mother. She suggested that Kristina take Rachel into the living room and asked if they'd like a cup of tea.

Rachel answered yes. She'd love some tea. At least it would give her something to do with her hands. Wesley had just called to confirm that the dead girl was indeed Analise Sonquist and now it was up to her to break the news to her friend and find out everything she could. Kristina led the way into the large living room and she looked nervous as Rachel sat down to face her.

'I'm afraid I have some bad news,' Rachel began. 'I believe you know Analise Sonquist. She works as an au pair in Tradmouth.'

Kristina nodded warily.

'I'm very sorry but I'm afraid Analise was found dead this morning.'

The colour drained from Kristina's already pale face. 'Dead? How?'

'That's what we're trying to find out,' Rachel said. 'You knew her well?'

Kristina shrugged her thin shoulders. 'I knew her.'

'Did you see her often?'

She hesitated. 'We usually meet on Tuesdays . . . and when she wants me to do something for her.'

Rachel had expected expressions of shock, pious platitudes and maybe even tears and she was surprised at the iciness of Kristina's words. It was almost as though the news of Analise's death hadn't shocked her very much; almost as though it had been half expected. She leaned forward. 'What do you mean?'

Kristina glanced at the door. Perhaps, Rachel thought, the relationship between Kristina and Jane wasn't quite as sunny as she'd first assumed. Perhaps there were secrets Kristina didn't want her employer to know about.

'Jane works on three days in the week and when she is out Analise brings Alexander here and I look after him. He is a nice baby – very good – so I do not mind.'

'So what did Analise do while you looked after Alexander?'

Another shrug.

'Didn't you ask her?'

'She was meeting a man, I suppose.'

'You saw her last night?'

'We met in the Tradmouth Arms. Two other girls were there – Solange and Pilar. They're au pairs with the same agency and we usually meet up every week. Analise only stayed an hour – maybe less. It is the same every week. She was impatient to leave. She had a hot date.'

'Who with?'

'She didn't say . . . but it was probably the same man she meets when she leaves Alexander with me. We used to meet for lunch sometimes but now I only see her when she wants me to look after Alexander,' she said with a note of bitterness. Kristina was no fool: she knew that she'd been used.

'Could anyone have followed her from the pub?'

Kristina shrugged. 'It was very crowded. People were coming and going all the time. If anyone followed her out, I wouldn't have noticed.'

'What was her relationship with Mr Crest, the man she worked for? Could he be the man she was meeting?'

Kristina gave a knowing smile. 'She said he tried to get her into bed. He was . . . frustrated, she said. Then it changed. She thought he had got himself a girlfriend.'

'So who was the man she met?'

Kristina shook her head. 'It wasn't Mr Crest, I'm certain of that. Analise said once that her man was an artist. Mr Crest, I do not think he is an artist.'

Rachel gave the girl an encouraging smile. At last she was getting somewhere.

'Did she mention this artist's name or where he lived or . . .?'

'No.' She thought for a moment. 'But she said she had met him because of Mrs Crest.'

'Did Mrs Crest introduce them?'

Rachel could tell that Kristina was becoming impatient with the questioning. 'You have not told me how Analise died. Was it an accident?'

Rachel braced herself to impart the bad news. 'I'm afraid Analise was murdered.' She saw the girl's hand go up to her mouth. For the first time she was showing emotion over her former friend's death. 'That's why we need to ask all these questions and why you need to tell us everything you know.'

'I have told you everything I know. I wondered if this man might be married and that is why Analise did not tell me very much about him.'

Somewhere across the hall a baby began to cry and then the other followed suit. With the twins, a toddler and some-times Alexander to look after, Kristina must have had her work cut out. No wonder she resented Analise's presump-tion. The only mystery, Rachel thought, was why she hadn't told Analise to get lost. She decided to ask her.

Before Kristina answered, she glanced at the door. Jane was taking her time with the tea but then she had three young children on her hands.

'I look after Alexander because I feel sorry for him,' said Kristina. 'Analise told me that his mother does not care for him. He is a nice baby. I like babies.'

Rachel, who had always kept her distance where babies were concerned, nodded as though she understood.

'So you really can't tell me any more about the man Analise was seeing?'

'She said he was a great artist, that is all.'

Rachel smiled, trying to hide her disappointment. He might have been a great artist but he might also have been the man who ended Analise Sonquist's life.

*

Wesley sat at his desk staring at the model of Anubis, holding it this way and that so that he could get a better look through its veil of protective plastic. He examined the thing with its little jackal's head and its man's body, wondering when Neil Watson would get back to him. He had left a message on his voicemail for him to call but that was half an hour ago.

He picked up the phone and tried again and this time he was in luck.

'Neil. I've been trying to call you.'

'Likewise.'

'Pam said something about four murders. What's it about? I take it you're in Exeter at the moment?'

'No. I'm up at a place called Varley Castle. Ever heard of it?'

'What are you doing there?'

'The last owner's niece has just inherited and she's giving it to the National Trust. She called me in to give her some advice.' Wesley thought he sounded rather pleased with himself. It's always good to be wanted.

'Advice?'

'There's a big Egyptian collection here. She thought the Archaeological Unit would be the place to go to but I've had to confess it's not really my field. A bloke from the British Museum's come up to have a look at the stuff.'

Wesley's heart began to beat a little faster. 'Is he there? Can I talk to him?'

There was a moment's silence on the other end of the line. 'Andy's not here at the moment but I'm expecting him any time now. Why do you want to speak to him?'

Wesley wondered how much he should reveal. But he knew Neil would continue to ask questions until his curiosity was satisfied. And besides, he had a feeling he might need his help on this one. 'There's been a murder down here and an Egyptian artefact was left at the scene. Can you come down to Tradmouth and bring this Andy with you?'

'Yeah, I suppose. I'll ask him as soon as he turns up. Who's been murdered? When? How?'

'I'll tell you all about it when I see you. How soon can you get here?'

'Not till lunchtime. It's an hour's drive at least.'

Wesley ended the call before Neil could start grumbling about the journey. But he knew he'd be there, no problem. He only hoped his tame expert would be as compliant. But most people, in his experience, are only too happy to show off their field of expertise: everybody likes to feel important.

He suddenly realised that he hadn't managed to find out anything about the four murders Neil had mentioned to Pam. But, knowing Neil, they were probably way in the distant past and he had other things to worry about.

He had just picked up the Anubis figure again when Gerry Heffernan appeared at the incident room door. He had been upstairs to give Chief Superintendent Nutter an update. He didn't look pleased but then he rarely did after a meeting with Nutter.

'Have you heard how Rach got on with the victim's mate?' Gerry asked, making for Wesley's desk.

Wesley shook his head. 'Not yet.' He touched the bag and the little jackal-headed god shifted in his plastic shroud. 'I've been in touch with Neil. He's bringing an expert in Egyptology down later to have a look at this statue found on the body.'

'Are you going to mention the linen sheet and the . . .' He hesitated. 'The mutilations, because the Nutter thinks we should keep all that quiet for now.'

'We'll have to tell Neil's expert. I'm sure we'll be able to rely on his discretion.'

'I hope so. The last thing we want is a copycat killing.' Gerry picked a pen up off Wesley's desk and fidgeted with it for a few moments before putting it down again. He looked restless, as if his mind was working overtime.

'Did you ask about the psychological profiler?'

'I asked and the Nutter said he's still thinking about it. Let's go and see Mr Crest. He doesn't know the bad news yet . . . unless his wife's called to tell him.'

'That's likely.'

'Pity. I would have liked to see his reaction.' There was a long pause and Gerry's face suddenly became solemn. 'I've sent Trish to the Hands Across the Sea agency to get the contact details for Analise's family.'

Wesley sighed. It had to be done.

Neither man felt much like talking as they travelled to Morbay via the shiny new car ferry, larger and more efficient than the old version, now out of service and anchored upriver awaiting its ultimate fate.

The sky had turned dark grey, promising rain. At this time of year Wesley couldn't help yearning for the climate of his parents' native Trinidad but he knew that would change once the better weather arrived bringing with it hordes of visitors, all searching for the beauty of the place. Once off the ferry, he drove through the country roads until a scattering of DIY warehouses and car showrooms in huge barn-like buildings, functional and without permanence, told them they had reached the conurbation. Soon the industrial estates gave way to clusters of brick houses fronted by sparse grass and an array of straggly shrubs, grime-coated from the main road traffic. Eventually they passed through older, more substantial, suburbs before arriving in the centre of town with its thick traffic and Byzantine one-way system.

The offices of Darley, Crest and Uglow, Solicitors, were nowhere near the sea which had for centuries been Morbay's *raison d'être*. They squatted behind the main shopping street and the company's name was blazoned proudly across the frontage of an unlovely modern office block.

Clive Crest was in a meeting when they arrived but as soon as they showed their ID to his secretary she buzzed through to announce their arrival in a strained voice and the man himself appeared almost immediately. As he shook hands he looked worried – like a man with something to hide.

'My wife called to tell me the news. Analise was a lovely girl. Full of life. Who could do something like this?'

'That's what we're trying to find out, sir,' said Wesley quickly, suddenly wanting to stem the flow of platitudes. Crest led them into his office and told the secretary that they weren't to be disturbed. She was a middle-aged woman with a short curly perm and too much weight around her middle: not the sort who would present much of a threat to Suzie Crest.

As soon as he was settled behind his huge oak desk Clive Crest spread his hands, a gesture of honesty and co-operation. 'Please, gentlemen, how can I help? I'll do anything that will bring this monster to justice.'

'Where were you and your wife last night?'

'At home. We always have an evening at home on Analise's nights off.' Somehow he sounded too eager to convince them of his innocence, which made Wesley suspicious from the start.

'You haven't asked how she was killed,' Wesley said, watching the man's face carefully.

Crest looked a little flustered. 'Er . . . I didn't think. How . . .?'

'She was strangled.' Gerry caught Wesley's eye. They'd keep it simple for now.

'Where was she . . .? Where did it happen?'

'On the road leading to the castle. Not that far from your house. Did you go out at all last night, sir?'

'I've already told you, Suzie and I stayed in all night.'

'Not even for ten minutes to take the dog for a walk or . . .?'

'We haven't got a dog, Chief Inspector.'

Wesley saw Gerry give the man a smile that would make a crocodile look amiable. 'Maybe you wanted a bit of fresh air . . . or fancied a stroll.'

'I didn't go out and neither did Suzie. Analise went out around eight. She'd told us earlier that she was meeting some friends for a drink in Tradmouth. We assumed that was where she was going so we didn't give it a second thought. On her nights off she's free to do as she wishes.'

'Do you know the names of any friends she had in the area?'

'There was the Norwegian girl, Kristina. She was the only one Analise had ever mentioned by name.'

'Did you find Analise attractive?' Gerry asked the question innocently.

'She was a pretty girl, Chief Inspector. But I assure you there was nothing between us.' There was something in the man's eyes. Lust maybe. Wesley wouldn't have been surprised if Clive Crest was a bit of a ladies' man on the quiet . . . when his wife wasn't there to see.

'Your wife goes out a great deal in the evenings, I believe.'

'What's that got to do with . . .?'

'It means you were often alone in the house with Analise.' Gerry gave the man what looked to Wesley like a 'we're all men of the world' wink. 'Now you wouldn't be the first man to be tempted in that situation and you wouldn't be the last. We really need to know if you were having a sexual relationship with the dead girl.'

Clive Crest's face went bright red. 'I certainly wasn't having a sexual relationship with Analise and I resent the suggestion.'

'I'm sorry, Mr Crest,' said Wesley, trying to smooth the waters. 'It's just a possibility we have to eliminate. Your wife said she didn't know how to contact Analise's family,' he continued.

'The whole thing was arranged through an agency. We used them before last year when Suzie came off maternity leave but the girl didn't stay long. Very unreliable.' He sighed. 'Analise was a great improvement.'

Wesley allowed a short silence before he asked the next question. 'Did you know Analise had a boyfriend?'

'We didn't interfere in her private life as long as she looked after Alexander properly.' He paused, as if he'd suddenly remembered something. 'I don't know anything about a boyfriend but I did overhear her talking on her phone one evening. She was talking quietly as though she didn't want to be heard.'

'But you couldn't resist eavesdropping?' Gerry said. 'What did she say?'

'I'm not in the habit of listening to private conversations, Chief Inspector.'

'Oh come on, Mr Crest, the lass has been murdered. We'll be glad of anything you can tell us.'

'I'm sure she was talking to a man – you could tell from

the way she spoke. I didn't really hear what she was saying but I think she said the word "dangerous" – although I might have been mistaken,' he said, clenching his hands.

'When was this?'

Crest thought for a moment. 'Just after Christmas maybe.'

'Did Analise go home for Christmas?' Wesley asked.

Clive Crest shook his head. 'No. She stayed with us. She was here.'

'Did she go out much over the Christmas period?'

'A few times. Although I don't know where she went or who with. She mentioned that her friend in Stoke Beeching had gone back to Norway but Analise's parents were dead so . . .'

'For someone who's been living in your house since last autumn you don't seem to know much about her,' said Wesley.

'We don't pry into the private lives of our employees, Mr Peterson. Rule one – don't get too involved.'

Wesley's phone rang and he went into the outer office to answer it. After a short conversation he returned to his seat at the other side of Crest's desk.

'That was one of my colleagues. She's been talking to Analise's friend, Kristina.' He looked Crest in the eye. 'Analise told Kristina that you tried to get her into bed.' He watched the man's face for signs of guilt and somehow he wasn't surprised when Crest started blustering and denying everything. Wesley usually knew a liar when he met one and Clive Crest really wasn't very good at evading the truth.

'It's possible that your wife might have introduced Analise to an artist,' Wesley continued, cutting off the flow of embarrassed protest. 'Any idea who it might be?'

'You'll have to ask my wife. Although I think it unlikely.

123

Analise didn't mix with us socially. And I don't know any artists,' he added petulantly.

Gerry stood up. They'd learned all they were going to learn from Clive Crest for the moment. Wesley, however, was sure he was hiding something. And as he was about to leave the office something on the shelves behind Crest's desk caught his eye. Amidst a cluster of photographs and sports trophies stood three small painted Egyptian statues, about six inches high. One was a stately black cat with gold earrings, the other the hawk-headed god Horus, and the third was a thin human figure with the head of a jackal: Anubis, the god of the dead.

He stopped and pointed to the shelves. 'Are you interested in Ancient Egypt, Mr Crest?'

Crest appeared to relax a little. 'Oh, these . . . they're holiday souvenirs. We went on a Nile cruise the year before Alexander was born. Suzie hates the things – won't have them in the house.'

Wesley smiled and took his leave. At least he agreed with Suzie Crest about something.

Wesley found a message waiting for him back at the office. Neil and his expert had been delayed and they couldn't make it till later. Neil didn't give an explanation, but then he rarely did.

He looked around the incident room. There was an atmosphere of tense industry as officers sifted through paperwork, tapped on computer keyboards or held phone conversations in hushed voices. He could see Rachel sitting at her desk near the window, typing furiously into her computer. She looked as though she'd be glad of another trip out and Wesley didn't really want to visit Clare Mayers alone.

Ten minutes later they were in the car, heading out of town on the road to Hugford. Clare was still convalescing so she was bound to be in. And there was something Wesley needed to know.

The hamlet of Hugford, just a few houses clustered around the junction of two country lanes, was shrouded in damp mist. Water dripped from the bare branches over-hanging the road and the place was silent apart from the barking of dogs and the chug of a tractor in a nearby field. The barking reminded Wesley that the animal sanctuary – Della's new enthusiasm – was nearby. But he had other things on his mind.

He let Rachel ring the doorbell beside a glazed front door with flaking paint that had once been brilliant white. He could hear a bell echoing inside the small, pink-washed cot-tage and, after a few moments, Clare herself appeared in the porch, her hand clutched protectively to her throat.

'How are you?' Rachel asked as Clare led them through the narrow hall to the living room.

'A bit better,' was the reply, although her voice seemed as hoarse as ever.

The living room was a tip. The coffee table was invisible beneath layers of pizza boxes, stained mugs and celebrity magazines.

'Is your mum at work?' Wesley asked gently.

The answer was a nod.

Clare seemed to be on edge and Wesley wondered why. Maybe he'd leave Rachel to have a sisterly word. But first he took a plastic evidence bag out of his pocket and placed it on the coffee table on top of a well-thumbed copy of *Heat* mag-azine. 'Will you have a look at this please, Clare. Is it familiar at all?'

Clare picked up the bag with her finger and thumb as though she feared it might be contaminated. Then her expression changed from wary curiosity to wide-eyed horror.

'What's the matter, Clare?' he said softly. 'Have you seen something like it before?'

Clare didn't answer. She dropped the bag onto the coffee table as though it was a red-hot ember.

'Is it him, Clare? Does it look like the person who attacked you?'

Suddenly her whole body began to shake and tears cascaded down her face.

# CHAPTER 13

*My dealings with Sir Frederick had, up till now, been typical of those between master and employee. I had eaten my meals with the children and kept to the nursery wing with little thought to how Sir Frederick passed his leisure hours.*

*I was, therefore, surprised when one evening he suggested that I join him for dinner. I have to confess that I found the prospect a little alarming as I had little in the way of suitable clothing. However, I searched my meagre collection of garments and selected a green silk dress that I had not worn since I had lived with my aunt and uncle in Oxford. Then I had worn it when the bishop dined with us – my aunt having chosen it as suitable, modest and not too frivolous. I did not like the dress much but it was all I had so I put it on and examined my reflection in the cheval mirror that stood in the corner of my room.*

*I was rather pleased with what I saw. A slender young woman of twenty-three with glossy chestnut hair caught up in a bun. Tendrils of hair had escaped the hair grips and now they framed my face rather prettily, I thought, and the green silk dress fitted me rather better than it had done a year before and brought out the green in my eyes.*

*As I walked down the great granite staircase to the dining room to join Sir Frederick, I suspected that the warm glow of pride I felt would probably be short-lived. In my lowly position and not being adept at small talk I was bound to be overwhelmed by the situation and struck dumb. I approached the dining room door, passing a hurrying servant who didn't give me a second glance, and I suddenly realised that John might be present at dinner. What was I to say to the young man who had so belittled me? As I pushed open the heavy oak door my heart felt cold and I was filled with dread.*

*I was so relieved to find Sir Frederick alone. He stood up as I entered and the look he gave me was most appreciative. Then he planted the tenderest of kisses on my hand.*

*I was hardly aware of what we ate that night for we talked of Egypt and his expeditions. How happy I was to be transported to that far-off land.*

# CHAPTER 14

It was a late lunch; a tuna sandwich eaten at three o'clock at Wesley's desk. They had stayed with Clare Mayers until her mother arrived home at two fifteen but hadn't discovered anything further. It seemed that Clare had told them everything she knew.

Gerry had ordered the investigation team to assemble for an update and as Wesley munched his sandwich, everybody had started to gather in the incident room. At five past three Gerry strode in, solemn-faced, and there was an expectant buzz of conversation. Wesley took the final, hurried bite of his sandwich, brushing the crumbs off the papers on his desk before taking his place at Gerry's side by the massive notice board.

'Right, everyone,' Gerry bellowed, like a teacher addressing a class of unruly adolescents. The chatter suddenly ceased. 'We've got a team out searching the woodland where the body was found. Her clothes are missing and so is her bag – if she was carrying one: that's something we need to find out.' He paused for dramatic effect. 'And let me introduce you to Clare Mayers's attacker . . . and the possible murderer of Analise Sonquist.'

Wesley could see Gerry had a large picture hidden behind his back, a blown-up image of the small jackal-headed god found on Analise Sonquist's body. He produced it magician-fashion and held it up for everyone to see before pinning it in pride of place at the centre of the notice board, next to the gruesome crime scene pictures of the dead Analise.

'Meet our main suspect.' There was a ripple of suppressed laughter. Gerry held up his hand. 'Don't laugh. According to Clare Mayers this is exactly what the dog-headed man who attacked her looked like. I know I assumed that when Clare said he had a dog's head she meant he was wearing some kind of mask like the Neston attacker but even I can't be right all the time.' He paused for a flutter of respectful laughter. 'The killer left this figure on Analise's body and we need to find out why.' He turned to Wesley. 'According to DI Peterson here who knows about these things the mutilations on the body might – just might – be connected to Egyptian rituals and this figure is the Egyptian god associated with death. The question is, as Egypt's thousands of miles away, what's he doing here in Devon?'

'On his holidays, sir.' The newest detective constable on the team, cursed with acne and newly transferred from uniform, looked round expecting his quip to be appreciated. But his attempt at humour was met with silence.

'Wrong time of the year,' Gerry responded quick as a flash. 'And a lot of places don't allow dogs.'

Wesley saw the lad blush. If he'd been there longer he'd

have known that only Gerry was allowed to provide the inappropriate jokes during an investigation.

The DCI moved on. 'Analise Sonquist's post mortem's in half an hour's time so we might find out more then. In the meantime I want Rachel and Trish to go over to the Crests' house and search Analise's room. She said she was meeting someone so there's a chance she knew her killer.'

DC Paul Johnson put up his hand. 'Where does this dog's head come in, sir? Is it a mask he wears or . . .'

'I can't think of another explanation. Why do people usually wear masks when they're committing crimes? To avoid identification.'

'Or there could be some other reason,' said Wesley. 'Some kind of ritual the killer thinks he has to follow.'

'I think DI Peterson has a point, sir,' said Rachel. 'Or he might wear it because he gets some kind of kick out of terrifying his victims.'

'Could be a combination of all three.' Gerry began scrawling on the notice board with a felt tip pen. Three words: anonymity, ritual, terror. Wesley was sure that this just about summed it up.

Perhaps when Neil arrived with his expert on Egyptology, he'd come up with some fresh ideas.


Rachel Tracey didn't envy Gerry and Wesley having to attend Analise Sonquist's post mortem. She'd been brought up on a farm, always close to nature and the cycle of life and death, but the thought of witnessing a human body being cut open filled her with disgust.

She was, however, rather looking forward to searching Analise Sonquist's room. When she and Trish arrived at the Crests' house at three thirty she rang the doorbell and when Suzie Crest opened the front door she held up her warrant card.

'Chief Inspector Heffernan has asked me and DC Walton here to search Analise's room. Then we'd like to ask you some questions if that's OK.'

Suzie Crest didn't shift. 'Your Chief Inspector Heffernan went to see my husband at work. I resent all this intrusion.'

Rachel looked the woman in the eye. 'Your au pair has been brutally murdered, Mrs Crest. I think you'll find that it's rather difficult to carry on as normal in the circumstances.'

It seemed that Suzie knew when she was beaten. She pivoted on her heels and began to walk ahead of them up the stairs, her feet treading silently on the thick carpet.

'Was Analise carrying a handbag when she went out?' Rachel asked casually.

'She usually carried a shoulder bag – a sort of patchwork thing she bought in Neston. Unless it's up in her room she'll have had it with her.'

Analise's room wasn't on the first floor near the family bedrooms. It was up another, smaller flight of stairs in what used to be the attic. The servants' quarters. There were two doors up there, both closed.

'She had the use of both these rooms,' Suzie said, pushing one of the doors open. 'When the house was built I suppose the maids used to sleep here.'

Rachel stepped into the room. It was a small living room with sloping ceilings, a sagging chintz sofa and a battered desk in the corner on which stood a laptop computer and an assortment of magazines and books. The furniture, Rachel assumed, would be rejects from downstairs, given to the au pair rather than thrown away. She walked over to the window. At least Analise had had a wonderful view. Beyond the rooftops below, the river shimmered in the cold watery sunlight. This might even be the best view in the house.

Rachel left Trish to examine the contents of the desk and followed Suzie to the room where Analise had slept. It was a pretty room with flowery wallpaper, a sloping ceiling, a small Victorian fireplace and built-in cupboards. It reminded Rachel of her old bedroom at Little Barton Farm and she felt a sudden and unexpected pang of yearning for the simplicity of her childhood. But she had work to do; cupboards to search. She thanked Suzie who took the hint and left the room.

Analise had travelled fairly light so the search was easy. Rachel found several letters in her bedside drawer written in a foreign language which she assumed was Norwegian and she resolved to get Kristina to translate them. Rachel had heard that the Analise's parents were dead so at least they would be spared the most terrible pain a human being can bear – that of losing a child. Somebody was already trying to contact her wider family: Rachel was just glad that the job wasn't hers.

She sorted through the clothes and shoes in Analise's wardrobe, all from chain stores; not the cheapest but not expensive either. No surprise designer labels here: if there had been a boyfriend, he hadn't been the kind to shower her with gifts. There was no sign of a patchwork bag which suggested she must have had it with her when she went to her last fateful meeting. She had been found naked so her clothes and bag must be somewhere. It was just a question of finding them.

As she was pondering this problem Trish entered the room waving a couple of plastic evidence bags triumphantly.

'I've found her diary. I think I'll leave the laptop to the experts.'

Rachel nodded. She knew only too well that Trish and computers weren't the best of friends. 'Anything interesting in the diaries?'

'It's all in Norwegian. But quite a few Mondays and Tuesdays – the days she used to leave Alexander with Kristina – are marked with a star.'

Rachel sighed. 'Why couldn't she have put a name . . . preferably with an address to go with it?'

'You ready to talk to Mrs Crest about this artist?'

Rachel nodded.

'I found these as well. She's with a man in some of them – it might be the boyfriend. We'll see if Mrs Crest recognises him.'

Rachel took the pictures from the evidence bag and went through them one by one. Some were of Analise with another girl who bore a strong resemblance to her, probably her sister. From the pure quality of the light and the wooden houses in the background, Rachel knew they'd been taken in her native Norway. There were other pictures of a slightly different size, obviously from a more recent batch. These had been taken in a pub where a smiling Analise was posing with an older man. He was in his mid to late thirties, tall and good looking in a casual sort of way. He wore a cheesecloth shirt with wooden beads around his neck and his sandy hair was slightly long but neatly cut. The clothes he wore gave him a faintly arty look and he had his arm around Analise's shoulders as they posed for the camera.

'I wonder if that's Mr Monday,' she said to Trish.

'Or Mr Tuesday. Not bad is he?'

Rachel smiled. Trish had been having an on-off relationship with Paul Johnson for a couple of years now and Rachel often wondered whether she'd spread her wings one day. But they shared a house and she hadn't seen any sign of it yet.

They found Suzie Crest in the drawing room, sitting on the sofa watching Alexander playing contentedly in a wooden playpen in the centre of the room. Suzie regarded her son with detached interest, rather like a visitor to a zoo watching some mildly engaging and exotic creature.

'He's a lovely baby,' Rachel said as she entered the room.

Suzie turned her head. 'Have you any children?'

'Not yet.' Rachel rather surprised herself by her reply. Having children was something she had never really contemplated. She had always assumed that her nieces and nephews would be the only youngsters in her life. But since she had started seeing local farmer Nigel Haynes, ideas she had always rejected were starting to form into vague possibilities. She squatted down by the playpen and passed Alexander a sorting box which he took from her with chubby little hands. All his toys, she noticed, were of the educational kind. No frivolity here. To Suzie Crest, family life was a serious business, to be sub-contracted to others whenever possible.

'I called the agency earlier,' Suzie said absent-mindedly. 'They promised to find me someone else urgently. I really can't take much more time off work.' She fidgeted with a button on her silk blouse. For all her outward calm, Rachel could sense her inner agitation.

'We've talked to Analise's friend in Stoke Beeching, Kristina. She says Analise was involved with an artist.' She watched Suzie's expression but it gave nothing away. 'She told Kristina that she met this man through you.'

'I don't see how . . .'

Rachel took a photograph out of the evidence bag she was carrying and passed it to Suzie. 'Do you recognise the man in this picture?'

Suzie's eyes widened for a second. 'That's Geoff. Geoff Dudgeon. Before I started my yoga I went to the watercolour class he used to teach on Mondays. He's very talented; has his own gallery in Neston. He's a talented potter as well as a painter.'

'Did Analise meet him at these classes?'

'No, that was long before she arrived. But he called here a few times before Christmas because he was helping with the set designs for one of our Castle Players productions. I suppose Analise could have met him then but I really can't remember.'

'Do you have his address?'

'No. But you're detectives so you shouldn't have any trouble finding him. Now if that's all . . .'

Rachel knew when she was being dismissed. As she and Trish left the room Alexander began to cry. And when she looked back from the doorway she saw that his mother had made no effort to pick him up or distract him. She was still sitting there on the sofa, staring into space.


'I've never seen anything like this before,' Colin Bowman said as he gazed at the mutilated body on the stainless steel table.

Wesley stood as far away from the action as he could manage but the little heaps of internal organs that had been found piled beside the body were in his line of vision, now placed neatly in a series of metal bowls.

'The question is, Colin,' Gerry asked, 'have we got another Jack the Ripper?'

Colin didn't reply. He had just taken off the top of the head with a circular saw and was now examining the brain, a frown of deep concentration on his face.

'Do you know, gentlemen,' he said after a few moments. 'I think our killer's tried to hook out the brain through the nose. That was how they did it in ancient Egypt, I believe. Isn't that right, Wesley?'

Wesley nodded. 'When I saw the nostrils I did wonder . . .'

Gerry emitted a grunt of disgust. 'You are joking, Colin.'

'I never joke at autopsies. And it fits in with the other mutilations . . . and the figure of the jackal-headed god found in the linen sheet.'

'Apart from the Egyptian business, is there anything you can tell us?' Wesley asked hopefully, his eyes still averted away from the action on the autopsy table.

'Well, she put up a fight. From the state of her fingers, I'd say she tried to grab the ligature around her neck . . . without success, unfortunately. Cause of death, strangulation with a thin cord of some kind. Garden twine maybe.'

'You've seen pictures of Clare Mayers's neck – the girl who survived. Is it the same?'

'I'd say identical.'

'Any sign of sexual assault?'

'Definitely not. She wasn't a virgin but she hadn't had sex within the last few days before she died.'

'And the mutilations?'

'The internal organs were removed post mortem and placed in separate neat piles beside the body. I said at the scene that the killer would only need a basic knowledge of anatomy and a sharp knife of some kind. A fairly competent job but not professional.'

'What kind of knife was used?'

137

'Probably a kitchen knife or a chef's knife; something widely available, I'm afraid.'

Colin nodded to his assistant to clear up and, once he had cleaned himself up, he led the two detectives into his office. Tea was served. Wesley felt they deserved it.

'I had a quick look on the Internet last night but I feel we should get an expert in . . . just to confirm that the mutilations really are consistent with Egyptian funerary rites,' said Colin. 'I could be jumping to conclusions because of that statue.'

'It's already in hand, Colin,' said Wesley. 'Neil's working with an Egyptologist from the British Museum and he's bringing him down.'

'Good. That was quick off the mark.'

'Neil's doing some work at a castle up near Dartmoor, something to do with a collection of Egyptian artefacts.'

Colin raised his eyebrows. 'That's very convenient.'

Wesley nodded. It did seem rather a stroke of luck.

'So we're looking for an ancient Egyptian?' said Gerry lightly. 'Rameses the Ripper.'

Wesley and Colin chuckled dutifully. A little gallows humour always helped to stave off the horror of what they were dealing with.

'We've sent the sheet she was wrapped in off for forensic examination,' said Wesley. 'I'm pretty sure it's linen.' He paused. 'The Egyptians would have used linen.'

'Of course,' Colin replied. 'But what does this ancient Egyptian stuff mean? Is someone playing games with us or what?'

'If we knew that, Colin,' said Gerry, 'we could all go home and have our tea.'

Wesley's mind was still on the sheet. 'There can't be many

places round here that sell pure linen sheets,' he said. 'If he paid by credit card . . .'

'That sheet looked pretty old to me,' Gerry said, pouring cold water on his optimism. 'It might have belonged to the killer's granny.'

They took their leave and as they walked back to the incident room, Gerry seemed particularly subdued. He slouched along the damp pavements, hands in the sagging pockets of his anorak, deep in thought and Wesley hardly liked to break the spell. But as they reached the doors of the police station, his mobile phone began to ring.

After a short conversation, he ended the call and turned to Gerry who was watching him with curiosity.

'That was Neil. He'll be down here in half an hour with that Egyptologist.'

Gerry grunted. 'And that profiler would be useful. Sod the Nutter's budget, I want him called in now.'

As soon as they reached the incident room Paul Johnson came hurrying up. There was news. But not of the definite kind. Someone had called at Geoff Dudgeon's studio but he wasn't at home and a woman claiming to be his wife had said he was away in London. And there had been a sighting of Alan Jakes in Dukesbridge, not far from his sister's address. A patrol car had been sent over to investigate.

And there was another juicy morsel of information about Alan Jakes. Before he started at the garage he had worked for a while for a butcher in Neston.

And if anybody knew how to wield a knife it was a butcher.

Wesley was sitting at his desk making notes on a blank sheet of paper, trying to get the facts of Analise Sonquist's murder straight in his head, when his phone began to ring. It was the Reception desk. There were two men to see him – a Dr Watson and a Dr Beredace.

Wesley almost ran down the stairs to meet them and when he reached the foyer Neil introduced his companion as Andrew Beredace from the British Museum. Wesley thought Beredace looked a little nervous. But then police stations often have that effect on people.

He took them up to the incident room, reasoning that Andrew Beredace needed to see the evidence if he was to give his professional opinion. Wesley hoped he had a strong stomach. The last thing they needed was an expert witness fainting on them.

But first Wesley introduced Andrew to Gerry who stood up and shook his hand vigorously.

'Look, Andrew, we need your help,' said Wesley. 'There's been a murder and we suspect that the mutilations on the victim's body tally with how the Egyptians used to prepare bodies for burial.'

Andrew looked surprised. 'Really? Of course I'll help if I can.' He smiled. 'Neil's told me all about you . . . and your wife. Pam is it? You didn't fancy a life in archaeology, then?'

'There are times when I wish I'd stuck to digging things up.' He paused. 'And this is one of them. It's a nasty case. You OK with gory details?'

Wesley looked at Andrew's face and saw that his agreeable smile had suddenly disappeared. He swallowed hard and nodded.

'Last Sunday night a girl was attacked and she claims her attacker was wearing a jackal-head mask. She said it was like this model of Anubis which was found on the dead girl's body.'

Wesley handed Andrew the Anubis figure, still in its protective plastic. Neil stood beside him, craning his neck to get a good look.

'May I?' He indicated that he wanted to take it out of its bag.

Wesley nodded. It had already been dusted for fingerprints and none had been found.

Andrew took it out and studied it for a while.

'This is a fake. Cheap tourist tat available in most rip-off markets in Cairo.'

'So it's not the real thing?'

'Definitely not. It's not even the right sort of wood for Egypt. It looks hand-painted but it could have been made in China for all I know.'

Wesley thanked him. At least now they knew they weren't looking for someone who had access to a collection of Egyptian antiquities. Which widened the field a little.

'Do you mind looking at some crime scene photographs? I'm afraid they're pretty gruesome. Are you ready?'

The answer was a nervous nod. Wesley led him over to the notice board at the other end of the room. Gerry followed with Neil who wore an expression of horrified fascination.

Andrew stared at the photographs pinned up on the board. As his eyes flicked from one to another, he held his hand over his mouth, his face screwed up in distaste. Neil, after one initial glance, turned his back to the board and stood watching the officers in the incident room working at their desks.

When Andrew had finished studying the images he followed the others back to Gerry's office in stunned silence. His face looked rather pale as he sat down in the visitor's chair.

'These mutilations definitely seem to be consistent with Egyptian funerary rites,' he said quietly. 'I take it she was already dead when . . . I mean, she wasn't just unconscious when . . .'

'No,' said Gerry. 'She was dead – which is one blessing, I suppose.'

Andrew took a deep breath. 'I noticed that her nose was a bit . . . The Egyptians inserted an instrument up the nose to hook out the brain. It was a skill Egyptian embalmers probably developed with experience and . . .'

'This was our killer's first time . . . as far as we know,' said Wesley. 'And he didn't manage to remove any of the brain.'

'But he tried. In the pictures it looks as if he left the organs in piles beside the body. They should have been placed in special Canopic jars.'

'And you can't buy those in Sainsbury's,' said Gerry.

'But he could have used something similar,' said Andrew. 'Any container would have done, surely.'

'Which suggests he went to the scene unprepared?' said Wesley. 'The murder might have been opportunistic? There's a chance he still had the cord in his pocket from the attack on Clare Mayers, but it takes some planning to carry a load of containers around.'

'It might not be the sort of thing you'd do if you were out on the prowl on the off chance of coming across a likely victim.' Andrew Beredace seemed to have recovered from the shock of seeing the crime scene photos and Wesley guessed he was starting to enjoy himself. Easy when you haven't got the responsibility of bringing the perpetrator to justice, he thought.

'Is there anything he didn't get right about the ritual?'

'Oh, he did the very basics but I don't suppose he could

have done all of it in the circumstances. Embalming was a long process, of course.'

'Go on,' said Gerry with a hint of impatience.

'Well, the body would normally be washed and the hair removed.'

'No sign that he did that. What next?'

'Well, he clearly knew about the hook inserted into the nose. In Egyptian funerary rites when sections of brain were left behind they were dissolved with some substance but we're not sure what: Herodotus merely says "drugs" so it could be a number of—'

'And the incision in the abdomen?' Wesley asked, fearing that Andrew was about to go off on a tangent.

'This was done by specialists known as the *paraschistai* using a flint or obsidian knife. The incision wouldn't be large – according to Goyon, the chief *paraschistai* would place his left hand inside the body and cut the organs free with a metal knife. It was a crude procedure: the heart was always left in place and the kidneys were usually inaccessible so they had four Canopic jars ready to receive the organs: one for the liver, one for the stomach, one for the lungs and one for the intestines. Then the body was cleaned, filled with natron and padded out with cloth soaked in resin. As I said, this all took some time. Eventually the body was wrapped in linen bandages, probably sealed with more resin. Protective charms and scarabs were inserted in the layers of—'

'And where does Anubis come into all this?' asked Gerry.

'Much of the embalming process was symbolic, reflecting the preparations made by Anubis when he brought Osiris back to life. The priest in charge of the funerary rituals represented Anubis . . . and he wore an Anubis mask.'

143

Wesley caught Gerry's eye. It all fitted.

Andrew continued, 'From those photographs, I'd say that the killer's made a crude attempt to make it look like an Egyptian ritual but he's got some details wrong. That incision's far too large for a start and he's taken out the heart which would never have been done because they believed that the soul resided there. And the body's wrapped in a sheet instead of layered bandages.'

'He was out in the open air,' said Wesley. 'He wouldn't have had time for the niceties.'

'That's true. But I think whoever did it only had a vague idea about Egyptian funerary rites.'

'So we can rule you out then,' said Gerry lightly.

Andrew smiled. 'If I were you, I'd try and find out where he got hold of the Anubis mask.'

Gerry grunted. 'These days they probably sell them over the Internet.'

'I'll get someone to follow it up,' said Wesley. 'Although we don't know exactly what it looks like. Is it a home-made job, an accurate reconstruction or a plastic Halloween horror? We need Clare Mayers to give us a better description.'

But Gerry didn't seem to have heard him. 'I reckon if we don't catch our man soon, he's going to try it again.' He looked straight at Andrew. 'And he might just get it right next time.'

Wesley had given the task of trawling the Internet for purveyors of Anubis artefacts to the new recruit in CID. At first the lad had seemed eager, almost a little excited, at the prospect of a few hours spent in front of a computer screen but now his chin was resting on his hands and his face was a study in boredom. Wesley felt a little sorry for him. But someone had to do it and it wasn't going to be him: rank had to have some privileges.

Alan Jakes's sister in Dukesbridge had received a visit from a couple of uniformed officers but she had denied all knowledge of her brother's whereabouts, which Wesley hardly found surprising. But the fact that Jakes had once worked for a butcher nagged at the back of his mind and there was always the possibility that he might have taken to reading books on ancient Egypt in his leisure hours. They needed to find Jakes and find him quickly.

He was about to get up and fetch himself a cup of tea from the machine in the corridor when his phone began to ring.

'Wesley, it's Ian. Ian Petrie. Can you be at the hotel in half an hour?'

Wesley looked at his watch. It was four thirty, still early in the day during a murder investigation. He'd told Pam not to expect him until nine at the earliest.

'I'm rather busy with this murder, Ian.'

'Surely you can take a break for half an hour. I need someone with local knowledge to go round the art galleries in Neston with me.'

'I can get you a list of galleries and proprietors.'

There was silence on the other end of the line. Then Ian spoke. 'I would have thought you of all people would have been more co-operative. I backed you when you were in the Met. I defended you from some of those racist bastards and gave you the breaks you needed.'

Wesley found himself feeling a little resentful at the implication that any success he'd had in his career had been down to Ian Petrie, that his own abilities had counted for nothing. Even though Petrie needed a favour, catching the murderer of Analise Sonquist was more important. He said as much to Petrie, trying to keep the irritation out of his voice.

'It sounds like you've forgotten all I did for you.' Petrie wasn't going to let it drop.

'I haven't, Ian. Honestly. You were a good boss and I'll never forget it.' A little flattery usually worked wonders in his experience. 'But you must appreciate that murder takes priority. And this is a particularly nasty one – a young au pair.'

'How about tomorrow lunchtime then? Surely they give you time off for lunch around here?'

'I wouldn't bet on it. But I'll see what I can do.'

'Good man. See you at twelve thirty in your Reception.'

Wesley put the phone down. He knew that he was in danger of getting too bogged down in the facts of Analise's murder and that it might do him good to get away from the incident room for an hour. He'd just have to square it with Gerry.

And, who knows, while he visited the art galleries of the area, he might just find Geoff Dudgeon at home. And Geoff Dudgeon had known Analise Sonquist.

The girls had gone back to Vicky Page's house, a large white stucco mansion perched on the wooded hillside overlooking Morbay. They often went back there after school. Vicky had her own flat over what used to be the stable block, a luxury Peony and Sarah could only dream of. Jen hadn't gone with them. Jen tended to stay away these days. And of course Clare was still indisposed.

Vicky put on some music, loud enough to disturb the rest of the family in an ordinary house but in Vicky's house her parents and her brother were too far away to be bothered. Or even most of the time to be aware of her existence.

146

The first thing Vicky did was to change out of her school uniform. She couldn't wait for the freedom of university after the prison of Neston Grammar. Nobody would tell her what to do there, she thought – not that anybody told her what to do at home. Her parents were busy with work and social functions and she could come and go as she pleased. It was only school that reeked of childhood restrictions – and that would soon be an unpleasant memory.

She had picked up the local evening paper from the doormat on her way up to her room and carried it up to her flat, throwing it down on the coffee table before going to her bedroom and changing into jeans and a low-cut top. When she returned she noticed that her friends, who had made themselves comfortable, sat up to attention on the edge of the sofa. She sat down, crossed her long legs and gave Peony and Sarah a patronising smile. They relaxed again, like troops who'd just been ordered to stand at ease, and, as Vicky picked the paper up, they watched her, gauging her mood, ready to hear her plans for that coming weekend, preparing to hang on her every word.

But before Vicky could turn to the relevant pages, she froze, staring at the front page.

'What is it, Vic?' said Sarah. 'Something the matter?'

Vicky slung the paper back onto the coffee table. 'It's her . . . the girl who was murdered.'

Peony's eyes widened in alarm. 'What about her?'

'She works for him. She's his au pair.'

'You mean your older man? You mean Clive?'

'He talks about her. Even had the nerve to mention her name in bed once. I told him once that it got on my tits the way he went on about her sometimes. Analise this and Analise that.'

147

'You think he fancied her?'

'He always said he didn't. I told him that his cow of a wife is one thing, but when it comes to screwing the au pair . . .'

'Was he?'

Her lips twitched upwards in a bitter smile. 'I told him if he ever did I'd kill her.' She paused. 'But I can trust you two to keep that to yourselves, can't I?'

When Vicky began to laugh, the others looked down in embarrassment. As a friend Vicky was exciting and unpredictable. But the absent Jen had always warned them that one day she'd go too far.

# CHAPTER 15

*My dinner with Sir Frederick was to be the first of many and each time we dined alone. I realised after a while that he always waited until John was away from the house before he summoned me, which I considered most thoughtful. We did not speak of John, of course, but I was certain that his father was aware of his true nature.*

*One evening when I returned to my bed chamber after handing my young charges over to their nursemaid to be put to bed, I found upon the bed a blue silk gown of such exquisite beauty that I could not resist seizing it up and holding it against me as I swirled in front of the mirror. As I'd swept it off the bed a note had fluttered to the floor and when I read it I discovered it was from Sir Frederick. 'A gown of beauty for a woman of beauty,' it said. 'Please wear this tonight when we dine.'*

*I had no difficulty in complying with my benefactor's request and we spent a blissful evening together. First we dined and then we went to the museum where Sir Frederick – or Frederick as I called him now – entertained me with more tales of Egypt. He told me how he had broken into the richly painted tomb of a woman in Thebes – a court musician –*

*only to find all the paintings of the dead woman defaced and papyri beside her coffin bearing execration texts – curses to exorcise malignant ghosts. She had been a murderess, he said, who had killed for the joy of it and had been cursed by her victims' kindred. He had brought these texts back with him and he promised to show them to me and translate their meaning. I told him I would be honoured to gaze upon something so rare and he told me that I was a rare woman indeed to appreciate such things. I insisted that I would never tire of hearing his stories and we talked late into the evening.*

*Then, as it was a warm summer night we walked in the garden, breathing in the scent of the roses. And when he kissed me I raised no objection and felt a longing in my body that I had never before experienced.*

# CHAPTER 16

Clare Mayers put on her usual brave face when her mother appeared in the living room wearing her new trousers and a sparkly top, a little too low cut for decency.

Karen Mayers had already had a couple of drinks – why pay pub prices when you've got a bottle handy in the kitchen? Clare knew the telltale signs: the voice that was just a little louder than normal and the new-found eloquence. Karen always said that she could take on the world with a few vodkas inside her.

Tonight she was off to the karaoke evening at the Red Lion in Whitely. Clare hoped that she wasn't going to make a fool of herself. She hated the thought of word getting round and Vicky smirking and whispering behind her back at school. Clare would be glad when this final year at Neston Grammar was over and Vicky had gone off to university to spread her poison in some distant town. Sometimes, in her darkest hours, she had even wished that Vicky was dead.

There had even been times when she had contemplated betraying her nasty little secrets . . . but she was afraid of the repercussions at school.

Clare heard a car horn outside and then the slamming of the front door. Her mother had gone off in a taxi. If she'd said she was scared to be alone after what had happened to her, Karen would have told her not to be such a baby. She was old enough to cut loose from her mother's apron strings. Not that Karen had ever worn an apron in her life: she had never been that sort of mother.

Clare switched on the TV, spread her English essay notes out on the coffee table in front of her and stared at them, not quite knowing where to start.

Hamlet, in her opinion, was an irritating, self-centred idiot. Too much thought never did anybody any good; she had tried it and it only made everything worse. Especially when she thought of Alan Jakes.

Finding herself in bed with the man who had been her mother's lover had seemed romantic at first: Heathcliff carrying Cathy off across the moors in his strong arms, united despite society's disapproval. Back then she'd seen it as an opportunity to give herself a modicum of worldly glamour – to imitate Vicky's exciting existence. But now, in retrospect, the whole thing seemed sordid. Now she knew that Alan Jakes was a dark, good-looking, charming egomaniac who enjoyed wielding power over women, power he couldn't exercise in his everyday life as a garage mechanic's mate, taking orders from colleagues and customers. Alan Jakes had been all charm at first and he'd made her feel like the grown-up woman she longed to be. But she'd soon discovered that he liked to be in control. He'd scoffed at her ambitions to go to university and he'd made her do things in bed and in the back of his van that she hadn't particularly enjoyed; humiliating things that now made her heart shrivel with embarrassment. Sometimes he'd frightened her and laughed at her fear, his eyes shining with pleasure. It had taken a few weeks for the truth to dawn: Alan Jakes was bad news.

His reaction had been violent when she'd told him their liaison was over. No girl ever finished with him, he'd told her as he banged his tightly clenched fist down on the table a few inches from her face. He'd sworn to teach her a lesson she wouldn't forget and those chilling words still echoed in her head. When he left the house that day, slamming the door behind him, she had sat there tearful and shaking until her mother returned from work. But she knew she'd receive no sympathy from the woman she'd replaced in Jakes's dubious affections, so she had nursed the secret of her clandestine affair and Karen had interpreted her distress as teenage sulks. She knew that if she'd told Karen what had really gone on, her mother would have been furious – then she would have laughed and said that if you play with fire you get burned.

After that Jakes had disappeared from her life for a few weeks and she'd begun to feel safe again . . . until she'd seen him in the Anglers' Arms, staring at her with a knowing smile playing on his lips. He'd said nothing but she knew he was watching her every move, his eyes boring into her back. And then Vicky hadn't let her share the taxi so she'd been left to start her long walk down that dark lane alone.

The police had shown her that model of the man with the dog's head and she wondered why Alan had chosen to terrify her like that. There was little doubt in her mind that it had been him. He'd promised to teach her a lesson. And she'd known that he'd meant violence.

153

She could hear the wind blowing hard outside, bending the trees until they creaked and groaned, and she could see rain drops shivering on the window panes. She walked across to the window and grasped the thin curtains in both hands but before she pulled them closed she couldn't resist peering outside, scanning the lane for the dark-blue van with stickers on the windows. His van. It wasn't there but that meant nothing – he could have parked it down the lane out of sight.

She shut the curtains with a violent jerk and hurried to the kitchen. Had her mother remembered to lock the back door? There had been so many times when she'd forgotten.

She didn't switch the kitchen light on. Instead she tiptoed across the room, her eyes adjusting to the dim moonlight filtering in through the window, and when she tried the back door handle she was relieved to find it locked.

After grabbing the cordless phone from the worktop she heard the door handle rattle. Once. Twice. He was out there and he wasn't giving up. Her heart was thumping now, so loud that she was sure he could hear it. But she stood motionless, praying he'd think the house was empty and go away.

Then she heard a voice, muffled on the other side of the glass. 'Open the door, Clare. I only want to talk.' Jakes's tone was wheedling, persuasive, just as it had been when he'd wanted to get her into bed. It was hard to believe that it was the same voice that had issued such vile threats. 'Let me in, Clare. Come on. It's pissing down out here.'

Clare felt the tears stinging her eyes. The handle rattled again and she retreated into the hall on tiptoe. Then she heard breaking glass and she froze with terror, pressing her back against the cold hard wall of the narrow hallway.

She felt the phone in her hand. Her lifeline. She couldn't

see the buttons in the dark so she rushed into the living room and dialled 999. He'd hurt her once and he wasn't going to do it again.

When Wesley arrived home at eight o'clock the hall smelled faintly of disinfectant. He found Pam watching TV, engrossed in her favourite soap opera, a pile of school books on the coffee table awaiting her attention. The kitten lay curled up asleep beside her. Wesley could see the little furry body moving up and down with each breath.

Pam looked up and gave him an absent-minded smile. 'I suppose you want something to eat?'

'Gerry and I had a takeaway back in the office,' he said as he slumped in the armchair and stretched out his legs. 'Have you heard about the murder?'

Pam sat forward and the kitten, disturbed by the movement, opened its eyes. 'What murder?'

'Didn't you see it on the news?'

'I had a staff meeting tonight so I was back late. Mum picked the kids up from school. Who's been murdered?'

'An au pair from Tradmouth. Her body was found near the road leading to the castle.'

'Any suspects? Jealous boyfriend?'

Wesley hesitated. 'We think there's a connection with the attack on that schoolgirl near Hugford.'

Pam's hand fluttered up to her mouth. 'I thought you'd linked that to the assault in Neston.'

'We're not ruling anything out at the moment.'

Pam looked him in the eye. He could see that the news worried her. 'Do you think he'll do it again?

'It's early days.

'That's not what I asked.'

155

'I suppose it's a possibility,' he said quietly. 'I saw Neil today.' He thought the change of subject might take the anxious expression off her face. She had to drive back from school alone in the dark and, like every other woman in the area, the spectre of a murderer waiting in the shadows would be there at the back of her mind till the killer was caught.

'I thought he was working at Varley Castle.'

'He is. But I needed to ask him something.' He decided not to mention the Egyptian connection for now as Gerry had decided that the information shouldn't yet be made public. Besides, it would only prey on Pam's mind just as it was preying on his.

'Has he threatened to pay us a visit?'

'He sends his love. How's the cat?'

Pam reached out a hand and ruffled the little creature's fur. It began to purr loudly. 'Getting under my feet. Making the kids over-excited. Depositing a lot of puddles and worse in the litter tray which I have to clean out because nobody else'll do it. But apart from that . . .'

Before she could continue, Wesley's mobile phone began to ring. He saw Pam roll her eyes as he answered it. Now she'd been told about the murder she knew full well what the next few weeks would hold. And he knew that after all this time she'd become resigned to it. Although sometimes, in dark hours, he feared that one day she'd lose patience.

When the call was finished he turned to her, assuming his most apologetic expression. 'Sorry. That was the station. There's just been a 999 call from the girl who was attacked in Hugford. She was in her house alone when a suspect tried to break in. Uniform's out looking for him. But if they bring him in I might have to go back to the station. I'll go and say goodnight to the kids,' he said, levering himself up from the clinging depths of the chair. He touched Pam's hair and she looked up.

'Don't get them onto the subject of The Kitten, will you. They'll never get off to sleep.'

Wesley promised. The word 'kitten' wouldn't pass his lips. And if he read them a bedtime story it would be dull and soporific with no mention of felines whatsoever.

'And can you clean her litter tray out again while you're up?' she called to his disappearing back.

As he climbed the stairs he had an uneasy feeling that the tiny ball of fur was destined to rule the house with a paw of iron. He smiled to himself as he tiptoed towards Amelia's room.

But when he reached the landing, his mobile started to ring again and he shot into his bedroom to answer the call: the last thing he wanted was to bring a pair of curious children out of their bedrooms to investigate.

The voice on the other end of the line was female and unfamiliar. Whoever it was didn't identify herself but Wesley could tell she sounded young and definitely nervous.

'I thought you ought to know,' the voice said, 'Vicky Page has been sleeping with the man that au pair worked for – the one who was murdered. I just thought you should know.'

'Who am I speaking to please?' Wesley asked, trying to make the words sound casual.

But the line went dead and he discovered that the caller's number had been withheld. Whoever it was had said all they had to say. A simple statement. No involvement.

Clare Mayers's friend, Vicky, had been having an affair with Clive Crest. At last he'd found a connection between the two girls.

\*

Neil arrived at Varley Castle on Thursday morning only to find that there was no sign of Andrew Beredace's car. As he was staying at a pub nearby, Neil had expected him to be there first. However, when Caroline Varley answered the door she explained that Andrew would be late because he had to telephone various museums and universities – calling in favours.

She looked a little agitated and Neil was soon to discover the reason why. She led Neil into the drawing room and invited him to sit. 'Andrew told me about the murder . . . about the statue of Anubis on the body.'

Neil stared at her. 'I don't think he should have told you. The police like to keep things like that to themselves.'

'Well, I'm hardly likely to go blabbing to all and sundry, am I?' she answered sharply. 'At least Andrew said the statue was a fake so it can't have come from here.'

'There was no suggestion that it did.'

'It's just so awful.' She pulled a tissue from her pocket and crumpled it in her fingers.

Neil watched her, not quite knowing what to say. The murder of the au pair and the way her body had been desecrated was horrible. But Caroline hadn't known her – there was no reason, as far as he knew, why she should be so upset.

Before he could enquire further Robert Delaware walked in. The phrase 'as if he owned the place' passed through Neil's mind. There was certainly something proprietorial about the way he strode into the room. And he looked smug, as though he'd just scored a victory of some kind.

'How's the book going, Robert?' he asked, trying to sound casual. He didn't particularly like Robert Delaware and he was surprised that Caroline had allowed him to plant his feet so firmly under her table. However, his arrival had distracted her from the news of the au pair's murder and she stuffed the tissue back in her pocket.

'Well,' Delaware said. Neil saw him glance at Caroline and he suspected the book would take as long to write as it suited him to take advantage of her hospitality.

'Whereabouts in Tradmouth do you live?' Suddenly Neil had an urge to build a mental picture of Delaware's life. Perhaps it was idle curiosity. Or perhaps something about the man had aroused some suspicion he wasn't quite ready to put into words.

'I have an apartment in Ford Street.'

'You mean a flat over one of the shops?'

Delaware gave him a sideways look. 'You know Trad-mouth?'

'A friend of mine lives there. I think I mentioned him . . . he's a policeman.'

There was an awkward silence and Neil knew this was the perfect opportunity to ask the question that had been on his mind for days. 'You never did tell me the full story about John Varley and those women he was supposed to have mur-dered.'

Delaware's eyes flicked toward Caroline. 'I don't think Caroline wants to be reminded of . . . It was her great uncle, after all. Skeletons in the family cupboard and all that.' He cleared his throat and turned to Caroline. 'I take it you've had a look through Sir Frederick's journals, Caro?'

She shook her head. 'I keep meaning to but I haven't had a chance.'

'They're fascinating. And his description of the other archaeologists and all the rivalry between them makes for a good read. I think you should get them published.'

'Maybe I will.' She reached out and brushed Delaware's arm with her hand. 'Perhaps you could edit them for me.'

Neil averted his eyes. If he could see through Delaware, he wondered why Caroline couldn't.

'I'd love to. I've got to know them pretty well in the course of my research, so the job wouldn't prove too challenging,' he said with a smug smile. 'I'd better get to work.' He bent to kiss Caroline's hand, the height of pretentiousness in Neil's opinion, and stalked out of the room.

Neil was left alone with her, again, unsure what to say. He really wanted to tell her that he didn't trust Robert Delaware, that the man was insincere and full of his own importance. But he knew it was best not to make waves when he was a guest in the woman's house.

Instead he found himself apologising. 'I'm sorry for mentioning your great-uncle and those murders – I hope it didn't upset you . . .'

Caroline gave him a weak smile. 'It all happened a long time ago. Besides, I mentioned it first, didn't I? Remember? When you first came here.'

Neil nodded. It was something he could hardly forget.

'I think Robert's just being over-protective. Silly really,' she said with a fondness that made Neil's heart sink.

'What do you know about the murders? I mean, if you don't want to talk about it, that's all right but . . .'

'To tell you the truth I don't know much at all; only the bare facts. Sir Frederick's elder son, John, murdered four local girls but it never came to trial because he committed suicide before the police could arrest him. The killings stopped as soon as he died so the police didn't look for anyone else in connection with the murders. As I said before, Sir Frederick probably had it all hushed up. People in his position could do that sort of thing in those days. I'm sorry I can't tell you any more.' She tilted her head to one side. 'Why are you so interested anyway?'

It was a good question; one that Neil didn't know how to answer. He wasn't sure himself why the tantalising mention of four murders had caught his imagination. But it had and he wanted to know more. Perhaps it was the unaccustomed feeling of having to take a back seat while Andrew Beredace did all the serious work. Of course he had to co-ordinate things with the Unit and the National Trust but he was used to getting his hands dirty. Perhaps he was bored and looking for something to exercise his imagination.

'Well, they say that inside every archaeologist there's a detective trying to get out,' he said lightly. The saying was hardly original but he felt it was appropriate. 'I'll leave you in peace. There's something I need to check before Andrew arrives.'

Caroline stood up and put a hand on his sleeve. 'If you find anything out about the murders, you will let me know, won't you? Maybe it's time I faced a few family demons.'

Her words surprised him. But then she'd only recently moved to the castle from a busy life in London; before that she had only been there as a visitor so there was no reason why she should be privy to family secrets from a hundred years ago, especially when those secrets had been carefully hidden by following generations.

In Andrew's absence he felt no obligation to spend the morning in Sir Frederick's Egyptian museum. Besides, bearing in mind that he had to complete reports on everything of archaeological interest on the estate, he wanted to have another look at the medieval ruins in the woods.

He was halfway down the corridor when he had an idea

of such brilliant simplicity that he felt rather proud of himself. He crept back and let himself out of the front door, closing it quietly behind him. It was nine forty-five now. The local library was bound to be open.

He steered the Mini down the drive and followed signs to Mortonhampstead, the nearest small town. The library was easy to find. In fact the fine Victorian building constructed in the last year of the great queen's reign was hard to miss. Once he had parked the car, he rushed up the library steps and pushed open the door.

Inside, he approached a woman with an ID badge hanging around her neck. She was slim, fair-haired and rather beautiful but Neil didn't have time for dalliance, not even if she hadn't been wearing a gold band and a rather flashy diamond engagement ring on the third finger of her left hand.

'I'm looking for the local history section,' he said. 'I'm interested in Varley Castle in the early twentieth century. I believe there were some unsolved murders . . .'

The woman's eyes lit up with recognition. From the glimpse he'd caught of her badge he knew her name was Helena. A pretty name which suited her.

'Someone was asking about that last week. An author. You'll find a couple of local history books over there and we keep back copies of the local paper dating back to 1887 on microfilm – I'll show you.'

'Do you know this author's name?' he asked as Helena set up the machine for him.

'Sorry. But he said he was doing some research up at Varley castle.'

So Robert Delaware had been looking at back copies of the local rag for details of the murders John Varley had committed. Neil wondered why he had been reluctant to talk about it. Perhaps he would find the answer in the old newspaper reports.

First he had a look through a couple of books in the local history section which provided the bare facts. In May to July 1903 four local girls had been found strangled and mutilated in fields and country lanes around the Varley Castle area. The nature of the mutilations was glossed over but there was one telling remark: a local policeman said he feared that Jack the Ripper had left the streets of Whitechapel and had travelled to Devon to continue his evil work.

Then Neil searched through the local newspaper for the relevant time and suddenly it was there in front of him. A headline, sensational as any modern tabloid: 'Horrible murder. Woman's body found in field, brutally mutilated. This is the devil's work, says vicar.'

His heart pounded as he read on. The body of Jenny Pride, a young woman betrothed to a blacksmith, was discovered by farm workers early on a Thursday morning. She had been strangled and her innards had been cut out and spread beside her on the ground. At first the unfortunate girl's fiancé, the blacksmith, had come under suspicion and had endured several days of police interrogation but had been released when his mother had sworn on the Bible that he was with her on the night in question and hadn't left the house.

Once Neil had digested the facts, he sent the machine whirring into action again and found the second headline, similar to the first. This time the victim was one Nellie Lacey and the circumstances were almost identical, apart from the fact that Nellie, a maidservant at a vicarage, was found in woodland near Varley Castle: the same woodland where John Varley had hanged himself.

163

By the time the third body was discovered the headlines had become more hysterical. A monster was scourging the land. A wild beast. Maybe even Satan himself gorging on the blood of innocent virgins – ignoring the inconvenient fact that the third victim, one Betty Vance, had already borne a child out of wedlock.

The fourth and final victim was found in a field on the edge of the Varley Castle estate. Her name was Peggy Carr and she was a scullery maid in the castle kitchens. She had died in an identical manner to the other girls but this time the report included something that hadn't been mentioned before. 'The body of Miss Carr had been encased in a linen shroud in the same manner as the other unfortunates and a strange statue of great antiquity had been laid upon her body.' Just thirty-three words but they captured Neil's attention. He scrolled through later copies of the paper, only to find that, after a flurry of arrests, futile police activity and press speculation, the killings stopped. John Varley's suicide, a week after Peggy Carr's body was found, warranted three lines on an inside page, showing that in those days the gentry could command discretion from the press. After that there was no more mention of the murders, the assumption being that the perpetrator had hanged himself, thus saving the state the trouble.

Neil took out his mobile phone and pressed out Wesley's number. This was something he'd want to know about. However there was no answer, just an invitation to leave a message. The news would have to wait.

Wesley was in Clive Crest's office when his mobile phone began to ring. Thinking that it might be the news that Alan Jakes had finally been brought in, he glanced at the caller display but, on seeing it was Neil, he silenced the instrument. Crest was looking terrified and he didn't want any interruptions.

He and Gerry had been waiting for the solicitor when he arrived for work – because Gerry had thought it would cause maximum embarrassment – and when Crest breezed into the office, Gerry and Wesley had appeared to ruin his day.

'I received a phone call last night, Mr Crest,' Wesley said. 'It was from a woman but she didn't give her name. It was a pay as you go mobile so we've no way of tracing the owner but we can narrow it down to a few possibilities.'

He watched Clive Crest's face. The man was becoming increasingly nervous. 'You see, I gave my mobile number to some of Clare Mayers's school friends and told them to call me if they had any information. Clare Mayers was the girl who was attacked near Hugford, by the way.'

Crest looked as frightened as a wild animal about to encounter the wheels of a four-by-four in a country lane. For a fleeting moment Wesley felt a little sorry for the man.

'This anonymous caller made a certain accusation.'

It was Gerry who leaned forward and looked Crest in the eye. 'She said you were having it off with one of Clare's mates. You see, we think Clare Mayers was attacked by the same man who murdered your au pair.' He paused. 'You seem to be the link between the two victims.'

Crest shook his head vigorously. 'I can't accept that. I swear I had nothing to do with Analise's death. And I don't know Clare Mayers. I've never met her in my life.'

'But you do know a school friend of hers. Vicky Page?'

The blood drained from Clive Crest's face. He sat there for a few moments in shocked silence before speaking.

Wesley could tell he was trying to choose the right words, something that wouldn't make him look too bad.

'I don't suppose it's any use denying it,' he said with a sigh.

'I don't suppose it is,' said Wesley. He gave the man an expectant smile and waited.

'I never met Clare, although Vicky did mention her from time to time. Vicky didn't like her much. She said she was – what's the word? – a loser. But Vicky does tend to be a little . . . a little harsh about people sometimes.' He hesitated. 'Don't think I'm comfortable with our relationship, Inspector. And there have been times when I've asked her what she sees in me – the difference in our ages and all that.'

'And what did she say to that?' Gerry asked. He sounded genuinely interested.

'She said she liked mature men. That was how she got onto the subject of her friend Clare: she said she was infatuated with her mother's ex but he was a petty criminal of some kind. She was very scathing about it.'

Wesley saw Gerry give the man a meaningful wink. Man to man. 'I bet you couldn't believe your luck when a nubile sixth former said she was interested in a bloke like you – losing your boyish figure, thin on top and the wrong side of forty.'

Crest looked at him, unsure how to take it. Then he nodded. 'I feel bad about deceiving Suzie of course. But . . . but her life is so occupied by her work and Alexander . . . and her leisure activities.'

'She has no time for you?' said Wesley, trying to sound sympathetic, suddenly recalling how Pam had occasionally voiced something similar. Time was precious.

'Let's just say I'm not at the top of her priority list. I met

Vicky when she came here on work experience and she seemed so vibrant. So alive.'

'And she makes you feel young again,' said Gerry as if he'd heard that particular story a million times before . . . which he probably had.

'Yes. She makes me feel young,' said Crest with a hint of defiance. 'She's a remarkable girl.'

'And you buy her presents and take her out for fancy meals?'

The solicitor nodded. He looked more unsure of himself now that Gerry had just put a slow puncture in his romantic bubble.

'We're not here to make moral judgements,' Wesley said quickly. 'We just need to know where you were on Sunday night when Clare Mayers was attacked.'

Crest swallowed hard. 'I met Vicky. She was going to a quiz night at the pub with some friends. I picked her up at the bottom of her road and . . .'

'You had a bit of hanky-panky in the back of the BMW?'

Wesley looked at Gerry. Sometimes he pushed things a bit too far. But the tactic often worked.

Crest's face reddened. 'I have a Mercedes, Chief Inspector. And yes, if you must know, Vicky and I made love in a country lane. Then I dropped her at the Anglers' Arms to meet her friends. She was late but she said it didn't matter. She told me she was getting a taxi back.'

'What did you do after you'd left her?'

'I went home. Suzie was out at a rehearsal for her drama society production. But Analise was there. She saw me come in.'

'Analise is dead, Mr Crest,' said Wesley softly. 'Did you go out again?'

167

Crest looked sheepish and Wesley knew there were more confessions to come.

'Suzie came back from her rehearsal and went straight to bed. I wasn't tired so I stayed up for a while. Then Vicky called me. She told me she was at home and her family were away. Suzie always takes a sleeping pill and once she's asleep she's out like a light till morning so I told myself she'd never find out.' He looked at Wesley as though he judged him to be the more understanding of the pair. 'I drove over to Vicky's and I sneaked back at five in the morning before Suzie woke up. They call it living dangerously, don't they? Taking risks. I've never been much of a risk-taker, Inspector but that's the effect Vicky has on me. I'm a different man when I'm with her.'

Wesley said nothing. Instead he stood up and walked over to the shelves. He picked up the model of Anubis that stood there, similar to the one found with Analise's body but a little larger. He carried it over to the desk and placed it in front of Crest, watching his face carefully.

'Do you know what this is?'

Crest looked a little relieved. 'It's an Egyptian god. I forget the name.'

'Anubis. His name's Anubis and he's the god associated with preparing the dead for burial.'

'I'll take your word for it. Suzie probably knows more about it than I do. She borrowed all those models a while ago. Late last year, I think.'

Wesley caught Gerry's eye. 'Why was that?'

'Her dramatic society put on a play called *I Remember Cleopatra* last November. They're performing it again for the Tradmouth Drama Festival in a few weeks' time.'

'Set in ancient Egypt?'

'No, as a matter of fact it's a comedy by some local

playwright about a theatre company visiting an isolated Scottish island and putting on a production of *Cleopatra*. Anyway, Suzie borrowed the models for some reason . . . to get ideas for costumes, I think. She helps with the backstage stuff . . . as well as having a large part in the play.'

'What's the name of the dramatic society?' Wesley asked casually.

'The Castle Players. Suzie's a bit of a leading light.'

'I expect you were there in the front row,' said Gerry. 'Showing your support.'

Crest nodded. His earnest expression told Wesley that he hadn't quite appreciated the irony in Gerry's voice.

Wesley stood up. 'I know we've already searched Analise's room but I'd be grateful for your permission to search the whole house.'

Crest's eyes widened in alarm. 'Suzie won't like it.'

'We can get a warrant.'

'I don't suppose I've got much choice then.'

'I would have thought you'd be glad to help the police.'

'Not when I'm being victimised.'

Gerry got to his feet slowly. 'Sorry you feel like that, Mr Crest. We'll be in touch.'

The two men left the building in silence. But once they were in the car heading back Wesley felt he had to voice the thoughts whirling around his brain.

'You think Suzie could have borrowed the model to make a mask?' Somehow disembowelling someone didn't really seem like a woman's crime. But they had to consider all possibilities.

'She's a fearsome woman but I think this murder's out of her league,' said Gerry.

'We need to interview Geoff Dudgeon – the artist Analise was sweet on. According to his wife he's been in London but he's due back today. I'm going over to Neston with Ian Petrie later so maybe I'll be able to speak to Dudgeon while I'm there.'

'Good. And we'll get the Crests' house searched ... sooner rather than later before madam has a chance to do any tidying up.' Gerry picked up his mobile phone and pressed out the number of the incident room.

'What about Vicky?'

'So Clive Crest is a randy old goat. That wasn't a crime last time I looked.'

'But now Analise is dead he has no alibi for the attack on Clare. We only have his word for it that he returned home and didn't go out again till Vicky called him.'

Gerry said nothing for a few moments. Then he spoke, his voice uncharacteristically quiet. 'And now Analise is dead there's nobody to tell us he did come back, is there, Wes? It works both ways.'

Gerry had sent a team to search the Crests' house and, as Wesley walked down the stairs to Reception, he felt glad that he wasn't with them. The prospect of facing Suzie Crest on an empty stomach was more than he could deal with at that moment.

Ian Petrie was waiting for him as arranged, studying the posters on the walls, and when Wesley pushed open the door at the side of the reception desk, he turned round, a smile on his lips. 'I don't know how you put up with it down here, Wesley,' he said. 'Stolen farm machinery and thefts from yachts.'

'We have our moments.' Wesley looked at his watch meaningfully but Ian didn't appear to notice.

'I saw the headlines. Young au pair, wasn't it? It'll be one of your local nonces. Just check the sex offenders' register and you should pick up the pervert in no time.'

170

Wesley smiled. If only it were that simple. 'Is it OK if we grab a pasty before we go off to Neston?'

Ian shrugged. 'I suppose I should sample the local delicacies while I'm down here.'

'If we make an arrest for this murder soon I might even buy you a cream tea,' Wesley said, steering Ian out of the police station door. 'There's an artist in Neston called Dudgeon. I need to speak to him in connection with this murder case. According to his wife, he's been in London but I'm hoping he'll be back.'

'Let's hope we can kill two birds with one stone then,' said Ian. He sounded distracted, as if his mind was on something else.

It had begun to drizzle so they ate their pasties in Wesley's car. It was too cold to open the windows so the car would stink of food for a while but Wesley didn't really care: he had more important things to think about.

They reached Neston at one o'clock and Wesley managed to find a parking space behind the council offices.

'I take it you've never been to Neston before?' he said to Ian as they began to walk towards the High Street.

'No. Seems a nice little place.'

'Yes. It is.' Wesley wondered how long it would take Ian to notice that Neston wasn't quite like other towns. Here you were more likely to find practitioners of New Age healing than conventional doctors or dentists and the wholefood emporium dwarfed the local Tesco.

'I've got a list of all the art galleries,' Wesley said as they walked up the steep High Street towards the castle. 'There are five in all.'

'Tourist tat?'

'Not necessarily,' Wesley said, slightly offended at Ian's

assumption that everything in Devon was geared up to ripping off tourists. 'There are a lot of good artists working around here. And some of them charge prices that a humble detective inspector can't afford.'

He saw Ian smile. 'You have gone native, haven't you, Wesley? No need to sound so defensive. Look at these shops – hippies' paradise.' He snorted. 'Bet your drug squad do a roaring trade round here.'

'Neston's always been a bit New Age. But that particular element doesn't cause us many problems.'

They visited four galleries, starting at the top of the High Street near the castle and working their way down, underneath the arch that formed part of the old town walls and past the red sandstone church.

Wesley allowed Ian to do the talking. Always the same questions: could they have a quick look around the studio and storeroom and did the staff know of anybody called Ra? The answer to the first question was yes each time: they were free to look anywhere they liked. And the answer to the second question was always no. Nobody had heard of anybody connected with the local art scene who called themselves Ra. After four visits they seemed to have drawn a blank. But there was still one more to go. And that happened to be the one Wesley was anxious to visit.

Wesley led the way, turning right just before they reached the bridge over the River Trad. In this part of Neston shops and restaurants had been created out of the shells of old warehouses and Geoff Dudgeon's gallery was situated down a little alley next to a newly converted block of apartments not too far from where Andrea Washington, the woman who'd been assaulted back in January, lived.

When he reached the Dudgeon Gallery with its tasteful

172

sage-green frontage, he looked round and saw that Ian was hanging back.

'This is the last one on our list. The Dudgeon Gallery. Proprietor Geoffrey Dudgeon.' He paused. 'He's the artist I mentioned before; the one who appears to have a connection with our dead au pair.'

'In that case I'll let you ask the questions this time.'

Wesley saw that the sign on the door of the gallery was turned to open. To his disappointment, when he pushed at the door a bell jangled to announce their arrival. He had always preferred the element of surprise.

The woman who shot out of a back room to greet them was in her thirties, stick-thin with hair that was an unnatural shade of red. When she saw that a pair of potential customers had entered the premises a half-hearted smile of greeting appeared on her lips as she asked if they were looking for anything in particular.

Wesley looked around. The gallery was filled for the most part with colourful pottery, eye-catching and unusual. Some pieces were large and heavy, others delicate. The artist certainly had talent. The prices were steep but he saw a tiny vase that he knew Pam would love. But then he realised that giving expensive pottery as a present for her coming birthday probably wasn't a good idea with children and a kitten tearing about the place.

He took out his warrant card and held it out for the woman to examine and the smile was replaced by a sneer of disapproval.

'We'd like to speak to a Mr Geoffrey Dudgeon. Is he back?'

She didn't reply. Instead she vanished through the door into the back, leaving them standing there.

'Let's go through before he decides to do a runner,' said Petrie, making for the door.

But Wesley put out a restraining hand. 'I think it'd go down better if we didn't go barging in.'

Ian stopped, deferring to Wesley's superior local knowledge. 'OK. But if we lose him . . .'

Wesley suddenly wondered whether he'd done the right thing – whether his gentler, more measured approach was going to backfire. He could almost read Ian's mind: his bright young black DS had become soft down here in his rural backwater and if he were to return to the Met he probably couldn't hack it any more. He sent up a silent prayer that Dudgeon hadn't made a rapid escape through the back door: if he had, Ian's assumptions would be confirmed.

After what seemed like a long time, the woman returned, her expression hostile as any criminal's partner on the defensive when the cops came to call. 'He'll see you. This way.'

She spun round and marched off into the back and Wesley followed, Ian on his heels.

They found themselves in a large light studio. An electric kiln stood at one end and the shelves around the walls were filled with pots, bowls and plaques in various stages of manufacture. At the other end of the room stood an easel and an assortment of colourful paintings were stacked against the walls.

Wesley recognised the man who stood at the sink drying his hands from the photograph Rachel had found in Analise's room. Geoff Dudgeon was in his thirties with sandy hair and neat features and he wore paint-spattered blue overalls of the kind favoured by garage mechanics. Wesley had half expected Analise's lover to be some louche middle-aged artist with long hair, a disreputable corduroy jacket and a taste for wine and women – but he knew from experience that stereotypes rarely exist in reality.

Wesley introduced himself and a concerned frown appeared on the man's face. He turned to the woman and gave her a nervous smile. 'It's OK, Bea. Why don't you get us all a cup of tea?'

The woman hesitated for a moment before walking slowly from the room.

Wesley watched her go and once he was satisfied that she was out of earshot he began to speak. 'We've been trying to contact you, Mr Dudgeon.'

'I had to go to London yesterday – a rather nice deal with a West End gallery. I came back this morning and my wife said the police were trying to get hold of me. I've been intending to call you.' He picked up a damp paper towel and began to knead it in his hands. 'Look, I know they haven't named that girl who was found dead near Tradmouth Castle yet but I heard on the news this morning that she was an au pair who lived with a local family.' He glanced towards the door as though he was afraid of being overheard. 'I've been . . . I've been seeing a girl called Analise Sonquist and as soon as I heard about this au pair getting murdered I tried to ring her, just to make sure she was all right, but when there was no reply I started to worry. Was it Analise?' He looked from one man to the other with pleading eyes. 'Well, was it?'

Wesley looked at Ian Petrie. He was hovering, shifting from foot to foot, trying to conceal his impatience. He'd wanted to question Dudgeon but murder trumped art theft and Wesley's investigation had intruded. Petrie would have to wait his turn.

'I'm sorry to be the bearer of bad news, Mr Dudgeon, but I'm afraid Analise Sonquist was the victim. We won't release her name to the press until the relatives have been informed but . . . I'm sorry.'

'Oh God.' Dudgeon slumped down on a nearby stool and buried his head in his hands.

Wesley waited. There was no point in pushing the man until he was ready to talk. He felt Ian touch his arm.

'Can I have a word, Wesley?' he hissed in his ear.

He could see Ian wasn't pleased. He followed his old boss to the far end of the room and waited.

'We're supposed to be asking about Ra and the Egyptian antiquities.'

'He's a suspect in my murder enquiry. Besides, he'll be less inclined to think up a clever story with his girlfriend's death on his mind.'

Ian said nothing and as Wesley returned to Dudgeon's side, he suspected that he'd won the argument, not that it made him feel any better.

'Sorry about that, Geoff,' Wesley said gently, playing Dudgeon's new best friend. 'You were close to Analise?'

Suddenly the woman entered with a tray of brightly coloured mugs, the fruit of Dudgeon's labours. Wesley thanked her as she put the tray down and waited for her to go. But she stood there defiantly.

'I'm sorry, Ms . . .'

'Dudgeon. I'm Geoff's wife. Whatever you have to say you can say in front of me.' She folded her arms and stood her ground.

'Please, Bea, can you give us a few minutes?'

She touched Dudgeon's shoulder, a worried look on her face. 'You're upset. What have they said?'

Dudgeon turned to her. 'Please, Bea. I just need a minute. There's nothing to worry about. I'll tell you all about it later.'

Wesley suspected that his final statement was a lie. His deception with Analise would probably test Bea's toleration to the limit. For an artistic pair they seemed remarkably conventional, he thought.

'Bea doesn't know about Analise,' Dudgeon said as soon as his wife was out of earshot.

'I gathered that,' said Wesley. 'How did you meet Analise?'

'Through Suzie, the woman she worked for. She attended a watercolour course I gave last year and she consulted me about the set designs for a production the Castle Players put on last autumn. It was a comedy – something about Cleopatra. I think she regarded me as her tame artist: Suzie's inclined to expect people to dance to her tune and she's a hard woman to say no to. Anyway I sketched out some designs for her and dropped them off. Suzie was out but Analise was there and we got talking. She was lovely, Inspector. Gentle. She used to leave the baby with a friend and we'd spend time together. And we'd meet up most Tuesday nights.' He glanced at the door. 'Look, I really don't want Bea to find out.'

'We can be discreet. I need you to come down to Tradmouth police station to make a statement and answer a few questions. OK?'

'Yes, of course.'

Wesley looked at Ian. 'And DCI Petrie here is from the Met. Arts and Antiques Squad. He'd like to have a word with you as well.'

Ian cleared his throat. 'Do you mind if I have a quick look around your studio, Mr Dudgeon?'

Dudgeon didn't answer for a few seconds. Wesley thought he looked like a man who had tried to think up a good excuse but failed. 'Yes. Help yourself. But you won't find anything.' He sounded confident but Wesley detected a note of apprehension behind the words.

'Does the name Ra mean anything to you?' Ian asked.

Wesley saw Dudgeon look at him with wide, innocent eyes. 'He's an Egyptian god, isn't he?'

'What do you know about Anubis?' Wesley couldn't resist slipping the question in.

'Anubis? He's another Egyptian god. But I don't know what he's the god of.'

'He's the god who was said to have presided over the embalming of the dead, Mr Dudgeon.' He still had the figure found on Analise's body in his pocket. He pulled out the plastic bag and handed it to Dudgeon. 'Does this mean anything to you?'

Dudgeon studied it briefly then looked up. 'Not really. Although I'm sure I've seen something like it before.'

'Where?'

'Sorry. Can't remember.' He stared at the figure, his brow furrowed in a frown of concentration. 'Hang on. I had a stall at a craft fair in Tradmouth a few weeks ago. I'm sure there was a stall there selling things like this but I can't be sure. It was on the other side of the building and I really wasn't taking much notice.'

Wesley couldn't help wondering whether he was telling the truth.

Wesley had left Ian Petrie in Neston searching Dudgeon's studio. From the relaxed way the artist gave permission for the search, there was probably nothing there to find. And as he hadn't heard from Ian since they parted, Wesley assumed that he'd drawn a blank.

At three thirty Wesley and Gerry sat facing Geoff Dudgeon

in Interview Room 2. It was a windowless claustrophobic room and Wesley was sure he could still catch a faint whiff of cigarette smoke in there, impregnated into the walls in the days before the smoking ban. But it could have been his imagination.

Dudgeon had made no attempt to summon a solicitor as he said he had nothing to hide. Wesley wasn't sure whether to believe him.

'Let's go over what happened on Tuesday, the night Analise died,' Wesley said. He could see Dudgeon was getting tired. If he was going to change his story it would probably be now.

'We've been over this time and time again.'

'Analise left her friends in the pub early saying she was meeting someone. Her friend Kristina assumed she was meeting you.'

Geoff Dudgeon sat in silence for a few moments then suddenly he looked Wesley in the eye. 'OK. I meet her most Tuesdays and I'd arranged to meet her that night. I said I'd see her at Tradmouth Castle at nine thirty but I couldn't make it because Bea wasn't well. She was up all night being sick. Something she ate, I think. I couldn't leave her, could I?'

'You left her the next day to go to London.'

'That was something I couldn't put off. Besides, she was a lot better by then.'

'So what did you do when you realised you couldn't make your meeting with Analise?'

'I tried to call her but she didn't answer her phone and when I tried again the phone was switched off. You've got ways of tracing where mobile calls were made from, haven't you? You can check.'

'Even if we found out that the calls came from your phone

179

and it was in Neston, it wouldn't prove anything. You might have got someone else to make them for you . . . creating evidence to back up your story,' said Wesley reasonably.

'I was at home in Neston. Check Analise's phone. Please.'

'We haven't found her phone.' He paused. 'Or her clothes.'

Dudgeon's mouth gaped in horror. This was the first time Wesley had mentioned that Analise had been found naked and it had clearly come as a shock. If he'd been a betting man Wesley would have put money on Dudgeon's innocence.

'So she was assaulted . . . sexually? Is it the same man who attacked that girl in Neston?'

'I didn't say that, only that we haven't found her clothes,' said Wesley quietly. For the moment they were keeping the information about the mutilations to themselves. As far as the world was concerned, the victim had been strangled – once the truth came out the press, local and national, would think all their birthdays had come at once.

'We need to check your alibi, you can see that, can't you? We'll have to talk to Bea.'

'She has no idea about Analise and if she found out it could ruin my marriage. Please. Look, I had nothing to do with Analise's murder so either charge me or release me.'

'You were Analise's lover and your only alibi for the time of her death is a wife who might well be lying for you.'

'She wouldn't. She—'

'Or you might be lying for her. You can understand why we're reluctant to let you go,' said Wesley reasonably.

'Check with my phone company. I was nowhere near Tradmouth that night and neither was Bea.'

Geoffrey Dudgeon folded his arms and sat back in his seat.

\*

Wesley and Gerry walked down the corridor back to the incident room in silence. It was Ian Petrie's turn to talk to Dudgeon now but Wesley didn't feel inclined to eliminate the artist from his investigations just yet. The story of Bea's sickness might still turn out to be a work of fiction. But Dudgeon was confident that his phone records would show he was safely in Neston at the time of Analise's murder so it might be hard to prove that.

As soon as they entered the CID office, Trish told Gerry that Chief Superintendent Nutter wanted to see him urgently. Also Kristina had translated the letters found in Analise's room: they were from her sister and contained a few references to Geoff Dudgeon but nothing else that could be relevant to her death. Analise's sister had been contacted through the Hands Across the Sea agency in Morbay and she was on her way to Devon. Wesley himself slunk off to his desk to think in peace and check his phone for messages. He'd realised during his interview with Geoff Dudgeon that he'd forgotten to switch it over from silent that afternoon. He just hoped he'd not missed anything urgent.

As soon as he sat down Rachel called across to him. 'Neil Watson's been trying to get hold of you. He called three times – said you weren't answering your mobile. He says it's really important.'

Wesley thanked her and checked his mobile. Sure enough there were five missed calls, all of them from Neil's number.

He speed-dialled the number and Neil answered after the third ring. 'Neil. I gather you've been trying to get hold of me.'

'Where the hell have you been?' Neil said. He didn't sound pleased.

'Pursuing enquiries.'

181

'The murder near Tradmouth castle?'

'Yes.'

'I've got some information.'

'Something archaeological?' He had rarely heard Neil sound so excited about anything that wasn't connected with his work.

'This is something that's going to blow you away.'

Wesley sat forward. 'What is it?'

'That murder you're investigating is a copycat killing, mate. In 1903 this bloke called John Varley killed four women in exactly the same way that au pair was killed. Then he hanged himself in the woods by the castle. The deaths were identical. Look, I think you should get up here.' He hesitated. 'According to the local rag at the time, one of the policemen investigating said that Jack the Ripper had left Whitechapel to continue his evil work in Devon.'

For a few moments Wesley was lost for words. He had seen the body of Analise Sonquist and he couldn't have expressed it better himself.

# CHAPTER 17

*After my romantic encounter with Sir Frederick — for romantic it was, I can think of no other way to describe it — my senses seemed heightened and my heart light. I lived thus in a state of happiness such as I had never known. I had led a life of boundaries and restrictions but now I experienced a new freedom. The freedom of love.*

*Each sighting of my beloved made my heart pound within my breast and the decorum we were forced to maintain during our everyday dealings only served to make me more sensitive to each glance, each stolen touch of the hand. I was happy in those months — oh how I was happy. I gave the children their lessons with a new enthusiasm and I was gratified to see how they had inherited their father's passion for the great civilisation of ancient Egypt. We translated hieroglyphics together and learned about all the ruling dynasties of that great land. I knew this would please Sir Frederick and when the children showed off their knowledge to their father he seemed touched and very proud.*

*The sole cloud on my joyful horizon was his elder son. John now dined with us frequently and treated me with nothing short of contempt.*

*I enquired politely at dinner when he was returning to Bristol but my question was met with hostility. As a paid servant it was none of my business, he said. He would leave for Bristol when he was ready.*

*When I was alone with Sir Frederick I asked why he allowed his son to be so rude to his employees. But my beloved bowed his head and appeared to be burdened with some great sadness. John, he explained, had suffered a dreadful accident as a child. As the father who had encouraged him to climb the tree, he felt a heavy responsibility for what had happened so he lacked the will to chide the young man. In addition, ever since John had discovered the facts of his mother's death in an asylum a year after his own birth, he had blamed his father for the manner of her demise, saying that he had neglected her and treated her with a disdain that had caused her to sink into despair. My beloved seemed distressed and wracked with guilt at these ridiculous allegations, but I assured him that he had no cause to reproach himself.*

*And yet I could see that his dealings with John might blight our love. The young man knew how to control his father's feelings. And there seemed to be little I could do to improve the situation. Blood is so much stronger than the snares of the heart.*

# CHAPTER 18

Wesley hurried to Gerry's office to tell him about Neil's call. He knew he needed to drive up to Varley Castle and find out more. And possibly discover who else had been taking an unhealthy interest in Devon's very own Jack the Ripper.

When he relayed the news to Gerry, the DCI stood up, frowning as he considered the implications.

'Four of them?' he muttered. 'So are you going up to Varley Castle?'

Wesley nodded. 'I think I should. Neil told me that some-one has been accessing the information recently – an author who's staying at the castle. He's writing a biography of one of the owners.'

'In that case you need to speak to him. I'd like to come with you but I've got things to do.' He looked at his watch. 'You'll be pleased to hear that Guy Kitchener's coming in in ten minutes. I've already sent him details of the case so he should be up to speed.'

'So the Chief Super's got his budgets sorted out?'

Gerry gave a wicked smile. 'I used my charms to hurry things along, Wes. He couldn't resist. This is just an initial meeting with Kitchener to see what he's got to say for himself.' He gave a loud sigh. 'We're holding Dudgeon while we check his phone records and have a tactful word with his missus. I wonder how your old boss is getting on with him. I told Paul to sit in on the interview.'

'Let's hope he gets more out of him than we did.'

'You think he might be involved in Ian's Egyptian antiquities scam?'

'I don't know. He's a talented potter. It wouldn't be hard for him to conceal artefacts inside clay tourist copies – he could do something like that in his sleep.'

'So you think he could be Ra?'

Wesley shrugged. Since he'd heard from Neil, Ian's problems had begun to seem trivial compared with an aspiring Jack the Ripper stalking the streets.

'How's the kitten?'

Wesley looked up from the paperwork that seemed to have mysteriously appeared on his desk overnight. 'Scaling the curtains but apart from that . . .'

Guy Kitchener smiled. 'My mother tells me your kids love the sanctuary.'

'They haven't stopped talking about it.' He paused. All these pleasantries were all very well but there were serious things to think about. And Gerry was perched on the edge of his desk looking impatient.

'So what kind of man are we looking for?' Gerry asked.

Wesley saw that his eyes were on Guy as if he was waiting for him to say where the killer could be found. Name, address, colour of eyes. The lot.

'I take it this is a man?' Wesley said. 'Could a woman have done it?'

'Doubtful.' Guy took a deep breath. 'Our man is somebody who has little or no power over his everyday life. He might be married or living with a woman but if so, he's probably not the dominant partner.'

'We're looking for a henpecked husband then?' Gerry muttered.

'It is a possibility. Although it could just as easily be a man who's stuck in a job where he feels frustrated and belittled. As he seems to be displaying some knowledge about the civilisation of ancient Egypt he might be an educated man – or self-educated – so maybe he thinks that he's stuck in a job beneath his capabilities. In his mind the killings give him power and a twisted kind of status.'

'What about his character? Age, social background?'

Guy thought for a few moments. 'He's likely to be a loner; socially inept. And the ritual of disembowelling doesn't suggest youthful impulse. He's probably in his thirties or forties. And it's possible that he stalks his victims, gets to know their habits.'

'But if the same man was responsible for the attack on Clare Mayers, it doesn't seem that he's made any contact with them,' said Wesley.

'I take your point, Wesley, but it might be someone Clare's spoken to at one time even though she might not remember.'

Rachel Tracey was sitting a few feet away, listening intently. She raised her hand. 'What's his attitude to women?'

Guy gave her a smile. 'Good question. I'd say from the

way the bodies are mutilated that he may be a little afraid of them.'

Gerry asked the next question. 'We've told you about Alan Jakes – do you think he's our best bet?'

Guy's answer was cautious. 'From what you tell me he has a predatory attitude towards women. Perhaps that's to conceal his fear or hatred of them. I'll be able to tell you more when you've brought him in and I can observe him being interviewed.' He picked up his briefcase. 'You'll keep me up to date with any developments, won't you? We've got to find this man before he kills again.'

'You think he will?' Wesley asked quietly.

Guy looked at him. 'I think that's certain. He's got a taste for it now. And the way he mutilated Analise's body . . . They say the first time's the worst for a killer. He'll find it easier next time.'

As Wesley set out to meet Neil he toyed with the idea of calling Pam. But he reasoned that she knew all about Analise's murder so she wouldn't be expecting him in till late anyway.

He knew he was in for an hour's drive and, as he steered the car towards Dartmoor, Guy Kitchener's words still buzzed around his brain. Analise Sonquist's murderer would kill again – if they didn't find him soon and stop him.

In his headlights he could see the rain pouring down in fine horizontal sheets and it seemed like an age before he saw the sign directing him to Varley Castle. He turned right and found himself on a dark, single-track lane with hedges towering on either side like prison walls. Unlike Rachel who had learned to drive at seventeen on her family's farm and drove down the Devon lanes with the confidence of a native, Wesley proceeded cautiously in the rapidly fading light and after a mile he saw a gateway flanked by a pair of monoliths worthy of a prehistoric stone circle. A sign by the entrance told him he had reached his destination. Varley Castle.

He steered down a winding tree-lined driveway until the bulk of the castle came into view, massive against the dusk sky.

Neil's yellow Mini was parked near the imposing front entrance and when Wesley climbed out of the car he stood there for a few seconds gazing up at the huge edifice – one man's medieval fantasy created out of cash and granite. He walked slowly to the great oak front door, raised the huge lion-head knocker and let it fall with a crash that gave him a frisson of satisfaction.

When the door creaked open Wesley was rather surprised to see Neil himself standing there.

'I expected the butler,' he said as he stepped inside and looked around.

'Sorry to disappoint you.' He began to move away. 'Come into the library. I've got all the stuff in there.'

'Who else knows about this?'

Neil looked round as though he didn't want to be over-heard. 'Only me and Andrew. I haven't mentioned it to Caroline or Robert Delaware yet. I thought I'd let you do that.' He leaned forward and lowered his voice. 'Like I said over the phone, the woman at the library told me that Delaware's already been there after the same information.'

Neil led the way to the library, a large, impressive room with a roaring fire, much cosier than Wesley expected. Neil picked up a cardboard file which lay on a table at the side of the room and handed it to Wesley.

'I had copies made of the newspaper reports. What do you think?'

Wesley read while Neil waited, watching for a reaction. Eventually he put the papers back in their file.

'You reckon it's the same as . . .?'

Wesley took a deep breath. 'They sound very similar. 1903 – I should be able to get hold of the case files from the police archives,' he said confidently, hoping they hadn't been lost or destroyed in the intervening years. 'I need to talk to Robert Delaware. Where is he?'

'Down in the kitchens with Caroline. He sniffs around her like a dog after a bitch in heat. Makes you want to vomit.'

Wesley looked around. 'I can see how owning a place like this might lend a woman certain charms.'

'It's not that,' Neil said quickly. 'I just don't trust him. Come on, I'll show you Sir Frederick Varley's museum of Egyptian antiquities. There's some amazing stuff in there.'

'I thought you weren't particularly interested in Ancient Egypt?'

Neil shrugged. 'It's growing on me. Come and say hello to Andrew anyway. He's up there cataloguing stuff. Then I'll take you down to the kitchens and introduce you to Caroline and Delaware.'

Before Wesley could say that he'd rather get the interview with Delaware over with, Neil had begun to stride ahead up the grand staircase. Wesley told himself that his man was unlikely to make his escape and resigned himself to following Neil through grand double doors into a large room which had the look of a museum – the old-fashioned kind with dusty exhibits and indecipherable labels. Andrew Beredace was sitting at a table by the window, studying a small artefact under an angle-poise lamp. He looked up and smiled when they entered.

'So this is Sir Frederick Varley's collection?' said Wesley as he looked around.

Andrew stood up. 'I'll give you the guided tour.'

But Wesley felt a little guilty as he dutifully admired the artefacts. Maybe he should have been firmer with Neil and made straight for the kitchens. Satisfying though it was to be shown the collection by an expert, he knew that Analise Sonquist hadn't been murdered by a desiccated mummy. He needed to interview the living, sooner rather than later.

He had just thanked Andrew for his time when the expert spoke. 'Neil's shown me those cuttings. John Varley had been brought up with all this lot.' He made a sweeping gesture with his hand. 'He'd been immersed in ancient Egyptian culture so he probably thought that it was right to prepare the dead women for the afterlife. He would have thought he was doing them a favour. I don't expect he saw himself as a second Jack the Ripper.'

Wesley was taken aback at first but then Andrew's words began to make some kind of sense. Maybe the killer back in 1903 had seen the mutilations as an act of kindness rather than hatred.

He let Neil show him down to the kitchens, reasoning that the arrival of an unaccompanied stranger might put Caroline Varley and Robert Delaware on their guard. He found the pair standing close to each other next to the wooden sink, deep in conversation. They both looked up when Neil and Wesley entered the room.

'Caroline. I'd like you to meet a friend of mine,' said Neil, ignoring Delaware. 'This is Wesley Peterson. We were at Exeter University together.'

Caroline immediately held out her hand. 'Pleased to meet you, Mr Peterson . . . or is it Doctor? All you archaeologists seem to be Doctor these days.'

'It's just Mr.' He took her hand and shook it firmly. 'And I'm not an archaeologist.' He produced his warrant card and as he presented it to Caroline he saw a flicker of shock cross her face. But she handed the card back to him calmly and smiled. 'A police inspector. I do hope you're not here on business?'

'I'm afraid I am.' He'd been watching Robert Delaware's face and noted that it remained expressionless. 'I'd like to ask you and Mr Delaware some questions if I may.'

'What about?' She sounded puzzled.

'It concerns the murder of a young woman in Tradmouth on Tuesday night.'

'I don't see how I can help you. I haven't been to Tradmouth for a year or more.'

Wesley turned to Delaware. 'What about you, Mr Delaware? Where were you on Tuesday night?'

'I . . . I was here, wasn't I, Caro?' Wesley was certain he saw a flash of anxiety in his eyes.

But Caroline wasn't prepared to lie for him. Their relationship obviously hadn't reached the stage where she would even consider it. 'No. You went to Morbay on Tuesday evening. You said you had to see somebody. Remember?'

'What time was this?'

It was Caroline who answered. 'You went out around seven and it was almost midnight when you got back. I made us both cocoa.'

Delaware smiled. Wesley had seen many similar smiles on the faces of suspects over the years – heartiness tinged with terror. 'Of course.'

'You'll be able to give us the name of the person you saw, of course,' Wesley said.

'Of course. It was a man who had some letters from Sir Frederick Varley. I'm writing Sir Frederick's biography.'

'So I've heard.' Wesley looked the man in the eye. 'There is another matter we'd like to ask you about. I believe you've been researching into four murders that happened here in 1903. They were committed by Sir Frederick's son, John Varley.'

This time Delaware couldn't hide his shock. 'I'm writing Sir Frederick's biography. His son's suicide had a massive effect on his life, as you can imagine. I had to discover why he killed himself so I needed the details of the murders he was allegedly responsible for.'

It all sounded very reasonable but somehow it didn't allay Wesley's suspicions. He paused before speaking again, his eyes on Delaware's face. 'We think there might be a connection between the 1903 murders and the recent murder in Tradmouth.'

Delaware's mouth fell open. 'That's impossible,' he said, shooting a look in Caroline's direction. 'They were Jack the Ripper-style killings. Do you mean to say that . . .?'

'There are certain similarities. And we suspect there's an Egyptian connection.' He saw Caroline's hand go up to her mouth in horror. 'So you can see why we're talking to anybody who knows details of those murders. By the way, where were you on Sunday night?'

Delaware glanced at Caroline. 'I went back to my flat in Tradmouth for the weekend because I had various things to catch up on. I came back here first thing on Monday.'

'Any witnesses?'

'Afraid not. I didn't think I'd need any.'

Wesley opened the file he was carrying and spread the

copies of the old newspaper cuttings out on the worktop. Delaware glanced at them then looked away but Caroline picked them up and examined them. Unless she was a good actress, it was clear that she had never seen them before.

'You have seen these cuttings before, Mr Delaware?'

'I've told you that already. I found them in the local library. But anybody can get hold of that information. It's in the public domain.'

'I'll need the name of the person you saw in Morbay on Tuesday night. And I'd like you to come down to Tradmouth police station tomorrow to make a statement.' He gave the man an expectant smile then he turned his head away and watched Caroline as she devoured every word of the newspaper cuttings.

Delaware looked irritated. 'Is that really necessary?'

'Just ask for me at the Reception desk when you arrive.' He handed Delaware his notebook and a pen. 'Now if you could write down the name and address of the person you were with on Tuesday . . .' Delaware hesitated for a second then he wrote down a name – B Cooper – and a Morbay address.

'Thank you, sir,' said Wesley as he put the notebook back in his pocket. 'See you tomorrow then.' He gathered up the cuttings and returned them to the file. Gerry would be anxious to see them. Then he said goodbye to Caroline but she looked rather stunned and made no attempt to move.

'You reckon it's him . . . Delaware? Is he the Tradmouth Ripper?' Neil said as they walked to the front door.

Wesley gave a snort of derision. 'The Tradmouth Ripper?'

'Well, once this gets out, the tabloids will want to call him something catchy. You know what they're like.'

Wesley nodded. He knew what the press were like all

right. 'I'd better get back. I think Caroline Varley's had a bit of a shock. Keep an eye on her, won't you?' he said. 'And thanks. This could be the breakthrough we need. I'll be in touch.'

'There were four of them,' Neil said to his friend's disappearing back. 'If he's copying John Varley he won't have finished yet.'

Wesley said nothing as he got into his car. The last thing he wanted to think about was the possibility of more deaths.

Geoff Dudgeon stepped out of the police station after being interviewed by Ian Petrie and Paul Johnson, a free man for the time being. As Wesley's mind was filled with the dark deeds of John Varley he almost walked past the artist in Reception without realising it, but Dudgeon mumbled a resentful greeting and brought Wesley's thoughts back to the present day.

'Mr Dudgeon. Interview over?'

Dudgeon stopped and turned to face him. He looked mildly indignant; an innocent man, wrongly accused. 'I hope that's the end of it. They've checked with the phone company and my wife and I'm in the clear.'

'I'm pleased to hear it. But you were involved with the victim so we might need to speak to you again. I'm sorry but that's the way it is,' he added, as though he meant it.

Dudgeon grunted something Wesley couldn't quite make out and hurried away, glad to get out of the place.

When Wesley reached the incident room he found Ian Petrie deep in conversation with Paul. Ian was sitting at Wesley's own desk, making himself at home. When he saw Wesley he stood up.

'I've just seen Geoff Dudgeon,' Wesley said to Paul as he

195

took off his coat. 'He says his story about the calls to Analise's mobile has been checked out.'

'His phone company confirms that he tried to call her number several times between nine and eleven thirty on the night she died from a location in the centre of Neston,' said Paul. 'Looks like he was telling the truth.'

'Or he knew that we could trace mobile signals and got somebody else to make the calls for him to give himself an elaborate alibi . . . his wife maybe. But it's a case of proving it,' said Wesley, perching on the edge of his desk.

'You're right, Wesley. We only have her word for it that he was at home mopping her fevered brow and wives have been known to cover up for their husbands,' Ian said. 'He could still have been up to something . . . not necessarily murder, but something.'

'Like what?'

'He denies all knowledge of anyone called Ra but he could be lying. Of all the artists we've tracked down in the Neston area, he's the only one who makes the sort of pottery that could be used to hide antiquities.'

Wesley said nothing. Paul went on to recount how Dudgeon had been more than willing to talk about his relationship with Analise Sonquist once his formidable wife was no longer there to overhear. When asked about the Egyptian figures he said he'd seen on sale at some craft fair in Tradmouth, his answers had been annoyingly vague. But that was something they could check out.

'So he didn't say anything likely to move your enquiry forward, Ian?' Wesley asked.

Ian shook his head. 'When I asked him about Egyptian antiquities he said South Devon was his horizon and Egypt didn't figure in his life.'

'Did you believe him?'

'I don't know. It might be worth checking whether he owns or rents other premises around here – a workshop for the antiquity scam.'

'He said he'd been to London. What was he doing there?'

'He claims he was visiting an art dealer – someone who might sell his work for a commission. I've asked Paul here to check it out.' Ian smiled and put a hand on Paul's shoulder. 'This lad'll go far. I'd watch your back if I were you.'

Wesley could see Gerry Heffernan in his office, talking animatedly on the phone. He slid off the desk. 'Sorry, Ian. There's something important I've got to tell the boss.'

He hurried to Gerry's office and pushed the door open. He had the cardboard file containing copies of Neil's newspaper cuttings tucked underneath his arm and when Gerry hung up he placed it carefully on top of the files cluttering the desk.

'I've got all the details. The eldest son of Varley Castle's owner killed four women in 1903, strangled and mutilated them and left them dotted around the countryside. He hanged himself and the killings stopped.'

'Saved the hangman a job then.'

'Looks like it.'

Gerry reached out and took the papers from Wesley's folder and began to read. When he'd finished he looked up. 'They're identical.'

'The library told Neil that the only other person who's been taking an interest in this particular case is Frederick Varley's biographer, Robert Delaware. I met him at the castle.'

'What's he like?'

'His eyes were too close together,' said Wesley with a grin. 'And I definitely think he was hiding something.'

'When did he visit the library?'

'Shortly before the attack on Clare Mayers.'

'First abortive attempt?'

'Possibly. He claims he was at his flat in Tradmouth on Sunday night. No witnesses.'

'What about Analise's murder?'

'He says he was in Morbay on Tuesday evening visiting a fellow history enthusiast – someone who owns some papers concerning Sir Frederick Varley. I've told him to report here for questioning tomorrow but I'll get his alibi for Tuesday checked out first. Then we'll have to ask the newspaper offices and other nearby libraries if anybody else has been taking an interest in those articles.'

Gerry buried his face in his hands. He looked tired. Wesley noticed that his shirt was crumpled. When Wesley had first arrived in Tradmouth the DCI had always looked as though he'd slept in his clothes. Then the helpless widower had met Joyce Barnes and recently, under her influence, he had gradually become positively dapper. However, a fortnight without Joyce had made him revert to his former slovenly ways.

'I'm worried,' Wesley said.

Gerry looked up. 'Worried?'

'I think we should put out a warning – tell women to be on their guard.'

Gerry looked at his watch. 'It's too late for tonight's news but we'll think about a warning tomorrow. And we need to tell Guy Kitchener about the Varley murders and the similarities.'

'Yes, I'll see to it.'

'I just hope he comes up with some results soon.'

'Let's wait and see, eh?'

Wesley returned to his paperwork, suspecting that it was going to be a long evening.

Pam Peterson let herself into the house, flicked on the hall light and swore softly under her breath. Della was supposed to have picked the children up from school and brought them home for their dinner. But Della had never been one of those reliable sorts of mother that her friends seemed to have. Wesley's mother was that type but unfortunately she was miles away in London.

When Della started volunteering at the animal sanctuary, Pam had harboured a fleeting hope that her new interest would make her act her age at last and become the perfect grandmother. Up till now she had always been in the habit of appearing in the children's lives spasmodically, distributing unsuitable presents and causing mayhem. Michael and Amelia seemed to accept her as a force of nature, as children often do, not asking questions and not judging her actions or intentions. But Pam herself wasn't inclined to be that tolerant.

Her first thought as she entered the living room and switched on the light was that the place looked a mess. It was clear Della had been back. She'd created chaos and then she had gone on her merry way, taking the children with her, getting them over-excited and keeping them from their homework. Pam had been teaching all day and, with this new murder investigation, Wesley wouldn't be back till late. It was Della's thoughtlessness that made her angry.

She was about to return to the car to fetch the plastic box containing all her marking and paperwork when she spotted a scrap of folded paper with her name printed boldly in felt tip sitting on the coffee table on top of a pile of books. She picked it up and read it.

'Gone to sanctuary. Meet us there at six. Rose Croft, Hugford. Love and kisses, Della.'

Suddenly she heard a plaintive mewing from the kitchen. The Kitten. She gave a weary sigh and opened the door, sweeping the little creature up in her hand as it tried to make its escape, swearing that next time she'd make the children feed it and clear out its litter tray . . . or better still, she'd make Della do it. However, it was impossible to resist the kitten's charms for long and she found herself giving the little creature a cuddle before closing the kitchen door gently behind her.

After she'd brought her box of school work in from the car and dumped it on the dining room table she locked up the house and drove towards Hugford through a thin veil of drizzle. The sanctuary was only a couple of miles away along the main road to Neston then left down the country lane where Clare Mayers had met her attacker, and as there were only a handful of houses in Hugford, Rose Croft was easy to find. She parked on the wide verge opposite a large gate bearing the words 'Rose Croft Animal Sanctuary. Please ring bell' and as she crossed the road she could hear her children's excited voices and the barking of what sounded like a pack of dogs.

She pressed the bell and waited.

Wesley looked at his watch. Nine o'clock. He stared at the telephone and willed it to ring.

Paperwork was piling up on his desk but he wasn't in the mood to face it. He took his mobile from his pocket and turned it over and over in his fingers. He had just called home but there'd been no reply so now he selected Pam's mobile number and he was rather relieved when she answered after the third ring.

'Hi,' he said when he heard her voice. 'Where are you?'

'I could ask you the same question.'

He looked round. The incident room was still full, everybody bent over desks and computers or holding hushed phone conversations. Checking alibis, checking sightings. Waiting for the snippet of information that might turn everything around. 'Having a wonderful time at Uncle Gerry's holiday camp.'

'Caught your murderer yet?'

'We're working on it. I thought you'd be home?'

'Della spirited the kids off to the animal sanctuary. I'm there now trying to prise them away.' She lowered her voice as though she didn't want to be overheard. 'Mary's quite a character. She set up the sanctuary ten years ago and she runs it as a charity. I never knew the place existed.'

'Is that Guy Kitchener's mother?'

'That's right.'

'I've just been on the phone to Guy. He's helping with this case. Is the sanctuary just for cats and dogs?' Somehow he didn't feel like discussing work just at that moment.

'Cats, dogs, donkeys, hedgehogs – anything you can name. The kids are having the time of their lives. I don't know how I'm going to get them out of here. Look, I'd better go.'

He was about to end the call when he heard Pam's voice again. 'Hang on, I knew there was something I had to tell you. You know Neil's working up at Varley Castle? Well, there's a lovely painting of the castle above Mary's fireplace – I asked her about it and she says she's distantly related to the family.'

'The Varleys?'

'I presume so. She said she was only a third cousin or something and she's never had any contact with them. I told her that Neil's up there at the moment. Coincidence, isn't it?'

'Yes.' He hesitated for a moment. 'I'd like to see this sanctuary one of these days.'

'Why? You're not planning to interrogate Mary are you?'

She could always see right through him, he thought as the phone on his desk started to ring. 'I'll see you later then.'

'How much later?'

'Sorry, love. Not sure.'

He said goodbye, put down his mobile and picked up the receiver.

The news was good. One of Alan Jakes's mates had let slip that he was at his sister's address in Dukesbridge. The house was being watched and it was only a matter of time before he was brought in for questioning.

It was a question of sitting tight and waiting.

# CHAPTER 19

*One summer evening I arranged to meet Frederick in the woods by the ruins of the old manor house. We thought it wise to conduct our meetings in private away from the prying eyes of the servants who, I am sure, would have loved nothing better than to gossip about their master and the governess who thought she was so far above them but was really no better than she ought to be. I sensed that they had little liking for me for I was neither one of their number or a lady who would warrant the respect due to her class.*

*I was on my way to the ruins, my heart filled with eager anticipation, when I encountered John. He was standing in my path, barring the way, his visage set in a contemptuous snarl and his eyes so full of hatred that I was suddenly afraid. He grabbed my wrist, put his face close to mine so that I could smell the strong liquor on his warm breath. He told me to stay away from his father. Then he held me close and when I felt him hard against me I knew that he was aroused to lust. He caught hold of me and began to drag me through the trees, muttering names that I recall now with a blush. I was a whore, a Jezebel, a harlot, and I used my* body to entrap unwary men. He would teach me, he said, that harlots did not prosper. When we came to a clearing he threw me upon the damp earth and tore at my clothing like a wild beast. I screamed and pushed away his pawing, exploring hands and when he stopped my cries with a violent, painful kiss I kicked and wriggled beneath his weight. I would not be violated by this wretch without a fight and yet I feared his strength would overwhelm me.

When I heard Frederick's voice, shocked and angry, I gave thanks to the great goddess Isis that my beloved had come to my aid. Brought to his senses by his father's arrival, John released me from his grasp, struggled to his feet and sprang away in an attempt to put some distance between us.

'She wanted me,' he shouted to his father, pointing his finger at me accusingly. 'She said she wanted a man who had the energy of youth. She told me she's had her fill of old men.'

I knelt upon the damp earth and put my hand out to Frederick but he stood as though frozen, staring down at me with cold distaste in his eyes. And I felt so alone.

# CHAPTER 20

When Wesley arrived in the incident room next morning Gerry beckoned him into his office before he had a chance to take off his coat. There was an eager expression on the DCI's plump face.

'Alan Jakes has been picked up. He arrived back at his sister's shortly after midnight and he's being brought over from Dukesbridge this morning.' His mouth turned upwards in a wicked grin. 'I've arranged for warrants to search his flat and his sister's house. He won't be bright enough to cover his tracks so if he does turn out to be our man, we're bound to find some evidence.' His expression suddenly changed, as though somebody had just told him some bad news. 'I had a call earlier to say that Analise's sister's arrived at Heathrow and she's on her way here. We'll leave her to Rach, eh? She's good at that sort of thing.'

Wesley nodded. Rachel was a natural with grieving relatives and yet he knew that she hated that aspect of the job:

against her better judgement, she always ended up getting emotionally involved although nobody would have guessed it from her detached manner. But Wesley knew. And he liked her for it.

'And Joyce rang last night. She'll be back in a few days.'

'You'll be glad to see her.'

'Aye. Our Sam's had a clean round and put the washer on but it's not the same. And since our Rosie's accepted the situation I don't feel I've got to creep around any more like a guilty teenager.' He paused. 'I'm really missing Joyce. I never thought I would but . . .'

Wesley suppressed a smile. 'Hardly surprising. I take it we'll interview Jakes as soon as he arrives?' He had heard so much about Alan Jakes that he was curious to see the man for himself.

'Of course.'

'Are we calling Guy in?'

'I rang him but he's teaching all morning. I said I'd let him know how it went and he'll be able to listen to the tapes,' Gerry said before disappearing into his office to wrestle with his paperwork.

There was a lot to do so Wesley returned to his desk, remembering that Robert Delaware was due to turn up later to give a statement. Delaware was another person he wanted to see. But there was something he needed to check first.

He looked around the room and saw DC Nick Tarnaby sitting at his desk, gazing out of the window at the river below with a faraway look in his eyes, as though he was seeing some sun-drenched tropical island in place of the dank February scene.

'Nick, can you do me a favour?' Tarnaby sat to attention,

suddenly defensive. 'Can you check out this name and address please? I've got somebody coming in to make a statement later and I need to be sure of my facts.' Somehow he'd sensed Delaware had been lying about the Morbay address where he was supposed to have met a Mr B Cooper on the night of Analise's death.

'I've got a lot to do, sir,' Tarnaby muttered sullenly. 'All the house to house reports from the castle area and—'

'This shouldn't take long. And it is important.' He smiled expectantly. 'If you can let me know as soon as possible. Thanks.'

He sat down at his desk before Tarnaby could raise any more objections and began to make a list on a sheet of scrap paper. There was Delaware to eliminate from their enquiries; Delaware who knew all about the terrible murders John Varley had committed. Then there was Geoff Dudgeon who'd been the victim's lover and whose alibi was shaky to say the least. Clive Crest too had a rather dubious story for the relevant time and he'd been Analise's employer as well as the lover of Clare Mayers's school friend Vicky. Finally there was Alan Jakes. By all accounts he was a nasty bit of work and he might well have attacked Clare Mayers. Also his family were local so it was possible that he'd heard the story of John Varley's crimes at some time and decided to emulate them.

A minute or so elapsed before Gerry emerged from his office like a bear coming out of hibernation. He had a hungry look in his eyes. Someone was about to be eaten alive.

'They've got Jakes in Interview Room One downstairs, Wes. Coming down?'

Wesley stood up.

'And I've sent a couple of DCs to his place and Dukesbridge are giving his sister's house a going over. I've told them to tear it apart – leave no mattress or cushion unturned. I don't like men who frighten little girls.' From the look on the DCI's face Wesley guessed he was going to enjoy going a few rounds with Alan Jakes. He almost felt sorry for the man.

They walked down to the interview room in silence and when they got there they found Alan Jakes seated at the table, watched by the well-built uniformed constable who was standing guard by the door. Jakes was fidgeting with an empty polystyrene cup, plucking pieces off it which landed like flakes of snow on the table. He looked up as the two detectives entered and gave them a welcoming scowl.

'How long are you going to keep me here?' he said with a hint of self-righteousness. 'This is against my human rights, this is.'

Wesley sat down opposite him, switched on the tape machine and gave the suspect a businesslike smile. Alan Jakes was a good-looking man. His hair was dark, almost black, and he had bright blue eyes and a mouth that turned up slightly at the corners, hinting at charm. But appearances are often deceptive.

'We'd like to ask you about your relationship with Karen Mayers and her daughter Clare.' He leaned forward expectantly, catching a faint whiff of Jakes's surprisingly subtle aftershave, a little stale perhaps but then he'd been held overnight in the cells at Dukesbridge.

'OK. I was seeing Karen then I realised that Clare fancied me so we went to bed. It wasn't illegal. She was over sixteen.'

'Clare was attacked last Sunday night. She'd been to a quiz night at the Anglers' Arms and she walked home alone. You were at the Anglers' Arms that night. You saw Clare there.'

'No comment.'

Gerry had been sitting beside Wesley in silence watching Alan Jakes's face carefully. But now he spoke. 'Clare said she didn't want to see you again, didn't she? That must have made you angry. She told us that you threatened her. She was just a silly little girl and you're the big man who calls the shots. You wanted to teach her a lesson, didn't you?'

Jakes shook his head. 'I never touched her. Is she saying I did?'

Gerry smiled sweetly. 'No comment. We've got a warrant to search your place. Someone's gone over there now.'

'They'll be wasting their time.'

'Where were you on Tuesday evening?'

'Tuesday? I've been staying over in Dukesbridge at my sister's. She's not been well.'

'That's very thoughtful of you,' said Gerry. 'Isn't he thoughtful, Inspector Peterson? Restores your faith in human nature. But you came over this way on Wednesday night, didn't you? You tried to break into Clare Mayers's house.'

Jakes pondered the question for a few moments. Wesley could almost hear cogs whirring in his head. 'I'd heard she was accusing me. I wanted to put her right.'

'You scared the life out of her. She dialled 999.'

'She's always been a drama queen. I didn't do nothing.'

'OK,' said Wesley. 'Let's move on. On Sunday night what did you do when you left the Anglers' Arms?'

'Went home.'

'Then the next day you went to your sister's?'

'That's right.'

'And you didn't turn up at work.'

'I needed a break.'

Gerry began to sort through a file he'd brought with him,

witness statements from the people they'd traced who'd been in the Anglers' Arms on the night Clare Mayers was attacked. He took out a sheet, made a great show of reading it, then passed it to Wesley.

'One of the barmen gave us a statement. He told us something very interesting. When he left for home at a quarter to midnight there was a car parked next to his. An old Ford van. Dark-coloured with stickers in the window. He noticed it particularly because his brother's just bought a similar vehicle to do up. Everyone apart from the staff had gone home by then and he wondered who it belonged to – it wasn't anyone he worked with 'cause he knew all their vehicles. According to our records you own a dark-blue Ford van don't you, Mr Jakes? You were driving it when you were picked up in Dukesbridge. What were you doing hanging round after the pub closed?'

'I wasn't. I knew I was over the limit so I got a lift home.'

'Very law-abiding of you, Mr Jakes. Who gave you a lift?'

'Can't remember.'

'We've got the names of most of the people who were in the pub that night so we can ask around. Are you telling us the truth or did you follow Clare?'

Wesley watched Jakes and waited.

After what must have been a full minute of stunned silence Jakes spoke. 'OK, I followed her. But I never touched her. Honest, I never laid a finger on her. I just wanted to scare her . . . to teach her a lesson.'

Wesley glanced at Gerry. 'Tell us what happened.'

'I saw Clare in the pub and when I left she was having a row outside with one of her mates. She wanted her to let her into her taxi but the mate wasn't having any of it. She said she was going the other way. I hung back and waited until

210

the taxi had driven away and Clare started to walk down the lane to Hugford. I don't know why but I started to follow her . . . keeping my distance like. I thought when I got halfway down the lane I'd come up behind her and give her the fright of her life . . . show her she couldn't mess with me. I wouldn't have hurt her . . .' His voice had become a self-righteous whine and Wesley was rather surprised that he felt a sudden urge to punch the man.

'So what happened?' he asked.

'I got halfway down the lane then I saw her.'

'It must have been dark.'

'There was a full moon. I could see quite well. She was with somebody.'

'Who?'

'Dunno. I rounded this bend and there she was. I thought she was . . . well, sort of kissing so I shot back. I stood in a farm gate, pushed up by the hedge so she couldn't see me. Then I took a peep and I couldn't believe what I saw. She was in a clinch with this . . . Well, I could only make out a vague shape but it looked like he had an animal's head but that sounds daft, doesn't it? I hadn't had that much to drink and I did a double take like. Then this van came along.'

'The driver didn't see you.'

'He wouldn't have. As soon as I saw the headlights coming I went through the gate and hid behind the hedge. I was going to wait till the van had gone but it stopped. I heard the brakes screech so I thought I'd better make myself scarce and I ran across the field back to the main road and picked up the van at the pub. Covered in bloody mud and cow shit I was. Then I heard that your lot were looking for the bloke who attacked her so I went to my sister's. Thought it'd be wise to lay low for a bit.'

211

'You should have come forward.'

'And I'd have been first on your list if you'd known I'd been there on the scene. Who'd believe that I saw a bloke with an animal's head? If I hadn't seen it with my own eyes I wouldn't have believed it myself.'

'Vanishing like you did is hardly the act of an innocent man,' Wesley pointed out reasonably.

Jakes's lips formed a snarl and for a moment Wesley feared he was about to spit in his face but instead he turned his head away.

'So what did this animal-headed bloke with Clare look like?'

Jakes shifted in his chair and shrugged his shoulders. 'He was a lot taller than her but I only caught a glimpse for a second before the van came along.'

'And you never thought of going to help her?'

'Well, I didn't know, did I? It could have been some sex game for all I knew.' He gave a knowing leer. 'I didn't want to go barging in, did I? I didn't want to get involved.'

'We know you were in Hugford on Wednesday but where were you on Tuesday night?'

'With my sister in Dukesbridge. She'll tell you.'

'Do you know a girl called Analise Sonquist? She was an au pair for a family called Crest in Tradmouth.'

For the first time Jakes looked nervous. 'Is that the girl they found up by the castle? Look, I had nothing to do with that, I swear.'

For a few moments nobody said anything. Wesley knew that often suspects had a compelling urge to fill a silence with anything – maybe even a confession. But when the ringing of his phone broke the tension he jumped, announced his temporary departure for the benefit of the tape recorder

212

whirring at the end of the table, and hurried from the room. After half a minute he returned and resumed his seat.

'They've finished searching your place. Interested in Ancient Egypt are you?'

Jakes looked uneasy. 'Not particularly. Why?'

'They found a model of King Tutankhamen's death mask.'

'So? I saw it at a car boot sale. I liked it so I bought it. Look, you can't prove anything. You've got nothing on me. Charge me or let me go.'

Gerry grunted. Wesley knew he never liked it when a suspect got the better of him. But in this case Jakes was right: without other evidence they'd find it difficult to get the CPS to prosecute on the strength of a mass-produced Egyptian death mask.

'You used to work in a butcher's, I believe?'

'That was years ago when I'd just left school.'

'You've cut up animal carcasses?'

Jakes shook his head. 'Nah. I just carried them out of the van . . . and I swept up and served in a shop, that sort of thing.'

Wesley had brought the Anubis figure with him, hidden in his pocket protected by a plastic evidence bag. He took it out and put it on the table.

'Do you recognise this figure? For the benefit of the tape I'm showing the suspect a model of Anubis.'

'Ann who?' Jakes picked it up, made a cursory examination then threw it down on the table again. 'Never seen it before in my life.'

'So it's nothing like the animal head on Clare's attacker?' He knew it was a leading question but it was worth asking.

'Dunno.' He picked it up again and examined it more closely. 'Could be now you come to mention it. What is it?'

213

'The Egyptian god connected with death and embalming.'

Jakes looked puzzled. 'You what?'

Before Wesley could reply Gerry gave him a slight nod and stood up.

'Well, thank you, Mr Jakes. We'll be in touch.'

'You mean I can go?'

'We've no reason to detain you for the moment. But don't leave the area, will you? We might need to speak to you again.'

'Do you think he's telling the truth?' Wesley asked as they walked back to the incident room.

'I'm pretty sure he'd never seen Anubis before.'

'He didn't recognise it as the mask Clare's attacker was wearing.'

'He only caught a glimpse ... and in spite of the full moon that lane must have been pretty dark. And I don't really think Analise's murder is his style. Do you? And can you see him researching into the John Varley murders? 'Cause I can't.'

Wesley didn't answer. He was keeping an open mind.

As soon as Wesley returned to the incident room, Paul Johnson broke the news that Geoff Dudgeon had indeed visited a London gallery the day after Analise was murdered. It didn't provide him with an alibi, of course, but it meant that he hadn't deliberately been avoiding the police. When Nick Tarnaby called him over to his desk, Wesley put Dudgeon to the back of his mind.

Nick had checked out the name and address of Robert Delaware's alibi with uncharacteristic efficiency and he presented Wesley with a piece of paper. Wesley thanked him – hoping that with a bit of encouragement the taciturn and slothful Tarnaby might one day become a decent detective – and ambled back to his desk.

As Wesley slumped back in his chair something caught his eye. A missing persons report was sitting on the right-hand side of his desk next to his phone. This was normally the province of Uniform and he wondered who had left it there.

Curious, he picked it up and read that a woman called Isobel Grant had gone into Tradmouth to meet someone for a drink the previous evening. She'd told her mother that she'd be home by ten whatever happened because she had to be up early for work the next day. She hadn't arrived home and she hadn't turned up at work.

He looked up and saw that Trish Walton was watching him. He waved the report in her direction. 'Do you know something about this, Trish?'

She stood up and walked over to his desk. 'Yes. I know Uniform usually deal with that sort of thing but . . .'

'This Isobel Grant is twenty-eight. Surely her mother's jumped the gun a bit reporting her missing? Isobel probably hit it off with this man she was meeting and she's with him now in his flat or some hotel bedroom.' He handed the report back to Trish.

'That's unlikely, sir,' she said quietly. 'If you'd read the whole of it you'd have seen that Isobel's diabetic. She hadn't taken any insulin with her. She'd only expected to be away a few hours.'

Wesley's lips formed an 'oh'. He should have known that Trish wasn't the type to make a fuss about nothing.

'Do we know who she was meeting?'

'Yes. Isobel's mother had a call from one of her friends from work at ten thirty last night. The friend, Gwen, had

215

been trying to call her mobile but it was switched off. It turns out Gwen had called Isobel earlier in the evening and she'd been in the Angel having a drink with a man she'd met earlier that day. She went to the loo to take the call for some privacy so she told Gwen quite a bit about him. Anyway, Isobel promised to call her back when she got home to report how the evening had gone . . . only she never did.'

'So what do we know about the man she met?'

'She told Gwen his name was Adrian. He was a wealthy businessman who owned a yacht called the *Lazy Fox*, moored in Tradmouth.'

Wesley raised his eyebrows. The woman attacked in Neston had said she met a man who claimed to be a yacht owner and businessman – a Rory not an Adrian but there were similarities. 'I take it she'd never met this man before?'

'Not that Gwen knew of.'

'Then you'd better go and break the news to the boss. And get Uniform to ask the Harbour Master if the *Lazy Fox* exists – and, if it does, if it's still moored here.'

Trish began to walk slowly towards Gerry's office, as though she feared that her news was potentially explosive, while Wesley gazed at the paperwork on his desk. Isobel Grant had chosen a very bad time to disappear.

Just as Wesley was gathering his thoughts a call came from Reception to say that Robert Delaware had arrived and was asking for him.

Five minutes later he was in the interview room recently vacated by Alan Jakes. Unlike Jakes, Delaware looked far from comfortable in the utilitarian surroundings. He shifted in his seat and took constant sips from the cup of tea Wesley had provided for him as though he needed something to occupy his hands.

'I feel like a criminal sitting here like this,' Delaware began with a forced smile on his face.

'Just routine,' Wesley said lightly. 'Let's get down to business, shall we?'

'Fire away then. What is it you want to know?' Delaware was doing his best to sound casual and confident. But Wesley could sense the fear as his eyes flickered from side to side, taking in every feature of the room as though searching for a way out.

Wesley took the sheet of paper Tarnaby had given him from his pocket and placed it on the table, smoothing it out carefully, wracking up the tension.

'We've checked out the address you gave us . . .'

'Ah yes, I was meaning to tell you about that . . .'

'It doesn't exist, does it? And neither does Mr or Ms B Cooper.'

Delaware leaned forward, preparing to share a confidence. 'Look, I didn't want to say where I really was in front of Caroline Varley. Caroline and I have . . . well, we're becoming rather good friends. And if she'd found out that I was seeing someone else . . .'

'We'll need the name of this woman, Mr Delaware. I can assure you that we can be discreet when we want to be.'

'Actually . . .' He lowered his voice. 'It's not a woman, it's a man. You can understand why I wanted to keep it from Caroline . . . and there's his wife as well. She was away for the night on business. If some flat-footed copper goes barging in asking him to confirm that he was with me . . . Well, you see the problem, don't you?'

Wesley leaned forward. 'We're only interested in eliminating you from our enquiries.' He hesitated. 'As far as we're aware, you're the only person who's been looking up the details of the murders committed by John Varley recently so you can understand why we have to confirm your alibi.'

'Yes, of course.'

'Now if I could have the details of the person you were with . . .' He slid the paper towards Delaware who scribbled down another name and address. A Mr Raymond Seed at a Morbay address. 'Please, if his wife's there when you talk to him can you say you've come about witnessing an accident or something? Also he's a teacher and . . .'

'Where does he teach?'

'Neston Grammar. He teaches history.'

Wesley raised his eyebrows. That particular school kept cropping up every now and then and he wondered whether it was significant. After promising discretion he put the paper in his pocket, omitting to say that it probably wouldn't be him who conducted the interview: it would be some detective constable who may or may not be the soul of tact. Delaware and his lover would have to take their chances.

After a few more questions he told Delaware he was free to go and he shepherded him out into Reception, assuring him that the police weren't in the least bit interested in his complex sexual arrangements providing no law was broken. They weren't in the business of spreading people's private secrets – not deliberately at least. However, he didn't mention that during a murder enquiry there was often no time to avoid collateral damage.

When he returned to the incident room he rang the number Delaware had given him and when there was no reply he rang Neston Grammar only to be told that Mr Seed was off sick and wouldn't be back till next week.

'He teaches history, doesn't he?' Wesley asked innocently.

'No,' said the disembodied voice on the other end of the line. 'He teaches art . . . part-time.'

Wesley thanked her and replaced the receiver.

The owners of Gull's Nest lived in Exeter but at this time of year they came down to check on their investment most weekends. In spite of its modern conveniences and its view over the River Trad via Tradmouth's rooftops, the small whitewashed house in Upper Town, five minutes' walk from Tradmouth town centre, was hardly rented out during the winter months, except for a couple of weeks around the festive season. All that would change once Easter came, of course, and the place was virtually fully booked for the coming holiday season.

Keith Bunton had finished work early that Friday afternoon and when he arrived at Gull's Nest with his wife, Penny, they dragged their weekend cases from the car boot along with a cardboard box of provisions.

It was Penny Bunton who unlocked the back door that led onto the small paved courtyard at the rear of the house. She strolled outside with a carrier bag full of rubbish and made for the bin hidden behind a trellis by the wooden back gate.

But when she saw what lay on the stone paving, wrapped up in bloodied linen like a grim parcel, she dropped the rubbish. And as the used tea bags, toilet roll tubes and tin cans scattered over the cold damp ground, her mouth formed a silent scream.

# CHAPTER 21

*I had not found myself alone with Frederick for some time and I spent the time in a daze, going through the motions of duty so that others were quite unaware of my anguish.*

*The children were quiet and attended to their lessons for which I was most grateful as I was feeling unwell. In the mornings I was most nauseous and on one occasion I felt faint and sorely in need of fresh air.*

*Frederick's manner was civil whenever we met and we still took dinner together in the evenings as he had no wish to eat alone and John was usually occupied elsewhere – although where and with what I had no inkling. However, although Frederick conversed with me freely, mainly on the subject of his Egyptian studies and the findings of recent excavations, I was sure that I could detect a certain coolness in his manner. On one occasion I begged him to tell me if I had done something to offend, but he would say nothing.*

*I guessed that John's wicked words had brought about this unhappy transformation and I assured Frederick that there had been no truth in them, that John had made up his lurid tale because of his hatred for me.*

*Frederick acknowledged that this might be the case but his coolness remained. Nothing could be as it was before those filthy words were uttered.*

*Then one day I fainted after dinner and when the doctor was called the news he had to give me was most unwelcome.*

*After examining me most thoroughly, he told me that I was with child.*

# CHAPTER 22

Wesley and Gerry had left Mrs Bunton in the living room, sitting on the sofa with her husband's arm around her shoulder. One of the policewomen had brought her a cup of tea but it stood, cold and untouched, on the coffee table. The pair were clearly in shock and it was also obvious that they knew nothing about the body in their courtyard. The two policemen slipped out of the room and made for the back of the house where the crime scene team were going about their well choreographed business beneath the temporary floodlights brought in for the occasion.

Gerry stood silently by Wesley's side, hands in pockets, staring at the spectacle as if in a trance. After a minute or so the back gate was opened by a uniformed sergeant and Colin Bowman entered the courtyard wearing a white crime scene suit and carrying a large bag.

'What have we got?' Colin asked after delivering a cheerful greeting to the assembled team.

Gerry seemed uncharacteristically silent so it was Wesley who answered. 'It's another young woman. Same as the one up by the castle, I'm afraid.'

Colin's amiable expression disappeared as he stared at the bloodied linen wrapping. 'I'd better have a look. Do you know who she is?'

'She fits the description of a twenty-eight-year-old woman called Isobel Grant who was reported missing this morning.'

Gerry touched Wesley's arm, a signal for them both to step back into the shelter of the cottage kitchen and let Colin get on with his gruesome work.

'Where's Rach?'

'She's gone to meet Analise's sister at Morbay station.'

'Give her a call and tell her to get round to Mrs Grant's as soon as she can. We need to inform her that her daughter's been found.'

Wesley made the call. He knew Rachel hated playing Angel of Death, as she always called it, but he was just glad that he didn't have to do it.

When the call ended Gerry spoke again. 'When exactly was Isobel last seen?'

'According to the missing persons report she left home yesterday at around six thirty, presumably to meet this Adrian she told her mate about on the phone.'

Gerry fished in his pocket and extracted a tatty scrap of paper from its depths. 'Uniform contacted the harbour master. The *Lazy Fox* does exist and it's moored up at the marina. We should get someone down there. We really need to talk to Adrian . . . if that's his real name.'

'And when we find him we need to ask him where he was on Tuesday night. And on Sunday when Clare Mayers was attacked.'

'Chief Inspector, can I have a word?'

Wesley looked up. One of the crime scene investigators was standing at the back door, shifting from foot to foot. It was obvious that he didn't want whatever he had to say to be overheard by the Buntons. As the CSI held out a plastic bag for his inspection Gerry closed the door between the narrow galley kitchen and the living room. 'What is it?' he asked.

'Dr Bowman found this caught up in the sheet she was wrapped in. It's been photographed in situ.'

Gerry took the bag from him. 'Our friend Anubis again,' he said quietly. 'Our killer must have bought a job lot.'

Caroline Varley stood at the entrance to the Egyptian room. 'Do you know where Robert is?'

'Sorry, I've no idea.' Neil looked at his watch. He had been busy helping Andrew sort out Sir Frederick's collection and he'd lost track of time. Andrew was sitting by the window cataloguing some jewelled scarabs, so absorbed in his task that he didn't seem aware of Caroline's presence.

'Only he was going to see that policeman friend of yours in Tradmouth. He said he'd be back by six and it's almost eight. I'm worried that he's had an accident. The roads round here can be treacherous in the wet.'

She gave Neil a pleading look and his heart sank. As far as he was concerned, Robert Delaware was a creep on the make and Caroline deserved better.

But it would have been churlish to refuse her heartfelt request. 'I'll try Wesley's number,' he said, wondering if Delaware had been kept in for further questioning. If he had it wouldn't surprise him in the least.

When Wesley answered his phone it was obvious that he

wasn't in the mood to chat. He told Neil curtly that Delaware had left Tradmouth police station around three hours ago and rang off.

He sensed something had happened and Wesley's reluctance to talk made him suspect that history might have repeated itself. He couldn't forget that there had been four corpses back in 1903. Anyone copying John Varley wasn't likely to stop until he'd reached that number – or exceeded it.

When he relayed the news to Caroline she walked off with a worried frown on her face.

'I'm just taking a break,' he called across the room to Andrew who acknowledged his words with a small wave of the hand, too involved in his ancient scarabs to be bothered with the present day. Andrew had taken a room in a pub a mile away so without the problem of a long drive home, he'd probably work late into the evening. Neil had to face the drive back to his flat in Exeter so he wanted to leave within the next half hour . . . but he couldn't resist taking advantage of Delaware's absence.

Delaware had been given two rooms at the top of the castle in what was once the servants' quarters. If there was anything to find it would be there.

Hoping he wouldn't meet Caroline on the way, he tiptoed down the wide stone passage where the dim bulbs cast sinister shadows. Then he hurried up the old servants' staircase, separated discreetly from the family's domain by a heavy oak door. The servants' accommodation at Varley Castle had been very well appointed by Victorian standards but there was no mistaking the austerity of the décor and the pokiness of the rooms, all, no doubt, meant to keep the lower orders firmly in their place.

It was the first time Neil had visited this particular part of the house. Here there was a faint, musty smell and the walls were pale-green, unadorned apart from the odd cheap framed print. There were no rich Turkish rugs on the bare floorboards and the rooms contained Spartan beds with ticking mattresses and battered brown chests of drawers. Eventually he came to a room which was larger and better furnished then the others and had probably once accommodated the butler or housekeeper. The modern divan bed was topped by a colourful duvet and there was a worn rug on the floor, a lamp on the bedside table and a single wardrobe with a suitcase perched on top. The floral curtains at the window were open to reveal angry clouds scudding across the moonlit sky. Neil switched on the light. This was Delaware's room all right.

There was a door in the far wall which, Neil discovered, led into another, similar-sized room containing a large desk and two chests of drawers. He switched on the light and saw that the desk was piled with papers and what looked like old letters: Varley family letters. Caroline had given Delaware access to the lot and Neil wondered whether she'd been wise to do so. But then she'd probably thought that there'd be nothing worth hiding.

He started to search through the papers, not quite sure what he was looking for. Evidence that he'd somehow been involved with Wesley's murder victim perhaps, or maybe a desperate note from the girl asking him to meet her. But there was nothing remotely like that. Everything dated back to the time of Sir Frederick Varley, mainly letters from his colleagues, estate manager and family concerning exploits in Egypt and his household back in Devon. An old metal box contained more letters concerning a tomb in Egypt and the discovery of a remarkable painted interior. There were photographs too, disappointingly monochrome, of brilliantly executed tomb paintings and hieroglyphics.

Neil felt a little deflated. He'd got it into his head that Delaware was up to something, that he wasn't what he appeared to be. But if Robert Delaware had any secrets, he hadn't hidden them here.

He suddenly felt a pang of guilt that he'd been snooping on a man merely to satisfy his own prejudices. It was time he got out of there but he couldn't resist a swift peep inside the drawers before he left. He opened each one, finding some empty and others containing papers and sketches of hieroglyphics Varley had found in various tombs and temples.

The bottom drawer of the chest nearest the window slid open more smoothly than the others and when he saw what it contained, Neil's heart beat faster. It was an old sketch-book, shabby and foxed, and when he opened it carefully he saw that the pencil sketches within had been executed by a talented hand. In a way, that made it seem worse – the juxtaposition of technical ability and horror.

The book was filled with sketches of dead women; some merely strangled with twisted, cyanosed faces and a cord biting into their thin necks. In others the women were eviscerated, the organs portrayed in loving anatomical detail. Then there were sketches of human shapes, neatly wrapped in bloodstained linen.

This sketchbook was the souvenir of a killer.

It was eight fifteen and the mutilated body of Isobel Grant had been taken off to the mortuary to lie in peace until Colin conducted the post mortem the following morning. Rachel

227

had already broken the news and had left her mother with a family liaison officer for company. By all accounts Mrs Grant was distraught, but that was only to be expected. And now they faced the unappetising prospect of intruding on her grief.

Gerry had been liaising with the Harbour Master, a man he knew well. There was no sign of life aboard the *Lazy Fox* and, according to the Marina, she was owned by the manager of the local golf club, a man by the name of Humphries – and his first name definitely wasn't Adrian.

'Dr Kitchener's coming in first thing tomorrow,' Wesley said, making conversation as they walked along the waterfront: anything to take their minds off the mutilated body of Isobel Grant.

'So how come he knows your mother-in-law?' asked Gerry as they climbed the steps up to the Grant house.

'She met him at a conference at Morbay University and when he told her about his mother's animal sanctuary she was quick to volunteer. I can't help wondering whether he's the attraction rather than the animals.'

'Poor bloke. Nobody deserves that.' Gerry laughed and Wesley joined in, knowing that as soon as he reached Mrs Grant's front door all laughter would have to cease. But now he felt like affirming that there was still humour in the world – that life went on.

Mrs Grant's terraced house stood in a row perched above the Marina Hotel overlooking the river. The downstairs lights were on and the curtains were drawn. The place looked cosy and welcoming, which proved to Wesley that appearances can deceive: the atmosphere inside would be far from comfortable. He rang the doorbell and waited.

After a minute or so the front door opened a crack, but as

228

soon as the young policewoman recognised them she opened the door wide and stood aside to let them in.

'Can't be too careful,' she said, looking round. 'The last time I did this job we were pestered by press from noon till night.'

'They don't know yet, love,' Gerry said reassuringly.

Wesley didn't recognise the young woman and concluded that she must be new, transferred from another station perhaps. She was small and plump with a pretty face and short chestnut hair. He put out his hand. 'We've not met. DI Peterson. Wesley.'

The woman nodded. 'I've heard of you. Pleased to meet you at last. I'm DC Julie MacBride, stationed at Morbay.'

Gerry gave her one of his grins. 'DCI Heffernan. No doubt my reputation's gone before me and all.'

Julie smiled and said nothing.

'How's Mrs Grant?' Wesley knew it was a stupid question but he felt he had to ask it anyway.

'Stunned. She just sits there with Isobel's photograph on her knee, rocking it to and fro like a baby. Heartbreaking.'

Julie led them into the living room and Wesley looked around. The small front room looked newly decorated and up to date with its leather sofas, wooden floor, red shag pile rug and floor-length red silk curtains. There were two empty mugs on the low coffee table, bright and chunky. Isobel's taste perhaps.

In pride of place over the fireplace hung a blown-up graduation portrait of the young woman they'd just seen dead and mutilated in the courtyard of the Buntons' holiday cottage. But in this picture she was smiling proudly in mortarboard and black gown trimmed with a pale blue and white fur hood, holding a scrolled certificate in her ringless hands.

Mrs Grant looked up. She was nursing a framed photograph, hugging it to her breast protectively. She seemed younger than Wesley had expected with shoulder-length blonde hair and an attractive freckled face. She was the sort of woman who would normally have looked cheerful. Wesley wished she still had cause to.

He fixed a concerned expression to his face and held out his hand. 'Mrs Grant, I'm so sorry for your loss,' he said, hating the fact that his words seemed so inadequate. 'This is DCI Heffernan. He's the senior investigating officer in charge of the case.'

Gerry shook hands solemnly, muttering platitudes.

'Has DC MacBride told you that we can get somebody else to identify Isobel if you're not feeling up to it?'

She nodded. 'I want to do it. I want to see her.'

Wesley sat down by the woman's side. 'I know you gave us the details when you reported her missing but I wonder if you could tell us any more.'

She shook her head. 'She was a careful girl, Inspector. She wasn't naïve. I couldn't believe it when her friend, Gwen, said she'd gone for a drink with a man she didn't know – a stranger who picked her up in the street.'

She offered the photo she was holding to Wesley. He took it from her: it was warm. 'Look at her picture. She was a lovely girl; beautiful and clever. She had a degree in physics, you know. Taught at Tradmouth Comprehensive. She loved teaching.' He examined the picture dutifully. Unlike in her graduation portrait, Isobel struck an informal pose, smiling happily with a champagne glass raised in a toast to the unseen photographer.

'Which university was she at?'

'Liverpool.'

Wesley saw Gerry's eyes light up. 'That's my home town. And my son was at university there studying to be a vet.'

Wesley shot his boss a look. Mrs Grant would hardly wish to be reminded that somebody else's son was still alive and well while her own daughter was lying in the mortuary.

But Mrs Grant smiled politely. 'Perhaps they knew each other.'

'I'll mention her name to our Sam. If he knew her he'll be upset. I take it she had a lot of friends in this area.'

Mrs Grant hesitated. 'Not really. But she was trying to build up a social life and she was friendly with Gwen: she teaches French at the same school.'

'I know. Somebody's gone over to speak to her. Did she keep in touch with her university friends?'

'I think so. She used the Internet a lot.'

'We'll need to get somebody to examine her computer,' Wesley said gently. 'Is that all right?'

Mrs Grant nodded and hugged the photo close to her. 'She was such a lovely girl.'

'I take it you got on well?'

Mrs Grant suddenly looked uneasy. 'We had our rows, of course. She kept saying she was sick of living at home and she wanted a place of her own. But that's normal, isn't it?' She sounded defensive, as though Wesley's question had hit a raw nerve.

'And if you've got a recent photo we can have . . .'

Mrs Grant stared at the picture in her arms then she handed it to Wesley. 'You can use this one. It's the latest one I've got. It was taken at Christmas. You'll let me have it back, won't you?'

'Of course we will.' Wesley took it from her carefully as if it was something delicate and very precious – which to Mrs Grant it was.

231

When Wesley's phone rang he excused himself and stepped out into the hall. It was Trish. She'd spoken to Gwen and she was reporting back. From the privacy of the Ladies' toilets at the Angel, Isobel had told Gwen that Adrian was very good-looking, quite a charmer. He was a divorced businessman with a big house up near the golf club – although the exact nature of his business hadn't been specified. No surname had been mentioned but Isobel was keen to boast to her friend that her date owned a yacht, the *Lazy Fox*, and a red Ferrari. Isobel must have thought she'd struck lucky. According to Gwen she'd certainly sounded excited . . . and maybe a little smug.

Wesley waited until they'd left the house before he filled Gerry in on the news.

'A red Ferrari.' Gerry rolled his eyes. 'Flash or what?'

Wesley looked at him and smiled. 'There can't be too many red Ferraris around here.'

Maybe finding Adrian would be easier than they'd feared.

By the time Wesley arrived home the children were fast asleep and Pam was slumped on the sofa with a glass of red wine in her hand watching the ten o'clock news headlines.

When he entered the room he bent and kissed her on the forehead.

'Neil's been after you,' she said, her eyes still on the TV screen. 'He must have called five times. Says it's urgent.'

'My phone's been switched off.'

'He sounded worried.'

Wesley sat down beside her and shook his head. 'It'll have to wait till tomorrow.' He looked into her eyes and saw anxiety there. She'd sensed something was wrong. 'We found another body.'

'There was something on the local news but they didn't give details.'

'It's the same as the other one . . . Analise Sonquist.'

Pam's hand went to her mouth. He put out his arms and drew her towards him. 'I'm shattered.'

She gave him a brief hug and broke away. Then she got another glass from the kitchen and poured him a large helping of wine. 'I take it you've eaten?'

'You can't work evenings with Gerry without having a takeaway. As far as he's concerned a cop with an empty stomach is a cop with an empty charge sheet.'

Pam gave a half-hearted smile and raised her glass just as the kitten charged in and scaled the curtains. She clung to the top mewing pitifully as Wesley stood up and disentangled her needle claws carefully from the fabric.

'Stupid animal, she's been doing that on and off ever since I got in. The kids think it's hilarious.'

The phone started to ring just as Wesley had lifted the tiny creature down from the curtain and placed her gently on the floor. Pam picked up the receiver and passed it to him, mouthing the word 'Neil'.

Wesley sighed and took the instrument from her. 'Hi, Neil.'

'I've found something,' Neil said. 'A book full of sketches of John Varley's victims.'

'You mean pictures of them when they were alive?'

'No. These are like crime scene photos only sketches. The bodies are wrapped up in bloodstained sheets. Four victims, several pictures of each with the names printed neatly underneath.'

Wesley said nothing for a few moments as he absorbed the information.

'Where did you find them?'

Neil hesitated. 'I . . . er . . . I thought I'd have a quick look through Robert Delaware's room while he was out.'

'And he'd hidden the sketches?'

'They were in a drawer with some other stuff he'd been using in his research. Shall I try and bring them down tomorrow? I think you should see them.'

Wesley thought for a moment. 'Leave everything where you found it and I'll come up to the castle tomorrow. If you see Delaware don't mention it, will you?'

'I'm not daft.'

'Is he back yet?'

'He arrived just before I left. I don't think he suspected I'd been sniffing around.'

'Good.' Wesley looked at his watch. It was after ten now. He told Neil he'd be in touch and put in a call to Gerry to tell him the news.

'Morning briefing at seven thirty?' said Gerry cheerfully. 'And we can send someone over to Varley Castle to pick up Delaware and the evidence. He'll be back here just in time for elevenses.'

First thing the next morning Wesley sat at his desk. Guy Kitchener sat opposite him sipping coffee.

'You've seen the photos of the latest victim, I take it?'

Guy put his coffee down on the desk. 'Yes. It's identical to the first. And as the details of the mutilations haven't been released, we can rule out a copycat killing. There's a seriously disturbed weirdo out there.'

Wesley gave him a weak smile. 'Weirdo? Is that a technical term you psychologists use?'

'It's the term a layman would use. I like to put it in words

234

the average policeman would understand. Present company excepted, of course. I imagine the DCI likes to call a spade a spade.'

'Don't underestimate Gerry.'

'I wouldn't dream of it.'

As if on cue, Gerry Heffernan emerged from his office, calling his faithful to attention. It was time for the morning briefing. And he had a satisfied look on his face.

'Right,' he said when the troops were gathered, facing the notice board with its array of gruesome photographs. 'There's been a couple of developments overnight. First of all there's the man Robert Delaware claims he was with on the night of Analise Sonquist's murder. He's a teacher called Raymond Seed and he's not answering his door. According to his school, he's been off work sick since Tuesday but his neighbours think he's gone away, no idea where to. Also he lives alone so Delaware's story about him having a wife is a load of rubbish.

'Our second development is that our friend Delaware has been found in possession of some rather unpleasant sketches of John Varley's original victims in 1903 – identical MO to the deaths of Analise Sonquist and Isobel Grant. According to Dr Bowman, Isobel was probably killed after Delaware left here on Thursday. He's being picked up so he should be with us very soon.'

Wesley glanced at Guy who was perched on the corner of his desk with an expression of expectant interest fixed to his face.

'We've got Dr Kitchener here,' Gerry continued. 'He's going to bring us up to date on his conclusions.' He didn't sound too confident. 'Guy. Would you like to say a few words?'

Guy Kitchener stood up and cleared his throat. 'I've been

analysing the locations where the bodies have been left. Dr Bowman says the victims were killed where they were found. If we assume that Clare Mayers was an intended victim this means that all the attacks have taken place within a three-mile radius.'

'So the murderer lives in the area?' asked an eager young DC.

'Not necessarily. It's possible that he lives somewhere not far away, like Neston or Morbay, and travels into the area. This is his hunting ground. He strikes then returns home.'

Wesley caught Gerry's eye. Delaware had a flat in Tradmouth yet to be searched, and he was staying out at Varley Castle. But then Guy's suggestions weren't necessarily to be taken as holy writ.

Guy continued. 'After Analise's death I thought there was a chance that she was singled out for some reason but now I don't think there's any personal motive for the attacks. The victims made themselves available to him. They were in the wrong place at the wrong time.'

'So it's no use looking too deeply into the victims' private lives?' Gerry sounded a little disappointed.

Guy shook his head. 'I'd concentrate more on the perpetrator if I were you. I've been thinking about the mutilations. Normally I'd say that a killer who could do that had a deep and pathological hatred of women. But having heard about the Egyptian connection from Inspector Peterson here, it puts rather a different slant on things. The mutilations emulate the Egyptian procedures that were meant to give the body immortality so perhaps it's his way of doing them a favour. Showing them love even. I'm not sure.'

'Are these murders linked to the attack on the woman in Neston?' Gerry asked.

236

'I'm keeping an open mind on that one,' Guy replied.

It was Wesley's turn to ask the question that had been on his mind since Neil's phone call the previous night. 'Our killings are identical to the ones committed by John Varley in 1903. Why has the murderer chosen to copy these old murders?'

'Simple. He heard about them and they began to prey on his mind until interest turned into obsession. It didn't come out of the blue. He'll have been planning this for a while. When you catch him you'll probably find a lot of stuff about ancient Egypt and the Varley murders in his home. Maybe even a sort of shrine to John Varley.'

A uniformed officer bustled into the room and made straight for Gerry Heffernan. He passed the DCI a piece of paper. Gerry read it and looked up. 'Right, everyone. Carry on.'

As everyone returned to their tasks, Gerry caught hold of Wesley's arm and drew him towards his office. Guy followed a little behind as though uncertain of his welcome.

'Robert Delaware's here,' Gerry said to Wesley. 'He's down in the interview room. And that sketchbook's being brought over.'

Guy caught up with them. 'I'm sorry, I couldn't help over-hearing. Do you mind if I observe the interview?'

'You can watch through our fancy two-way mirror,' said Gerry. 'Delaware fits your profile of the killer – in his thirties, single, a rather unsuccessful author who nobody's heard of.

Wesley could tell that Guy was trying hard not to look smug.

'And he gave a false alibi for Analise's murder,' Gerry continued. 'At first he told us he was having an affair with a married man who has now conveniently vanished. I think he made up that tale on the spur of the moment to throw us off the scent. He probably reckoned that if he could convince us he wasn't interested in women sexually, then he'd hardly go to the bother of killing them.'

Wesley knew that Gerry might have a point. 'Delaware was certainly in Tradmouth on the day of Isobel's murder – he came here to make a statement and he didn't get back to the castle till late. And Raymond Seed, his alibi for Analise's, has gone walkabout.'

There was a knock on the office door and the three men looked round. It was Nick Tarnaby. He hovered on the threshold like a child reluctant to join a party.

'What is it, Nick?' Wesley asked. He'd always considered Tarnaby surly and unco-operative, a difficult man to get along with, until he'd acted with considerable heroism during the arrest of a murderer the previous November. Since then he'd tried to make a real effort with the man – but it still wasn't easy.

'The landlord of the Angel recognised Isobel Grant's picture. She was in there the day before yesterday. And she was with a man.' He consulted a sheet of paper. 'Five feet ten, short dark hair. Mid-thirties; smart leather jacket.'

'Could fit Delaware's description,' said Gerry with a frown. 'And it could fit the man Andrea Washington met in Neston before she was assaulted. Had the landlord ever seen this bloke before?'

Nick hesitated. 'He said he thought he'd been in before a couple of times but he'd been dressed casually, scruffy even – old jeans and sweatshirt, as if he'd been working on a boat or something. He said the man had a bar meal with Isobel and they left together around nine. They seemed to be getting on OK but they were hardly all over each other.'

238

'We'll need an e-fit.'

Nick nodded. 'Right you are, sir.'

Wesley caught Gerry's eye as Nick scurried out. What they could do with now was a bit of luck.

*I Remember Cleopatra.*

Suzie Crest had thought it a superb title for a play and she had been relieved when the decision had finally been made to enter the Castle Players' autumn production for the annual Tradmouth Drama Festival in April. With a few more rehearsals their success could be repeated . . . and even improved on. And as it had been written by a local author – a woman who lived just outside Neston – she reckoned they stood a good chance of walking off with the festival prize. Local always went down well.

On the day of the first rehearsal Suzie was the last to arrive at the church hall and some of her fellow thespians shot wary, even pitying looks in her direction, which was hardly surprising as her small supporting role in Analise Sonquist's death had made the local papers. She hoped nobody would mention it as she hadn't yet rehearsed the appropriate responses.

Analise's sister had turned up on her doorstep earlier and, for once, Suzie had been lost for words. She had mumbled platitudes and the girl had cried while Suzie had watched her, a little ashamed that she could feel nothing but irritation. Clive had called her a selfish, unfeeling bitch. It had been the first time he'd ever talked to her like that. Since Analise's death he seemed different somehow. Everything seemed different.

The police hadn't bothered them for the past couple of days, not since the second body had been found. At least

Clive had a cast-iron alibi for that one, she thought. He'd been with her all night, sulking and moody like a child whose mother wouldn't allow it out to play. But he'd been there all right. They both had. Until they could get themselves a new au pair, their social wings were clipped.

She paused in the doorway of the church hall, watching her fellow actors and backstage helpers rushing here and there, some panicking, some purposeful. But she knew that an element of chaos was as inevitable as the seasons. Costumes and props were bound to have gone missing since November and lines were sure to have been forgotten. She made for the side room where the costumes were kept and when she reached her destination she found the tweed suit, sensible shoes and grey curly wig that would transform her into another woman for the duration of the performance – into Mrs Murchison, the wife of a laird who expects to land the role of Cleopatra, only to be disappointed. It was hardly a glamorous part. But Suzie had never really been the glamorous type.

As she began to check that her costume was complete, she heard a raised female voice, high-pitched and slightly lisping. 'It isn't here.'

Suzie looked round. Agnes White, the woman in charge of wardrobe, was making a frantic search of a large cupboard.

'What have you lost?' she asked.

'The mask Fiona wears at the end of the second act – when all the Egyptian gods and goddesses parade in front of Cleopatra and Mark Antony.'

'Which one is it? The hawk?'

'No. The jackal. Remember? Raymond copied it from that statue you brought back from your Nile cruise. You know Raymond – he's my daughter's art teacher at Neston Grammar.'

240

Suzie froze. 'You're sure it's missing?'

'Absolutely sure. But it's not the end of the world. The others are here so nobody'll notice if we're one god short, will they? The trouble is, it's Fiona's only part so we'll have to think of something else to give her. A handmaiden perhaps. What do you think?'

Suzie didn't answer. Her mind was racing. According to the papers there was some bizarre Egyptian connection to Analise's death. And the police had shown an interest in Clive's Anubis statue.

The police really should be told about the missing mask. She dreaded facing all those questions again – and Clive had been so edgy since Analise was found – but she knew it had to be done. Perhaps it would be best if Agnes did it, she thought.

Murder was so unpleasant.


When they reached the interview room Guy Kitchener slipped next door to watch unobserved behind the two-way mirror.

Robert Delaware looked nervous, frightened even. He was drinking a cup of coffee from the machine. Some, including Wesley, would have called that a cruel start to the interrogation.

The duty solicitor sat by the suspect's side, fidgeting with a pen. He looked almost as uncomfortable as his new client.

Gerry came straight to the point. 'Your alibi's gone AWOL, Mr Delaware. Raymond Seed's not been at work . . . and he hasn't got a wife.' He looked at the suspect expectantly. Get out of that one.

Delaware bowed his head. 'I've been trying to ring him but there's been no answer. I didn't know he was away.'

'He's let you down,' said Wesley gently.

241

'Seems like it.' He rubbed his eyes, leaving the delicate skin surrounding them red and puffy. He looked weary. If he was going to talk, it might be now.

'You lied to us.'

Delaware began to play with the empty cup in front of him, his nervous fingers turning it round and round.

After a while he spoke again, as though he had an urge to fill the expectant silence. 'I haven't done anything. I didn't kill those women. Why should I?'

'You tell us, Robert.' Before he entered the room Wesley had been handed a brown paper evidence bag containing the sketchbook from the castle. He picked it up from where he'd been concealing it down by the side of the chair and lifted it onto the table. He unwrapped it, opened it and pushed it towards Delaware who sat, frozen.

'For the benefit of the tape I'm showing Mr Delaware a sketchbook containing drawings of murder victims from 1903. Have you seen it before, Mr Delaware?'

'Yes, but—'

'It was found in your room at Varley Castle. How did it come to be there?'

'It was amongst the Varley family papers in the muniment room. I took it up to my study because I'm working on a chapter about the death of Sir Frederick Varley's son, John. He killed these women then he hanged himself in the woods near the castle. This was part of my research.'

Gerry Heffernan leaned forward. 'And you expect us to believe that?'

'It's the truth.'

'Have you ever been in a pub called the Angel in Tradmouth?'

Delaware looked wary. 'I might have been. I can't remember.'

242

'You don't seem too sure.'

'Can I go now? I've told you everything I know.'

'Where were you on Thursday evening?'

'I was travelling back to Varley Castle. I was here in the afternoon. Remember?'

'You could easily have met Isobel Grant afterwards.'

'I don't know anybody called Isobel Grant.'

'You didn't get back to Varley Castle till almost midnight. Why was that?'

Delaware glanced at his solicitor, a pleading look in his eyes.

The solicitor cleared his throat. 'I think my client's told you everything he knows, Chief Inspector. The evidence against him is all circumstantial so—'

'You've got a flat in Tradmouth, I believe. I'd like to organise a search.'

Delaware looked uneasy. 'OK. But is it really necessary?'

'If you've got nothing to hide you've got nothing to fear,' Gerry replied with a smile that would grace a crocodile.

Delaware shot another glance at his solicitor who turned his head away.

'Where were you last Sunday night?'

Delaware looked confused. 'I was at Varley Castle. Yes, I'm sure I was.'

'Can anybody vouch for that?'

He hesitated. 'Caroline was out. Somebody from the village invited her round for dinner.'

'Are you going to release my client?' the solicitor said. He sounded a little bored, but then it was a question he'd asked many times before over the course of his career.

'Not at the moment,' said Gerry. He stood up, his chair scraping on the linoleum floor.

As the uniformed constable sitting by the door escorted Delaware back to the cells, the solicitor looked at his watch meaningfully. They didn't have long to make the decision; either charge Delaware or let him go. It was just a matter of getting the necessary evidence.

They met up with Guy Kitchener in the corridor.

'What did you think?' Wesley asked.

'He was nervous. And evasive.'

'And he fits the profile you gave us,' said Gerry.

'Yes. He's arrogant too. He's confident he can get away with it.'

'John Varley didn't get away with it back in 1903,' observed Wesley, unable to get Varley out of his mind.

'But Delaware thinks he can succeed where Varley failed. That's what I mean about arrogance.'

'If he is guilty what's his motive?' Wesley asked.

'Power,' Guy said with confidence. 'It makes him important and gives him a kind of immortality. Think of all the books that are published about serial killers.' Guy looked at his watch. 'I've got to get back to the university for a meeting. Sorry. Call me if anything new comes up, won't you?'

'I never reckoned much to profilers and psychologists before but he talks some sense,' Gerry said as soon as Guy was out of earshot.

'Do you think Delaware's our man?'

Gerry considered the question for a moment. 'I think we can rule Dudgeon out and all this Varley stuff is too subtle for Jakes. But Delaware fits our bill perfectly.'

Wesley knew Gerry was right. But he still felt uncomfortable.

As they arrived back at Gerry's office Paul Johnson came rushing up to them. He had news.

'I've spoken to the person who took the bookings for the craft fair at the church hall in January. Remember, Geoffrey Dudgeon thought he'd seen someone selling those Egyptian figures there? Well, one of the stalls was hired by a Raymond Seed. Wasn't that the man Robert Delaware said he was with when . . .?'

'Yes. It's about time we found our Mr Seed,' said Gerry. 'Anything else?'

'I've been trying to trace this Adrian Isobel Grant told her friend she met. According to records, the only Adrian who lives up near the golf club is sixty-seven years old and there are no Ferraris registered locally to anybody called Adrian. And he lied about owning the *Lazy Fox*. I'm beginning to think that Adrian doesn't exist.'

# CHAPTER 23

*Frederick had not visited my bed for many weeks; not since John had uttered his poisonous words. This lack of intimate contact denied me a suitable opportunity to reveal my dilemma to him. I had no wish to be overheard by servants or to arouse the suspicions of those below stairs so I kept silent, nursing my secret.*

*My waist was beginning to thicken and I knew that my hidden shame would soon be evident to the world and the gossips who dwelt in the attic rooms and looked down their noses at me – a lady who has been forced by poverty into sharing their servitude – would revile me as the worst kind of sinner: a magdalen; a fallen woman. However, I hoped and prayed that when all was revealed Sir Frederick would share the responsibility for my fall from grace and offer me his protection – even, I dared hope, the honour of marriage.*

*One evening when I was taking dinner with Sir Frederick, a new maidservant upset a glass and hurried out to fetch a cloth to wipe up the spill. All the servants being absent from the room, we were at last alone and I could contain myself no longer. I rose and went to the head of the table where Frederick sat and I knelt beside him. He begged me to rise before the maidservant returned but I stayed there, resolving not to move until I had said my piece.*

*'My dearest, I am with child,' I said. 'And you are my child's father.'*

*It was at that moment, when I saw the horror and distaste on his face, that I knew that all the affection he had claimed to have for me had been false. He had used me for his pleasure like some servant girl of no importance. And now I would be alone in the world facing censure and disgrace.*

# CHAPTER 24

As soon as Wesley returned to the incident room Gerry called him over.

'A Mrs Agnes White has just called in. She's acting as wardrobe mistress for the Castle Players. They performed a play called *I Remember Cleopatra* back in November and now they're entering it for the Tradmouth Drama Festival. They put all the costumes away in a cupboard at the church hall before Christmas and when they came to get them out again, they found that a mask had gone missing.' Gerry paused for dramatic effect but Wesley guessed what was coming. 'It's a jackal mask. Anubis. And there's another interesting connection: Mrs White mentioned that her daughter was interviewed about the attack on Clare Mayers. Mrs White is Peony White's mother.'

'Small world,' said Wesley. 'Who's had access to this mask?'

'The church hall's always in use so anyone can walk in.

And there's something else. The mask was made by Peony's art teacher . . . one Raymond Seed.'

Wesley said nothing for a few seconds then he looked up. 'Delaware's elusive alibi.'

'Morbay keep trying Seed's address but he's not there. He rang into school on Tuesday morning then he vanished.'

'It's time we made a thorough search of Delaware's Tradmouth flat: it's above a shop in Ford Street. There might be some clue there to Seed's whereabouts.'

Gerry nodded. 'Better see to it right away.' He hesitated. 'Is it Delaware, Wes . . . maybe with this Seed as his accomplice? We're not leaping to conclusions?'

'He's been taking an unhealthy interest in the John Varley murders; he's got no alibis for the attack on Clare Mayers or the two murders; and he fits Guy Kitchener's profile. He's in custody now but the clock's ticking away so if we don't find some solid evidence soon, we'll have to release him. And if he's free, he might kill again.'

As Wesley turned to leave the office, Gerry's phone rang. After a short conversation he summoned Wesley back with an urgent shout.

Robert Delaware had just collapsed in his cell.

Dave Bartle, landlord of the Angel, prided himself on remembering his regulars. But the same couldn't be said for occasional patrons who popped in once in a blue moon for a pub meal.

A taciturn plain-clothes policeman had called that morning to help him create an e-fit of the man he'd seen with the murdered woman. But the truth was that he'd taken little notice of the man, although he'd had a nagging feeling that he'd seen him before.

But Dave didn't have time to think of that now. It was one o'clock on a Saturday and there was a long queue at the bar.

'Yes, sir, what'll it be?' he said automatically to the next customer in the queue.

'Pint of bitter and a packet of salt and vinegar crisps.'

Dave looked up at the man for the first time and his heart missed a beat. It was definitely him. Only this time he wore a stained sweatshirt instead of an expensive shirt and leather coat. There was a smear of oil on his hand too, as though he'd been working on an engine.

'That'll be three pounds forty-eight, if you please,' Dave said with an effort at bonhomie. He didn't want to scare the man off.

'Take over, will you?' he whispered to Barry the barman who was serving by his side. 'I've got to make a phone call.'

He took the policeman's card out of his pocket and picked up the phone behind the bar.

Wesley stood in the tiny living room of Delaware's flat, glad for time to think away from the hectic bustle of the incident room.

Delaware had been taken off to Neston Hospital as there were no available beds at Tradmouth. According to the doctors, his life was in no danger and no explanation had been forthcoming for the dramatic medical emergency. Wesley suspected an element of play-acting . . . but perhaps his years in the police had given him a jaded view of human nature.

As he'd arrived at the flat he'd received a call from an excited Gerry Heffernan. The landlord of the Angel had spotted the man who'd been with Isobel Grant. Paul Johnson had rushed off to investigate but no doubt the man would have vanished by the time he got there – or alternatively he'd

250

turn out to be some innocent bystander who happened to bear a passing resemblance to the man they were looking for. Wesley wasn't getting his hopes up.

He began the search. He had always believed that you could tell a lot about a person from the state of the place they lived in but he wasn't quite sure what to make of Robert Delaware's domestic habits. The bedroom, just large enough for a double bed and a wardrobe, was neat but in the living room objects spilled from cupboards and the floor was littered with papers, as though he – or somebody else – had been making a frantic search for something and hadn't had the time or the inclination to return everything to its proper place.

Chaos made Wesley uncomfortable so he began to pick up the papers and arrange them in neat piles on the coffee table. He came across printouts of e-mails: one from Delaware's publishers rejecting a proposal he'd made for a book on local history, and another asking when the first draft of his biography of Sir Frederick Varley would be ready. There was also a letter from his bank asking him to come in and discuss his overdraft situation. As Wesley continued his search he found a small pile of adult magazines hidden beneath a pile of bills in the corner and he flicked through them absent-mindedly, reminded of Guy Kitchener's words – the killer could be afraid of women. And here was Delaware using glossy images as a substitute for real relationships. Somehow it seemed to fit. There was no sign of any equivalent gay magazines, rather confirming that the relationship Delaware had claimed to have with Raymond Seed was a lie . . . as Wesley had suspected all along.

The built-in cupboard by the fireplace was packed with books on Egypt and printouts about early twentieth-century expeditions and discoveries. The man had certainly done his homework before embarking on his biography of Sir Frederick Varley.

He was about to close the cupboard when a book title caught his eye, written in large red letters on the spine of a dull brown volume: *The Art of Mummification*. Wesley took the book out and when he leafed through it he noticed that a page corner had been turned down. He opened the page in question and saw an illustration that reminded him of one of Colin Bowman's autopsies. His hands began to shake a little as he stared at the full-page outline of a body with broken lines indicating where the embalmers of the dead had extracted the internal organs. Whoever had killed Analise Sonquist and Isobel Grant had been in possession of this information. If things were looking bad for Robert Delaware before, this final piece of evidence seemed bound to condemn him.

He dropped the book into an evidence bag and left the cold, shabby flat, locking the door carefully behind him.

There had been a mystery key found amongst Robert Delaware's possessions that hadn't fitted his Ford Street premises. Gerry had contemplated this puzzle for a while before telling Trish Walton to take it with her when she and DC Darren Norris visited Raymond Seed's address in an upmarket part of Morbay. They had obtained a search warrant and, if Seed wasn't in, they had orders to gain entry. But Trish thought she'd try her luck with the key before taking any more drastic measures.

There was no sign of life when Trish and Darren arrived and as soon as Trish tried the key in the lock she found that it fitted perfectly.

Seed's flat occupied the entire ground floor of a large Edwardian house. It was spacious with a tasteful blend of modern and antique furnishings and rich Turkish rugs on the polished oak floorboards. Quite luxurious, Trish thought, for a part-time art teacher. But there was nothing there to link Seed with Robert Delaware, not even an entry in the address book by the phone. There wasn't even any sign of Seed's own artistic efforts which Trish thought rather unusual.

When she spotted an insignificant-looking door in the far corner of the slick, modern kitchen she decided to investigate. The door was locked but she noticed a small key cupboard hanging on the wall above the worktop and she tried the keys in the lock one by one, eventually striking lucky. She pushed the door open and stared down into the dark abyss below for a few seconds before summoning Darren from the living room for support.

She reached out her hand, fumbling for the light switch and when the large, well-appointed cellar was bathed in light she could see tables laden with paints and clays. Against one white-painted brick wall stood a pile of wooden crates and on another wall there were rows of shelves filled with colourful statues, masks and figurines. All Egyptian.

Trish crept down the cellar steps, glad that Darren was behind her. When she reached the bottom she realised that the place was some sort of workshop and the crates stacked up by the far wall bore writing that she guessed was Arabic or something similar.

But it was a shelf filled with small figurines that made her catch her breath. Anubis after Anubis, all similar to the one found on the body of Analise Sonquist. And beneath them was a row of identical masks: the heads of a jackal, painted in black and shades of blue.

She took out her phone but as there was no signal down there, she asked Darren to go upstairs and put in a call to Gerry Heffernan. Once alone, she stood there looking around. The Egyptian objects gave her the creeps, watching her with their dark, painted eyes. Then suddenly she heard raised voices coming from the kitchen upstairs.

When she darted back up the steps she saw Darren standing in front of the cellar door, facing a man who looked more worried than angry.

'Raymond Seed, I presume?'

The man nodded warily.

'We'd like a word with you concerning the murders of Analise Sonquist and Isobel Grant.'

When the man sat down heavily on a stool and put his head in his hands, Trish thought he looked a little relieved. But it was probably her imagination.

Luckily the man who'd been with Isobel Grant on the night she disappeared had still been in the Angel when Paul Johnson arrived. Paul recognised the man as soon as he walked in but he didn't want to leap to conclusions until the landlord had given him the nod. Once he did, however, Paul approached Alan Jakes, who was sipping his pint and staring appreciatively at a couple of young women in the corner, and asked quietly if he could have a word. Fifteen minutes later Jakes was sitting in interview room one nursing a plastic cup filled with a hot brown liquid that claimed to be tea. Biscuits hadn't been offered.

Gerry Heffernan stood outside in the corridor with Paul, squinting through the peephole in the door. Jakes looked annoyed but largely unfazed by his situation which, in Gerry's opinion, marked him as a guilty man.

Gerry had summoned Guy Kitchener from Morbay University and now he stood aside so that the psychologist could watch the man himself. 'Well? What do you think?'

Guy turned to face him. 'So this is the man who's been having an affair with Clare Mayers? He looks confident.'

'And that means?'

Guy took another peep. 'Most people would look worried even if they were innocent.'

'My thoughts exactly. We'd better get on with it.'

As soon as Guy had disappeared through the neighbouring door to watch the interview through the two-way mirror, Gerry flung the door open wide and let Paul Johnson take his seat first while he stood for a few moments, towering over his suspect.

'They've given you a cup of tea then?' he said as he sat down.

Jakes nodded.

'Sorry about that. We've had complaints to the European Court of Human Rights about the tea from that machine,' he said with an attempt at levity.

Alan Jakes didn't smile. 'Why am I here? I was having a quiet pint and I was dragged here against my will. I could sue.' He glared at Paul.

'Own a yacht do you, Alan?'

Jakes snorted. 'Do I look as though I can afford a yacht? Look, why am I here? Has that Clare been saying things? If she has, she's a lying cow.'

Gerry ignored his protestations and slid a photograph of Isobel Grant across the table. 'Do you know this woman?'

Jakes picked it up, glanced at it swiftly then put it down again as if it was red hot. His lips tilted upwards in a cocky half-smile but Gerry could see that his hands were shaking.

'Why?'

'She was murdered on Thursday night and dumped in the back yard of a house in Tradmouth, that's why.'

For a second Jakes looked alarmed. 'Look, that's got nothing to do with me.'

From what Gerry Heffernan could see his shock was genuine. Or maybe he was just a good actor.

'Did you see Isobel Grant on Thursday night? I should tell you that you've been identified as the man she was with.'

Jakes looked unsure of himself. Then he came to a decision. 'Yeah I saw her but I didn't hurt her. I never did nothing.'

'You used the name Adrian. Why was that?'

Jakes sat silently for a few moments. Eventually he leaned towards Gerry confidentially. 'I thought it'd be a laugh if I became a posh bloke with a Ferrari and a yacht. I'd been working on this boat, the *Lazy Fox*, so I had the keys.'

'I thought you worked in a garage?'

'Yeah, but I do some boat maintenance too. I've got a mate who works at Peters and I help him out sometimes.'

'Really,' said Gerry, trying to sound casual. 'I've thought about trying Peters for my boat but they've got a reputation for being a bit on the expensive side.'

'You get what you pay for.' Jakes smirked and looked Gerry up and down. 'They do tend to deal with the upper end of the market.'

'All the gin palaces, eh.'

'Something like that.'

'So you said you owned a yacht. What other cock-and-bull stories did you tell her?'

'I said I had a big house near the golf club and said my Ferrari was in the garage for repairs.' He looked Gerry in the eye. 'There are times when I just fancy being someone else. No harm in it.'

'And did Isobel swallow it?'

'I reckon so. I said I'd take her out on the yacht on Sunday. I knew the owner was away and wouldn't be needing her till next week so . . .'

'You were going to borrow the *Lazy Fox*?'

'Why not? As long as my mate doesn't find out.'

'Where did you meet Isobel?'

'I saw her in Winterleas – chatted her up over the frozen peas and asked her out for a drink.'

'How did your date with her end?'

'I don't mind telling you that I thought my luck was in. I was going to invite her back to the *Lazy Fox*. But she said she had to meet someone. She buggered off.'

'Just when you thought you were going to get your leg over, eh?' Gerry gave him what he considered to be a sympathetic look. 'Did she say who she was meeting?'

Jakes shook his head. 'She just said she'd been waiting for a chance to see this person for a while and she was meeting him by the waterfront.'

'She didn't mention a name?'

'Nope.'

'What time did she leave?'

'About nine o'clock.'

Gerry turned to Paul. 'See if we can get hold of any CCTV footage from the waterfront for around nine o'clock on Thursday, will you?'

Paul nodded and hurried from the room.

'You weren't tempted to follow her by any chance?' Gerry said as soon as they were alone. Man to man. 'Like you followed Clare on Sunday night . . . to teach her a lesson.'

257

'Why should I?' he said defensively. 'We left the Angel together then I went straight to the Anchor. There's a bloke who goes in there who owes me money. Since other things were off the menu I thought I'd go and get it back.'

'Was he there?'

'He was as a matter of fact.'

'And he'll back you up, will he?'

Jakes nodded.

'You do this sort of thing often . . . meet a woman and lie about who you are?'

Jakes shrugged. 'It's a game, isn't it? They love it really.'

'Spend much time in Neston?'

'Not been there for years. Why should I?'

Gerry didn't answer. He stood and walked out of the room and when he reached the corridor he put in a call to Paul up in the incident room asking him to show Jakes's photograph to Andrea Washington, the Neston assault victim. She'd been chatted up in a pub by someone fitting Jakes's description. Perhaps there was a link between the two cases after all. While he was talking Guy Kitchener emerged from the other door and stood, arms folded, leaning against the wall, waiting for him to finish.

Gerry ended the call and looked at Guy. 'What do you think?'

'Well, he doesn't like women.'

'I thought he did,' said Gerry, puzzled.

'You told me about how he treated Clare Mayers and now he's going round pretending to be someone he's not. He sees women as prey to be lured into his trap by the bait of this other persona he took on – Adrian the successful business-man. I'd say he despises women.' He paused. 'Maybe he's even afraid of them.'

'Aren't we all?' Gerry muttered, looking at his watch. 'But is he our killer?'

'It's a possibility,' Guy answered. 'But lying to a woman's not a crime. You've no reason to hold him.'

Gerry scowled. He didn't need a psychological profiler to tell him bad news. He knew it only too well himself.


Wesley had been forced to push Ian Petrie's investigation to the back of his mind. Murder took precedence over smuggled Egyptian antiquities, especially murder of a senseless and brutal kind. Ian had just chosen the wrong time to arrive in Tradmouth.

But as soon as he'd learned the circumstances of Raymond Seed's arrest and what had been discovered in his cellar, he'd called Ian and now the man was sitting by Wesley's desk with an eager glow in his eyes. He might be looking tired and older these days, but he still hadn't lost his passion for the chase.

Seed himself had been very anxious to assure them that he had no connection whatsoever with the recent murders. He had already admitted that the story he'd told the school about being ill was a lie: he'd been in London and they could check with his hotel if they liked. And they had checked: he had been in London, and Wesley guessed there was a link between his trip to the capital and the fake Egyptian artefacts found in his cellar.

'Seed's downstairs in the interview room,' Ian said. 'Your DC Johnson's a good lad but I need someone who's au fait with the art world and smuggled antiquities. Will you conduct the interview?'

Wesley sat there for a while fingering a forensic report he'd just received. The last thing he needed now was a distraction. But there were questions he needed to ask.

'I'll check with Gerry but I'm sure it'll be OK.'

'This should tie it all up. There have been quite a few fat payments into Seed's bank account that can't be explained by a part-time teacher's salary. There's also evidence that he's been travelling to Egypt on a regular basis – always in the school holidays, I may add, which should have given us a clue, I suppose. It looks as if he takes the stuff over with him and no doubt he creates a few more sculptures while he's there to conceal the genuine antiquities and paints them up to look identical to the fakes. Clever. After what we found in that cellar, it shouldn't be difficult to get him to make a full confession and once we find out who he was meeting in London, we've cracked the entire organisation.' There was a long pause. 'I'm wondering about that chap Delaware's involvement.'

'He knew Seed's address but he obviously didn't know he couldn't provide him with an alibi because he'd gone off to London.'

'I know you're holding Delaware on another matter and that he's been taken off to hospital but I'd still like to speak to him.'

'Yes, of course.' Wesley hesitated. He knew he had to ask sooner or later so he thought he might as well get it over and done with. 'Something's been worrying me, Ian.'

'What?'

'Last Monday you told me you'd only just arrived in Tradmouth but someone at the hotel said you'd been there since Saturday.'

Ian glanced round. Even though they'd been talking in hushed voices there was still a chance they'd be overheard in the busy incident room. 'Can we go somewhere more private?'

Wesley abandoned his paperwork and led Ian out into the corridor. He found an empty office and switched on the strip light overhead. The two men sat down, facing each other. Wesley noticed that Ian's eyes were bloodshot and his flesh seemed a pallid yellow in the harsh light. He didn't look well.

'Look, Wesley, I'm sorry if I've put you in an awkward situation turning up like this.'

'That's OK. Under normal circumstances we'd have been only too happy to provide assistance in an enquiry like yours. It was just the timing that was a bit awry. With these murders and—'

Ian bowed his head. 'I made assumptions.'

'Come on, Ian, as far as you knew I was stuck here bored rigid in some West Country backwater. You weren't to know I'd be involved in a double murder case.'

Ian gave a weak smile and Wesley saw that his eyes were watering. 'I've been trying to get to the bottom of this Egyptian antiquities scam for a long time. We've known the stuff was coming in and we had the name Ra. Then we caught on to the Neston connection by chance . . . only he wasn't an artist with a studio in Neston as we'd thought – he taught at Neston Grammar.'

'And Ra's short for Raymond.'

'Egyptian antiquities – someone's got a sense of humour.'

'I expect you want to take him back to London with you.'

'Yes. I know you'll probably need him for your murder enquiry so I'll ask a car to come over and pick us up when you've finished with him.'

'You still haven't told me why you didn't tell me you'd spent the weekend in Tradmouth,' Wesley asked after an awkward silence. He looked Ian in the eye. His eyes were green, something he'd never noticed before.

It was a few seconds before Ian answered. 'I just needed time to myself and I felt that a couple of days in a hotel down here would give me the opportunity to consider my options.' He paused, a smile playing on his dry lips. 'I used to come here on holiday as a child, you know. Year in, year out. I caught crabs on the waterfront and watched the boats sailing down the river out to sea. It was a magical place back then. I can understand why you settled here, Wesley, I really can. When this case came up I couldn't resist coming back and I gave myself a couple of days just to . . . I don't know, to gather my thoughts, I suppose.'

'What about?'

There was a long silence. Wesley had a sudden dreadful feeling that the nebulous suspicions that had started to form like unwelcome ghosts in his head were about to be confirmed and he could feel his heart beating faster.

'Whether to opt for treatment or let nature take its course. And whether to tell my ex-wife.'

'You should have told me something was wrong.'

'And have you pussyfooting around feeling sorry for me? Come on, Wesley. I needed your local knowledge to help me clear up this case I've been working on for over a year. I didn't need a nursemaid.'

'I'm sorry,' Wesley said almost in a whisper. He cleared his throat. 'You said ex-wife. I thought you and Sheila were solid as a rock . . .'

Ian gave a bitter laugh. 'Turns out she'd been carrying on with a chartered accountant for years. I'd be on some all-night stakeout or tracking down art thieves and he'd be round at my house . . . in my bed. She finally walked out last year.'

'I'm sorry.'

'Will you stop saying that?' Ian hissed the words and Wesley realised that his sympathy was getting on Ian's nerves.

'It must have hurt . . . Sheila I mean.'

'It did.' His lips formed into a bitter smile. 'Just make sure you don't let your missus think you're putting the job first, Wesley. Your Pam's a good 'un as far as I remember – pretty girl . . . and clever. And you've got a couple of kiddies – don't let them forget what their dad looks like. That's my advice to you – take it or leave it.'

After another long silence Wesley asked the question that had been on his mind since they'd entered the empty office, trying to sound matter-of-fact. 'What exactly is wrong with you?'

'Bowel cancer.'

Wesley tried to search for suitable words but he rejected each comforting phrase that popped into his head as too trite or clichéd.

Eventually it was Ian who spoke. 'Maybe I should tell Sheila.'

'She'd want to know.'

Wesley's mobile phone began to ring and he cursed silently. It wasn't the moment for interruptions. But Ian jerked his head towards the instrument.

'You'd better take that. Could be important.'

Reluctantly Wesley answered the call to find that Ian was right, as Wesley had usually found him to be when they'd worked together. He saw Ian watching him expectantly, his face so pale and drawn that Wesley cursed himself for not noticing that something was wrong before. But he'd been engrossed in his own concerns.

When the call was finished he turned to Ian. 'They've found documents in Seed's place addressed to someone called Ra . . . and they think they've found some artefacts that look genuine in a hidden part of the cellar. But they could be wrong so we'll need an expert to tell us if they're just good forgeries. Do you want to go down and have a chat with Seed?' He felt like a parent offering a treat to a sick child.

'That's what I'm here for.'

'Are you sure you're up to it?'

'Of course I bloody am. Don't treat me like an invalid. I wish I'd never told you now.' Ian sounded annoyed, whether about his former colleague's concern or about the weakness of his own body, Wesley couldn't tell.

Five minutes later they were facing Raymond Seed. He was a slightly-built man in his late thirties whose ponytail emphasised his receding hairline. He wore a faded blue Breton smock and tattered jeans, as though he had chosen to dress in what he imagined was the uniform of an artist.

Wesley was surprised at how co-operative Seed – or Ra as he was known to his associates – had become now that he realised that there was no point in lying any more. But he was insistent on one point. Robert Delaware had given his name as an alibi because they were old friends. Delaware knew absolutely nothing about the antiquity smuggling. Wesley, however, didn't believe a word of it. He suspected that Seed was indulging in a spot of damage limitation: there was no point in them both being prosecuted.

But Wesley had more questions to ask.

'You teach at Neston Grammar, I believe?' he began. 'Do you know a girl called Clare Mayers?'

'Yes, I teach part-time there. Clare's in the sixth form. Art's one of her subjects so I see a lot of her.' His thin face suddenly became solemn. 'I was sorry to hear she's been in hospital. I hope she's all right now.'

264

'She's made a good recovery.' He paused, his eyes fixed on Ra's face. The man looked nervous. Wesley had the two Anubis figures found on the bodies of Analise Sonquist and Isobel Grant in his pocket protected in plastic evidence bags. He took them out and placed them on the table. 'Do you recognise these?'

'May I?'

Wesley nodded and Seed picked them up, turning them over to examine every detail.

Eventually he put them down and pushed them back to Wesley. 'Yes. They're mine. I made them.'

'You had a stall at the craft fair in Tradmouth church hall in January, I believe.'

Seed looked surprised. 'That's right. I sold quite a few of these.'

'Do you make Anubis masks?'

'I have made some for the export market. You found a couple in my cellar, I believe. As Inspector Petrie here will no doubt be only too keen to tell you, anything bulky like a mask is ideal for concealing smaller antiquities for smuggling back into this country to sell on to collectors who don't concern themselves too much with the legality of where things come from.'

'Would someone be able to wear the masks you make?'

'I wouldn't fancy wearing the plaster ones. They'd be far too heavy. If I was making one to wear I'd make it out of papier mâché.'

'I understand you made a papier mâché Anubis mask last autumn?'

'Yes. I teach a girl called Peony White – she's a friend of Clare Mayers. Her mother wanted some masks for a local drama society production. It wasn't just Anubis; I made

Horus the falcon and Apis the bull along with a couple of others – a baboon and a crocodile I think it was. She said they were doing *Cleopatra* – a little ambitious I thought, but there's nothing like aiming high, is there.'

'There certainly isn't. The Anubis mask you made has gone missing from the church hall where it was stored with the other costumes for the production.'

Seed shrugged. 'Nothing to do with me.'

'Just one more thing, Mr Seed. Can you remember who bought your Anubis figures at the craft fair? Do you keep records or . . .?'

Seed smiled and shook his head. 'If you'd ever been to one of those fairs you wouldn't be asking that. We were selling the things for a fiver and, as far as I can recall, everyone paid cash. And I certainly don't remember any names. Sorry.'

'Anybody you can remember who bought a number of them?'

'Several people I should think but I can't remember who. I think I had some nicked as well. Can't trust anybody these days.' He glanced at Ian Petrie who was listening intently.

'Why did Robert Delaware have a key to your flat?'

There was a flicker of alarm in Seed's eyes, swiftly suppressed. 'I must have lent it to him once. I forget why.'

Wesley thought the truth had been too much to expect. He thanked Seed and handed the interview over to Ian Petrie. Ian looked tired but that didn't stop him pressing Seed for the name of his contact in a London auction house. But Seed wasn't talking.

'You were meeting your contact when you were down in London last Tuesday, weren't you?'

'No comment. I'll admit to my part but I'm not going to name names.'

For a self-confessed novice in the criminal world – an art teacher who'd hit on a money-making scam and was now paying the price – Raymond Seed was being remarkably stubborn. But once Ian had taken him back to London, that might change when he learned that co-operation could earn him a lighter sentence.

In the meantime his solicitor managed to get him released on bail. Wesley could tell that Ian wasn't happy about this – and neither was he. He was sure that Seed was lying about his connection with Robert Delaware, but Seed wasn't considered likely to abscond or pose any danger to the public at large so he walked out of Tradmouth police station a free man for the time being.

Wesley told Ian he'd see him later: they'd meet for dinner that evening.

Anubis. He'd almost come to think of himself as the god who looked after the dead. Just as the killer of those four women up near Varley Castle over a hundred years ago had.

At one time he'd feared that the first chosen victim, Clare Mayers, had caught a glimpse of his face, in which case it would have been absolutely necessary to repeat the attempt he'd made at the hospital to silence her for good. But there'd been no announcement, no e-fit flashed across the TV screen, so she'd probably only seen the mask, the shell, and it was likely that he'd panicked for nothing.

So the score was two. Not enough.

He took the mask from its hiding place, running his fingers over its painted curves. He'd seen the original and felt its power, even though it was now almost crumbled to dust. And he'd seen a painting of the embalmer, his identity hidden by an identical mask, bending over the prone corpse, obsidian knife in hand, ready to perform his merciful task.

Now it was his turn to act; to cut into the soft dead flesh, still warm from the life so recently departed.

It was time to get to work again.

# CHAPTER 25

*Each day I went through the motions of normal life. I gave Edward and Victoria their lessons and behaved toward them as I always had because my predicament was none of their doing. How could I blame the children for the sins of the father? Besides, I had become fond of them. Whatever happened, I would not let them suffer for what their father and half-brother had done to me.*

*I was now six months with child and my body had thickened considerably although I felt quite well and strong. However, when I lay alone in that room at night feeling the child move inside my belly, I cried often and prayed that I might die in childbed so that my ordeal of shame and loneliness would end. Sir Frederick made no reference to our former relationship when we met, nor did he make any mention of my condition. It was as though, by ignoring the situation, he hoped it would vanish like a bad dream in the morning.*

*I continued in this silent world of unspoken secrets until one night when Frederick visited my room. I had locked the door but he had obtained another key from the housekeeper's room, sneaking in there and pilfering it when she was otherwise occupied. To my horror he entered unannounced and in my astonishment I let out a small cry and cowered there, protected only by the bed covers, until he switched on the electric light, an innovation of which he was so proud, and the identity of my intruder was revealed. He sat on the chair in the corner of the room and refused to look me in the eye as he spoke. For what he had to say struck me in the heart like a dagger.*

*He had arranged for my baby to be adopted by a family on his estate who had long been childless. I was to give birth in secret at the castle then I was to be given the choice of continuing with my duties as though nothing had happened or of leaving for another post with excellent references.*

*At no time did he mention the love we had shared. And at no time did he ever enquire about my feelings on the matter. I put my hand on my belly and felt my baby moving. Soon it would be torn from my body and given away. If I chose to stay at Varley Castle I would see it from time to time but it would never know me as its mother. Was that situation more painful, I wondered, than the prospect of never seeing my child again in this life?*

# CHAPTER 26

Wesley had planned to have dinner with Ian Petrie at the hotel but when he'd called Pam and told her the news of his former colleague's illness, lowering his voice so that the rest of the incident room couldn't hear, she had insisted that they should eat at home. She'd feel awful, she said, if she didn't make the effort to offer some hospitality in the circumstances. However, as Wesley sat there at his dining table that evening, making conversation, his mind kept returning to the case and that afternoon's developments.

He'd hoped that Andrea Washington would be able to identify Alan Jakes as the man she'd met in the Neston pub before she was attacked. But his luck was out. Andrea was away for the weekend so the confirmation would have to wait.

A couple of DCs had been given the unenviable task of examining all the available CCTV footage for Thursday night from the waterfront area. According to Alan Jakes,

Isobel Grant had arranged to meet someone there. Or it might just have been a ploy to end an unsuccessful date: they only had Jakes's word for it that things had been going well.

Jakes's story about meeting a man who owed him money had been checked out: he'd definitely been there and the debtor had paid up. But Jakes still lacked an alibi for the night of Analise Sonquist's death.

Then there was Robert Delaware. Gerry had looked positively triumphant when Wesley had presented him with the book he'd found in Delaware's flat, *The Art of Mummification*. An art known to the killer of Analise Sonquist and Isobel Grant.

Wesley had called Neston hospital to see when Delaware could be picked up, only to be told that the doctors wanted to keep him in overnight for observation. In spite of Gerry's worries concerning the overtime budget, Wesley had arranged for a constable to stay outside the suspect's room to ensure that he didn't try to make his escape. Wesley had always been the cautious type.

When he felt Pam nudge his arm his mind returned to the present. Ian was sitting opposite him, sipping his coffee appreciatively. The dinner had gone well but Wesley had felt all evening that he had to choose his words carefully. Ian didn't want to be treated as an invalid but Wesley dreaded making a thoughtless remark that would remind his guest anew of his situation.

Ian had seemed appreciative of Pam's hurried culinary offerings – a casserole followed by a fruit salad; something simple after a Saturday spent listening to her mother going on about the animal sanctuary. Ian and Pam had met before, of course, when he'd been Wesley's boss back in London, and they'd got on well. Ian had been good company back then, urbane and knowledgeable. And yet he had always worn his expertise lightly, never using it to make others feel inferior. But that evening he had been subdued, not the man he used to be. And, in spite of everyone's efforts to keep cheerful, Wesley felt sad.

Ian left fairly early and Wesley offered to walk him back to the hotel, reluctant to let him venture back on his own after three glasses of red wine. But Ian was firm in his refusal. It was very kind of Wesley but he'd be fine.

As Wesley stood on the doorstep, watching Ian walk away down the steep road, he felt Pam's arm slip through his.

'How ill is he?' she said softly.

Wesley shut the door, blocking out the cold. 'He says he can't decide whether to go for treatment or not.' He paused. 'There doesn't seem to be any fight left in him.'

'A diagnosis like that can knock you for six, I suppose,' she said. 'But he shouldn't just give up. Has he told Sheila?'

Before Ian's arrival Wesley had told her briefly about the separation, just to ensure that she didn't make a faux pas. 'I don't know.'

'Why did they split up?'

'She went off with someone else.'

After a few seconds Pam spoke. 'I used to like Sheila.'

'He said it was because he spent too much time at work.' He hesitated. 'If you ever thought I was doing that, you'd tell me, wouldn't you? You wouldn't just seek solace elsewhere?'

Pam looked away, avoiding his eyes. 'You've got no choice, have you?' she said quickly. 'You've got to do your job.'

'There have been times when I've felt like asking Neil for a job in the Archaeological Unit.'

She touched his cheek. 'Neil's obsessed with his job. In some ways he's worse than you.'

At that moment the phone started to ring. Wesley stood there, reluctant to pick it up. Then Pam made the decision for him. She answered it herself and, after a brief conversation, she passed it to Wesley. 'It's Gerry. He says it's urgent.'

Wesley stared at the receiver as though it was contaminated. Then eventually he took it from Pam's outstretched hand.

After a few muttered words and broken sentences he put the phone down then he stepped forward and took Pam in his arms. He held her close for a few moments, taking strength from the warmth of her body, before breaking the expectant silence.

'There's been another murder.'

'Where?'

'Over in Neston. Near the hospital.' He kissed the top of her head. 'I've got to go. Sorry.'

She stood on tiptoe and kissed him but he could see the disappointment on her face. Another Saturday night ruined.

At that moment the kitten tore in from the kitchen like a tiny fury and made a vertical ascent of the curtains.

It was a well-known short cut from the hospital area to the town centre. But for a long time various local groups had complained vigorously about the overgrown bushes and the lack of adequate lighting.

Andrea Washington had been assaulted in this very location. But on that occasion she had survived, shaken but unscathed.

The latest victim hadn't been so lucky.

Colin Bowman was already there, making his preliminary examination beneath the floodlights set up around the scene. The CSIs were going about their well-choreographed business dressed in their white suits while uniformed officers guarded the perimeter, ticking off names on clipboards and keeping out anyone who had no valid reason to be there.

Wesley and Gerry had been handed crime-scene suits on their arrival. Gerry was still struggling with his while Wesley was walking slowly and reluctantly towards the hub of the action. He could see a young woman lying sprawled face down on the scrubby grass at the side of the gravel path. She was dressed for a night out in sequined top and tight satin trousers and she looked as though she was asleep. He half hoped she would struggle to her feet and be on her way but his head told him that wasn't going to happen.

'She must have been cold dressed like that,' Wesley said to Colin as he gazed down at the shell that was once a young and living woman.

'They don't feel the cold at that age,' Colin answered with a sigh. 'My daughter's the same.'

Wesley bowed his head, dreading the day when Amelia was old enough to insist on going out dressed provocatively with no inkling of the dangers that lurked around every corner.

Colin addressed the photographer and the officer with a video camera who were recording the scene for posterity. 'I'm going to turn her over now.'

Wesley watched as he rolled the young woman gently onto her back but as soon as he saw her face he looked away. In spite of the cyanosed flesh and the bulging tongue, he could tell that she had been pretty with freckles and bobbed chest-nut hair. 'Any ID?' he asked, trying to keep detached, professional.

'Her bag was found just over there in the bushes. Her name's Naomi Hart. According to the ID card in her bag she's a nurse at Neston Hospital. On her way to a night out by the look of it.'

'Is it the same killer or . . .?'

Colin straightened himself up with a heavy sigh. 'It's our man. The method's identical. A thin ligature around the neck tightened from behind. The only difference is that our killer hasn't had a chance to undress the corpse and make his characteristic mutilations. I think he started to undress her – there are no shoes and the top's unbuttoned – but he was probably disturbed. Someone said you'd made an arrest,' he said as he snapped his bag closed.

Wesley looked round. Gerry was lumbering towards him, face like thunder. 'We had. But our main suspect's in there.' He jerked his head towards the bulk of Neston Hospital. 'He collapsed in the cells and they're keeping him in for observation.'

'He couldn't have got out, could he?' Colin asked.

'There's a constable outside his room.'

'Looks like we were wrong about Delaware,' said Gerry as he stood staring at the dead girl as if he couldn't take his eyes off her contorted face. 'It could be a copycat of course.'

Colin pointed at the dead girl's neck. 'The ligature mark is absolutely identical to the other two. And there's this.' He picked up a plastic bag that was lying in the shadows and handed it to Wesley. 'It was found next to the body.'

Wesley took the bag from him and held it up for Gerry to see. Another model of Anubis.

'And further on down the path somebody's dropped a white sheet . . . neatly folded, so it looks like he was making a run for it when he was disturbed. He didn't have time for his nasty little ritual.'

Wesley watched as Colin stooped to continue his examination of the corpse. If there was any connection between this new victim and the others, they would soon know. Analise and Clare Mayers had been linked by the furtive relationship between Analise's employer Clive Crest and Clare's school friend – or perhaps friend wasn't the word – Vicky Page. No link had been established between Analise and Isobel Grant, although Alan Jakes was the connection between Isobel and Clare.

Or were the attacks random? Had the victims been selected purely because of their availability?

There had now been three deaths – and one failure. If the killer was emulating John Varley's reign of terror, that failure must have rankled.

Wesley rang Pam. He thought he ought to tell her that he'd be fully occupied for the rest of the night.

It was Sunday morning and they'd had no sleep. Wesley found Gerry at his desk, his head buried in his arms, trying to catch a few moments of rest.

As soon as he heard Wesley enter the office he raised his head. His eyes were bloodshot and he looked rough. 'I was trying out a bit of this power napping I keep hearing about. Ruddy useless. Anything new?'

'There's an interesting report from Forensic. The sheets used to wrap the bodies were definitely from the same source. Linen, probably around a hundred years old, give or take a few years . . . and they bear traces of naphthalene.'

'What's that?'

'Mothballs.'

'So they've been kept in a cupboard somewhere.'

'An old person's cupboard. People don't tend to use mothballs nowadays; probably 'cause they stink. The sheets are high-quality linen and all of them bear a laundry mark which has been traced to an old laundry that operated in a village not far from Varley Castle.'

'Varley Castle again.'

'They would have used high-quality linen sheets like that at Varley Castle. Don't you think?' Wesley had Gerry's attention and the DCI was looking considerably more lively now. 'That place must be full of stuff like that. Old Sir George Varley would hardly have been a fully paid-up member of the throw-away society. And Caroline Varley's still in the process of finding out what she's inherited.'

'This all points to Robert Delaware, Wes. He's had the run of that place. Unlike Alan Jakes who wouldn't know King Tut from Queen Victoria.'

'But Delaware didn't leave his hospital bed last night – I checked with the constable on duty outside his room. And Jakes was drinking with some mates who are all swearing blind that he was there all evening.'

The bells of St Margaret's church began to ring and Wesley saw Gerry glance at his watch.

'No choir today,' he muttered regretfully.

'I'm sure they'll manage without you.'

Gerry pulled a face. Wesley knew he enjoyed his Sunday morning sing. It was a habit he'd kept up since his childhood days as a chorister at Liverpool Cathedral, interrupted only by his seafaring years and serious criminal enquiries.

'Have we found any link between this latest victim and the others?'

Gerry shook his head. 'Not yet. We've got people talking to all her friends and family. And it seems she's just broken up with a boyfriend.'

'Suspect?'

'Shouldn't think so. According to her mates it was an amicable separation.'

'What about her friends?'

278

'She was popular with her colleagues and she had a wide circle of friends. Nice girl by all accounts and—'

Before he could finish his sentence the door opened to reveal Guy Kitchener. There were dark circles under his eyes and he looked as though he'd dressed hurriedly and forgotten to drag a comb through his hair. And he looked worried.

'I heard there's been another one in Neston. He's getting bolder.'

Wesley smiled. 'But he chose the wrong location last night. He was disturbed before he could carry out the mutilations.'

Guy entered the room and sat down. 'That could be bad,' he said with a frown. 'He'll probably feel the need to try again.' He swallowed hard. 'Like when Jack the Ripper carried out his double event. He was disturbed before he could mutilate the first victim so he went on to commit another murder the same night. That second murder surpassed all the others in savagery. He'd been thwarted, you see. Like the Whitechapel killer our man feels a sense of entitlement. And that makes him dangerous.'

Wesley caught Gerry's eye. 'So he could have had another go last night and we haven't found the body yet?'

'It would certainly fit psychologically. And the body of Isobel Grant was only found by chance. If the owners of that cottage hadn't turned up she could have lain there in that courtyard for weeks.'

'How can you know how a lunatic's mind works?' Gerry said sharply as he turned his face away.

'He won't consider himself a lunatic, Chief Inspector. There'll be a logic behind his actions – maybe not one that we would understand but it'll make perfect sense to him.'

For a few moments nobody spoke. Then Wesley broke the silence. 'He's not going to stop, is he, Guy?'

'I'm afraid not.' Guy looked down at his watch. 'I'm sorry to be pessimistic but that's my professional opinion. Look, I've got students' work to mark so I'd better be off. Call me if there's anything new, won't you?'

Wesley watched Guy leave. If he was right, there would be more deaths to deal with. More bereaved families to break the worst news of all to. As he sat down opposite Gerry, Rachel hurried in. 'I've just had a PC Smethwick on the phone. He arrived at Neston Hospital to take over from the officer on night duty.' She hesitated. 'He reckons that Delaware could have got out without anyone knowing.'

Wesley twisted round in his seat. 'How?'

'Delaware's in a side ward – a single room. When Smethwick arrived he peeped into the room. Delaware was asleep – or pretending to be – and when Smethwick walked over to the window he saw that it led straight out onto the fire escape. His clothes were in the room so he could have got dressed and got out of the room any time he wanted during the night. The nurse told Smethwick that Delaware's fine – he'll be discharged tomorrow.'

Gerry Heffernan stood up, looming there like a bear about to deliver a blow to a hapless child. 'Didn't anyone notice there was a fire escape outside the room?'

'No. The constable was stationed outside in the corridor and as far as anyone knew Delaware was in there asleep with no way out because it's on the second floor.'

'And nobody thought to check the room?'

Rachel shook her head. 'He could easily have got out, picked up whatever he needed and killed Naomi Hart, couldn't he?'

Gerry slumped in his seat and it groaned under his weight. 'You don't need to say any more, Rach. We've cocked up. I don't suppose a nurse was taking his pulse at the time of the murder?'

'No. He was last checked at nine o'clock.'

'And Naomi Hart was found just outside the hospital,' said Wesley. 'He's our man, Gerry. He's got to be.'

Gerry stood up again. 'We've got to get something concrete on Delaware before he has a chance to do it again. You heard Guy. He's been thwarted so he'll strike again soon. Possibly tonight. He's well enough to be discharged from hospital so I suggest we bring him in again for questioning. And we have to find out how he picked up the sheet and the Anubis figure so all local taxi firms need to be checked – he must be keeping the equipment somewhere we don't know about. And get Forensic to go over his clothing and the hospital room for any link to the murder scene.'

'So we're absolutely sure it's Delaware?' said Rachel.

'Aren't you, Rach?'

'Everything seems to point that way.'

'He knows all about John Varley's killings and he's copied every detail. Who else would know about that? If those sheets do come from the castle he's had plenty of opportunity to help himself. And if he's using that missing mask, the world and his wife and his dog have access to that church hall. He could easily have pinched it.'

'How would he have known it was there?' Wesley asked.

'Maybe he went to the performance of the play, whatever it was called.'

'*I Remember Cleopatra*. Are we discounting Raymond Seed then? He's out on bail.'

Gerry shook his head. 'An antiquities scam is a very different kettle of fish to this kind of murder. Delaware's a loner obsessed with John Varley's killings.'

'He gave Seed as his alibi for the first murder and he had the key to his flat. Seed admits they were friends.'

'But Delaware didn't know Seed was away in London, did he, so they can't be that close. What more do you want from Delaware, Wes? A signed confession?'

Wesley could see the strain on Gerry's face. Because of police incompetence, the possible killer had been able to slip out of his hospital room undetected. Naomi Hart's blood might be on their hands. And Gerry was finding that hard to live with.

'Right,' Gerry said. 'I want everyone who's already been questioned to account for their movements. But that's only a precaution. We need to build a case against Delaware and that starts now.'

'He must be keeping the mask and the sheets somewhere, not to mention the cord he uses to strangle the poor women. We know he doesn't keep these things in his flat on Ford Street and he wouldn't have had time to fetch them from Varley Castle last night so there must be somewhere else we don't know about. A lock-up, for instance, or maybe he has an accomplice.'

'Seed?'

Gerry shook his head and sighed as he leaned back in his chair. He looked tired, probably more from the weight of guilt about being unable to prevent Naomi Hart's death than any lack of sleep. It was a heavy burden to carry. Almost intolerable. Wesley knew how he felt because he felt the same.

The sooner Robert Delaware was back in custody, the better.

On Monday morning Robert Delaware was due to be released from hospital. The doctors had found nothing

282

wrong with him and Wesley wondered whether his collapse had merely been a piece of theatre. Delaware had proved himself to be a liar. But was he an accomplished actor too?

At ten o'clock, after delivering his customary briefing, Gerry Heffernan sat in his glass-fronted office at the edge of the incident room like a controlling fat spider at the centre of a web. From time to time members of the team would hurry into the DCI's office to offer him morsels of information and then he would emerge from his nest to address his underlings, bringing them up to date with each new development. Wesley, sitting at his desk near the hub of activity, saw an expression of grim determination on Gerry's face. Whatever happened, he wasn't going to make another mistake.

Wesley gazed out of the window. It was raining and drops of water chased each other down the glass. He could see the thick grey clouds reflected in the river and the boats covered in their winter tarpaulins, bobbing up and down on its rough and inhospitable surface. It was almost March and soon Tradmouth would emerge from its winter slumber. Around Easter the first visitors of summer would arrive. And with them more crime. But Wesley really couldn't see how things could get any worse.

'Can I have a word?'

Wesley looked up and saw Tom from Scientific Support hovering by his desk. He was a tall, good-looking young man with short hair, intelligent grey eyes and a glowing reputation as a maestro of the computer keyboard. Gerry Heffernan regarded his mysterious talents with the awe afforded to a witch doctor by tribal elders.

Tom took a seat opposite Wesley which suggested that this was no flying visit. 'I spent most of yesterday going through Isobel Grant's computer files,' he began.

Wesley raised his eyebrows. 'I'm impressed by your dedication. I thought you usually went diving on Sundays.'

Tom grinned. 'I do most weekends but the weather was bad and Gerry called in a favour.'

Wesley gave him a conspiratorial smile. 'Understood. He can be very persuasive when he wants to be. Find anything interesting?'

'I did, as a matter of fact. Isobel Grant went in for computer dating and I managed to get names and addresses first thing this morning.' He placed a sheet of paper in front of Wesley. 'They're all there – the men she'd been in contact with. And I've printed out some of her e-mails – the personal ones that could be useful – and I've requested the addresses from the service providers. I'll let you have them as soon as I get them.'

Tom took a sheaf of papers from the laptop case he was nursing on his knee. He selected one and handed it to Wesley. 'You can have a look through them at your leisure but I thought this one sounded interesting. And so is Isobel's reply.'

Wesley took it from him and began to read. The e-mail was from a Gemma Fielding, obviously a friend.

'Izzy, it was good to see you yesterday but for God's sake be careful. The idea of asking him for money is ridiculous and I hope you weren't being serious. I know it must be complete shit living with your mum but there are easier ways of getting a deposit to buy a house. Personally, I'd rather sell my body . . . if anybody would buy it (ha ha). Please tell me you were joking. Don't do anything daft. Love Gemma.'

The reply was printed underneath. It was dated a couple of days before Isobel's murder.

'Don't worry about me – I can take care of myself. And what I told you is definitely not for sharing with anybody . . . even Matt. I wouldn't have said anything if we hadn't had that extra bottle of Chardonnay. In vino veritas, eh? But seriously, swear you won't say a word to anyone. See you on the twenty-sixth. Love, Izzy.'

Wesley looked up. 'We need to talk to Gemma Fielding. While we're waiting for her address I suppose we could e-mail her.'

Tom frowned. 'And if she's the sort of person who doesn't want to talk to the police she might not answer. She might even do a runner.'

Wesley was rather surprised at Tom's jaundiced view of human nature. He had always thought that that level of suspicion was confined to police officers. 'You could be right. Any more interesting e-mails? Any asking someone for money, for instance?'

Tom shook his head and placed the printouts on Wesley's desk. 'They all seem to be from friends – normal stuff about jobs and boyfriends and people they know. She moans a lot about having to live with her mum and Tradmouth's dire social scene. You might find out more from her text messages if you've got her phone.'

'We haven't. The killer took it along with her clothes.'

'I've also looked at her Facebook page but there's nothing there that she wouldn't want to share with the world. It's only that e-mail from Gemma that suggests she might have been involved in something iffy.'

'So if she did ask someone for money, she must have done it over the phone or even to their face.'

'Or sent a letter . . . or maybe she took Gemma's advice

and chickened out.' Tom hesitated. 'She was a teacher, wasn't she?'

Wesley nodded.

'Then she'd probably have had more sense.'

'My mother-in-law's a teacher and she's the stupidest woman I've ever met.'

Tom began to chuckle. 'Point taken.' He stood up. 'I'll let you have those addresses as soon as I get them.'

As Tom hurried off with a satisfied expression on his face Wesley began to leaf through the e-mails on his desk, looking for anything suspicious. Or anything connected with Ancient Egypt. But there was nothing. Just gossip between friends, most of it tedious to anyone who didn't know the people involved. Gemma Fielding was the only person who had written anything out of the ordinary.

Until he'd read her e-mail he'd assumed Isobel Grant was a straightforward young woman, a teacher living with her mother, so keen for love and escape in a small town with a probable dearth of eligible men that she'd accept a date with a stranger – a stranger who turned out to be Alan Jakes. But those few words from Gemma printed in Times New Roman on an A4 sheet of paper had opened up new possibilities: Isobel was planning to ask somebody for money, possibly in an attempt at blackmail. But could that have anything to do with the recent murders? All the indications were that the unfortunate victims had just been in the wrong place at the wrong time.

He walked into Gerry's office and, after clearing a space amongst the clutter of files and forms, he placed Gemma's e-mail and the reply on the desk in front of him.

Gerry's verdict was as he expected. 'If it's some madman who gets a kick out of killing and mutilating young women,

I can't really see that this is relevant, Wes. But follow it up if you want to. You never know your luck.'

'Tom's getting Gemma's details from the service provider.'

'That'll keep him out of mischief.' He sighed heavily. 'It's a pity the murderer took their mobile phones along with their clothes. I wonder what he's done with them?'

'Kept them as souvenirs probably,' Wesley said quietly.

'Or chucked 'em in the river.'

'Maybe. In which case they might be washed up at some point. Unless he weighted them down.'

'He's clever. He'll have weighted them down.' Gerry sounded despondent.

'He's bound to make a mistake sooner or later.'

'If it's Delaware, he's laughing at us.'

'If it's Delaware, we can reel him in any time. He says he's going straight to Varley Castle and Neil'll be there to report if he gets up to anything suspicious. We'll circulate his car number to all patrols so if he makes a move, we'll know about it. And once we have the evidence to charge him, we'll bring him in.'

Wesley remembered the fire escape but hopefully the same mistake wouldn't be repeated. He sifted through the other papers Tom had given him and came across a list of men Isobel Grant had contacted via a dating website. In the excitement of finding the e-mail from Gemma, he'd almost overlooked it. But now he scanned the names and the sight of one in particular made his heart beat a little faster.

He pushed the list towards Gerry. 'These are the names of the men Isobel contacted on the dating website. Recognise anybody?'

Gerry picked up the sheet. 'Well, well. Who's a naughty

solicitor then? I thought Vicky Page would have been enough for any man.'

'And don't forget his wife.'

'I don't think I'll forget Suzie Crest in a hurry.' He continued to examine the list, a wide grin fixed on his face.

'I wonder how much she knows about her husband's extra-marital activities?' Wesley suddenly had a thought. 'What if Isobel met Clive and she asked him for money to keep quiet about his infidelities? That could be what Gemma meant.'

Gerry looked up. 'Put him on our list. And we'd better get statements from the other men too.'

With these new developments and the prospect of questioning Delaware further once he'd been released from hospital, Wesley was trying to feel optimistic . . . even though Guy Kitchener's prediction about another death still lurked at the back of his mind.

Whatever happened, they had to prevent another tragedy.


Neil ended the phone call and stood there for a few moments.

'You OK, Neil?'

He turned and saw that Andrew Beredace had looked up from the papyrus he'd been reading.

'Robert Delaware's out of hospital. He's coming back here and Wes has asked me to let him know when he turns up.'

'Why?'

'It looks like he's a suspect in these murders.' He put his hand to his mouth. 'Oh, shit. Wes told me not to say anything.'

'Well, I'm not going to pass it on,' said Andrew, returning to his papyrus.

But Neil wasn't listening. 'I think he'll try and convince Caroline of his innocence hoping she'll take pity on him and smuggle him out of here like some escaped prisoner of war in the movies.'

'I don't think Caroline's that stupid.'

'People do strange things.' He paused. 'And there's the sheets.'

'Sheets?'

'The bodies were wrapped in linen sheets. A policeman came round asking Caroline questions about them. She said she didn't know exactly what was in the place but the sheets had the same laundry marks as some of the table linen she found in the still room so they might have come from here.'

Andrew focused his eyes on the papyrus again, as though he didn't want to hear. 'This papyrus tells a really interesting story.'

Neil knew when somebody was trying to change the subject but he really didn't mind. 'Does it?'

'It came from the tomb of a court musician in Thebes. It's absolutely fascinating.'

Neil saw a slight smile on Andrew's face: the smile of the keen enthusiast – or maybe the obsessive. 'Don't keep us in suspense.'

Andrew took a deep breath. 'It's what's called an execration text . . . a sort of curse left by her enemies. This one explains what she was supposed to have done. This musician, right . . . she's a beautiful young woman and she has a baby by one of the court officials – a very important man. Anyway, when she has this baby the father denies it's his but he says he'll take it into his household anyway but when it's taken off her it disappears and she accuses the father of killing it. She hangs around and works out a way to get her revenge. She stabs the father and his wife. Then she moves on to the rest of his family because death had become a pleasure to her.' He began to read. '"The carving of their flesh and the spilling of their life blood was sweet as honey."' What do you make of that?' He paused for a second. 'Do you think someone can actually enjoy the act of murder . . . take pleasure in it like food or sex?'

Neil frowned. 'I don't know. Do you?'

But a voice interrupted before Andrew could answer. 'I've just had a call from the police.'

Both men turned round: Caroline was standing in the doorway, one hand resting on the jamb. She looked nervous. Maybe even frightened.

'Was it about Robert? My friend from Tradmouth CID's just called to tell me that he's out of hospital.'

'Why should he tell you that?' she asked sharply, suddenly on her guard.

Neil didn't answer. He'd probably said too much already.

'They want to come here and conduct a thorough search of the castle.' She looked Neil in the eye. 'Robert's not a suspect is he? They said he'll be staying here and he's not supposed to leave the grounds . . . condition of his bail or something.'

'Would you like me to stay tonight?' Neil asked.

'I could stay too,' said Andrew. 'I'll get my things from the pub.'

Caroline nodded. 'Would you? It's not too much trouble?'

'No trouble at all,' said Andrew Beredace with a smile.

Ian Petrie had called twice while Wesley was away from his desk. The message lay there on top of a file containing forensic reports – a reproach for his neglect of his old colleague. But some things couldn't be helped.

He punched out Ian's number. The phone was answered almost immediately.

'I've been trying to get hold of you,' Ian said as soon as he heard Wesley's voice. 'Any idea when I can take Raymond Seed back to London for questioning?'

'Sorry, Ian, it might have to wait. But if you need to question him you can do it here. You know you have our full co-operation.'

There was a long pause. Then Ian spoke again. 'How about a drink after work?'

Wesley looked at his watch. He'd already disappointed Ian once and when he looked at the heap of paperwork on his desk he realised he was going to have to do so again. 'Sorry, Ian, I really can't make it today. Maybe tomorrow. I'll call you.'

He replaced the receiver and looked up to see Paul Johnson standing by his desk.

'There's still no sign of Andrea Washington.'

'We need to confirm that Jakes was the man she met on the night she was attacked. Keep trying.'

Paul nodded. 'Uniform gave Delaware a lift back to Tradmouth to pick up some things then drove him up to Varley Castle. He called in at his flat and stopped by his garage to get something from his car. Trish thought we should have a look to see if he's taken anything away from the flat – or left something incriminating.'

'Trish thought?' Wesley suppressed a smile. Paul and Trish had been carrying on a tentative courtship for years. Gerry had often said he wished they'd just get on with it and make up their minds.

291

'And did you have a look?'

'Just a quick check.'

As if on cue, Trish appeared in the incident room doorway. She was well wrapped up in a brown woollen coat and a striped scarf. She spotted Paul and gave him a shy smile. Nick Tarnaby was lurking behind her like a sulky child trailing after its mother as she entered a room full of formidable aunts.

Trish marched straight over to Wesley's desk. She had a plastic evidence bag in her hand and she placed it in front of him. He looked at the objects inside then he looked up at Trish.

'Anubis,' he said, fingering a pair of painted figures through the plastic. 'Where did you find them?'

'In the cupboard by the fireplace. They weren't there when the place was searched before.'

'So someone must have been in and put them there.'

'Delaware himself, I presume.'

'He didn't have the Anubis figures on him when he left hospital. His things were checked. And he was watched so he didn't have a chance to go anywhere to pick them up.'

'The garage?'

'It was searched and there are no obvious hiding places.'

'The car then. We never searched his car.'

Trish cleared her throat. 'He is the killer, isn't he? There's no doubt now, is there?'

Wesley didn't answer for a few moments. 'There's always doubt, Trish. But he's the best suspect we've got at the moment.'

He looked at the Anubis figures in front of him. 'How many of these things are there?'

Trish shrugged. 'Seed had quite a production line going.

292

Whoever killed those women must have bought quite a supply . . . unless Seed himself is our man.'

'Or our man got hold of them somehow. Someone with links to Seed maybe . . . which includes Delaware. We still don't know what their exact connection is, do we?'

Trish gave a brief half smile. It was all very well, Wesley thought, to indulge in this constant speculation. But what they needed was solid evidence.

Trish turned to go. He watched her cross the room but his thoughts were elsewhere. After a few moments his reverie was disturbed by Rachel Tracey's voice, slightly raised and brimming with excitement.

'I've had someone looking through the CCTV footage of the waterfront on the night Isobel Grant died.' She sounded excited. 'There's something on one of the cameras – the one above the estate agents. Isobel can be seen quite clearly and Jakes is following her at a distance.'

Wesley sat up straight, suddenly attentive. 'And?'

'Then this dark hooded figure comes into view and Jakes scurries off like a scalded cat. There's no way we can get an ID on the figure – can't even tell whether it's a man or a woman but it does seem to be carrying some sort of holdall. It's standing there on the corner by the Harbour Master's office and Isobel stops a few feet away. She seems to say something then the figure disappears down the side road and Isobel follows.'

'And?'

'They both vanish. I've had someone checking other CCTV cameras but they don't appear on any. If you go up that road then along a bit you reach a flight of steps between two shops which leads directly to the back gate of the Buntons' cottage where she was found. If he'd found the gate unlocked, which the Buntons admit it was because the bolt doesn't work properly, and the house in darkness, then he'd have had complete privacy in that courtyard to do whatever he liked undisturbed. Do you want a look at our killer?'

Wesley followed Rachel to the CCTV room. As he walked a few feet behind her he caught a waft of her perfume. Something heavy and sexy. Maybe she was planning an exciting night with Farmer Nigel . . . if she could get off work at a reasonable time, which was unlikely.

They sat together at a chaste distance in the semi-darkness and watched the monochrome image of the dead girl. When Isobel spotted the figure waiting at the corner she seemed to hesitate, almost as though she was a little afraid. Then she straightened her back and strode on boldly, only to disappear down a side street a couple of moments later.

'She's followed him so she must trust him,' said Rachel as she replayed the tape, her eyes fixed on the screen. 'Do you know, I reckon he's about the right height for Delaware.'

'I think he's slimmer.'

'Mmm. It could even be a tall woman. She probably wouldn't have been on her guard with a woman. What do you think?'

As Wesley fixed his eyes on the screen he thought Rachel might have a point.

He put on the mask. It felt secure and the smell of plastic with all its memories excited him. He had seen her face through the eye holes. He had seen the astonishment and the fear as he sneaked up on her and the memory of her terror and her struggling body still aroused him. His more recent planned attempt had been thwarted of course and, with all the publicity about the murders, he'd wondered if he'd ever get a chance to use it again.

He'd chatted her up first in the pub and she'd been impressed by his lies, just as they all were. They were only interested in money . . . in men with a bob or two. Gold-diggers, they used to call them. They needed teaching a lesson. They needed a fright.

Tonight was different. He hadn't used the pub strategy but instead he'd come out on the off chance: it was always wise to change your MO and keep one step ahead of the police. As he watched and waited he longed to feel that power again. Women were two-faced treacherous bitches . . . like his mother was when she abandoned him and his dad to go off with some rich bloke.

Suddenly he spotted a woman in the pub doorway, miniskirted and tottering unsteadily in high heels like a baby gazelle. She was dressed in a short dark coat with a small bag slung over her left shoulder. It looked as though his luck was in.

He followed her some way behind, head bowed so she wouldn't see the mask if she turned round. And once they neared the castle, he quickened his pace and started to gain on her, anticipating the terror on her face and the pleading look in her eyes when she finally realised what was happening.

He had almost drawn level with her. He had already unzipped his trousers and he wondered whether he'd have the chance to take things further this time. He could feel adrenaline pumping around his body as he grabbed at her coat and clung on tightly to the cloth. He could smell her perfume mingled with dread and an overwhelming sense of power flooded through him. But he still wasn't sure if he could manage to take the situation to the conclusion he longed for. With the Andrea woman he had lost the courage and with that stupid vacuous bitch, Izzy, another bloke had turned up to scupper his plans. But even if he didn't have the bottle to do what he longed to do, he could still enjoy this new woman's fear.

He clamped one arm tight around her waist and with his free hand he began to fumble with the buttons of her coat, searching for an entrance to the bare flesh beneath. Then the breath was knocked out of him as an elbow struck hard into his ribs. It happened so fast, the reversal of his world when the weak became the strong and the strong weak, and he felt a sudden rush of pain as his intended victim pushed his arm up his back and he collapsed helpless to his knees.

His heart was pounding as the pretty young woman tore off the mask and put her face close to his. 'I'm DC Dawkins, Neston police. You're nicked.'

The would-be attacker bowed his head as he abandoned all thoughts of escape.

# CHAPTER 27

*Secrecy. It was essential, I was told, to avoid a scandal. And only two people, apart from myself, were to know the truth: Sir Frederick himself and Mrs Ball, the housekeeper who had worked at the castle since it had been built by Sir Frederick's father.*

*Mrs Ball was a woman of few words. She had a reputation for harshness amongst the younger staff and I had no particular liking for her. However, she would attend me in childbed because it was said that she had experience of such matters, having attended her own niece when she had borne an illegitimate child by a footman some years ago. She took great delight in telling me that on that occasion the baby had died. What a blessing it would be for me if my baby were to suffer a similar misfortune, she whispered to me when we were alone. I was too shocked to make a reply but her words struck fear into my heart. What if Sir Frederick had given instruction that, for the avoidance of a scandal, the child should not be permitted to live?*

*I was nearing my time now and my belly was large so there was no concealing my condition. I had been relieved of my duties and a retired* schoolmistress from a nearby village had been engaged to teach Edward and Victoria in my absence. The children had been told that I was unwell and that I was not to be disturbed under any circumstances. I imagined that they were missing me and I longed to reassure them that I was well and would not die as their mama had done. Or would I? Childbirth was hazardous, especially under the supervision of a midwife such as Mrs Ball.

One night when the household was asleep I crept down to Sir Frederick's little museum of antiquities. There were things there I wanted to see, things that gave me comfort. There was a birthing stool used by women in Ancient Egypt to aid them in labour. If I'd possessed the courage, I would have asked to use it. And there were papyri there in the collection with prayers to the cat goddess Bastet who was said to help women in childbed. I felt I would be in need of her care.

How my father would have chided me for placing my trust in false gods rather than the true God. I did not know then whether he was right or wrong. I merely knew that I would need some help and the graceful statue of Bastet was there looking down on me in that chamber of shadows and corpses lit only by the candle I had brought from my bedside. And next to Bastet was the image of Anubis – the god who would prepare my body for the afterlife if the worst happened.

# CHAPTER 28

As soon as Gerry Heffernan arrived in the incident room on that damp Tuesday morning he received a call from Neston CID. Wesley saw a satisfied smile spread across the DCI's face as he put the receiver down. The news, whatever it was, was good.

He emerged from his office and called for attention. He was the bearer of glad tidings. The extra patrols put on in Neston after Naomi Hart's death had borne fruit. A man had been caught by an undercover officer. He'd followed her and jumped her near the castle and he got the shock of his life when she said who she was.

Gerry hurried off to break the news to CS Nutter, leaving Wesley to make the call to DI Tony Wilshire, his counterpart in Neston.

'Hi, Tony. I believe congratulations are in order.'

'Yeah. Our man's being interviewed as we speak.'

'You know what I'm going to ask, don't you, Tony? Who is he and could he be our killer?'

'Actually, Wesley, he's already on your radar. He met your second murder victim on the night she died. Alan Jakes is his name – lives in Tradmouth and just comes to Neston for his jollies; doesn't want to piss in his own back yard, I presume. He's admitted to the assault on Andrea Washington but he's claiming that he never harmed anyone and that he only did it for the excitement.'

'Why the mask?'

'It's Goofy, the cartoon dog. He says he found it on a yacht he was working on and it seemed like a handy way to conceal his identity. He's being very co-operative. Positively chatty. We'll have finished questioning him by lunchtime so feel free to come and get him.'

As Wesley put the phone down Gerry re-entered the office with a beaming smile on his face. Nutter obviously hadn't given him any trouble. After Wesley outlined what Tony had told him, Gerry sat down heavily and rubbed his hands together. 'I'll ask Guy to observe our interview with Jakes.'

'You've seen the CCTV, Gerry. He was telling the truth about Isobel Grant meeting someone.'

Gerry looked up. 'But what if he carried on watching her out of sight of the camera? He might have taken a short cut and followed her when she parted from this other bloke. What are the odds of there being two attackers of young women operating at the same time in a ten-mile radius?'

'I take your point but I reckon Jakes just gets his kicks out of scaring them. Our man strangles and mutilates them.'

'Maybe Jakes would have finished the job with the others but something stopped him.'

Wesley had to acknowledge that the DCI might have a point. 'What about his alibis?'

'We've only got the word of his mates from the pub and they could be lying for him.'

'Mind you, he doesn't strike me as the type to take much of an interest in Egyptology.'

Gerry pulled a face. 'You've got a point there, Wes. We mustn't forget Robert Delaware. I think we should bring him in again . . . apply some pressure.'

'He's up at the castle keeping a low profile. Neil says he's been spending all his time in his room working on the biography he's writing.' He noticed a stain on the DCI's tie . . . tomato ketchup probably. 'When's Joyce back?'

'Not till the weekend.'

Wesley gave him an understanding look. Then he made a decision. 'Ian Petrie's not well.'

Gerry frowned. 'Sorry to hear that. What's wrong?'

When Wesley told him, Gerry sat there quite still for a few moments. 'Poor sod,' he said eventually, bowing his head.

'I said I'd try and meet him for lunch today.'

'Yeah, Wes. You do that.' He stood up. 'And we need to speak to Clive Crest about that dating website too.' He pretended to examine the debris on his desk. 'I'll send someone over this morning to have a word.'

'I'd like to speak to him myself. There's something about him . . .'

Gerry nodded his assent and looked at his watch. 'About time I addressed the troops. What time can we expect Alan Jakes?'

'Neston are sending him round in a car as soon as they've finished with him. Might be early afternoon.'

Wesley left the office. He'd ring Neil later to check up on

Delaware. But in the meantime Clive Crest was on his mind. The priapic solicitor seemed to know a large number of young women. And he wondered if Naomi Hart was amongst them.

Clive Crest had just called his secretary to say he wouldn't be arriving at the office till after lunch. Suzie had insisted on going into work so he'd been left holding the baby who was, at present, fast asleep in his cot. The agency had told them that it might be some time before they could procure a replacement for Analise. Suzie was treating her murder as a major inconvenience; she hadn't even shown Analise's sister much sympathy when she arrived on their doorstep wanting to retrieve the dead girl's belongings. Sometimes Clive wondered why he'd ever thought that marrying Suzie was a good idea. There were times when her self-absorption made him cringe.

*Carpe diem* had always been one of Clive's favourite sayings – he used it many times on social occasions to give the impression that his grasp of Latin was better than it actually was – so he decided to seize that particular day and take advantage of Suzie's absence. There was something he needed to do while she wasn't there – something he didn't want her to know about.

Their two garages were built beneath the house which, like many Tradmouth houses, clung to the hillside overlooking the river. A steep flight of steps led up to the front door and the garages – one for his BMW and one for Suzie's SUV – were at street level, carved out of the rock beneath the garden. Clive shut the front door and made his way down the steps.

When he reached the garage door and twisted the handle, it yielded to his touch because the lock was broken; it was

302

one of those jobs he kept putting off. The door flew up and he edged his way gingerly around his car, making for the large space at the rear. This was Clive's own space, oil-scented and dirty; the only space where Suzie would never think to look. It was where he kept his treasures.

He shifted an empty oil drum to one side and crouched down. Behind the drum was a battered plywood cupboard. He tugged open the ill-fitting door and reached inside, feeling for the envelope he knew was there. His fingers made contact and he pulled it out, holding his breath.

Analise's death and the subsequent police intrusion had marred things for the moment, but Clive harboured hopes that once the fuss had died down he and Vicky might be able to take up where they'd left off. He missed their snatched time together. He missed her young body and the pleasure she gave him. And he missed her laughter – even though most of it was cruel.

He knew that Vicky Page wasn't a nice person. She teased him about his thinning hair and mocked his scrawny physique but that hardly seemed to matter when every encounter with her made his whole body tingle with excitement. He pulled the photographs out of the envelope, moistening his lips as he stared at the glossy image of the young naked girl. She had told him to take the pictures, an act that had caused her great amusement. Vicky always told, never asked. Then there were the pictures of them both, bare limbs entwined, taken with a timer. She said she'd kept a set of those . . . in case they ever came in useful. These words had made Clive uncomfortable and the realisation that she possessed the means to blackmail him one day had crawled across his mind. But he'd pushed that thought from his head. Vicky might be short on sexual morals and scathing about her friends but he was sure – at least he hoped – that she'd never do anything illegal like that. Besides, one day she'd go off to university and abandon him without a second thought. To her, their relationship was an amusement, a rebellion. But to him it was a window into a different, thrilling world. A glimpse of his own personal paradise.

He returned the photographs carefully to their hiding place, wondering what he would do if Vicky ever threatened to show those pictures to Suzie; if she ever saw him as an easy way of financing her university years. It wasn't something he liked to think about but he knew it was a vague possibility – an unexploded bomb, sitting buried deep beneath the comfortable edifice of his life.

When he looked at his watch he realised that he'd already been there ten minutes with his forbidden pleasure and that there was a risk that Alexander might wake up and start crying. He closed the cupboard door and he had just shifted the oil drum back, careful to line it up exactly with the circular mark it had left on the concrete floor, when something caught his eye. He'd been so engrossed in those intimate memories of Vicky that he hadn't noticed the black bin bag standing on the grey metal shelving, pushed between half-empty paint pots and defunct domestic appliances.

He reached out to grab it and as his hand made contact, it fell to the floor and its contents spilled out onto the cold concrete. He recognised the jacket and pink sweater at once because he'd seen Analise wearing them so many times. Squatting down beside them he reached for the length of garden cane that stood in the corner and began to turn the things over. Beneath the outer clothes lay Analise's underwear – faded pink bra and matching lacy pants – her socks and scarf. Even her canvas shoulder bag was there.

Clive threw down the cane and stood up, staring at the things as though he feared they'd explode in his face at any moment. Eventually he took a deep calming breath and braced himself before donning a pair of unused gardening gloves and stuffing everything back in the bin bag, reopening his secret cupboard and throwing the lot inside.

Then he heard the unexpected sound of the adjacent garage door opening. A loud grating sound. Unmistakable. Suzie was back.

Clive's heart was racing as he hurried out of his garage, an artificial smile fixed to his lips. They emerged from their respective garages at the same time, almost as though it had been choreographed, and as soon as Suzie saw him she gave a scowl of welcome.

'I was just getting something from the car,' he gushed. 'Alex is fast asleep upstairs; he's quite safe.'

Suzie said nothing as she made for the steps leading up to the house. He let her go ahead. It was always his lot to follow behind.

When they reached the front door he heard a car roll to a halt down on the road. He looked round and when he saw that it was a police car, he felt a little sick.

'Police,' Suzie muttered, her hand poised to unlock the door. 'What do they want now?' She looked at Clive accusingly.

He clenched his fists and tried to look casual. If she noticed his fear, so would the police.

They watched the tall plain-clothes policeman climb the steps and stride towards them up the sloping garden path. A dark-haired young woman walked behind him. They looked at ease with each other, almost as if they were lovers, Clive thought.

They introduced themselves as DC Paul Johnson and DC

Trish Walton and they needed a word with Mr Crest in private. And while they were there, would he mind if they made another search of the premises?

Suzie opened the front door wide. 'Help yourselves,' Clive heard her say. 'We've got nothing to hide.'

Clive swallowed hard and attempted to smile.

Wesley looked up and saw Gerry standing there.

'Any word on Delaware at Varley Castle?'

'I spoke to Neil ten minutes ago. He and Andrew Beredace have decided to sleep there. I think Neil's a bit worried about Caroline Varley.'

'So he should be if Delaware's our man.'

'We don't know for certain that he left that hospital room. Someone could have planted those Anubis figures in his flat. In fact I don't see how Delaware could have put them there.'

'He's clever, Wes. And don't forget, he knows all about those old murders. Every last nasty little detail.'

'All our evidence is circumstantial.'

'If it wasn't he'd be down in the cells.'

'Anything new from Forensic about the clothes he was wearing when he was taken to hospital?'

'There's nothing to connect him with the crime scene.'

'At least it looks as though Guy Kitchener was wrong about the double event. That's one blessing.'

'Mmm. Unless we haven't found the body yet.'

They were interrupted by the sudden droning of Gerry's phone. He picked up the receiver and, after a short conversation, he looked at Wesley, a triumphant expression on his face.

'That was Paul. He asked Clive Crest about his contact with Isobel Grant over the Internet. Crest denied that he'd ever met her.'

'Surprise, surprise.'

'And they've had a look round Crest's garage.'

'I thought that had already been done?'

'Apparently not. The garage is well away from the house so it got left out of the initial search. I'll have to have words with someone,' he added ominously. Then he paused and Wesley knew that he was about to deliver a dramatic punch line. 'Trish found a bin bag hidden in a cupboard. It was full of the clothes Analise was wearing on the night she died and her bag and mobile phone were there too.'

'I take it they're bringing Crest in?'

Gerry nodded. 'He's on his way.' He paused. 'You know what the trouble is, Wes? We've got too many suspects here.'

'And now we can add Clive Crest to our list,' Wesley said quietly. 'I never really had him down as a serious contender but he knew Analise, he'd been in touch with Isobel via the dating website and he's got no firm alibi for the attack on Clare Mayers. As for the murder of Naomi Hart, his wife was out and I wouldn't put it past him to have left the baby alone. I take it Paul and Trish didn't find that missing mask on the premises?'

Gerry shook his head. 'We can't have everything.'

'We need to ask Suzie Crest if her husband has any connection with Varley Castle . . . or if he's been showing any interest in hundred-year-old Dartmoor ripper murders.'

'I'll leave that to you, Wes. That woman scares the life out of me.'

The phone on Gerry's desk rang and he picked it up. After a brief conversation he looked up at Wesley. 'That was Neston. They're sending Jakes over in a patrol car. He should be here in ten minutes.'

*

Wesley placed the Goofy mask on the table between him and Alan Jakes. The comic Disney dog bore no resemblance whatsoever to a jackal-headed god who presided over the embalming of corpses. And Jakes's claim that he found the mask on board a boat and hit on the idea of using it to hide his identity while he attempted to assault women seemed plausible.

However, Guy Kitchener was observing the interview and he might have different ideas.

As Jakes had been caught in the act, co-operation was his only sensible option. And when asked about Isobel Grant, he stuck to the story he'd already told them.

The *Lazy Fox* had been searched earlier but nothing incriminating had been found. Wesley had been half hoping that Isobel Grant's clothes and bag would be found stuffed away in the cabin but those hopes had come to nothing.

It wasn't until the interview was almost over and Wesley had given up hope of learning anything new that Jakes came up with something unexpected.

'I might be a naughty boy, Mr Peterson,' he said. 'But I'm not a murderer. I never really hurt anyone, did I?'

'You scared the living daylights out of Andrea Washington . . . and Clare Mayers.' Wesley was growing sick of the man's self-righteousness.

'Look, I wasn't the one who tried to strangle Clare. It's not my style. But I saw him. And on the night that nurse was killed I was out in Neston and I saw him again.'

Wesley sat up straight, all attention. 'Go on.'

'I was walking near to where she was found. Nurses sometimes use it as a short cut so I thought I might try my luck and see if one of them fancied a drink after work – chance encounter, if you know what I mean.'

'So what happened?'

'I'd just arrived there – I was going to hang round by the path and pretend I'd lost my puppy – animals are always a sound bet. Anyway, I heard this sound . . . like a cry. Then I tripped over something and I think I swore. I made a noise anyway and then I heard a rustling – must have been about twenty feet away – and this bloke burst out of the bushes and hurtled right past me.'

'Can you describe him?'

'Yeah. He had this head on like the bloke I'd seen with Clare. And he was carrying a holdall – plain black, no logo before you ask. He ran down the path towards the car park like the hounds of hell were after him and I made myself scarce – I wasn't going to hang around, I can tell you.' He hesitated. 'Then I heard they'd found that dead girl near there. Well, it must have been the murderer, mustn't it? I reckon I must have scared him off.'

'Why didn't you tell us this before?' Wesley asked.

'I'm telling you now, aren't I?'

'Is there anything else?'

Jakes looked him in the eye. 'He took his mask off while he was running. If I'd seen his face, you'd be interested then, wouldn't you?'

Wesley's patience was wearing thin. 'If you know something, I strongly advise you to tell me now.'

'I'll think about it . . . if I'm granted bail,' Jakes said with an infuriating grin.

'Dream on,' said Wesley under his breath. There was no way they'd risk Jakes doing another vanishing act.

'OK, I didn't see his face. He was running away from me and it was dark.' The grin returned. 'But it was worth a try, wasn't it?'

When the prisoner had been taken out, Wesley made his way to the room next door where Guy had been observing through the two-way mirror.

'What do you think?' he asked.

Guy shook his head. 'I wouldn't bet on his story being true. He's playing with you, Wesley. He thinks if he pretends to co-operate with the police the judge might go easy on him. He's a chancer and, to be honest, I wouldn't believe him if he said water was wet.' He glanced at his watch. 'I'm sorry, but I'll be away for a couple of days. Conference in London. I'll be back on Thursday night. I'll call you then to see if there have been any new developments.'

'I'm sure we'll manage without you till then,' said Wesley, suddenly wondering if his words were true. Guy was proving more useful to them than he'd imagined. 'We're having Clive Crest brought in. Do you have to go at once or . . .?'

'I'm afraid so. I've got a train to catch. But I'd watch Crest carefully if I were you. He's intelligent and resourceful and he'll know you're trying to catch him out.'

There had been three deaths. In 1903 there had been four and the pattern had to be adhered to. Not too strictly, of course. There was room for a little pleasure. Maybe even room to exceed the original killer's score.

The jackal mask sat on the table and the killer picked it up. Papier mâché. So light, so easy to move around in, and the large eye holes meant that there was a good field of vision. Good for watching every twitch of their muscles and the terror on their contorted faces as they died. The killer slid the drawer open and took out the obsidian knife; honed and razor-sharp so that it could cut smoothly through newly dead flesh. As it gleamed shiny black in the light of the table

310

lamp the killer examined it and smiled. It had been cleaned after each killing, of course, just as it would have been cleaned and cared for when it was first used three thousand years ago.

The killer stood up. There was no point in delaying now. The next victim had been selected. It was just a matter of seizing the opportunity when it came along.

# CHAPTER 29

*I was quite unprepared for the pain, as women have been from the time of the Pharaohs and before. Mrs Ball chided me when I cried out, saying that my howlings as she called them would disturb and frighten Master Edward and Miss Victoria. And so I tried my very best to make no sound and endure my agonies in silence. For I had no wish to harm those two children who had shown me nothing but love and obedience. My own child, I thought, would be their half-sibling and was bound to possess their sweetness. Then I thought of John and prayed that no trace of his vile nature would taint this flesh of my flesh who was about to make his appearance in the world.*

*Sir Frederick, I was told, was away from the house. I would not be able to present him with his child and rely on his finer paternal feelings. I did not realise until afterwards that his absence was deliberate. Mrs Ball said that he would return when the business was over. John Varley, I was told, was at home and he had instructions to deal with any awkwardness that arose. Those words chilled my heart. Sir Frederick's eldest son was my enemy and I could count on no sympathy from him.*

*I will not describe how I laboured to bring forth my son – for it was a boy, a perfect boy of such wondrous beauty that my heart was filled with the most indescribable love. I held him close as Mrs Ball cut the cord that had bound him to me but then I felt her wrest his tiny body from my arms.*

*'I am to take him,' she said. 'Sir Frederick will not have the little bastard in the house. He is to go to his mother.'*

*'But I am his mother,' I sobbed.*

*'You are nothing to him. You never will be.'*

*I tried to grasp my baby's small body, my heart breaking as I listened to his urgent cries.*

*But Mrs Ball held on tight to him as she struck me in the face.*

# CHAPTER 30

As Clive Crest sat in the interview room, Wesley could see a bead of sweat form on his forehead and trickle down his pale face. He wiped it away with the back of his hand and sniffed.

The solicitor who sat by his side was the partner in his practice who dealt with criminal law. As the man was a friend of the suspect, he was more vociferous in his defence than the usual duty solicitor. And he was beginning to get on Wesley's nerves.

'Can you explain how the clothes Analise Sonquist wore on the night she died came to be hidden in your garage?' He tilted his head to one side expectantly, aware of Gerry fidgeting by his side, seething with unasked questions. But he knew that with Crest's solicitor watching like a cat at a mouse hole, it was up to him to curb the boss's enthusiasm.

'I'm sure they weren't there on Sunday. Somebody must have planted them there. The lock on the garage door doesn't work. I've been meaning to get it fixed for some time

314

but it's just one of those jobs that doesn't get done.' He looked at Wesley, man to man. 'You know how it is when you're busy at work.'

'But that still doesn't explain why the killer left them in the very place where you hid those photographs.' He glanced at the solicitor by Crest's side. He was a large man with heavy jowls and, at the mention of photographs, his small eyes had suddenly become alert, as though sensing an interesting revelation was about to be made about his colleague.

Crest blustered. 'The garage is the obvious place to hide anything. It's accessible from the road and you can't see the door from the house.'

'Perhaps the killer knows where you hid the photos of you and Vicky Page. Perhaps he knows you well. Perhaps he knows all your most intimate secrets.'

'Look, anybody can get into that garage.' He straightened his back. 'I didn't kill Analise but the killer obviously knows where she lived. Which means she must have been the target: it couldn't have been a random attack. Why aren't you out interviewing her friends? Or that artist she was involved with . . . Geoff Dudgeon? Why are you wasting time with me?'

Wesley caught Gerry's eye. Clive Crest had a point. On the night of her murder she was supposed to meet Geoffrey Dudgeon. And they only had his word for it that he never turned up – and his wife's of course, but she wouldn't be the first wife to lie for her husband, and she might even have made the necessary phone calls to provide him with an alibi. She'd given him alibis for the other deaths as well. A constant woman.

'Have you ever been to Varley Castle, Mr Crest?'

Crest looked puzzled. 'No. Why?'

'You have no reason to detain my client.' The solicitor spoke in a confident drawl. 'I suggest you release him at once before I make a formal complaint to your superiors.'

'Very well,' said Gerry, unusually subdued. 'But don't leave town, will you, Mr Crest? We'll need to talk to you again.'

Clive Crest and his solicitor stood up as one. They thought they'd won. Wesley knew their victory might be temporary. But from the expression of disappointment on Gerry's face, he obviously didn't share his optimism.

'He's got away with it,' Gerry said as soon as Crest and his colleague had been ushered from the room.

'Well, if he's telling the truth and they weren't there on Sunday, I don't see how Robert Delaware could have put them there.'

'But is he telling the truth?'

Wesley had to concede that Gerry was right. There was no reason to believe that Crest hadn't been lying.

Gerry turned to look at him. 'All our suspects seem to be slipping through our fingers like oiled eels.'

In Wesley's opinion Gerry probably had the situation spot on.


Caroline Varley tipped up the electric kettle and watched as the steaming water flowed out of the spout into the two colourful mugs lined up on the old wooden worktop. Then she waited, watching clouds of mahogany-brown seep from the tea bags that floated to the top of each mug like corpses borne up on the surface of a river.

She fished the bags out with a teaspoon, her thoughts on Robert Delaware. She had asked herself over and over again, when she lay awake in the small hours of the morning, what she actually knew about him. Shortly after she'd moved into the castle he'd written to her outlining his proposal for a biography of Sir Frederick. He'd named other books he'd written and invited her to contact his publisher for a reference.

But she hadn't done it: she'd taken him on trust; invited him into her life and given him a room in the castle, albeit in the servants' quarters, at his own suggestion. She realised it had been foolish but she had hated the idea of being alone in that vast place. Any company was better than none. She longed for the day when the National Trust took over the responsibility and filled the place full of staff and visitors and life.

She placed the mugs on a tray. Neil Watson was on his own up in Sir Frederick's Egyptian room, helping to catalogue each item, Andrew having gone over to Exeter some time ago to meet someone from the National Trust to make an interim report on the collection. She presumed Robert was up in his room but she couldn't be sure. He had avoided her since his return and he could be anywhere. She hardly liked to think about it.

When she opened the fridge and saw that there was no milk her heart sank as it meant a drive to the village shop two miles away. She looked at her watch: if she hurried the shop would still be open. There was no need to tell Neil where she was going because she would only be fifteen minutes or so.

After locking the back door behind her, she dashed into the courtyard and started the car. It was drizzling again and she flicked the windscreen wipers to intermittent before steering the vehicle down the drive, slowly, in an attempt to avoid the potholes in the old tarmac.

The light was fading and she was about to switch on the

headlights when she saw a familiar figure moving through the trees at the edge of the drive. Robert Delaware. As he disappeared into the wood, she brought the car to a slow halt, wondering where he was heading.

Her curiosity made her forget her misgivings. Besides, she had her mobile phone with her and Neil was just a few hundred yards away. She climbed out of the car, shutting the door as quietly as she could, and began to follow Delaware through the trees, breathing in the scent of damp vegetation, glad that she was wearing old and sensible shoes. She could hear twigs cracking somewhere ahead and she knew she was getting closer. Then she saw him and she hung back; she didn't want him to spot her. Soon he came to the edge of the woodland and Caroline stood in the shelter of an ancient oak, watching him as he strode across a field. There was nothing furtive about his movements – but then he had no idea he was being watched. In the gathering dusk Caroline could make out a small stone building at the far side of the field and she realised that it was an unoccupied, semiderelict cottage on the edge of the estate that she had visited as a child when she'd been in the habit of exploring the grounds. Since her return she had been so preoccupied that she had almost forgotten its existence. Delaware made straight for the crumbling building, hurried up the overgrown path and pushed the front door open.

After a few moments Caroline saw a light in the window – the flickering golden glow of an old-fashioned oil lamp. She left the shelter of the trees and crossed the field to the cottage, the wet grass soaking the bottoms of her trousers. She tiptoed up to the window and when she peeped inside she could see Delaware in the small shabby room. And it seemed he had company.

He was bending over a painted Egyptian sarcophagus, open to reveal a grey bandaged mummy, while all around him the room was packed with what looked like the entire contents of an Egyptian tomb. Statues, models of boats and chariots, Canopic jars. The lot.

She stepped out of sight with her back pressed against the damp cottage wall, considering her options. Then she took her mobile from her bag and speed-dialled Neil's number.

But before she could get any reply she heard the front door scrape open and the phone slipped out of her hands and landed on the muddy ground.

Analise Sonquist's newly discovered mobile phone had been bagged up and sent off for forensic examination. All the calls she made and received were to be itemised. It was just possible that they might reveal her killer's identity. But Wesley wasn't getting his hopes up.

Gerry was hoping for evidence, however tenuous, that Analise had been in touch with Robert Delaware. But first they needed to build the case against him so that the courts wouldn't allow him to wriggle from their grasp.

Wesley sat at his desk turning his pen over and over in his fingers. They were overwhelmed by evidence against a number of suspects, some solid, most circumstantial. But it was Robert Delaware who most interested him at that moment. Delaware had lied about alibis and Delaware knew all about the women John Varley had killed and mutilated back at the start of the twentieth century.

His phone started to ring and he picked up the receiver, hoping for good news. They were due some luck. When the call ended he hurried to Gerry's office.

'Caroline Varley's disappeared. She called Neil's phone

but she was cut off before she could say anything. As far as he knew she was down in the kitchen making a cup of tea. The tea was there but no Caroline. He went outside and found her car abandoned halfway down the drive. He's called the local police.'

'Where's Delaware?'

'He's gone as well. We'd better pull out all the stops. Road blocks?'

Gerry nodded. 'Better safe than sorry.'

Pam left school at five. After putting her plastic crate full of files and children's books into the car boot, she looked at her watch. Someone at school had said the man responsible for the Neston assaults had been arrested. She'd been tempted to ring Wesley to ask if it was true. But she hadn't had time.

Della had met the children from school, taking them to the sanctuary in Hugford where Pam was supposed to meet them and take them home. But as Pam was about to leave work the headmistress had cornered her and she'd been forced to listen politely as her boss waffled on about paper-work and the latest government initiative. When she'd managed to escape she realised she was running late but when she'd tried to call Della's mobile there was no answer. She had the number of the sanctuary but again there was no reply so she'd left a message on Mary's answering machine to say she was on her way. At least Mary Kitchener's place was keeping Della out of mischief, she thought. Volunteering to work with rescued animals was a far more suitable occupation for a woman of Della's years than some of her former pastimes. Besides, Michael and Amelia were enthralled with the creatures and helping to care for them would give them a sense of responsibility. The place was good news all round.

The short journey to Hugford involved navigating down several single-track country lanes in the half light before darkness fell. As Pam turned onto the road where the first Anubis attack had taken place – the one the girl had survived – she put her foot down, checking her rear-view mirror for following cars. But the road was clear behind her.

She parked up on the grass verge opposite the sanctuary. Wesley had told her that the first victim, the girl called Clare, lived next door to Mary's place. She could see a light inside the cottage and she wondered how the attack had affected the girl. Was she cowering inside, afraid of every sound? Or was Clare made of stronger stuff? Maybe she'd ask Wesley how she was getting on.

She walked the few yards to Mary's front door and rang the bell. After a few moments the door opened to reveal a smiling Mary dressed in her habitual checked shirt and padded gilet.

'I'm sorry, you've just missed Della and the children. She's taken them out for a burger.'

Pam cursed silently. 'I was supposed to meet them here. I was delayed at work so I left a message on your answering machine.'

Mary looked sympathetic. 'Oh, I am sorry – I haven't checked it for ages.' She hesitated. 'Won't you come in? Would you like a cup of tea?'

As Pam stepped into the hallway she noticed a strong aroma of dogs hanging in the air. This time Mary led her into a back room she hadn't seen before. There was a fire burning in the grate and the room resembled a cosy Victorian parlour crammed with souvenirs and photographs, all protected by a thin veil of dust. After a day spent on her feet in front of a class, Pam longed to sit down but every available chair was cluttered with the detritus of Mary's life so she moved slowly around the room, examining the pictures and photographs on the walls, tightly packed together so that the yellowing wallpaper was barely visible.

There were several pictures of Guy at various stages of development. And there were similar pictures of a younger boy, blond and thin with large eyes. Sometimes the boy was pictured with Guy, sometimes alone and, from the facial resemblance to Mary, Pam guessed that he was Guy's brother. But neither Mary nor Della had ever mentioned him and she wondered why.

There was the inevitable graduation photo of Guy in mortarboard and gown. Pam peered closely at it. Manchester University. There was also one of Guy in doctorate robes with the words University of Liverpool beneath. She wondered if he'd told Gerry Heffernan that he'd spent his postgraduate years in Liverpool. Gerry always leapt at every opportunity to reminisce about his home city.

Pam pointed to the photograph of the boy. 'You've never mentioned that you had another son.'

Mary's face suddenly became solemn. 'He died.'

'Oh, I'm sorry.'

'It was a long time ago.'

There was an awkward silence. Then Mary gave a brave smile. 'Your children have a wonderful rapport with the animals. Della tells me that Michael loves the kitten. I think it's so good for children to have pets. It teaches them responsibility.'

'Yes, you're right.' Pam glanced at her watch. If she went home now she could catch up with some lesson preparation. She felt a twinge of irritation that Della hadn't kept her up to date with her arrangements. But it was typical of her mother to be so thoughtless.

'Now, how about that tea?'

Pam stood up and gave a regretful smile. 'That's very good of you, Mary, but I think I'd better head back.'

'I'm so sorry you've had a wasted journey,' said Mary.

Pam thought she could see relief on her face. She'd much rather be with her animals than entertaining a virtual stranger.

Pam said a polite goodbye and made for the car, too irritated with her mother to take much notice of her surroundings. If she had looked around she would have seen a light going off in Clare Mayers's cottage and a dark figure standing in the shadow of the hedgerow opposite.

As she fumbled in her bag for her car key, the figure closed in behind her, moving silently on tiptoe like an animal stalking its prey.


Tom had just called to give Wesley the address and phone number of Gemma Fielding. Isobel Grant had e-mailed her shortly before her death and Wesley had a feeling – a gut instinct – that this particular avenue of enquiry might not lead to a dead end as so many others had. But he knew he'd been wrong before.

He dialled Gemma's number and listened to the ringing tone droning away in some distant Liverpool room. Just as he was about to give up, he heard a female voice saying a breathless hello. 'Is that Gemma Fielding?'

'Yes.' She sounded wary, as though she feared he was intending to sell her something.

After he'd introduced himself there was a short puzzled silence. 'Are you still there, Ms Fielding?'

'Yes. What do you want?'

Wesley paused, aware that he might be about to break

devastating news. 'I don't know whether you're aware that Isobel Grant was found murdered?'

There was a short silence at the other end of the line. Then she spoke quietly. 'I saw it on the TV. It's awful. I can't believe she's dead. I mean she was so . . . So full of life. She was one of those people who was up for anything.'

This wasn't the Isobel her mother had described but sometimes parents don't know the true nature of their children. 'You sent her an e-mail on the seventeenth of February. You advised her not to ask somebody for money. Can you tell me what that was about?'

'I don't see how it can have anything to do with her murder. Wasn't it some serial killer?'

Suddenly Wesley wondered whether he was on the right track. But he decided to persist. 'Please. Whatever you can tell us might be important.'

Gemma hesitated for a few moments and Wesley wished he could see her face to face.

'A couple of weeks ago she came up to Liverpool for the weekend and stayed in my flat. Anyway when we'd had a few drinks she told me about this plan. She'd shared a house with two other students in her second year and one of them . . .'

'One of them what?'

'Izzy said she'd seen this person again recently and she'd had this idea. She was really desperate to get a place of her own. That's why she did it. I said it was blackmail and she could get into trouble but . . .'

Wesley tried to make sense of her words but failed. 'Let me get this clear. Isobel was planning to blackmail someone?'

Gemma hesitated again, unwilling to speak ill of the dead. 'I suppose so but . . .'

'Who is this person?'

'I didn't know him – she shared with him the year before we met. He was in his third year – older than us. I didn't meet Izzy till she was looking for someone to share with in her last year and she answered our advert. We had a spare room, you see, and . . .'

Wesley took a deep breath. 'Do you know what she was planning to blackmail this person about?'

There was a long pause and Wesley repeated the question.

Then Gemma spoke, her voice hushed. 'Izzy said he killed someone. And then he committed suicide . . . drowned himself in the Albert Dock.'

'I thought you said she'd seen him.'

'That's what she told me. It doesn't make sense, does it?'

'Where did she say she'd seen him? Was it up in Liverpool when she visited you?'

There was a pause. 'No. She said it was down in Devon near where she was living. She said he didn't recognise her but she recognised him. Look, she probably made a mistake. It was probably just someone who looked like him.'

'Do you know this man's name?'

'She just referred to him as Lazarus – cause she thought he'd come back from the dead, I guess. And, like I said, I never met him and she never mentioned him when we were sharing in the third year.'

'Do you know anything else about him? What he studied at university, for instance?'

'No. But I know the other bloke Izzy shared with in the second year was studying dentistry – Izzy used to joke about it. His name was Dominic but I'm not sure of his surname. I'll see if I can track him down so I can ask him if he knows any more. But I can't promise anything.'

'I can get Merseyside police to do that.'

'I can ask around – friends of friends. Might be quicker.'

'OK. But we really need a breakthrough before this killer tries again.'

Gemma promised she'd do her best. Wesley only hoped that her best would be good – and quick – enough. But he put in a call to Merseyside as well. Some things were too important to leave to amateurs.

Pam flicked the remote control and the car locks clicked open. She walked round to the driver's door, key at the ready to make a fast getaway, thinking of all the school work squatting in the car boot waiting for her attention while Della had all the fun of taking the children out for tea.

As she reached for the door handle, she glanced back at the dark, quiet lane and saw a car parked up just beyond Clare Mayers's cottage. But she paid it no attention and pulled the door open, anxious to head for home.

She was quite unprepared when a strong arm grabbed her from behind. But in a split second her instinct for survival took over and adrenaline pumped through her body as she wriggled and fought with all the strength she could muster, clawing at her assailant's dark clothing, kicking at his shins, trying to catch enough breath to scream out.

For a brief moment she managed to writhe out of the thing's grasp and turn her head, only to see that her attacker had the head of a painted jackal. She could see glittering eyes inside the mask, narrowed like a beast going for the kill. And that fearsome head was the last thing she saw before she was knocked flying and her head hit the hard, damp surface of the lane.

# CHAPTER 31

*Two weeks after the birth of my son I was told that I should resume my duties. Sir Frederick still kept his distance and it was clear to me that there was to be no mention of what had passed between us. It was in the past and the future stretched before me, bleak and barren in that high fortress. They had taken away my child and without him my life was nothing.*

*It was a full six months after that terrible night of pain, birth and loss when I saw my child again. I had experienced in those days a strong desire to be alone with my thoughts and I had taken to walking in solitude around the estate and the surrounding countryside. One day I was walking in the woodland not far from the castle when I ventured onto an unfamiliar path. It took me to the boundary of the woods where I came upon a cottage. A small red-headed woman, not young but not yet old, was hanging out washing in the garden and I watched her for a while from the shelter of the trees for she was singing as she went about her work and she seemed so contented that I felt a pang of envy, especially when I spied the large perambulator standing near to the kitchen door.*

After a while the child in the perambulator began to cry and, abandoning her task, the woman walked slowly across the small neat garden to pick it up. As soon as I saw the child I knew that he was mine and I was sorely tempted to call out, to break through the fence and grab my baby. But I knew this would serve no purpose other than to get me sent away. At least this way I would be close to him.

I returned to the castle with a heavy heart, wondering how I could see more of my son. Then I realised that I must be bold. I must confront Frederick and tell him that I wished to play a part in our son's life. Naturally, his foster mother would see to his everyday needs but he would come to know me as a kind aunt, perhaps, one he could always go to in times of trouble. I would brook no argument. He was my own flesh and I would not surrender his love and regard meekly.

That evening I ate alone in my room as I had done since the later stages of my pregnancy. Then I made my way down to the museum room where I knew Frederick always went after dinner. I often went in that room myself at times I knew I would be undisturbed to study the artefacts and read the papyri. I regretted that I could no longer share my passion with Frederick. The loss of this intimacy hurt me almost as much as the loss of my child.

As I had expected Frederick was there, poring over a new papyrus that had been sent to him by one of his colleagues. To my great relief, my fear that John would be there with him was unfounded; but then John, unlike myself, had little interest in his father's passion. Frederick looked up as I entered that room and I saw guilt in his eyes. Then something else – a hardness of heart that made my own heart sink.

'I have seen our son,' I said, kneeling by his side. 'He is a fine boy. I beg you to allow me to see him. I would like him to know me . . . to grow to love me.'

Frederick turned his head away. 'That is out of the question. He belongs to the Mortons now. They are a good couple and they care for him deeply. It is best that he never knows you. And if you defy me on this matter you will be sent away without a reference.' When he turned to face me, his eyes held no warmth, only contempt. 'Or you can seek another post if you prefer. I will give you a good recommendation.' He paused for a moment and looked me in the eye. 'Perhaps that would be for the best.'

His words struck me like a blow. I stood up but my legs felt unsteady as I realised how powerless I was. I could have struck him there and then but I knew that a woman in my position is in need of a good character if she is not to sink into the darkest depths of poverty and degradation.

'But he is your son.' I said the words without thinking.

'I have two fine sons and John will inherit all this when I am gone. I have no need of a bastard.'

I picked up my skirts and ran back to my humble quarters. But the next day I returned to the museum. I found the papyrus Sir Frederick had been reading lying there on the table where he had left it the previous night. I sat down to read it and when I translated the hieroglyphs my heart thrilled with excitement and my course of action became clear in my mind.

# CHAPTER 32

There was no reply when Wesley tried to call Pam to tell her he'd be late. Then he remembered that Della was taking the children to the sanctuary again. That's where Pam would be . . . trying to curb her mother's enthusiasm.

He'd gone over what Gemma Fielding had told him in his mind but it still didn't make sense. Whoever killed those three women and attacked Clare Mayers knew about John Varley's crimes in great detail and had access to sheets that most likely came from Varley Castle. It seemed very likely that Gemma's story was just another diversion.

But he had to know for sure. Gerry was at his desk, head down over a file, and Wesley sensed that he would welcome an interruption, even one that wasn't potentially important. The DCI looked up as Wesley gave a swift knock on his open office door. 'I hope you've got good news,' he said. 'The Nutter's questioning our overtime sheets . . . again. Anything from Varley Castle about Caroline Varley and Robert Delaware?'

'A couple of patrol cars have gone up there to investigate but there's no news yet.' Wesley sat down. 'I've just been talking to a woman called Gemma Fielding up in Liverpool. She was a mate of Isobel Grant's and they kept in touch by e-mail. She thinks Isobel was trying to blackmail someone.'

Gerry's eyes lit up. 'So little miss nice harmless physics teacher had a dark side, eh? According to her loving mother she was a saint.' He smiled. 'Mind you, Wes, I don't see how it can be relevant. Our killer doesn't care who his victims are or what they've done. They just have to be female and in the wrong place at the wrong time.'

Wesley knew Gerry was probably right. But he couldn't banish Gemma's words from his mind.

'So you don't think this alleged blackmail attempt has anything to do with all this?'

'I always keep an open mind, Wes. But at the moment Delaware's our priority.' He thought for a moment. 'And let's face it, what do we really know about him? Only that he's a not-very-successful writer and that he has some sort of connection with Raymond Seed which we haven't really got to the bottom of yet. He's got no criminal record so his prints aren't on file. He's a mystery man.'

'But is he our man?'

'I can't think of anyone better at the moment ... can you?' He hesitated. 'We can't afford distractions, Wes. Three women have died so far. John Varley killed four.'

'And you think Delaware will try to match his record?'

'Come on, Wes, don't you? Who else had access to those sheets? Who else has been studying John Varley's crimes? How long has Caroline Varley been missing now?'

'An hour or so.'

Gerry looked solemn. 'So if Delaware's our killer, we're probably too late.' He banged his fist down on the desk. 'I feel like a spare part sitting here. We should be out on Dartmoor looking for them.'

Wesley understood the boss's feeling of frustration: he'd often felt like that himself. 'Dartmoor's a big place, Gerry. Leave it to the uniforms on the ground.'

Gerry glanced at his watch. 'Even so, we should get someone up to Varley Castle to see what's going on.'

Wesley returned to his desk and picked up the phone. Maybe he just hadn't asked Gemma Fielding the right questions.

The two uniformed officers had details of all the nearby premises and they knew that the cottage on the fringe of the woods was empty and awaiting renovation. But as the patrol car drew up outside there was a flickering light in the window. Somebody was in there doing God knows what.

The officers exchanged a look and climbed out of the car, putting on their hats. It was probably just a couple of local kids using the cottage for a bit of how's your father but DCI Heffernan had given strict orders that everywhere had to be checked out.

PC Dawson, a large man with a substantial beer belly, walked on tiptoe to the window but when he tried to peep inside he found that the ragged curtains had been drawn across.

He turned to his colleague, Shirley – a middle-aged policewoman who'd seen it all. 'You taking bets on rumpy-pumpy? We could do 'em for trespass . . . breaking and entering. Let's give 'em the shock of their lives, eh?'

As Shirley emerged from the car, thinking about the

paperwork, PC Dawson rapped loudly on the front door, a wicked grin plastered on his face. 'Police. Open up.'

When there was no reply he tried the latch and found the door was locked. Shirley rolled her eyes impatiently. 'Come on, Pete. Caroline Varley's hardly likely to have gone to ground in some derelict cottage.'

'Breaking and entering, Shirley . . . think of our clear-up figures.'

Suddenly they heard raised voices, one male one female – an argument but no lovers' spat.

'We'd better get in there.'

Shirley stood back as Dawson put his shoulder to the half-rotten door and, to her surprise, it gave way easily. She stumbled into the house after her colleague and positioned herself behind him as he gave the door to their right a mighty kick.

The scene revealed as the door flew open reminded Shirley of pictures she'd seen of King Tutankhamen's tomb. An army of statues gazed malevolently towards the mantelpiece and in the centre of the room, where a coffee table would be in any normal house, lay a painted Egyptian sarcophagus, open to reveal a battered mummy. She gathered her thoughts and glanced at the two photographs in her hand. It was them all right.

Robert Delaware was sitting on what looked like an Egyptian stool, his head in his hands, and Caroline Varley was standing by the empty fireplace, staring in shock at the uniformed intruders. He looked penitent . . . and she looked furious.

'Mr Delaware . . . Ms Varley,' Shirley said with a hint of triumph. 'We've been looking for you everywhere.'

*

'Something wrong?'

Wesley looked up and saw Rachel Tracey standing by his desk with a concerned look on her face. 'I can't get hold of Pam. She should be home by now.'

'Probably been held up somewhere.'

'Probably.'

The phone on his desk rang and he picked it up. After a short conversation, he turned to Rachel who was still hovering nearby. 'Robert Delaware and Caroline Varley have been found in an empty cottage on the edge of the estate.'

'They've got a whole bloody castle full of bedrooms if they want—'

'I don't think they were there for fun. The cottage was full of Egyptian artefacts. Delaware's just made a statement and he admits that he'd been nicking items from the castle under Caroline's nose. It all had to stop, of course, once Neil and the bloke from the British Museum arrived to catalogue everything. Raymond Seed was arranging to sell the things for him and the stuff was being stored in the empty cottage until Seed could take them to London. The murder business delayed their plans.'

'I bet it did.'

'Anyway, Caroline's just stumbled on his guilty secret and she's told him exactly what she thinks of his thieving ways. When the police arrived he came like a lamb.'

'No love interest then?'

'If he was ever in with a chance, he's not now. He's being brought in for questioning.'

'So does this mean Delaware's out of the frame for the murders?'

Wesley considered the question. 'I'm not sure.'

'Is Caroline OK?'

'She's fine, just angry that Delaware betrayed her trust like that. Neil's volunteered to stay there and keep her company.' Wesley stood up. 'I'm going out. The DCI's gone upstairs to see CS Nutter. If he asks, tell him I'm following up the Gemma Fielding lead. I've just had some more information from her that could be relevant.' He looked down at a scrap of paper on his desk – a list in his neat handwriting. 'And I'd better let Ian Petrie know about Delaware: it looks like he's the missing link to Raymond Seed. Why smuggle in Egyptian artefacts when you can help yourself from an uncatalogued source nearby?'

'So who's our killer then?'

Wesley didn't answer. He had a feeling that Gemma Fielding might hold the key but the connections were still nebulous gossamer threads that were only just starting to shape themselves into a feasible solution.

The phone rang again and he answered, hoping it would be something useful. It was extremely rare for Della to ring him at work but now she was on the other end of the line and she sounded worried.

'I've just got to your house. Pam's car's not here and there's no sign of her. And I found the kitten locked in the kitchen – she hadn't been fed. Have you any idea where she is?'

Wesley was suddenly overwhelmed by a feeling of dread. This must be what it was like to have two officers turn up on your doorstep with sympathetic expressions and bad news.

'I've been trying her mobile but there's no answer,' Della continued. 'I tried the school too but they said she left ages ago.' There was a pause. 'I don't think she got my message about not bothering to pick the kids up from Mary's. There's no answer from the sanctuary but that's not surprising 'cause Mary's often outside with the animals. Pam should have turned up by now. Something's wrong – I know it is.'

This was a new, humble Della. There was no sneering at the police now. She was desperate for help. He took a deep breath and told himself to stay calm. There was probably some simple explanation.

'I'll be right round there,' he said.

Pam came to and opened her eyes, vaguely aware of moonlight trickling through branches and clouds scudding across the darkened sky.

Her neck hurt as though a knife had pierced the flesh and when she tried to swallow she winced with the agonising pain.

She shifted her body a little. Wherever she was, it was cold and the surface she lay on was hard with sharp stones that bit into her flesh. It was then she realised that she was naked and wrapped tightly in something white.

Through a haze of pain she gulped air into her lungs and moved her limbs experimentally. At first she feared that she'd been tied up. But then she realised that whatever was enveloping her body was also restricting her movements. She could feel damp seeping through the cloth that was her only protection against the elements and she shivered with the cold as she lay there assessing her situation, unwilling to make any sort of noise in case it attracted the attention of the creature with the jackal head, the last thing she'd seen before she'd lost consciousness.

With a great effort she managed to turn her head a little and she saw that she was lying in the entrance to a field. Sniffing at the air like a trapped animal she struggled to free her limbs and when the wrappings gradually loosened she managed to touch her tender throat. She could feel a line where something had bitten into her flesh and she realised that the creature had probably left her there because it thought she was dead.

Slowly she summoned the strength to grasp the white cloth in her icy, numb fingers and struggle unsteadily to her feet. She could see her car just a few yards away. Whoever had attacked her must have dragged her the short distance to prevent her from being seen from the nearby cottages or by any passing motorist. But she was alive and safety was a short walk across the lane.

She pressed her body against the hedgerow, afraid that her attacker might still be hiding somewhere, waiting for her to break cover; watching like a cat watches an injured mouse. Then she began to take her first, tentative, tottering steps across the road, razor-sharp stones cutting into the tender soles of her feet. She couldn't see her clothes anywhere . . . or her car keys or her bag with her mobile phone inside. But she could hear dogs barking and she could see Mary's house ahead, a light from one of the upstairs windows casting a pale-gold rectangle onto the rough ground.

She tripped over the sheet that covered her nakedness and landed heavily on her knees, grazing them on the rough ground. As she struggled to her feet her knee felt as though it had been stung by a thousand angry wasps and she saw a small patch of blood seeping through the white cloth. But she pulled the sheet close around her body and stumbled forward.

Her head swam and the pain of swallowing brought about an overwhelming wave of nausea. But she had to stay calm and alert. She had to think.

*

'There's no sign of her.' Della looked at her son-in-law with desperate eyes. They were in the living room, standing up. Neither felt like sitting down.

Wesley had made a thorough search of the house but he'd found no evidence that Pam had returned home. He'd left several messages on Mary's machine but Della insisted that she didn't often check it when she was busy with the animals. He'd also contacted Traffic Division and the local hospitals in case there'd been an accident. But he'd drawn a blank.

He had often wondered how people felt when their loved ones went missing and now he had the answer. He felt overwhelmed, so numb with anxiety and dread that he found it almost impossible to function. The children were in the living room watching TV, unaware that anything was wrong – and Wesley wanted it kept that way.

He felt a hand on his shoulder. 'Don't worry, Wes.' He looked round and saw concern in Gerry Heffernan's eyes. 'She'll turn up.'

'I've tried all her friends but . . .'

'All patrols are keeping an eye out for her car. You've got your kiddies to look after.' Gerry hesitated. 'Or do you want someone to take them to your sister's?'

Wesley looked at Della. His sister Maritia, a GP and vicar's wife, would be a more calming influence than his mother-in-law. Besides, Pam was Della's only daughter: she was too emotionally involved. 'I'll give Maritia a call,' he said. 'If someone can take the kids over to Belsham vicarage . . .'

'No problem.'

'And send a patrol car round to the animal sanctuary. Della reckons Pam might not have got that message to say she'd already left.'

'If she'd gone there she'd be answering her phone surely?'

338

'Something might have happened on the way or . . .'

'OK, Wes. But don't you think you're overreacting? She could have decided to go shopping while Della had the kids or . . .'

Wesley sighed. Gerry could be right. But he had a gut feeling that something was amiss. Or maybe it was the thought that a killer was out there – and he knew what that killer was capable of.

When Gerry's phone rang Wesley almost jumped. This could be news.

After a short conversation, Gerry turned to him. 'Sorry, no news about Pam. It's just that Paul's been trying to get hold of your mate Ian Petrie to tell him about Delaware's connection with the antiquities racket, but he's had no luck. The hotel told him that he's checked out but he left a note at Reception addressed to you. Someone told them to take it to the police station.'

Wesley could tell Gerry was trying to distract him from his worry about Pam. 'He's probably gone back to London – something might have cropped up.'

'Maybe,' said Gerry as his phone rang again.

As he took the call Wesley's eyes were fixed on his face, looking for any telltale sign that this was relevant news, good or bad. Gerry's contribution to the conversation consisted of grunted monosyllables and when he'd finished he turned to Wesley, his face solemn.

'None of our suspects have been out and about this evening. Alan Jakes is in custody. Robert Delaware's accounted for down at Tradmouth nick and Raymond Seed's at home on bail like a good boy, as is Clive Crest.' There was a long silence.

Suddenly Wesley spoke. 'Gemma Fielding.' His mind had

been so numbed by worry that he'd almost forgotten what he'd been about to do before the crisis arose.

'What about her? Has she called again?'

'Not yet. She said she'd try to contact someone Isobel shared with in the second year.'

'And she's no idea what the name of this dead boy was?'

'Gemma never actually met him. But Isobel claimed to have seen him recently.'

Gerry looked at him, wide-eyed. 'So he might not be dead?'

'Isobel told her he'd died while they were at university. He committed suicide – drowned himself in the Albert Dock. But she told Gemma that she'd seen him in Tradmouth.'

Gerry frowned. 'I still don't see—'

'I called Merseyside police earlier to see if they have a suicide that matches. And I asked them to see if they could locate the other housemate as well. His name's Dominic and he studied dentistry so there's a chance he's traceable.' He hesitated. 'If Isobel Grant was really blackmailing someone . . . and this person wanted her dead . . .'

He stood there in silence for a while. Then he had a thought that made his stomach churn. He turned to Gerry again. 'I've just remembered something. Pam told me that Mary, Guy Kitchener's mother, said she was distantly related to the Varleys. The killer knows all about the John Varley case, doesn't he? And Pam was going to see Mary . . .'

Gerry pulled a face. 'I think you're jumping to conclusions, Wes.'

He took a step forward. 'I'm going over there . . .'

Gerry put a hand on his arm. 'I'll get Rach and Paul to go straight over there first in a patrol car. It'll be quicker.'

Before Wesley could answer, Gerry's phone rang again

and Wesley held his breath while he listened to the hushed conversation.

Gerry looked up. 'No news about Pam, I'm afraid. Rachel's got that note from Ian Petrie,' he said quietly.

'Tell her to open it,' Wesley said, taking the phone from Gerry's hand. He listened as Rachel read in a monotone as though she was reluctant to add her own interpretation to Ian's words.

'Have returned to London. Don't worry about me. And thanks for everything.'

'Let's get back to the station, Gerry,' Wesley said. 'We can't do any good here.'

Pam's limbs felt stiff and numb with cold but she knew she had to make for the sanctuary. Mary Kitchener would look after her and she could call the police from there.

She had no idea who had tried to kill her but she remembered that the first girl who'd been attacked lived almost next door to the sanctuary. Her boyfriend had been a strong suspect and although he'd been arrested for attacking a woman in Neston, there was a chance that he'd been released on bail: sometimes the courts seemed to be on the side of the criminal classes. If he was still hanging around then she was in danger.

She could hear the dogs barking and the occasional braying of a donkey and Mary's front door was now in view. She dared herself to look round and saw that she was completely alone in that quiet lane. But she knew that he could still be near, lurking in shadows, crouching behind the hedge, pressed up against a wall.

Her heart hammering, she staggered across the lane and flung herself at Mary's door. She rang the bell, leaning against the door jamb gulping in breath, and when the door opened she fell into the hall. As her grazed knees landed on the soft Turkish rug, she breathed in the comforting aroma of dog. And it smelt good.

'Pam . . . oh my God. What's happened to you? Are you all right?'

Pam looked up at Mary from her lowly position sprawled amidst the dog hairs on the floor. Mary pushed away a curious border collie and put out her hand to help her. Pam tried to speak but no sound came out. Whatever had been tightened around her throat had done some damage. She mouthed the words 'call the police' but Mary didn't seem to hear.

'Why on earth are you dressed in a sheet, dear? Where are your clothes? And your poor feet . . . Oh dear,' the woman wittered. 'I'll call Della.' A pair of other dogs had joined the collie and had begun to sniff round Pam suspiciously.

When Pam opened her mouth no sound emerged. But after a few attempts she managed a guttural hiss. 'Call the police and call Wesley. Call my husband.'

'Yes, yes, dear. But first let's make you comfortable. I think you should lie down. Can you make it up the stairs? You can have Ben's old room. The bed's made up. Guy's away at some conference and he won't be back till tomorrow. I'd call him over if he was here,' she muttered as she put her arm round Pam and began to help her towards the staircase.

Pam leaned her weight against the woman's stout body and Mary murmured words of encouragement. 'Don't worry. Just take it slowly. Everything's going to be fine.'

Eventually they reached the landing. Mary opened one of the doors and led Pam inside. If Pam had been able to speak she would have asked who Ben was because she hadn't heard

342

the name before. But communication was too much of an effort. Her throat felt worse now as she stumbled towards the bed.

She cast a cursory glance around the room. It was a plain room with stripy, masculine wallpaper. There were clothes hanging in the open wardrobe and neatly folded over the back of a chair in the corner as though the occupant of the room was about to return at any moment. Pam lay on the bed, aware that she was soiling the clean white duvet cover with her muddy limbs. Mary deftly covered her with the quilt that lay across the end of the bed and told her to close her eyes.

As Pam drifted into an exhausted sleep, she could hear dogs barking and a car screeching to a halt outside.

Wesley's phone rang and he answered it immediately, almost allowing it to slip from his grasp in his eagerness. After a curt conversation he felt like a man who'd just had the weight of the world's troubles lifted from his shoulders.

'That was Rachel. They've found Pam. She's OK.'

'Where is she?'

'Mary Kitchener found her. She was wandering round stark naked apart from a sheet and she collapsed on Mary's doorstep. It looks as if somebody tried to strangle her . . . just like Clare Mayers.'

Gerry swallowed hard. 'Well, thank God they didn't succeed.' He paused, studying Wesley's face. 'I'll organise a car to take you round. You're in no state to be driving.'

'I'm fine.'

'I'm getting you a car. You don't have to play the hero with me.'

When Gerry Heffernan had first joined the force his old

DCI had always kept a half bottle of whisky in the bottom drawer of his desk. Looking at Wesley sitting there, slumped in his visitor's chair, he wished, for once, that the old tradition had been kept up. Wesley looked as though he was in need of something reviving.

'Look, don't worry too much about Ian Petrie,' said Gerry. At least the subject of Petrie took Wesley's mind off Pam.

'I can't get what he told me out of my mind . . . about the cancer.'

'They can do marvellous things these days. I knew this bloke who—'

'Ian won't have any more treatment. He never could deal with ill health. I remember when his daughter was ill, he never talked about it . . . treated it as if it hadn't happened.'

'Maybe that's the best way. Anyway, we're arranging for Seed to be taken to London to face charges once we've finished with him. As for Delaware, it looks as if he's our responsibility for now, more's the pity.'

Wesley gave an absent-minded nod but before Gerry could say any more he received a call to say the car was ready to take them to Hugford. Wesley grabbed his coat from the stand and Gerry followed him out. There was no way he was missing out on this.

# CHAPTER 33

*The first murder took place on the evening of Sunday 14th September. It was a young woman of around my own age. I did not know her but I heard later that she lived in the village nearby with her parents and was courting a young blacksmith who, as is common in such matters I believe, came under suspicion at once.*

*The condition of the corpse caused much speculation in the district and very soon it was put about that Jack the Ripper himself had moved to Devon and was stalking our fields and lanes in search of hapless victims.*

*The details, of course, were not made public but everybody seemed to know that the girl had been horribly mutilated and that her innards had been cut from her body and arranged by her side. It was said that only a monster would treat a body in such a way. How little these poor, ignorant folk knew of history and civilisations other than their own.*

*John Varley had taken up permanent residence at the castle and had taken to wandering the estate at night. But I did not inform the police of this fact until much later.*

# CHAPTER 34

Wesley held Pam in his arms. She was wrapped in a sheet which smelled of sweat, dirt and mothballs. Normally she favoured Chanel Number Five. The sight of her in that sheet made his blood run cold. He knew that it was intended as a shroud – a wrapping for the dead.

'How are you feeling?' he asked for what was probably the tenth time since he'd arrived at Mary Kitchener's house.

'Apart from this sore throat, I'm OK,' she hissed. 'Stop fussing.' She gave his hand a squeeze as though she regretted the sharpness of her words. 'Have you any idea who attacked me?'

Wesley shook his head. They were sitting side by side on the sagging velvet sofa in Mary's back room in front of a blazing log fire. Wesley was no longer aware of the smell of dogs and the layer of dog hair that seemed to cover every surface: his eyes were drawn to the stiffly posed photograph of Guy Kitchener in his doctorate robes with the words

346

University of Liverpool in gold letters underneath. He had asked Mary about it and she had told him proudly that he had studied at Manchester before obtaining his doctorate in Liverpool. He wondered why Guy hadn't mentioned his sojourn in Gerry's home city. But he told himself that they had been so preoccupied with the murders that they had had little opportunity for pleasantries.

He asked Mary about the painting of Varley Castle that Pam had mentioned and she told him that it was in the other room: he could see it if he liked. He hadn't accepted the invitation.

There was another photograph standing on the mantelpiece too: a photograph of two little boys; one dark, one fair. From the pose and the certain family resemblance between them, Wesley had assumed they were brothers. And when he had asked whether she had another son Mary said simply that he'd died some years ago. He hardly liked to pursue the subject and resurrect old griefs. But he knew that he might have no option.

'How did your son die?'

The colour drained from the woman's cheeks. 'They said he killed himself but I never believed it. I'm sure it was an accident.'

'What happened?'

There was a long pause, as if Mary was summoning up all her inner strength to state the dreadful facts. 'He went out one night and never came back. He was found a couple of days later. He'd drowned.'

'Where was this?'

She hesitated. 'Up north . . . in Liverpool.'

Before Wesley could enquire further, the door opened and Paul Johnson poked his head in. 'Can I have a word, sir?'

Wesley gave Pam's hand a comforting squeeze and followed Paul out into the hall.

'Forensic are going over the place where your wife was attacked,' Paul said in a low voice. 'There's no sign of anything yet but there are tyre marks nearby.'

'I want this house searched. Every inch.'

Paul looked surprised. 'Why? Do you think . . .?'

Wesley didn't answer. What he was thinking was almost unthinkable.

The things were well hidden. A pile of linen sheets – clean but very old and smelling of mothballs – were neatly folded away in a space near the water tank in the loft. The papier mâché painted mask had been shoved into an old Winterleas carrier bag and concealed behind the rafters along with five Anubis figures, identical to the ones left with the bodies. There was an obsidian knife too – probably very ancient from some Egyptian tomb – wrapped in a plastic bag and shoved down in the floor joists amongst the insulation. The woman's clothes found in a carrier bag matched the description of those Isobel Grant was wearing on the night she died. Her bag was there too and her mobile phone. Pam's clothes, bag and phone had been shoved into a separate bag.

Mary stood on the landing and watched calmly as the items were brought down one by one. And her expression gave nothing away.

Once Pam had been taken to Tradmouth Hospital for a check-up a patrol car had driven her to Belsham Vicarage to stay the night with Wesley's sister. Maritia was used to dealing with emergencies. The children were already in Maritia's safe haven: Wesley needed to know they were in a place where they could come to no harm. He'd almost forgotten about the kitten but he'd been reminded by a subdued Della who'd agreed to look after it for a couple of days.

Now all the practical arrangements had been made he could concentrate on Mary Kitchener who was sitting in her armchair, a picture of domestic calm with a pair of dogs stretched out at her feet. With her wild grey hair and motherly figure she seemed an unlikely serial killer. But Wesley knew that stranger things had happened in the history of crime and that harmless-looking, motherly women had, on rare occasions, committed the most horrendous and grotesque misdeeds. Gerry sat beside him on the sofa, staring at the woman. Wesley felt a nudge in his ribs. It was up to him to start the questioning.

When he told Mary what had been found in her loft her lips formed themselves into a secretive, satisfied smile. 'That's very clever of you, Wesley. I always thought I'd kept one step ahead of you.'

'So you admit that you killed those women?'

'Is it any use denying it?'

'Did you kill them?'

She gave him another smile but said nothing.

'Can you tell me why you did it?'

'Not really.'

'You killed three women and attempted to murder two others and you don't know why?'

She appeared to consider the question for a few moments. 'They were sacrifices. I'm a follower of the goddess Isis. I was following old rituals.'

Wesley caught Gerry's eye. He didn't believe a word of it.

'I didn't think the ancient Egyptians went in much for human sacrifice.'

Mary pressed her lips together and didn't reply.

349

'Where's Guy?'

'He's in London. But you know that already, don't you?'

'Did he talk to you about the case?'

'My first victim was Clare . . . a girl from down the road. I said I was interested in the investigation and Guy, obligingly, kept me up to date. I do hope he won't get into trouble.'

'How did you go about killing them?' Wesley asked the question casually, as though he was enquiring about some mundane matter, like planting vegetables. He suspected he'd get to the truth quicker if they kept the atmosphere calm.

'You know that already.'

'I want you to tell me. How did you select your victims?'

'I saw they were on their own and vulnerable and I followed them. Then I strangled them with a piece of garden twine and performed the ceremony so that their souls could travel safely to the afterlife. I took out their organs and placed them beside their bodies just as the Ancient Egyptians did. Then I wrapped them in linen.'

'Where did you get the sheets from?'

'They belonged to my mother. They'd come down through the family. I was told that they'd originally come from Varley Castle but I don't know whether that's true.'

'You left the bodies where they'd be found.'

Mary nodded.

'Always?'

'Yes.'

'Why did you put Analise Sonquist's clothes in the garage of the house where she lived?' Wesley watched her face and there was no mistaking her surprise, there for a moment then swiftly hidden.

'I . . .' She seemed to be searching for a valid explanation.

'Guy said you'd interviewed the man who lived there. I suppose I wanted to incriminate him.' Somehow she didn't sound very convincing.

Wesley felt Gerry's hand on his arm. 'Can I have a word?' he muttered.

The detectives stood up, leaving Mary in the care of a young constable who was sitting by the window taking notes. Gerry led the way into the hall and turned to face Wesley.

'Are you thinking what I'm thinking, Wes?' He hesitated. 'It doesn't seem right.'

'She knows a lot of the details we've not released to the press.'

'So does Guy.'

'And the mask and those other things were found hidden here.' He sighed. 'She said she found the mask in the church hall while she was organising the craft fair – the timing fits with it going missing from the drama group's wardrobe. And Raymond Seed was selling those Anubis figures at the craft fair so she could easily have bought them – or even pinched them. But you're right, Gerry. There's something wrong. I'm sure she didn't know what I was talking about when I first told her about the clothes found in the Crests' garage. I don't think she did it. I think she's protecting someone.'

'Guy?'

'He's in London so he can't have attacked Pam.'

'Mary might have done that to throw us off the scent. The killer's always seemed to be one step ahead of us and Guy had access to everything.' He banged his fist on the wall, frustrated with his own gullibility. If his suspicions were right, he'd aided and abetted a murderer.

Wesley put a hand on his arm. 'We weren't to know. Come on, let's see if we can get the truth out of her.'

They returned to the living room. Mary was sitting bolt upright in her armchair. And she was smiling.

'Is there somebody who can look after the animals? I need to be sure that they're all right.'

'We'll contact the animal shelter in Neston. They'll send someone over.'

Mary nodded, a look of relief on her face, as if a huge worry had been lifted from her shoulders. 'In that case will you arrest me now, please? I don't see any sense in delaying this any longer. I'm willing to make a full confession. I'm tired. I just want all this to be over.'

They had little choice. Wesley left it to Gerry to make the formal arrest. And as she was led outside to the police car Mary Kitchener was still smiling. And that smile held a hint of triumph.

There was a serenity about Mary Kitchener that belied her horrendous crimes. Wesley had never seen a prisoner so content to be languishing on a thin blue plastic mattress in a police cell; the only time she had expressed any emotion was when she spoke of her son.

'I don't know what Guy's going to say when he gets back,' she said to Rachel Tracey as she led her down the corridor from the cells to the interview room the following morning. 'Have you managed to contact him yet?'

'Yes,' Rachel answered tersely.

'What did he say?'

'He's going to organise a lawyer for you,' she said, avoiding the woman's eyes. She found the very sight of Mary Kitchener unsettling. The woman who looked so innocuous had been capable of such evil and it made Rachel doubt her own certainties . . . and her own judgement.

Mary answered each question politely, elaborating when requested like a good citizen co-operating with the police. On the night of Naomi Hart's murder she had been disturbed before she'd had time to carry out the ritual mutilations. She'd found out later that it had been the man who'd assaulted that woman in Neston who'd put paid to her plans. Ironic really, she said, that he should have been a suspect.

There seemed to be little doubt of her guilt. The attack on Pam Peterson, the incriminating items found in her house, and the knowledge she possessed about Varley Castle, all pointed one way. She had claimed that if Rachel and Paul hadn't turned up at the sanctuary when they did, Pam Peterson would be dead. She had her there at her mercy and she would have finished what she started.

When asked why she hadn't killed Pam immediately, she said that she had been disturbed by Karen Mayers leaving her cottage. She'd left Pam there in the shelter of the farm gate and the hedgerow, intending to return and carry out the mutilations when all was quiet and dark. She had even provided a motive of sorts, although it wasn't one that made any sense to Rachel.

When Mary had been returned to the cells, Rachel turned to Wesley. 'Are you all right?' She could see the strain on his face. He had shown no emotion when Mary had been talking about what she'd planned to do to Pam and Rachel knew that this outward calm had taken a massive effort of will. If it had been someone she loved, she would have wanted to scream and hit out at the monstrous woman. 'What do you think?'

Wesley looked up from the sheet of paper he'd been doodling on. She saw that he was sketching the head of a jackal. He smiled absent-mindedly. 'How do you mean?'

353

'Is Mary Kitchener guilty?'

'There's not much doubt about that, is there?'

'Do you think she's mad?' Rachel asked suddenly.

'I'm sure that's what she'll tell the court. Plea of insanity.'

His mobile phone began to ring and Rachel watched him, trying to guess the subject of the conversation from his answers. When the call was ended he looked up at her, his face solemn.

'Guy Kitchener's in Reception. He took the first train back from London when he heard. He wants to talk to his mother.'

'I bet he does,' said Rachel with a snort. 'Are we going to have a word with him first?'

Wesley thought for a moment. 'Yes. There's something I want to ask him.'

Mary Kitchener sat in her cell, a serene smile on her face. Jackals were scavengers. Jackals cleaned up the mess left by death and decay.

Her work was done now. She had cleared up the chaos. She had become a jackal.

# CHAPTER 35

*They died quickly, those girls, one after the other. And as they died the newspapers became more and more excited. Jack the Ripper, they said, had never been caught in Whitechapel. What if he'd moved to the lonely countryside, taken refuge on Dartmoor and been unable to contain his bestial urges?*

*However, these girls were innocents compared to Jack's London victims. Country girls; girls who would wed their rustic clods of sweethearts and bring babies into the world to toil in farms and fields and maybe even to die in terrible wars. If he had chosen them, Jack the Ripper's grim tastes in female flesh had much altered.*

*The terrible mutilations suffered by these Dartmoor maids differed greatly from the Ripper's frenzied butchery. The victims were strangled first, rather than slashed and stabbed. Then their organs were removed and placed in dishes beside them before the bodies were wrapped with great respect in linen and amulets placed on their chests for protection in the afterlife. All was done according to the ancient rites of the Egyptians and when the police realised this, it was to Sir Frederick they came with*

355

their questions. He confirmed their suspicions. The killer was indeed familiar with the customs of those ancient people. This was no Jack the Ripper, wild with his hatred for whores. There was a purpose to these deaths and the bodies had been treated with respect, even love.

John Varley rarely ventured out these days, except for at night when he prowled the fields and the countryside. I watched him closely now as his mind descended into a spiral of resentment and hatred for his father and myself. His mother, I believe, had ended her days in an asylum. And it is said that these things are passed on to the next generation. A terrible inheritance.

# CHAPTER 36

Wesley could see the DCI sitting at his desk staring at the jackal mask that squatted on top of his heap of paperwork, swathed in a plastic evidence bag. They had just spoken to Guy Kitchener who had clearly been in shock. There had been tears in his eyes as he spoke – true emotion of the kind that is hard to fake. All his expert speculation about the killer's identity had come to nothing and the last person he'd suspected was his own mother. There was a kind of hideous irony to it, Wesley thought as he went over the conversation in his head.

'Of course I don't think Mother ever really recovered from my brother's death,' Guy had said. 'Ben had always been a little . . .' He hesitated, trying to find the right word. 'Unstable. And when he died Mum went to pieces. I tried to keep an eye on her but . . . I never thought for one moment that anything like this would happen.'

'Your brother drowned?'

'That's right.'

'And this was up in Liverpool?'

'He was studying there. It was just after his finals. I was up there at the time doing my postgrad work. I felt guilty – still feel guilty – that I didn't keep in touch with him more and do something to help him.'

'How did your mother know about the killings in 1903?' Wesley had asked.

'After Ben's death she became obsessed about us being related to the Varleys. She read everything she could about the family and Varley Castle and she must have found out about the murders that way.'

'So you knew about the 1903 murders before all this happened?'

Guy had shaken his head. It had been his mother's secret. If he had known, he would have told the police. He sounded sincere but Wesley wasn't sure that he believed him.

When Wesley asked Guy how exactly he was related to the Varleys the reply was vague. Guy had never taken much interest in his family tree but he thought the relationship was on his mother's side rather than his late father's. He had opened his mouth as if he was about to add something else, but then he'd thought better of it. The exact connection with Varley Castle still remained unclear. Wesley hoped that Mary would be willing to clarify matters when they next spoke to her.

He suddenly realised that he should really be with Pam, providing some comfort and support. After all, she'd probably been selected as a victim because of his job. Mary had hinted as much: the wife of one of the investigating officers would have been her greatest prize. The idea seemed to amuse her; but then many people enjoy getting one over on the police.

Pam had merely been unconscious when she'd been stripped and wrapped in the sheet and with interruptions from passing cars and Karen Mayers, it had proved impossible to ensure she was dead and to carry out the ritual mutilations. Wesley thanked God for Karen and those cars and tried not to think about what might have been.

His phone rang, interrupting his thoughts. He picked up the receiver absent-mindedly and said hello.

'Is that DI Peterson?' The female voice on the other end was familiar. And it held a note of excitement. 'It's Gemma Fielding here. Remember?'

Of course he remembered. But in view of recent events, it looked as if his tentative theories about Isobel Grant had crumbled to dust.

'What can I do for you, Gemma?'

'It was on the news that you've made an arrest. Is it true?'

'Yes.'

'In that case I'm probably wasting your time.'

'Did you have something to tell me?'

She hesitated for a few seconds. 'It's probably not important now but I've found out more about the person Isobel was blackmailing. I managed to get in touch with that other boy who lived in that house – Dominic. He's working at a dental practice in Mossley Hill and I tracked him down through friends of friends like I promised. He told me that the boy who killed himself was called Ben.'

The name caused Wesley's heart to beat a little faster. It looked as if Gemma had succeeded where Merseyside police were still struggling. He straightened himself up in his chair, suddenly alert. 'Go on.'

'Dominic said he remembers Izzy getting drunk one night and saying something about Ben killing someone. She told him Ben had stabbed a man but then the next day she insisted that she'd made it all up.'

'Who was this Ben supposed to have killed?'

'Some man . . . a stranger. Dominic reckoned it was just a tall story and he said Ben was a bit weird so he didn't have much to do with him when they shared a house.'

Wesley frowned. Gemma's words didn't quite make sense. Or maybe he was just too exhausted to make the effort to understand . . . especially when they had the culprit down in the cells. Dominic the dentist could well be right about it being a tall story. This could just be a meaningless distraction.

Wesley looked round to make sure he couldn't be overheard. 'Did this Ben have a brother called Guy?'

'Dominic said he had a brother who was a postgraduate at the university but he couldn't remember his name. Look, I don't even know whether the story was true or whether it was just a load of crap.' Another hesitation. 'But I went to the newspaper offices and had a look to see whether there were any reports of deaths around that time that might fit. There was one that was reported in the *Echo*: a homeless man was found stabbed in a derelict dock building. It probably has nothing to do with—'

'We can check it out. And if you can give me Dominic's number . . . I'd like to talk to him.'

Gemma recited the full name and phone number. 'You think it could be important?'

'I don't know.' He thanked her and ended the call. Then he made another call before hurrying to Gerry's office.

Gerry received the news in silence before putting through a call to his counterpart in his home city of Liverpool. Wesley sat opposite him as they waited for Merseyside police to call them back. Neither man felt much like talking. But it was Wesley who broke the silence.

'Where's Guy Kitchener now?'

'He's gone back to his flat to arrange Mary's legal representation. He said he'd be back later. I don't see how he could be involved, Wes. He couldn't have abducted Pam 'cause he was in London at that conference. I've checked and double-checked and he was there.'

'What about the other murders?'

'We had no reason to check his whereabouts, did we?' Gerry said, almost defensively. 'But we can get someone onto it.'

The phone rang. It was the DCI from Merseyside who'd dealt with the death in the derelict dock. Gerry put the speakerphone on and Wesley sat down to listen.

'I believe you've been enquiring about a murder back in 2005. Homeless bloke known as Rocky found stabbed in Olympia Dock.'

'That's right. Any suspects?'

They heard a sigh on the other end of the line. 'We assumed it was just a drunken brawl. Another homeless chap went missing shortly after and we worked on the assumption there was a connection and he'd done a runner. He had an alcohol problem and a record of violence.'

'What about the weapon?'

'The pathologist reckoned it was a common or garden kitchen knife – the type available in every other high-street shop or supermarket but it was never found.'

'And the missing man?'

'He was twenty-three and his name was Donny Narwell. Spent his life in care . . . usual story. He could be anywhere

361

now. He could even be dead.' Wesley heard another sigh. It was clear that the death of Rocky and the disappearance of Donny Narwell had defeated the investigative powers of Merseyside CID and had become just another statistic.

'A student committed suicide around that time. Name of Ben Kitchener? He was found floating in the Albert Dock.'

'Ah yes, not the best thing to happen at one of our major tourist attractions. The poor lad had a history of mental instability, I remember. He'd just finished his finals and apparently he'd had a lot to drink so . . .'

'Did you ever connect him with Rocky's murder?'

The DCI sounded quite surprised. 'We had no reason to. It was a straightforward case. His brother reported him missing and then came to identify him – he taught at the university, I think. He took charge of everything. There was an inquest of course but, as I said, it was straightforward. One of his housemates gave evidence that he'd been depressed. Tragic, though.'

'What was the housemate called?'

'Hang on.' There was a rustle of paper as the Merseyside DCI checked the file. 'Isobel Grant.' There was a pause. 'Wasn't that the name of one of your murder victims?'

'Yes. That's right. What was Ben studying?'

'I can't remember. History maybe . . . something like that.'

Gerry thanked him and asked for all the details to be e-mailed through. As soon as the call was finished Wesley stood up.

'I'm going over to Guy Kitchener's flat. Coming with me?'

Gerry followed him out of the office. Neither man had been to Guy Kitchener's place but they knew the address. Guy had mentioned that it was in a modern block with a balcony overlooking the sea. It wouldn't be difficult to find.

Luckily the traffic was light as they drove out to Morbay and when they arrived they parked by the promenade overlooking the slate-grey sea and the beach, deserted apart from a solitary man walking an elderly Labrador. Wesley, distracted by the evening's events, had forgotten his coat and when he emerged from the car he pulled his jacket close around him, trying not to shiver in the biting sea breeze.

Soon they were at the entrance to Beach View Court examining the names on the battery of bell pushes beside the front door. Guy Kitchener had written his name clearly beneath his bell and Wesley pressed it three times. It must have sounded urgent inside the flat – and it was meant to.

A disembodied voice from the entryphone speaker told them to come up. It was hard to tell how Guy felt about their arrival from those few words but when he opened his flat door to them his normally amiable face was solemn. But they'd just charged his mother with murder so that was hardly surprising.

'How is she?' he asked anxiously.

'A psychiatrist's coming in to assess her later. There's a chance she might be moved.'

'Good. A police cell's hardly appropriate. I take it you're here to discuss what she's done . . .?'

'Actually we'd like to ask you a few questions.'

'You'd better come through.' He led them into a spacious living room with wooden floors and angular modern furniture.

Wesley perched on the uncomfortable black leather sofa and took out his notebook. 'I believe you did your doctorate in Liverpool?'

'That's right. I taught at the university for a year or so afterwards.'

'You never mentioned it,' Gerry said accusingly.

'Why would I mention it? I didn't think it was relevant.'

'You had a brother called Ben. He drowned.'

There was a sharp intake of breath. 'Yes, but I don't see—'

'Your mother's third victim, Isobel Grant, shared a house with your brother in her second year at university.'

'I had nothing to do with my brother's housemates. He was five years younger than me and we didn't mix socially.'

'So you didn't know Isobel?'

'No.'

'Isobel told someone that your brother had done something terrible.'

'What do you mean?' His voice had become a nervous squeak.

'She claimed that he'd murdered a stranger . . . just to see what it was like to kill someone.'

Guy sat there with his mouth open for a few moments. 'That's absolute nonsense.'

'He couldn't keep it to himself. He got drunk and told Isobel Grant. Perhaps he killed himself because he couldn't live with what he did.'

'This is nonsense.' Guy spoke with confidence, almost as though he was trying to convince himself as well as the two policemen sitting opposite him.

Wesley continued. 'Isobel in turn told a friend what he'd said and I suppose the story got embellished with each telling until nobody really believed it and it became a sort of urban myth. When Ben killed himself everyone assumed he'd made it up because he was mentally unstable. But I think it really happened. And you knew about it, didn't you, Guy? I think Isobel Grant recognised you in the street and thought

364

she'd try and make some money out of what she knew. Did she ask you for money, Guy? Did she threaten to publicise what your brother had done unless you paid up?'

Guy shook his head, trying to laugh it off. But his laughter was forced and unconvincing. 'For your information, my brother suffered from depression. He found it difficult to cope with life. What you're alleging is absolute fantasy, Wesley. If I were you, I'd see a good psychologist.' He hesitated, as though he realised that he'd get nowhere with cheap insults. 'Look, it's only natural that you're still upset after what happened to your wife. In the circumstances you won't be thinking straight. I can only apologise that I didn't recognise sooner that my mother's mental state was so bad but—'

'We've checked with Merseyside police, Guy,' Gerry said. 'There was a death that fitted with Isobel's story. A homeless man called Rocky was found dead in a derelict dock.'

'So? Anybody could have killed him. He was probably stabbed in some drunken brawl.'

Wesley caught Gerry's eye. 'We didn't say he was stabbed.'

Guy didn't flinch. He merely gave a feeble smile and began to pick at his finger nails. 'It was a guess. Let's face it, Wesley, you're just fishing. You've no proof. And besides, my brother's dead. Mother adored Ben and it was probably his death that sent her over the edge. Of the two of us, he was always her favourite. I resented that for a while, of course, but . . . Well, he is – was – my only brother.'

Gerry cleared his throat. 'Liverpool Police found some DNA at the scene of Rocky's murder. There's no match on the national database but it's only a matter of time. You'll be willing to give a DNA sample, won't you, Guy?'

Wesley was sure that he saw a flicker of panic in the man's

eyes, there for a second then gone. 'I don't see why not. Look, I'm expecting a call from my mother's solicitor.'

'Mind if we take a look around?'

Guy sat quite still for a moment, breath held, as though he was making a decision. 'Help yourself. But you won't find anything.'

He sounded confident which probably meant they'd be wasting their time. Unless Kitchener was bluffing. They began to make a cursory search of the cupboards and drawers. When they'd finished Gerry gave a brief shake of his head and Wesley saw relief in Guy's eyes.

'Can you tell us where you were at the times of the recent murders?'

Guy made a great show of consulting his diary. Then he wrote down a list of his whereabouts and handed it to Wesley. 'I've written down the phone numbers of people I was with. They'll back me up.'

They left the flat and walked slowly back to the car. The sky seemed lighter now and there were more dog walkers on the wide expanse of damp sand beneath the promenade.

'Is it my imagination or are we missing something?' said Wesley as he unlocked the driver's door.

'No, Wes. I think Guy Kitchener's in the clear. All this stuff about what his brother may or may not have done is probably irrelevant. I reckon it's pretty straightforward. Mary copied those murders back in the nineteen hundreds – either because she's mad or because she knew Isobel Grant was trying to blackmail her precious son and she wanted her out of the way and used the other murders as a smokescreen. She picked on Pam to make a point . . . and at a time when Guy had a perfect alibi.'

'He's got alibis for most of the murders, that's true. And

he seemed quite willing to give us his DNA. Anyway, why should he be frightened of what Isobel knew about his brother? Ben's dead and what he did had nothing to do with Guy.'

'Although . . .' Gerry paused and thought for a moment. 'On the other hand, maybe there's something we don't know yet: maybe Guy was more involved in Ben's death than he's led us to believe, and Isobel knew it.'

He looked at Wesley, his eyebrows raised questioningly, before clambering into the passenger seat. Wesley could only shake his head. He felt so tired, it was almost as if he didn't know what to think any more.

# CHAPTER 37

*The frenzy that the terrible murders caused rather astonished me. The villagers lived in fear and all the talk amongst the servants was of the Ripper as he was called by the ignorant folk of the district. But I knew that this was no evil monster bent on bloodshed. I knew for sure that there was a purpose behind the deaths; that each detail had been planned meticulously.*

*By the time the fourth girl, Peggy Carr, went on her journey into the afterlife, the terror of the village and surrounding area was almost tangible and all imagined that the killer was of monstrous appearance with slavering fangs and fiery eyes. Their murderer stalked the woods and fields like a ravening beast, blood-soaked and terrible. How astonished they would have been if they knew the truth.*

*When the police came to the castle I stood concealed in a doorway near the top of the stairs and listened. They wished to know the whereabouts of John Varley. They had come to question him in connection with the murders.*

*How I smiled. But when I was with others my smile was hidden behind a mask of concern. How easy it is to dissemble.*

# CHAPTER 38

Wesley had still heard nothing from Ian Petrie – he'd expected a phone call to discuss Robert Delaware's role in the theft of antiquities from Varley Castle at least – and he toyed with the idea of contacting him. The thought still nagged at the back of Wesley's mind that he owed his old boss something; support, maybe, in his darkest hour.

His mobile rang and he looked at the caller's number. Neil. He had rather hoped it was Ian but he pressed the key to answer the call.

'What's been going on?' Neil said before Wesley had a chance to say hello.

'We've got someone for the murders.'

'I saw on the news that there'd been an arrest. Well done.' There was a short silence. 'You don't sound over the moon. Anything the matter?'

Wesley hesitated before replying. 'The suspect tried to kill Pam.'

He heard Neil gasp. 'Is she OK?'

'She's very shaken and she was taken to hospital to get checked out but apart from that . . . She's taking time off work and she's staying with Maritia for a few days while I'm clearing this lot up. How are things up at Varley Castle?'

'Busy.' Neil lowered his voice. 'Caroline's recovering from her shock. It's a good job me and Andy turned up when we did or Delaware would have stripped the place. I guess there must be a ready market for those things . . . not that I can see the appeal myself. I presume Delaware's safely behind bars? You've not released him on bail or anything like that?'

'No. He's been charged and remanded in custody and we've rearrested his contact, Raymond Seed, as well. What are you up to?'

'I'm holding the fort here on my own 'cause Andy's in Exeter at the moment. As soon as he gets back we'll bring all the stuff Delaware was hiding at the cottage back to the castle to be catalogued. To be honest, Wes, this Egyptian stuff gives me the creeps.'

Wesley opened his mouth to speak but he found it hard to get a word in while Neil was in such a talkative mood.

'We've had the press here as well, wanting to take photos of where the 1903 murders happened. Caroline told them to get lost but they took no notice.'

'Look, Neil, I'll have to go,' Wesley said. A uniformed constable had just dumped a box on his desk and was standing there expectantly, shifting from foot to foot.

'Where's this come from?' he asked as he placed his mobile phone on the desk.

'The Kitchener house. It was stashed in a cupboard by the

fireplace in the living room. DCI Heffernan told me to bring it in. He said there could be something important in it. I just did as I was told and—'

'That's fine. Thanks,' Wesley said with a half-hearted smile before the 'only obeying orders' speech could continue. The constable scurried off.

Wesley glanced at his watch. He had promised to see Pam and the kids later at Maritia's but he still had an hour or so. He looked at the box – blue plastic, around two foot square and sixteen inches high. He manoeuvred the lid off and peered down at the contents. It was filled with papers and photographs and on top there was an old book covered with marbled paper. He picked it up and when he opened it he realised that it was some sort of journal, each foxed and yellowing page covered with immaculate copperplate handwriting – beautiful to look at but difficult to read. The name on the flyleaf was Eleanor Jane Porton and the first entry bore the date September 1901. He placed it carefully on top of his files.

He began to take things out of the box – letters and old photographs. But a few of the pictures seemed more recent and a cardboard folder – the kind used by professional photographers – caught Wesley's eye.

When he opened it he felt the blood drain from his face. There, side by side, were two young men. The older was Guy Kitchener, looking straight at the camera with his arm placed protectively around the other man's shoulder. But it was the younger man who interested Wesley. He was obviously the grown-up version of the child in the picture at Mary Kitchener's cottage. This was Ben. Ben the alleged killer. Ben who had, in turn, died.

Only he hadn't died. If the boy in the photograph was Ben

371

Kitchener, he was still very much alive. And when Wesley had seen him very recently he'd been using a completely different identity.

He picked up his phone and pressed speed dial.

Ged Farrow from Neston Animal Rescue Shelter had just put the last of the dogs into the van. Apart from one ill-natured llama who was waiting to be taken to a farm near Ashburton, the sanctuary was clear of animals and his work was almost done.

Because the sanctuary and the shelter often helped each other out, he'd had dealings with Mary Kitchener for a few years now and he found it hard to believe that she was under arrest for murdering those women. Ged had always prided himself on being a good judge of people and he couldn't believe he'd been so wrong about Mary. On the other hand, he'd always had the feeling that there was something a little odd about her, as if she harboured some terrible secret – a sad burden she could share with no other human being. Perhaps that's why she had chosen the company of animals. Animals never judge.

As he was about to climb into the van he glanced back at the house and saw a shadowy shape at the window above the back door, a shape that resolved itself into a face, briefly, before vanishing. He stood there frozen, wondering if it had been his imagination.

He knew the house was supposed to be empty but there was no way he was going to play the hero and investigate. Slowly, in case he was being watched, he climbed into the driver's seat and steered the van a few yards down the lane before stopping the engine, oblivious to the barrage of barking that had just started up in the back. Then he took his phone from his top pocket, hoping he wasn't about to make a fool of himself.

Wesley had checked and double-checked. Their man hadn't a reliable alibi for the time of any of the murders or for the attack on Pam. But Mary had taken the blame and, if Wesley's instincts hadn't told him that the matter went much deeper, she would have served a long prison sentence. Maybe even the rest of her life. A mother would do anything for her child – even sacrifice her freedom.

He'd put in a call to the Met to enquire about unsolved murders of women in the London area. There were two that might have fitted but there was no proof that Ben Kitchener had anything to do with either. Maybe he'd behaved himself in London until he'd hit on a way to ensure that Isobel Grant never betrayed his secret, laying a false trail to confuse the police at the same time. But maybe he'd been a bit too clever.

Wesley guessed that Isobel had seen Ben in Tradmouth. She'd recognised him and dreamed up her blackmail scheme as a way of getting a place of her own away from her mother and the petty restrictions of home. However, she'd been stupid to underestimate a man who'd killed before for the sheer power and pleasure of it. Perhaps he'd been longing for years to repeat the experience, that ultimate adrenaline rush when the life of another human being is yours to take. Dominion over life and death. The chance to play God. The thought made Wesley shudder. If he was right about all this, it meant that Ben Kitchener was a very dangerous man indeed.

The call from Ged Farrow of the Neston Animal Rescue Shelter would normally have been treated as routine. But, under the circumstances, his possible sighting of someone inside Mary Kitchener's supposedly empty house was treated as top priority.

Wesley felt apprehensive as he sat beside Gerry Heffernan in the back of the patrol car. He'd come face to face with killers before but rarely one as cold and ruthless as this one. He'd heard once that most animals kill out of necessity, for food or survival, and it was only cats who killed for pleasure. Cats and human beings.

The car glided to a halt some way down the lane from Mary's house, Gerry having made it quite clear to their over-enthusiastic driver that lights and sirens would be counter-productive.

'Ready?' he heard Gerry say as they stepped out of the car.

Wesley nodded. He had Mary's door key ready and now he inserted it carefully into the lock, trying to make a silent entrance. The door opened slowly and the two men stepped across the threshold. Once they were inside they stood quite still and listened.

Gerry gave Wesley's arm a nudge. 'Go on then.'

'Do you think we should have brought back-up?' Wesley spoke in a whisper. If there was someone in the house he didn't want to announce their arrival.

'There's one of him and there's two of us. And we've got our stab vests on.' Gerry tapped his chest but Wesley had rarely seen him look so nervous.

Wesley went ahead, creeping across the carpet on the balls of his feet, pushing each door open gently, freezing every so often to listen like an animal sniffing the air for predators, unsure whether he was the hunter or the hunted.

Once they'd checked downstairs Gerry pointed upwards and they began to climb to the next floor, cursing in whispers whenever the stairs creaked. Then when they reached the landing they heard a faint scraping sound which seemed to be coming from the ceiling above their heads.

'The attic,' Wesley mouthed.

Gerry nodded and followed as Wesley crept over the worn carpet towards the narrow staircase at the far end of the landing. Then the door at the top of the stairs began to open slowly – a fraction at first, becoming wider and wider with a horror-film creak – and Wesley came to an abrupt halt, ignoring Gerry's urging hand pushing gently at his back. As soon as the DCI realised what was happening he began to back off, feeling his way back down the landing but Wesley stood his ground, staring upwards at the open door.

'You'd better come down, Ben.'

The man framed in the doorway stared down at him. His eyes were so like Guy's that Wesley cursed himself for not realising that the two were related.

Ben Kitchener smiled. 'Good to see you again, Wesley. How are you keeping?'

Wesley didn't answer. There seemed to be something almost obscene about the casual, friendly enquiry. It was something that belonged to Ben's other persona – the one Neil had known back at Varley Castle when Ben Kitchener had been living under the name he'd been using since the night all those years ago when he'd killed a man and thought it wise to disappear – the night he'd become Andrew Beredace.

'I was over in Exeter when I got a call from Guy. How's Mum?'

'She's OK,' Wesley answered. 'Was the attack on my wife her idea or yours?'

'Mum had nothing to do with it. When Guy told me

375

about Gemma I knew you were getting too close. I happened to be round here when your wife left a message on Mum's answer phone. I knew who she was and I thought it would be amusing if the wife of one of the investigating officers became my fourth victim. I was waiting for your wife outside when she arrived and as soon as she came out I . . .' A smile played on his lips. 'She wasn't supposed to survive, you know. Only Mum was looking out of the window when your wife left the house and she saw what was happening. She came dashing out and took the knife off me before I could finish what I started. Women are so squeamish, don't you think? She even wrapped her in my sheet so she'd be decent.' He shook his head, as though exasperated by his mother's weakness. 'She doesn't have the guts to kill.'

Wesley felt Gerry's restraining hand on his arm, as though the DCI was half afraid he'd go for the man at the top of the stairs. But Wesley took a step back.

'You're under arrest, Ben.'

The killer sighed. 'I've spent the past years wearing a mask, Wesley, so to be honest it's going to be a bit of a relief to be myself again.' He smiled, showing a row of perfect teeth, and began to walk slowly down the narrow stairs, hands in pockets as though he had all the time in the world.

# CHAPTER 39

*I watched from the upstairs window as the police gathered in front of the castle door. I had witnessed fox hunts when the riders assemble in preparation for the pursuit of the fox and I must say the atmosphere was remarkably similar. Only this time their quarry was John Varley.*

*It had been my testimony that had brought this about. I had spoken to the inspector in charge in confidence, claiming that I never wished it to be known that I had been the betrayer because I was afraid of losing my position in the household. How that inspector had drunk in everything I said, placing a fatherly hand on my sleeve as I feigned tears. I told him how I had seen John leaving the house on the very nights the women had been brutally killed and mutilated. And I had told the inspector that, like his father, John was obsessed with the rituals of the ancient Egyptian people, especially those regarding death and funerals. And I told him how he had boasted to me that he held power over life and death and how he had frightened me so that I feared for my safety.*

*Although Frederick was unaware of my part in his son's discovery, he*

377

*did not speak to me. In fact he had rarely communicated with me since the night they took my precious child away from me.*

*When John was found dead, hanging in the woods, I hoped that Frederick might come to me for comfort and acknowledge the son he had given up now that he had lost his eldest. But he still regarded me coldly.*

*Perhaps it had all been for nothing.*

# CHAPTER 40

It wasn't until Wesley had done some further digging that he discovered that Ben Kitchener had read Egyptology at Liverpool University, one of the few institutions in the country to offer the course.

The real Andrew Beredace had been Ben's fellow student but he had died tragically in a climbing accident at the age of twenty-one, shortly after his graduation. Ben had known of his death and had decided to assume his identity so that, whenever anybody checked, they'd found that Andrew Beredace had indeed been a bona fide student at the University of Liverpool. Also, by assuming Andrew's identity, Ben had increased his degree classification from a lower second to a first and on the strength of this he'd completed a doctorate in London and obtained a job at the British Museum. And there he'd stayed, his terrible past dormant like a preserved mummy in a tomb, until he'd made a trip to Tradmouth to see his mother and brother and had been spotted by Isobel Grant.

Mary, grateful that her younger son was still alive, had kept his secret. She had shielded him from the consequences of his crimes and protected his new identity, visiting him occasionally in the safe anonymity of London. Guy too had kept his secret – he was his brother after all.

Mary Kitchener's devoted love had caused the deaths of three women, two of whom had known nothing of Ben Kitchener's crimes and the reason why he judged that their lives had to end.

Now Ben was sitting opposite Wesley, his expression serene. The detective had hoped that he was establishing some kind of rapport with the killer, maybe because of their mutual connection with Neil, and as they sat there in the interview room, it almost seemed like a chat between old friends. Gerry sat beside him in silence, having sensed that nothing would be gained from interruption.

'Tell us what happened.'

'From the beginning?'

'Please.'

Ben smiled. His smile was charming. He had the sort of face you'd trust and even now Wesley was finding it hard to treat him as a cold-blooded murderer. 'It's a long story, Wesley. Sure you've got the time?'

'We've got all the time in the world,' Gerry said.

Ben smiled again. 'If you say so.' He took a deep breath. 'I'll start at the beginning, shall I? I suppose I've always been fascinated by the ancient Egyptians and their religion and I built up quite a library of books about them when I was a child. Mum's still got them in the attic – I was looking through them when you arrived, actually. She'd never throw anything of mine away. I know mothers shouldn't really have favourites but she'll do anything for me. There were times when I found her love a little . . . stifling but it's certainly had its uses over the years. Anyway, I got into Liverpool to study Egyptology – there was a lot of competition for places but I got there.' His expression suddenly altered. 'But that's not really the beginning. This all started in the early years of the twentieth century. Did you wonder why Mum keeps a picture of Varley Castle above the fireplace?'

'She said she was a distant cousin of the Varleys.'

Wesley found Ben's knowing grin annoying. 'Well, yes and no. We are related to the Varleys but on the wrong side of the blanket. My great-grandfather was the illegitimate son of Sir Frederick Varley, the famous Egyptologist, and a governess called Eleanor Porton. Maybe that's where I got my passion for Egyptology from.'

The name triggered a memory in Wesley's head. Eleanor Porton had been the name on the front of the journal Wesley had left on his desk, intending to look at it when he had a spare moment. 'Go on,' he said.

'Well, Eleanor shared Sir Frederick's obsession with Egypt and they became close. The inevitable happened, of course, but instead of marrying her – he was a widower so it would have been possible – he rejected her and forced her to give up her child who was my great-grandfather. He was brought up by a childless couple on the estate and it wasn't until he was in his teens that Eleanor made herself known to him and told him the truth. He went to live with her and they moved to the Neston area so the story ended happily, I suppose. But . . .'

'But what?'

'When my great-grandfather was about six months old four women were murdered. Sir Frederick's oldest son, John, got the blame and he hanged himself. He was known to be mentally unstable and he'd been particularly obnoxious to

Eleanor.' He smiled. 'I take it you know the details of those four murders?'

'Yes.'

'I used to read and re-read all the details in Eleanor's journal. How the women were strangled with a cord from behind, then their internal organs were removed with an obsidian blade from Sir Frederick's collection and the bodies wrapped in linen sheets from the castle and amulets left to aid their journey into the afterlife. It had all been done properly – or as properly as one can do in the circumstances when there's no access to embalming resins and spices.'

He spoke with the detached interest of a scholar, Wesley noticed. As if there had been no brutal death, no blood, no suffering.

'So you decided to emulate them?'

'Why not? Those murders stuck in my mind. I wondered what it would be like to do that to a human body.' He smiled again. 'Isobel had to be silenced so I thought I would muddy the waters. Even if you did find out about the little incident back in my student days, I thought you wouldn't be bright enough to separate Isobel's murder from the others. You'd be looking for a common thread. But there wasn't one.'

Wesley was tempted to point out that if they hadn't been bright enough to discover his secrets, he wouldn't be sitting there under arrest, but he stayed silent and let the man talk.

'Tell us about Isobel.'

'We shared a house in my third year.'

'With a dental student called Dominic?'

'That's right . . . but he had his own circle of friends and didn't have much to do with me and Izzy. Dominic and I had nothing in common.' He paused. 'But me and Izzy were close for a while. If it hadn't been for her it wouldn't have

382

happened, I'm sure of that. We brought out the worst in each other.' There was a small smile on his face as though he was reliving pleasant, or possibly erotic, memories.

'Go on,' said Wesley.

'It was one of those long drunken conversations that go on long into the night. I was telling her all about the Egyptian belief in the afterlife and their customs and she said she wondered what it would be like to kill somebody . . . to actually watch them die and see the soul leave the body.'

He swallowed hard and Wesley could see that the memories were no longer pleasant. This was something that disturbed him.

'Anyway, she said why didn't we kill somebody . . . just to see what it was like. I said it was a stupid idea but she wouldn't give up. She said she'd always wanted to see someone die and it would be easy. We'd just pick on someone who wouldn't be missed. We'd be doing them a favour, she said. Izzy could be very persuasive.'

'So you killed someone?'

'She was with me but there was no way she was getting her hands dirty. She took one of the knives from the kitchen drawer and we went out. I'd had a bit to drink and I'd smoked some dope so the old inhibitions were pretty low. We saw this homeless bloke in a doorway and Isobel got talking to him. She told him we knew where there was a crate full of booze that someone had nicked and abandoned at an old dock.' He looked up at Wesley. 'You wouldn't believe how convincing she sounded. Then when we got to the dock . . . I stuck the knife in him and . . .'

'What did Isobel do?'

'She laughed. I'd never heard laughter like that.'

'What about you?'

'I felt elated. Powerful. I can't explain. I've done it again but it's never been like that first time.'

'What happened next?'

'Isobel was a greedy bitch. She began to make life hard for me. She said if I didn't pay her to keep quiet she'd go to the police. That's when I confided in Guy. Guy had always had an over-developed sense of responsibility. I think Mum must have instilled it into him at an early age that I was the precious little brother so it was up to him to look after me. He's a psychologist so he'd be able to explain it better than I can. Anyway, one day an unidentified body was found in the Albert Dock – lad about my age and approximate description. No ID and nobody came forward to claim him. That's when Guy had the idea of me starting again. He reported me missing and when he identified the lad as me, I took the identity of this student on my course who'd died a couple of weeks after graduating. It seemed to work out fine. I went to London and, as far as Izzy was concerned, I was dead so she couldn't cause me any trouble. I thought she'd gone to work up north. I hadn't realised her mother had moved down here and she'd come down to live with her.'

'So she saw you?'

'That's right. I was with Guy in Tradmouth one weekend in January. He was helping Mum deliver something for a charity craft fair and I went with him. Izzy was in the street outside and she spotted me . . . and she recognised Guy. She followed us back to Hugford and then sent a letter to my mother's house addressed to me. She said she needed money. She was desperate to get a place of her own and she reckoned I owed her.'

'When did you hit on the idea of copying the jackal murders?'

'I knew all about Eleanor's journal, of course. Then I saw the jackal mask when I was poking about in the church hall during the craft fair – it had been used in a play, I think. There was some art teacher selling figures he'd made of Anubis so I nicked a few from a box behind the stall when he went off for a cup of tea. I couldn't risk buying them in case he remembered. I thought my idea was foolproof. And when you've killed once, it's easier second time around. By the time I got to Izzy – to my real target – I was quite an expert.'

'Your first attempt to kill Clare Mayers failed. Neil assumed you were in London when he rang you the day after but you'd given Caroline your mobile number – you were down in Devon all the time. We checked with the British Museum. You were on leave.'

'So it wouldn't be much use denying it, would it?'

'What about Analise Sonquist?'

'I saw her in the pub and when I saw that she was leaving on her own I followed her. Easy.'

'And you were disturbed when you killed Naomi Hart in Neston?'

He looked at Wesley, suddenly alert. 'Was that her name?'

'Yes,' Gerry said in a quiet growl. 'She had a name. And a family and friends – people who loved her.'

Ben Kitchener's eyes widened for a second before they began to fill with tears. Wesley's first instinct was to feel pity for him but then he told himself that it was all an elaborate act – that Kitchener's tears were tears of self-pity. He'd evaded justice for a while and three women had died. But now time had run out.

He listened as Gerry Heffernan read out the words of the formal charge. There'd be no escape for him now. Ever.

385

# CHAPTER 41

*How good it was to know that every time I ventured forth in search of a hapless victim, I was a step closer to avenging myself on the man who took my child from me. Whenever I thought of my beautiful son calling another woman Mother, I felt a stab of utter despair, as though my very flesh had been cut and my heart torn from my body. So I set upon my path of fitting vengeance. I would deprive Frederick of his son as I had been deprived of mine.*

*The first woman I killed was called Jenny Pride and that name suited her well. She was proud and, like many from the village, regarded me with contempt. I had thought news of my troubles had stayed within the confines of the castle walls but servants always talk and Jenny's sister was a kitchen maid. I was walking one evening and I had the cord in my pocket, in case an opportunity should present itself. I had taken the obsidian blade and the amulets from Frederick's collection and I had secreted a number of linen sheets for the purpose as well as some plates from the kitchen to hold the organs. It was my intention that the method would focus suspicion on John and all was planned. Now all I needed was a victim.*

*I enjoyed killing – I shall make no secret of it. For the powerless to feel suddenly powerful is intoxicating. Yet, for all the pleasure it gave me, the murder of Jenny Pride was difficult and as I cut into the warm flesh I looked away. I had enveloped myself in the sheet to protect my clothes – although as she was already dead when I cut into her there was no great flow of blood – and when it was finished I placed the organs on the dishes and wrapped her corpse in the bloodstained linen, not forgetting to leave the amulet amongst its folds.*

*The second time was easier and the third easier still. By the time I killed that sly little Peggy Carr – who I once heard calling me a common whore in lady's clothing – I was an adept executioner. I almost wished that I could have continued killing but after Peggy's demise the police were bent on their pursuit of John and they regarded his suicide as a confession of his guilt.*

*I knew then I had to do nothing which would make them doubt their assumptions so I lived out my life in quiet anticipation. Frederick, humbled and shaken by the death of his son, eventually made me an allowance, his conscience seemingly having been awakened by his loss.*

*So now I existed in some comfort, biding my time, in a comfortable cottage situated near to my son, watching him grow into a fine young man. With John dead and Edward away at school, Frederick began to take an interest in Charles – for that is what his foster parents called him – and paid for him to be educated. When Charles was sixteen Frederick died and I was able to make myself known to my son at last. My own flesh and blood. He was wary of me at first for he'd always known another woman as his mother. But soon I won him and I tried not to let the suffocating intensity of my love to become so overwhelming that it drove him away.*

*I often wondered whether I would ever be tempted to kill again to rid myself of people who were disagreeable or who stood in the way of my desires, but I had left all that behind me. However, I would certainly have killed again if any danger or difficulty threatened Charles. Perhaps it is a good thing that the need never arose.*

# CHAPTER 42

Neil Watson had finished his work at Varley Castle and after the affair of Andrew Beredace – or rather Ben Kitchener – he felt he could no longer trust his instincts.

The nights were growing lighter now and the weather was improving, although he had lived long enough in the south-west to know that this didn't necessarily presage a good summer.

After saying goodbye to Caroline and promising to visit the castle again in a couple of weeks to see how things were going with the National Trust's renovations, he decided that he couldn't face returning to his empty flat in Exeter. As he hadn't had any contact with Wesley and Pam for a week or so, he took the road south to Tradmouth. Now the case was cleared up, with any luck he'd find them in.

It was Pam who opened the door. She looked well. But then it was half term and Pam always tended to blossom when she didn't have to go into school every day. It seemed that she had recovered completely from her brush with death as she invited him in, exchanging news and pleasantries. When Neil had found out what happened the thought of what might have been had kept him awake at night. He stepped into the hall and gave her a hug and a kiss on the cheek. Life is fragile and friends can be lost so easily.

Pam told him that Wesley was in and as she began to shepherd him towards the living room a black kitten shot across his path, stopping suddenly when it saw its intended route was blocked and looking up at him with huge green eyes.

Pam scooped the kitten up in her arms just as Wesley came out into the hall. From the solemn look on his face, Neil guessed that something else must have happened. Something bad.

'What's up?' Neil said, absent-mindedly leaning over to stroke the kitten's head.

Wesley hesitated before answering. 'I've just had some bad news.'

Neil glanced at Pam but it was hard to read her expression.

'Remember that old colleague of mine who came down to investigate the Egyptian antiquity scam?'

Neil nodded. He remembered Ian Petrie but in all the fuss surrounding the arrest of Ben Kitchener, the antiquity-smuggling racket had been pushed to the back of his mind.

'His ex-wife's just called me. He's dead. He was ill – cancer – but I didn't realise he had so little time.'

'I'm sorry.' Neil couldn't think of anything else to say.

Wesley turned and disappeared back into the living room. Neil caught Pam's eye.

'He's upset,' she said in a whisper. 'Ian was the first boss at

390

the Met he got on with and he thought a lot of him. Wes reckons he really wanted to clear up that Egyptian antiquity case before he was forced to retire through ill health. He came here for dinner, you know. I had no idea . . .'

She reached out her free hand and gave Neil a gentle push towards the door. 'Go and cheer him up.'

Neil smiled. He didn't feel particularly cheerful himself. He'd become rather attached to life at the castle and he knew that next week he'd be starting a rescue dig near Honiton, seeing what lay beneath the soil before a close of new houses was built on the land. Maybe his new-found liking for the indoor life was a sign he was getting old.

The kitten started to wriggle and Pam put it down on the floor. 'We've finally named her. We put it to the vote and she's now called Moriarty. Wesley's suggestion – something to do with Sherlock Holmes.'

'His nemesis.' Neil laughed and the kitten began to scamper up the stairs with a youthful energy that made Neil slightly envious.

He took a deep breath and walked into the living room. Life had to go on.


Guy Kitchener sat in his office at the university. He'd closed the door, always a signal that he didn't want to be disturbed, and taken the copy he'd made of his great-great-grandmother Eleanor's journal out of his briefcase. Now it lay open on the desk in front of him, out of place amongst the e-mails and students' essays. There was also a photograph of Eleanor that he'd found slipped between the pages of the journal, posed in sepia, staring into the distance, her lips slightly parted as though she was recalling a pleasing encounter with some past lover.

He put his head in his hands. All his training told him that it was mainly nurture and upbringing, or maybe some abnormality of the brain, that made a killer. But maybe evil did exist, passed down through the generations like any other inherited trait. Maybe there was such a thing as bad blood. Eleanor had had no real reason to kill; she could have bided her time until Charles was old enough then revealed her true role in his life, as indeed she did. The pre-text for killing those innocent women was to avenge herself on Frederick Varley by bringing about his son's arrest and execution – a fate which was pre-empted by John's unstable nature. But none of it was necessary . . . just as Ben killing the homeless man for a dare and then killing those women as a smokescreen for his elimination of Isobel Grant hadn't been necessary.

Both Eleanor and Ben had enjoyed the act of murder. And there were times when Guy wondered whether he too was capable of such things, whether he was tainted with the same genetic inheritance. But he dismissed the idea. The very thought of killing made him feel slightly sick.

He stood up and walked over to the window. Mary had been charged with perverting the course of justice and when she'd been released on bail, Guy had moved in with her for the time being, just so that she wouldn't be alone. He had imagined that recent events would have rendered her broken and contrite but, in spite of the act she had put on in court, Guy knew that her spirit remained uncrushed. And if there was anything she could do to save her beloved younger son from a life of incarceration in some cold cell – a living death – Guy knew she'd do it.

The previous evening Guy had met Ben's lawyer who'd said that if they could establish that Ben was mentally unstable, obsessed with the 1903 case and liable to confess to anything, there was still a chance he might get off. Even the attack on Wesley Peterson's wife might be explained as a coincidence if they twisted the facts somehow to suit their purpose.

After the meeting Guy had hit on an idea so bold that it might just work. If there was another death – if everything was planned carefully so that none of their family could possibly be implicated – there was always a chance they'd be able to get Ben released. There must be somebody, an impressionable and unstable student perhaps, who'd be willing to kill for a substantial fee. Money was no object to Mary where her younger son was concerned. She'd always protected Ben like she protected weak puppies and kittens. Only he was her own blood, part of her, so she would defend him to her last breath.

If another murder would ensure Ben's freedom . . . Guy stared out of the window, wondering just how far he'd go for his brother. He'd kept his secret all those years and this was just one more step. Besides, he knew his mother would agree to anything that would win Ben's liberty.

Sometimes love can be far more dangerous than hate, he thought, as he watched a lone young man walk across the windswept quadrangle below. A loner. Maybe even a potential killer.